CALL BACK THE YEARS

CALL BACK
THE YEARS

by

MARGARETHE ERDAHL SHANK

Illustrated by Richard Bobnick

AUGSBURG PUBLISHING HOUSE
Minneapolis   Minnesota

CALL BACK THE YEARS

CONTENTS

CHAPTER 1

The Sea

The sea was mistress of them all, thought Arne, for it drank the fresh streams that spilled from the mountainsides; it nibbled on rocks and soil and sometimes tore to fragments the sea-homes of men who toiled for its riches. Its ancient voice seemed to chant: You belong to me, all belongs to me. And who could deny its power, thought Arne, knowing that many a rotten hull and many a bleached bone lay deep in its caverned recesses.

And above the sea, he thought, loomed the overpowering mountains—craggy, sometimes wooded, many bathed in perpetual snow. Perhaps it was no wonder, then, that folk like him often grew too great or too small within, for many seemed to spend their lives on a rocky shelf hanging between sea void and mountain vastness.

Despite all this he loved this land—the struggles it had cost him, the problems now existing for him in school and village. Frequently he wondered how his brother Roald had been able to leave Norway and why he never spoke of returning for a visit. It was always, "Some day, Arne, you too must come to America."

The red-skirted child stirred under the circle of his protective arm. "What are you thinking about, Father?"

How like an autumn sprite she seemed—hair the color of cider, eyes loaf-brown. "I am thinking that you must be restless by now," he said.

"I want to see Aunt Guro," she said, "but still I like it here, too." Both turned their faces back to the sea, postponing for some moments their climb up the mountain. As Arne sat there, he reflected how many were leaving Norway, seeking to better themselves on the plains and in the forests of America. Consider the Moen boy, for instance, who grew seriously ill during the dark, moist days of winter. Yet there were many who felt it wicked to desert one's motherland—that it was like giving one's own flesh and blood to a stranger. Among the critics of emigration in the area none was more eloquent—and perhaps more powerful—than their new pastor.

1

Yet how could *he* feel the sting of poverty which moved the hungry to leave, this clergyman who had married a shipper's daughter from Bergen?

Arne's free hand moved to pluck a blade of sunburned grass, which he absentmindedly put between his lips, savoring the sweet, dry flavor of autumn locked within its cells. "Why do you do that— chew on a weed?" asked Siri.

"I do not know myself, little one. And I would not recommend it to you." He noticed that the late morning sun cast only a weak shadow—such a strange day it was, most unseasonably warm, with a pale, burnished light glancing off glacier above and sea below.

She straightened her red skirt primly and stretched her legs, studying her shoes critically. "I would not chew grass myself," she said, turning to study her father with critical detachment, reminding him for an instant of her grandmother Bergit's well-known candor. "A *nisse* or a *troll* might have stepped on it, and that would surely be bad for you." Then suddenly, "Why did you name me 'Siri'?"

Arne looked into the disturbingly frank eyes of his six-year-old. "I have told you, *sweet heart*, we liked the name. No one else around here has it."

"Ah, but you are lying," said Siri, tempering her accusation with a teasing smile. "You yourself told me you dug the name out of a mound!"

And you, too, are an ancient one, he thought—hard and sound like your grandmother Bergit, who gazes sightless upon the world, tender like your mother Elisabet. Yet Siri, he felt, had another quality besides—something detached, almost poetic, a strain that had often been strong in his own people, the Gabrielsons. More than all things he desired for his little family was this—that they might always be together, that he might remain close to this child even throughout her womanhood, for he felt he would always understand her better than anyone else. He sighed, thinking they must get on with their errand up the mountainside; yet here they sat like English tourists with nothing better to do than gaze at forest and sea. "I see a sail! I see a sail!" Siri jumped to her feet with the explosive agility of the young. "It's a stranger's sail, isn't it, Father?"

"I do not know it," replied Arne. "I do not know *him*," he added for by now Arne could see the light shock of hair on the man's head.

"Well, I know who it is," said Siri importantly. "It is the merchant Gunhild was talking about. He has a satchel full of silver jewelry and all sorts of wonderful things."

"Silly girl!" he chided gently. "Must you prattle like a running stream?" He gave her a playful nudge. "Come now, we must be on our way. Aunt Guro will be mad with worry." They moved upward, following the tortuous path which circled half-sunken boulders. When they reached a promontory overlooking the fjord, he looked down at the farm again. A cloud obscured the sun; a shadow had fallen on a strip of water and extended arrow-like to the farm and the small pier beside which the sailboat had now come to rest. The sight of this boat brought something to mind—the talk in the village about this vendor, who, it was said, had a way with women. No wonder, then, that Gunhild had washed her hair and dried it in the morning sun. The girl ached for a man to quench the sudden firing of womanhood. Ah, well, Bergit was there, and little escaped *that* old one—who did not need eyes to see when she could read a multitude of household sounds.

For a quarter of an hour they climbed upward, the child skipping ahead on chubby legs, her plaited hair bouncing up and down on her straight shoulders.

The air, it seemed to Arne, had less density now—still it was uncommonly warm for a fall day. The leaves had turned on many of the trees; the trunks of the birches gleamed silver-gold in the strange light. How beautiful the country is, he thought; and again he wondered how Roald never yearned to return. But if America was indeed the Promised Land some said it was, it must have much to recommend it.

The loveliest of all were the aspen leaves, which—never still— tinkled *sotto voce*, like a soft prelude to a greater melody to come. He liked them all, these trees of Norway, but best were the birches, he thought. They reminded him of Elisabet, as the black alder reminded him of Bergit. There was the same supple grace to the birch, a resplendent softness, never intruding, lovely to the touch, like his wife's soft skin and radiant silver-gold hair. With a rush of warmth and pride he thought of the infant she bore within, and remembered the widow Moen's words, "Elisabet should bear a basketful of little ones, she has such a warm and tender way with plant and child." But the fact remained that birth and death were in the Lord's hands—and to have one skipping on the path ahead and another cradled within Elisabet, these were gifts enough.

Suddenly he was aware of the child's warm hand within his own. "I shall walk with you now," she said. While he took care to show no change of expression, he felt a secret amusement. How well he could read her change of mind! Still he should not smile at her—for were there not fears that lurked in all minds and in his own mind as well? "Now the *sea monster* never comes up here," she lisped, "but lives only in the sea below. Still this wood is a place well loved by the trolls and gnomes, for Aunt Guro told me so."

"Ah, she *has* seen them, then?"

"Of course," replied Siri, giving the tarn a hasty, sidelong glance. "Both of us have seen them. One night when we went out to cover the baby chicks we saw a troll peeking around a tree."

"Incontrovertible," agreed Arne. "Did he bite your leg?"

"Oh Father!" she exclaimed with womanly exasperation. "Why should he do that?"

"In other words, he let you go unharmed." He pinched her glowing cheek. She is no worse, he thought, than many others old enough to know better. Scowling thoughtfully, he recalled some of the superstitions which spring from the minds of men. True, they gave color and fireside drama, and yet they annoyed him somewhat, for it appeared to him that they were convenient excuses for weaknesses of thought and will. If a peasant was too lazy to cover the milk crock, it was easy to understand how she might invent a creature who had stolen the cream.

Now they were almost out of the disreputable wood that bordered the tarn. Evil and brackish, the water seemed to sicken the trees by its propinquity. "You see," exclaimed Arne, smiling at the child so close beside him, "the world itself has not grown dark because we skirted a tarn. We might remember that, Siri, when we have dark days ourselves. Walk but a few steps farther and seek the sun." Feeling somewhat sententious, he smiled at her but went on with,

"That sunlight we need is to be found somewhere," he said, "but nearly always in the mind." The child looked earnestly at Arne, then, and despite her young years, was not unheeding. "Siri," he continued, "I have always talked to you as I would talk to any one else, not like some who talk to children as though they had no minds." Although she did not always understand what he said, not all his sayings were too cryptic and dark for the morning light of her youth; and his words remained in the very deep of her heart, like forest seedlings waiting for their summer growth.

Unclasping his hand, she darted away, disappearing in a heavy growth of willows bordering a small stream. He quickened his own steps, for they were almost there; and he soon joined Siri, who stood on a little treadworn wooden bridge shaking with the thunder of the small mountain torrent. Unafraid, lost in the mystery of disappearing water, the child stood with her hands holding fast to the rustic railing. He wondered how many had crossed this bridge with halbert and shield during the ancient, tumultuous years; how many girls herding awkward kine; how many others had stood and stared into the boiling waters. But Siri had now sounded the alarm. He turned to see Aunt Guro scurrying down the path, arms outstretched, her little walnut face split into a huge grin. Uncle Nels rose from the bole chair beside the door and strode with swinging gait to join his wife and the child. Little and great arms enfolded her. Arne quickened his own pace, eager for the company of the cheerful, smiling old folk who were almost as dear as his own at Fjeldstrand. Nels's deep voice rose above the little tinkling sounds of Aunt Guro's greetings. When the initial flurry had subsided, and the handshakings, the inquiries, and complexities of rural greetings were over, Guro took the child by the hand and led her into the small cottage to see where a geranium bloomed in the window sill, where the cat had crept under a bed to have her kittens; then both were out with a scurry of small, quick feet to greet every living creature on the farm by name.

Arne, accepting some of the old man's tobacco, settled down in the high-backed chair beside a window, where he soon began to talk with that latitude possible for him only with a man like Nels, who cherished freedom above comfort. Nels sat astraddle an old carved bench he liked so well, a favorite brown pipe clamped between somewhat stained teeth. "Well," he said, "which is harder down there, teaching the young folk or the older ones?"

Fully aware of the old man's intent, Arne sat waiting for Nels's familiar comments about the parish below. "Does our esteemed clergy- man still thunder against the emigrants?" Arne replied that the young he could handle—still he had no wish to oppose a man whose authority exceeded his own in the teaching of the young, nor was it wise to quarrel with a man of God even if he exhibited more than his share of human frailties.

"Certainly, it's not treason to leave one's mother country?" asked Nels, who did not wait for an answer but continued, "If so, I should have been put away as a traitor years ago." He shook his bushy gray head sadly. "It's a pity old Sigurd Olafson had to die in his sleep, for *there* was a clergyman kind enough to turn one's steps heavenward, reluctant as our feet are." He drew deeply upon his pipe, banged his hairy hand on the bench. "I tell you," he said bitterly, "I have seen more honest piety among the rough men on shipboard under the stars than I can find down in our church these days, though I take a comb and card the mouthy wool of his words for a whole week afterward."

Arne smiled indulgently. "It has been chiefly on the subject of emigration we have been opposed," he said. "It is now said the Moen boy is about to leave for America. I cannot blame him much. What is there for him here? His lungs are too weak for him to join the men on herring runs; the rocky plot of land his mother and he have—in truth, what is there to stay for?"

"Yet it is a *sin* to leave the mother country!" scoffed Nels. "I have heard he has preached against me too." The old man laughed. "You remember I set out once with an ill-fated crew to seek our fortune in the new land. Now I am told it was greed for riches that left us stranded, by the hand of God, in South America. But I have seen greed that never left its own doorstep."

"Some ventures have failed," agreed Arne. "But then it is easy to fail anywhere, even here at home." He looked at the old seaman with sudden interest. "That venture that was abandoned—was it not the voyage of the Sophie?" The old man nodded. "I was but a child in Kristiania then—back in 1860, or thereabouts, wasn't it? I can still remember my father reading about it. But it is like anything else; for those who fare well in this life there are just as many who fail."

"Arne," said Nels rising, "are we to become like old vagabonds who have at last found a warm hearth, and finding it, cease to hear the wind knocking on the windowpanes? God knows our early ancestors need not be emulated or revered, but are we grown so soft that we must regard with bitter envy those who dream and dare?"

Arne rose too and stood at the window beside Nels, thinking that it must have been harder than he suspected for the old sailor to return to the little patrimonial plot of his childhood. He looked down at the plunging mountainside that extended below the little plot of land on which Ørnheim perched. "Sometimes I, too, think of leaving," he said, "to join my brother Roald in America. If old Bergit were not blind and Elisabet not so content with life on our little farm, I might be tempted to scrape together every *krone* I could find and emigrate myself. Yet I suppose there is work enough to be done here—perhaps it will be something to teach our young not to be rocked to sleep by platitudes—"

"Well, then you have your work cut out for you!" laughed Nels. "For it seems to me we are a people here in Norway who, if we hear something good once, think it twice as good if we hear it again. So it is with Koppen in the pulpit every Sunday. I care not to go again," he said, with some anger in his deep voice.

"It is the priesthood of Christ we revere, not the human," said Arne quietly.

"So I have heard before," said Nels. "Yet it is the human voice we hear, and too often it is Koppen who speaks, not God."

"I have some few worries of my own," said Arne. "It is the parish priest who passes upon the success of my teaching. I would not have it told about, but I have already been warned that I must touch lightly, if at all, upon our man Bjørnson."

"You see!" exulted Nels. "I am right! What harm is there in reading these peasant tales?"

"It is not so much the novel he dislikes," explained Arne, "as it is Bjørnson's connection with the theater, at one time in Bergen and then in Kristiania." Nels was about to interrupt, but Arne held up a restraining hand. "The man is very literal, without imagination, and his wife is such a pietist. I feel it is she who finds so much sin about."

"I have seen her father's home in Bergen. Her old man could not have worried much about sin!" Nels laughed. "Or he would not have made so much money in shipping. Homely women I have found it hard to like," said Nels, "but a pinch-eyed, homely, pious one makes me shudder until my big bones rattle."

Arne was spared a reply, for Siri and her great-aunt rushed in, one almost as light-footed as the other. "My what you men must think of me!" exclaimed the little kernel of a woman. She took off a bright shawl and laid it neatly over the back of a chair. "Now calm yourselves, you two, and we shall soon have coffee. And for you, Siri, *lefse* rolled in sugar and some sweets in that tin under the cupboard. Fetch them now, quickly, Siri."

"Calm ourselves!" Nels repeated, going back to the bench. "Here we have sat, the two of us, with not a word to say until coffee loosens the tongue. For shame, Siri, taking your aunt all over the farm while we choke with thirst!" For a moment the child's brown eyes held a stricken look, but a small wink from Pappa sent her scuttling to search for the tin of sweets. Guro scratched in the glowing ashes of the little grate, added a few small bits of wood, and placed the coffee pot on the snapping fire.

"I have meant to come down and help Elisabet with the sewing," said Guro in her delicate, lilting voice. "But Nels, here, is such a big man; it takes so much doing to keep him fed. Siri." she said, "take a bit of advice from this little aunt of yours. Never marry a big man, you'll only grow smaller waiting on him." She put down the spoon with which she was stirring the coffee and placed her small, wrinkled hands upon the child's shoulder. "But you will never be as small as I," she said.

Siri arranged the little sweet cakes on a handpainted tin. "I shall not have too big a man," she said seriously, "for I shall marry Lars. He has promised to wait!"

"Lars!" exclaimed Nels, slapping his great thigh with an echoing smack. But Guro silenced him with a shake of her head.

"Lars will be a kind husband and a good farmer," said Arne, seeking to still the laughter in his own voice. "Siri is making a quilt for their bed," he said, scowling Nels into behavior. The child's eyes could not conceal the delight with which she met their words and the dignity of her inclusion in the serious affairs of the world.

Guro handed her a white cloth to lay on the table under the window. "And of course it is true, Siri, that if you grow tired of the pattern of your quilt and would have another, you can always use it on your doll bed." Cream and cheeses and *lefse* and bread appeared quickly on the table. Siri carried over the tray of sweets; and having placed it as close as she dared beside the place where she was to sit, she climbed up on her knees, rested her arms on the back of the chair, and looked out the small-paned window to the plunging view below. "You like it here!" exclaimed Guro, giving the child's cheek a swift kiss.

"You and Uncle Nels live so close to heaven," replied Siri in a small voice great with awe, "that you are never out of God's sight. Did you know," she confided softly, "that Grandma was struck down by God, and when she was able to crawl to her knees again she was blind!"

"Oh, no, child, no!" exclaimed Guro softly. "You mustn't say that!"

"But she told me herself!" the child whispered sharply.

"It is merely Bergit's manner of speaking, Siri. You must not always take your grandmother's words too seriously. She is like her brother Nels here," she whispered. "Your Uncle Nels, too, says many things he does not truly mean; it is a way of speaking some folk have; they are not always serious when they seem to be, nor glad when they would have you think so. One must never worry too much about words." She called them to the table on which delicate English cups gleamed in the strange, yellowed daylight—cups that Nels's wanderings had brought her when she lived as a bride in Bergen, waiting, always waiting for his return from some journey across the seas.

Nels passed the plate of rolled *lefse* to the child. "But we have not said grace," she said.

"Perhaps you're right, little one," he said, "but it's my belief God knows we're grateful for this food. We have waited long enough." Nevertheless he bowed his massive, shaggy head while Arne spoke the familiar words of thanks. When the table prayer was over, he turned to Arne. "I like the custom of some folk abroad who do not talk to God in measured verse. You would think he could not understand us unless we took our words from some book a dead saint has written."

"Nels! Nels!" reproached Guro. "Elisabet will never let the child come up here again. Arne," she said, putting her small hand on his sleeve, "can you understand what has come over Nels?"

Arne glanced affectionately at Guro. "Nothing that does not come over all of us at times," he replied. "The world has need of rebels too." They ate in companionable silence, with Siri making quick work of the *lefse*, for her eyes were on the *fattigmand* and *krumkake*.

"Take some, child," said Guro, "for they were baked for you and Elisabet. They're meager fare for Nels, and I eat so little these days you will have to help us get rid of them." Siri nibbled delicately, as thoughtful children do, to make delicacies last on the tongue. Finally, when the coffee pot was almost empty, Guro arose and Siri with her, to begin clearing the table. The child whispered something in the old woman's ear. "It cannot hurt to ask," said the aunt. But Siri demurred, blushing deeply when Nels turned to stare at her. "Ask him!" urged Guro, giving her a playful push.

"Can you—would you take out the fiddle?" she asked, rushing to Papa's side lest Nels embarrass her with playful words.

"I cannot think where it is!" exclaimed Nels. "I have not seen it since you were here last. Could it be that you have taken it down the mountainside to give to Lars?"

"Papa, I know where it is. Truly," she whispered, clinging to the tail of his coat.

"But you might look," said Nels. "I have known things to disappear and as mysteriously come back again." Siri skipped across the wooden floor and bent down to open a cupboard in the corner beside a bed.

"Here it is," she said, carrying the dragon-headed fiddle to the grinning Nels. "Play a *springdans*. Will you play a *springdans*?"

Nels took the fiddle, drew the bow across the strings, and produced a cacophony of notes that sent Siri's hands flying to her ears. He stared at her with a sad, unblinking look. "It's a pity that you

Siri's braids flew, her skirts flew, her feet flew

do not like my playing, for it was always understood that I was to fiddle in your wedding procession. Now you will have to engage a stranger." He put the fiddle down on the table.

"Nels! Nels! Play for her!" coaxed Guro with an indulgent laugh. "It's growing late, and something in my bones tells me we shall have a weather change." She put out her arms to Siri.. "And I will dance with you." Nels put the old fiddle under his chin, and suddenly the little room was alive with merry sounds and the rhythmic tapping of his great foot. Siri's braids flew, her skirts flew, her feet flew; but even so, she was not so light as Guro. When Nels's fiddle stopped for a moment, she flew to Papa, who stood beaming at the three of them.

"Dance with me, Dad!" she cried. So Papa danced, a little self-consciously at first, then faster and faster. Stamp. Stamp. Stamp. The fiddle whined and sang, the old boards of the cottage shook under the tread of Arne's foot, and Guro stood laughing, her worn old hands clasped together with delight. Suddenly she could stand it no longer, and she was in the dance, too, light as a fall bramble, beside them, back of them, around them—until finally Siri and Arne stopped to watch her.

When the fiddling was over, she drew a hand across her gray-brown hair and said a little self-consciously, "Ah, but I must look like a silly she-troll.. About some things I guess I had no sense when I was young; and if you have no sense when you're young it could well be you will have less when you're old." Arne said he had heard it was often the other way around, but—no matter—they must be going. Never had he and Siri had a better time.

"There is one more thing that must be done," said Guro, giving Nels a sage look. With quick-tumbling words she explained that a mysterious package had come to them some days ago, but the man in the village who gave it to them said it was not to be opened by anyone but Siri. If Nels would fetch it now, perhaps Siri would like to take off the wrappings. The old man said he would be glad to bring in the box, but he was a little afraid of foreign parcels. He had been out in the world enough to know that there were such things as strange snakes and gunpowder and any number of mysterious things that snapped and bit and clawed. Nevertheless he went off into a little room and came back with a box almost as long as the width of Siri's shoulders.

Putting it in her arms, he backed off and said, "You never know what's inside a foreign parcel. I'll crouch here beside the bench while you untie the string." He hid his face in his hands, peering out between his fingers. "Get back, Arne!" he warned, but Arne felt that Siri was excited enough, so he remained beside the table, cap in hand. Guro brought the scissors, and only the women remained characteristically imperturbable in the face of an unopened package. At last the wrappings were off.

Then Guro backed off, holding the string and the paper in her hands. "Even I give up," she said laughing, "for who ever heard of putting one package inside another?"

"Is—is the package safe?" called Nels, still down on all fours, his voice rumbling upward from the floor. Nimble little fingers worked at the second string; then with a sweeping movement she had the lid off and stood staring at the contents as though mesmerized into immobility. She stared first at Papa, then at Aunt Guro, and finally at Nels, who was now back on the bench. "A doll! Oh, a doll!" she cried.

Guro embraced the child and box. "Take it out. Take the doll out, for she has come across several seas to nestle in your arms." Siri picked it up as though it might shatter at the merest brush of a finger. "Don't be afraid. Just love it," said her aunt. Quick tears caused Guro to pick up the corner of her apron and dab at her eyes, and Nels coughed a few times and then strode to the front door to spit eloquently into the bushes.

"It is too costly a gift for so small a one," said Arne, abashed.

"For the joy she has given us it is nothing," replied Guro.

"I am told," said Nels, "that even such an innocent thing as a doll is disapproved of down in the parsonage."

But Arne, always of a pacific mind in parish matters, replied, "It is merely one aspect of the wave of pietism sweeping over Norway."

"No wonder so many of our young folk leave," countered Nels. "Add hunger of spirit to such poverty as some of them have known— well, what is there to keep them?"

"I cannot think," said Guro, packing a basket of sweets and

cheeses, "that anyone would object to such a delicate and innocent thing as that doll." She glanced quickly at the child, fearing their conversation would upset her rapt delight.

"The old folk often looked at anything in the shape of a human as an idol, though I expect that in these modern times there are not too many left who do," said Arne.

Nels picked out a small twig from the basket beside the grate, held the little piece of wood above the embers, and when the twig burst into flame, relighted his pipe. "Who can say what is an idol? Is a man who builds a better boat than his neighbor's creating an idol? An idol shaped by pride in his work? Is a man like Koppen who polishes his words of doom to give them a Sunday airing creating an idol—an idol fashioned in the tumult of his own self-centered esteem?"

"Go, you two!" said Guro, giving Arne a playful push and placing her arm about the child. "Go before Nels begins another sermon." She gave her husband a teasing smile. "It's envy that eats him. He would like to be in that pulpit himself, for one has only to listen to him with one ear to see how easy it is for him to preach."

"Thank them again," whispered Arne, so with the doll clutched tightly in her arms, Siri went over and gave them each a kiss. "Many thanks," she said again and again. Their arms burdened with gifts, they finally took leave of the old couple outside the house and started toward the little footbridge, waving to one another again and again. A sudden warm wind blew over the mountain; the aspens in the path below stirred and shook; the conifers set up a hum. Arne had a pulling eagerness to be home again; and as they approached the tarn, Siri pressed the doll to her chest with one arm and gave her free hand to her father. The sighing breeze blew both hot and cold, rattling the dead growth at the tops of the trees and moving in sharp little whispers through the sear undergrowth. Baleful, staring, unwinked by even the smallest ripple, the tarn seemed to eye their retreating footsteps. When they were sheltered by intervening thickets Siri said, "That tarn would have liked to drown my doll."

"It only scowls," he said, "like any other thing that shuts itself away from others. It needs an inlet and an outlet. Forget it as something not worth thinking about." Perceiving the changeful quality of the breeze, Arne again felt disquieted and restless. Elisabet, he recalled, had urged them to come back early, saying that the day might prove as fickle as hares in a hayloft; and Bergit had said that something deep in her bones had felt a change, but then she added that no one should heed her mutterings, for she had little else to do than listen to the groanings of her ancient flesh.

They were clambering down now, holding on to bush and tree trunk, down an ancient stony path which must have once heard the heavy-footed tread of the Viking warrior. Arne longed for evening, with the lamp lit on the scrubbed pine table, Elisabet sitting beside him sewing, and Bergit rocking contentedly in her worn high-backed chair. His mind moved along a stream of disarticulate thoughts, settling for a moment on Nels, whose arena of struggle had moved from a larger world to a very narrow one; and then his thoughts moved into an eddy of problems related to his own status in the district—a status he had never questioned until the new clergyman's arrival.

"You are not listening, Father!" chided Siri. "I have asked you twice what to name my doll."

He scrambled down a thorny ledge to join the child, whose eyes were intent upon the shawl-wrapped doll. "I am afraid my thoughts were wandering," he said. "Do you like your own name, Siri?"

She pursed her lips thoughtfully and replied in a musing manner. "I like it well enough. But it was dug out of a mound."

"So it was," he agreed, placing his hand on her shoulder. "You bear a name spoken by tongues of old. But the past lives in all of us, even as the future does. If a troll peers into the window at night, it is because it wishes to look upon a human. It is the human tale that should excite the mind and warm the heart; and if anyone should ever tell you, dearest, that it is not a tale worth telling, remind him that God himself became incarnate."

"Yes, Father," she said, enduring his lecture politely, "but would you hold my doll now? I want to look over the ledge."

"Be careful!" he warned, placing the doll on the basket of sweets and cheese.

As he joined her on the escarpment, she looked back with a worried frown. "Your doll is perfectly safe," he assured her. How different

now was the look of sea and mountain and air! There was no radiance anywhere, not from the peaks of snow nor from the circling
sweep of sea. The little sunburned buildings and the larger red-
roofed house looked dwarfed and forlorn in the sulphur-colored air.
He caught sight of Elisabet standing at the corner of the house, saw
the movement of her hand, and waved in return. "I have a doll,
Mother!" She hopped up and down on the ledge, until Arne took
a lunge and grabbed at her jacket. "Can you hear me, Mother?"

"She can't hear you!" he scolded. "You must not excite her." They
picked their way back to the basket and then on down the old familiar path from which they could hear the sound of their little
stream.

"She still has no name," said Siri.

"That is true."

"Without a name she will not seem truly mine."

"Would you like a foreign name? She is a Parisian doll, you know."

"I'd rather have you dig it out of a mound, I think."

"You understand, kitten legs, that I actually do not dig it out of
a mound."

"Of course, Father," Siri assured him with the smallest taint of
hauteur. "Bergit told me it was dug out of a mound and then put
in a book."

He smiled teasingly. "How would you like 'Katla'?" She made a
horrid face. "Katrina—Trina?"

"Trina!" she said happily. The heavy air was growing warmer,
ever more pressing as they descended to the little sloping hayfield
above the farm. Balder had caught wind of them, leaping across
the grass, barking his delight. Now they were home, and nothing
could restrain the child. The dog and she ran through the little copse
and across a small footbridge. The child's cry sounded muffled and
strange in the still air. "Mother! Grandmother! Gunhild!" she cried.
"Come see what I have brought! Come see Trina. Down, Balder,
down."

Arne stepped on the little footbridge—now above a strangely
muted little stream, flowing into a sullied sea. He stood there before
descending, suddenly seeing them as a stranger would—the young
woman, his wife, wearing the stiff headdress of the district, a head-

dress that did not conceal a swirl of her silvery blond hair; Bergit, similarly coifed, straight and unseeing, both hands resting on the knob of her cane; and copper-haired Gunhild clapping her hands over the new doll Siri paraded before them.

Elisabet glanced up the pathway where Arne stood, indicated to Gunhild that she should help the old one and the young one in; and then she moved up the path toward her husband, a small woman, straight of shoulder, supple in movement. "I am so glad you are back," she said, moving into his welcoming arm.

"Is everything all right?"

Elisabet matched her steps to his and did not reply immediately. "I suppose it is, Arne, yet the air presses like a burden upon us all, the gulls have disappeared, and the small birds are silent. I can't like the look of things—that's all."

CHAPTER 2

Arne

After the death of their former pastor, Arne had often puzzled about their future at Fjeldstrand. Although he had not communicated his worries to Bergit, he felt that the old woman surmised more than she had ever indicated. Hearing him in the orchard on the day before his and the child's visit to Ørnheim, Bergit had slowly tapped her way to the tree under which he was picking culls.

Arne found vacations rewarding to both mind and body, for physical exertion gave him a sense of wholeness and time to reflect coolly on problems he had pushed back for further deliberation. Never before had life provided so ample a living for him; but did the same folk, he often wondered who smiled indulgently at the pastor's impassioned defense of poverty also smile deprecatingly at him, who had also married a woman with more means than he?

Bergit, who could be as straightforward as a sudden shaft of sunlight or as elusive as the shade of a wind-rustled forest, had chosen the latter course today. "I remember the time," she began, "when we entertained Ivar Aasen. I was only a little girl, but I remember his short visit well." As Bergit's cane searched the ground before her, Arne held a bracing hand in readiness, lest she fall as she groped to find a seat on a large rock beside the worn path; but he did not offer his assistance, having learned that Bergit's independence embraced ambulation as well as speech.

He waited until she had seated herself. "It would have been a privilege to meet him," said Arne, "for all of Norway is indebted to his work."

He watched with fascination as she drew her knitting from an apron pocket and ran her slender fingers across the surface of a half-finished stocking, finding the loops for her knitting needles. "Yes, it was quite a book he wrote, that dictionary of our folk language. Olaf always treasured his copy." Her deep-lidded eyes were fixed on the sea that stretched below the orchard slope, and Arne again found it difficult to believe that she was completely sightless, for

18

the expression of her eyes was extraordinarily responsive to her changing thoughts. "Your head is so full of stories and learning, Arne—do you ever think of writing a book yourself?"

Arne smiled with pleasure but replied that his head was not so full of learning as she thought; he was merely good at skimming over the bare spots—and as for writing a book, many a man had thoughts about it, but little talent and less will for it. "Now that we are alone," she said, "I would speak earnestly with you. You must not let Koppen worry you too much if you have an occasional difference of opinion. In my years I have seen them come and go— men of God, some of them, and also men who served themselves before they served God. Sometimes it is not so much the man's own fault. Perhaps he should not have chosen a holy profession; perhaps he was driven to it by an ambitious and proud family; perhaps he is diverted by a frivolous or selfish wife. Even a man like Koppen is only making the best of it. Mark how I talk to him when he makes *me* a visit!"

Arne laughed. "He doesn't know how to take you, I am sure."

"There is only One who knows how to take any of us, Arne. Because I have had so much time to think these past few years, it has become a wonder in my mind that folk get on as well as they do, each of us being like those stones along the sea—'tis a stone we are and a stone we'll be, though we wear a little off each other's edges."

Arne bit into an apple he had pulled from an upper branch of a tree. "Is it bad then—being a stone?"

"It's all we can be, some of us a little harder than others." She rested her busy hands. "So whatever you are, Arne," she said, "you'll have to be a little more of, so that folk know you intend being truly what you are."

"I cannot tell whether you have said much or very little!" He laughed. "Nevertheless," he said, sobering, "it is not that I care only for myself, but my students are growing restive under his close surveillance. Time and again he has come into my schoolroom this winter, once chiding me in front of my students for reciting to them a contemporary poem."

"Perhaps," replied Bergit, "I am only an ignorant hill woman, but such things have never bothered me. I can remember when I was a bride and had a new-fangled stove brought back to Fjeldstrand— the very one Gunhild was baking *lefse* on as I came out. None at that time had anything like it, at least none of the folk I knew. When we were in the city at one time I saw such a contraption and could not get it out of my mind how clean it was in comparison with the smoke and ashes of the open flame. So Olaf brought it back with us." Bergit threw back her head and laughed. "It so happened that we returned in somewhat of a storm—'twas all Olaf could do to make it to the village across the fjord. We landed drenched and blue with cold. When the little tempest had blown itself out, we had quite a gathering at the wharf, and it was then that some in joking— and some more serious than they would let on—told us that Olaf had paid quite a price for his wife's pride, that its weight and un- gainliness in the sailboat could well have sunk us. I can remember Sigurd Olafson, then a young man, who had come down to the wharf to see us off, turning to the folk who would rub off the shine of my purchase and saying, 'It is a question who has the more pride —Bergit here, who would cook in the new way or the folk who are so proud they have no pride.' It was not long before others, too, had such stoves; and so I say to you, Arne, if it is that you are young and would do things other than the way of the old, why do you worry about those that criticize?"

"I must do nothing that would jeopardize the lives of those I love."

"Fiddlesticks!" said the old one. "We are not starving." She was knitting steadily, her face turned toward the orchard slope and the gleaming sea beyond. "It may be that a man like you belongs in America. It is a place large enough, I have been told, for many opinions."

"Unthinkable!" said Arne.

"Unthinkable?" she parried. "Unthinkable because I have often said I myself would not go? I am one of those stones that will soon be turned underground; but even so, if I wanted to go, blind as a newborn kitten though I am, still I would go. I would miss you all— unbearably sometimes, but the truth is that parting is inevitable. Perhaps it was necessary for me to become blind to learn what I should have known long ago; it is *I* I must live with, I in this encumbered body with its restless mind." She sighed, rolled up the stocking and the needles and tucked them into her apron pocket. "Arne," she said in her deep, even voice, "I am like a fallen leaf, no longer a part of a living tree, and must be willing to live on the nurture that is within me until I am gathered upon the great autumn bonfire."

"You must not speak so sadly," said her son-in-law. "You have us all with you; you're not alone."

Putting her hand on her cane, she rose, "It's true, and I am glad for it. Still that is not my meaning. I have often looked within, now that the world is dark, and what I am saying is something you, too, must learn, and Siri as well. Elisabet will never learn it, I fear, for she is of such a gentle nature she must cling—once it was to Olaf, then to me, and now it is to you. For such as she, you can only pray that life will be kind. But little Siri, now, will need your guidance. She and the world will have to come to terms, for so it is with strongminded folk." She put out her free hand and Arne clasped it warmly. "It is good to have someone listen to an old woman's prattle, boy. Take in that basket of fruit, now, for I shall bid the women move the coffee pot forward on that wicked old stove." He watched her move slowly on the upward path to the house. She does not bend forward toward her searching cane, as so many old folk do, thought Arne, but walks as upright as her will. As he picked up the basket, he noticed the changing weather; the coolish autumn evening seemed to be warming now at early twilight. The days were becoming so short that one could scarcely afford to loiter. He swung the basket to his shoulder and felt inwardly warmed by his long visit with Bergit. He would never grow accustomed to the difference between her and Elisabet—but nevertheless he would not have them otherwise, the old one so sharp and wise and the young one so warm and yielding.

When he joined them at the table, Lars was there too, having returned from the village where he had left some fish for Mrs. Moen. Pale night was upon the little huddled buildings and the sea below as they sat down for supper. They regarded Lars and Gunhild almost like family members at Fjeldstrand, Lars coming when he was free to help them about the little farm and Gunhild planning to remain through Elisabet's confinement, and perhaps even longer. Whenever Lars and his sister were together as they were now, Arne found himself recalling the old tale about Gunnar, Gunhild's father, who, it seemed, had brought home the year-old Gunhild to his bride of four months—a child "conceived and delivered in a hay loft, if I know the ways of some people," sniffed the widow Moen, an expert on such subjects. Anna, Gunnar's bride, could not have been wholly pleased by this addition to the bridal bed. A year later Anna had borne twin sons and then, finally, Lars, now a strapping seventeen-year-old who had accompanied Gunnar on many a fishing trip, but expressed no special inclination for the sea.

"Most of this meal I have made with my own hands," said Siri. "Father, are you listening?" Still it was Lars whom she was eyeing.

Roused from his thoughts, Arne smiled and said, "So that's what's wrong with it! I feel as though I had swallowed an anchor. Lars, how do you feel?"

Siri eyed both men anxiously and then said swiftly, "It's true that Gunhild did most of the mixing, but I did the stirring." Elisabet, who had been quiet throughout the meal, smiled at them all vacantly and said that she wished to lie down, if they did not mind—but let them visit all they cared.

Arne looked at the small swollen figure apprehensively but Gunhild said, "She is all right—just a little tired. She was out in the smokehouse all afternoon, but I saw to it that she lifted nothing heavy." Though Arne turned back to the table, it was clear that his mind was troubled.

"And how was it in the village today?" he asked, for Lars, unlike Gunhild, did not talk easily without priming.

"I thought I would never get away from Kari Moen. When I finally shook her off, it was too late to see anyone else, though I did see Mikjell later."

"I suspect escaping Kari Moen is a common complaint," said Bergit, feeling for her rocking chair. "Come sit in my lap, Siri, for it is sad when you are too busy for a little chat."

"And what was the widow's complaint?"

"She took me aside to complain of Mikjell's discontent; he is determined to leave before another winter sets in."

"In my mind there is no doubt that the boy has consumption."

"Are they penniless?"

Arne handed his plate to Gunhild.. "They are not upon the parish, if that is what you mean. But I am sure a journey of some extent is well beyond their resources."

"When I got down to the boat, Mikjell was waiting for me. Poor boy!" said Lars with a shake of his head. "I didn't know whom to be sorrier for—him or his mother." Lars glanced toward the window and rose. "The moon will soon be up. I must be getting home." Siri slid off her grandmother's lap.

"You come tomorrow?" she asked, placing her hand in Lars's.

"Have you forgotten? Tomorrow we climb up to Ørnheim," said her father, "but, come, we'll walk Lars down to the boat."

As they moved toward the landing, "It is not cold enough for this time of year," said Lars. "Father is sure we shall have a change." They paused beside the little boathouse and pier.

"You will soon have the moon," commented Arne. "I can see a glimmering on the peaks."

Lars pinched Siri's cheek lightly and stepped into his rowboat. As he lifted an oar, he said, "Arne, I almost forgot. The widow wants a talk with you—it was the last thing she said."

"It's a wonder there *was* a last, but thanks, anyway!" Arne called as the boat moved away.

"Farvel, Lars! Goodbye! Goodbye!" Siri cupped her hand over her eyes and peered across the water. She turned away finally and held out her arms to her father, who lifted her up and carried her to the house. At the door she said with a little whisper, "Father, I am so glad God made Lars."

"You run in," suggested Arne, "and I'll make sure everything is safe for the night." He made a quick survey of the cowshed, said a few words to Vankel, the goat, patted the workhorses—all the while he was trailed by Balder, who yawned and stretched sleepily. "You're getting old, fellow," he said. "Why weren't you at the pier?" He would have to see about the chicken house, for Elisabet said something was tunneling into the foundation—one more task to be done before he returned to the children and their books. When the circuit was completed, Balder moved back to his bed in the hay and

Arne walked toward the house. The moon had cleared the mountains, and the small sea-intruded valley was golden along the waters,
shaded along the shoreline. Chill dampness rose from the ground,
but the air itself was not sharp with autumn chill. Arne stood by
the doorstep for a moment, wishing earnestly that he knew more
about the moon and the constellations—yes, what lay above the earth
and beneath his feet. Even the making of weather was a mystery.
He shook his head disparagingly: folk thought it was simple to teach
the young; but it was not easy if you knew the young should emerge
more curious and perhaps more knowing than those who taught
them—else what was man doing, merely marking time?

When he came into the house he discovered that Elisabet had already gone to bed, and he heard his daughter's questioning voice
upstairs and Gunhild's laughing replies. "Did she say how she was
feeling?" he asked Bergit, who sat rocking with the old brass-bound
Bible in her lap.

"Tired," said Bergit, "and she hoped you'd come to bed soon."

"Shall I read to you, Mother?"

"Not tonight. My mind reads to itself, for the old words are not
forgotten. But snuff out the lamp if you will."

"Goodnight," he said, patting her shoulder as he went toward his
bedroom.

When he was undressing, Elisabet sat up. "I can't fall asleep. The
moon has risen, I see." The light through the eight-paned casements
shone upon the bed where she sat, illuminating her face and the
two heavy braids falling across her high little bosom to the small
protuberance under her nightdress. In the golden light her eyes
looked shadowed and troubled.

"You are very beautiful tonight," he said, slipping in beside her,
pulling her head to his shoulder. He could smell the fresh cleanness
of her hair. "Is anything troubling you?"

"Nothing that I can find words for." She sighed and snuggled
her head under his chin.

"I was going to read," he said, "but then I had such a longing for
you that I came to bed earlier than I had planned. It's good that in
this world of struggle we have each other."

"It is," she agreed. He could feel her head growing heavier on his shoulder; she roused for a moment, lifting her head to look into his face. "I hope you did not want to talk. I am very tired." He helped her settle down, lying very still until he heard her gentle breathing. Then he stretched his legs and placed his hands back of his neck. Sleep was far away, and he glanced about the shadowy room and its familiar surroundings—the cupboard with its ornate scrollwork, his desk which a cabinetmaker across the fjord had built, his large bookcase, the highbacked chairs of another century. All these had become very dear to him, and he could take none of these possessions for granted, least of all Elisabet's gift of commanding all the small things in her world, both animate and inanimate, into cozy well-being.

He could scarcely remember a time when his mother had smiled. Most of his early years had been hard and bitter, yet he carried a residual memory of warmth and fun. What had happened to change her, he wondered. He recalled coming home from school to find her lying down, her dark hair uncombed, a loose wrapper tied carelessly around her waist. Had poverty made her indolent and uncomplaining, or had there been a sickness of mind which enabled her to live in a house with its work undone and the fires almost out? Surely, thought Arne, there are sicknesses of mind almost as common as sicknesses of body, sicknesses for which we have not bothered to find a name—or worse, a cause.

For a while schooling had appeared out of the question for his brother and him, beyond what the poorest had. One chilly day, however, their father had drawn them out for a walk, a luxury he rarely permitted himself since he often labored overtime on the accounts of a small shipping firm which employed him. "It is for you two I have worked so hard," he said. "Roald thinks he can find his future across the ocean in America. He being the older, let us all work hard to send him there. Then he in turn can help you, Arne."

Now that he had so much, thought Arne, what serpent of the mind had slipped into the thickets of memory to bite his apple of content. Would he never forget the tensions of his childhood, the feeling of treading between two worlds—the one bright and beckoning, the other dark and tragic? What drove other men to struggle, he did not know, but he knew a cold wind upon his back had driven him to the gates of learning.

He heard Bergit's footsteps moving slowly to her own room—she who lay down and rose to a darkened world. Now the house had grown entirely silent. He heard the wash of waves upon the rocks below, and beside him Elisabet's soft breathing. Once when he and Bergit had talked, he recalled saying that theirs was a strange household, for the man of the house idled in comparison with the women, who must wrestle with the daily tasks of survival. "We have always had farmers and fishermen at Fjeldstrand," she said, "so it is gain to have one who nurtures the mind."

Arne tucked the homespun blanket around Elisabet's shoulders and slid down under the covers. How strange it was to think of another life lying there with them, bound so closely to Elisabet, yet a being whom her conscious thought could neither form nor determine.

Careful not to awaken her, he turned on his side and rested his hand gently on her thigh. It was beyond all understanding, he thought, how so small a creature as Elisabet had so great a gift for sustaining and comforting him. Never would their children, he vowed, grow up as Roald and he had—too often comfortless and lonely.

Delicate waves of slumber washed against the shores of thought. A moment before he sank into the flood of sleep he was faintly aware of the rustling patter of some musteline searching about the foundations of the house. Then all of Fjeldstrand was asleep, while the moon traveled slowly through the rooms, shining upon ancient boards and scrolled carvings; and the waiting sea nibbled patiently upon the shore below the house.

CHAPTER 3

The Storm

On the eve of their return from Ørnheim they had almost forgotten the threatening weather and the yellow-gray sea, there being so much talk of their visit to Ørnheim and of Siri's new doll.

Arne, always aware of Bergit's deep need for communication, words that recalled for her the ascending path to her old childhood home, words that enabled her once again to sit on the promontory overlooking home and sea, began to picture for her the small events of their visit. First, of course, Arne had asked about the man who had put in beside their pier, wondering about the women's airy dismissal of this visitor, who, according to Elisabet and Gunhild, was like any other merchant. He had merely carried on his vessel a few things they needed, nothing remarkable. "Except himself," remarked Bergit with a satisfied chuckle. "The man had a caressing voice, and I felt the room grow warm with Gunhild's blushes." Still, she went on, she had no eyes for him herself; and whether he was handsome or not she would never know, for the two women could not agree on that point afterward.

With more success, Arne returned to the subject of Guro, and Bergit said, "I can remember well when Nels brought her home years ago. My, how we stared at that little woman: all chatter and liveliness and fun! Secretly I wondered what she saw in my ship's-frame of a brother, but she lived contentedly enough with him, first in Bergen, and then along the south coast." She searched about the table for her tobacco, which Arne quickly put into her hand and helped her light the pipe. He had now grown accustomed to her evening smoke, although Bergit remembered with amusement his initial shock; still it had made sense to him when Bergit explained it as a comfort to one of the few senses left to her. Elisabet, however, always so personally fastidious, had insisted upon one restraint: Bergit was not to smoke in *fine* company, not when the new minister and his city-bred wife called, nor in front of other people who might understandably be offended. At best, said Elisabet, it was an unspeakably odorous custom, bad enough in a man but unthinkable in her own mother were she not so limited in her pleasures.

"As I was saying," continued the old one, "Guro made Nels a fine wife. Then when Mother died and Nels had quit the sea, Father would not come down here beside the sea to live. Guro declared that she was weary of city life and would be willing to try the farm. Now we shall see, I thought to myself, what that little house plant will do up in that lonely croft!" Bergit puffed on her pipe. "But, do you know, she cared well for my father until he died; and then she made friends with all the living things, both great and small, and lived as happily among the clouds at Ørnheim as she had done anywhere else. She had so much energy that when her work was done up there she often came tripping down the old mountain path to help me with my sewing and baking."

"A most endearing little woman," agreed Arne.

"It was after one of these visits here that she met a bear."

"A bear, Grandmother?" Siri set the doll on a pillow and hurried over to her grandmother's rocking chair.

"It's a story I am sure you have heard, little one. She had spent the day with us, having accompanied us to church in the morning. It was almost dusk as she started back; but nothing bothered Guro, and she sang as she walked. She had a lovely voice in her youth, Arne—so clear and high. Suddenly she heard a crashing noise in the path above her, and there stood a great black bear, teetering on its legs, pawing the air."

Siri held on to the arm of the chair with both hands. "What did she do, Grandmother?"

"Have patience. A tale must be told in its own way."

"She backed slowly down the path, the bear following. As Guro tells it, the thought came to her that the way back was farther than the way home; and if it was her singing he had liked, sing she would. She told Nels later that never had he paid her voice the attention that bear did."

"Was she awfully frightened, Grandmother?"

"As frightened as a mouse on a millrace. She said later that was one song that could well have lasted into the night. Finally, however, the creature got down on its four legs and moved on through the woods in a crash of twigs and bushes."

"Dinner!" called Elisabet. "If you will come to the table, please."

"Is that the only story you have to tell?" asked Siri, hanging on to the chair as she drew an imaginary circle with her feet.

"I promise you another tonight," replied Bergit, allowing Arne to lead her to the table. All bowed their heads as Arne said the familiar grace.

"Uncle Nels doesn't like to say grace," remarked Siri as she accepted a plate of food from her mother.

"That one!" scoffed Bergit. "Sometimes I think it's a wonder God did not upset one of the boats he sailed on and toss him to the whales."

"You do not mean that, Mother," scolded Elisabet, who was of a literal mind. She looked about at the rest. "Just let one of us only hint that Nels is remiss about church going, and you're the first to make excuses for him!"

"Did this visitor today bring any news either from the big world or the village?" asked Arne. He was aware of his wife's exchanging glances with Gunhild. Finally Elisabet remarked that merchants tend to pick up a lot of talk—scarcely any of it worth believing.

"No more than you two women are to be believed," said Arne with amusement.

"It has never been my custom to intrude between husband and wife," said Bergit, looking apologetically in Elisabet's direction, "but you will recall that it was my opinion that Arne deserved to know what has happened in the village today."

"And what good would that do?" asked Elisabet reproachfully. "Well, since she has started it, I may as well tell you that this Tosten Vegg told us that the Moen boy ran away late last night."

"I am not surprised," said Arne steadily. "How was this accomplished?"

"When his mother was somewhere visiting," replied Elisabet, "he went into the cottage, packed his belongings, and went down to the harbor, where he found passage, they thought, with some fishermen going toward the coast."

"I should have gone over to the village myself today," said Arne regretfully, "for Lars told me last night that the widow wished to see me. Perhaps she and the boy had been arguing. First thing in the morning," he said thoughtfully, "I'll go over and see what comfort I can give her." Elisabet sighed with relief, agreeing that there was nothing that could be done now.

But Gunhild, who had risen to fill Arne's cup, said impulsively, "What makes us mad is that many in the village are blaming you. Is that not so, Elisabet?" The girl blushed deeply when she saw her mistress' look of anger.

"Why are they blaming *me*, Gunhild?" asked Arne.

"Wash up the dishes, Gunhild!" ordered Elisabet. "None of this is your concern, anyway."

Arne saw that the young girl was close to tears. "Don't feel sorrow over your words," he said.

"The village talk," said Bergit quietly, "is that you must have given the boy money for his passage, since you favor emigration." She felt for the cane which always hung on the back of the chair. "Whether you wish to believe such silly nonsense, I do not know. How do we know that this Tosten Vegg is not given to exaggeration?"

"What are you going to do, Arne?" Elisabet moved after him as he took a jacket from a hook. "No, No!" she cried, attempting to take the coat out of his hands. "You agreed with me when you came down from Ørnheim that the weather looked bad and just a moment ago you said you would go in the morning, not tonight."

"I'll be back in less than two hours' time."

"Just what do you think you can do over there? This is a senseless errand, Arne."

"There are two things I can do, Elisabet." He eluded her grasp and moved over to the door that led into a little storehouse. "I can bring some comfort to the Moen woman, and I can let the village gossips tell me to my face what they think. Elisabet, Elisabet," he said, seeing the look of strain on her face, "I have crossed on many a stormy day, if it is the weather that worries you. I can always stay overnight with the Engs, as I have done many a time."

"Where are you going, Papa?" Siri clasped him about the legs, tilting her head upward to study him with serious and questioning eyes. He set down the lantern and swept her into his arms and pinched a dimpled cheek.

"I am going on an errand, little one," he replied, "and when I come back I shall have grown a little taller, I think." He kissed her gently and set her down.

"How shall you do that, Father?"

"Run to Grandmother," said Elisabet, giving her a little shove. "She will have a story for you."

"And you, Bergit," said Arne, "keep all these children well in hand."

"That's a task to my liking. But be careful, Arne, for even the good man should not tempt his luck."

He beckoned to Gunhild to follow Elisabet and him out. When they had reached the path to the sea, he said, "Make sure that Elisabet goes right in."

"See how strange the light is," Elisabet remarked. "One can scarcely tell where the land ends and the sea begins. The waters are so still—as if the entire world is dead and we are walking in a dream."

"Come now," he said tightening his hold about her waist. "I know it is common for those who carry a child to have a heavy heart sometimes."

He helped her across the stony rise which led to the small pier. "Look, Arne, not a lamp's light shows in the village across the water!" She flung herself into his arms, digging her fingers into the rough homespun of his shirt.

He set the lantern down and his coat beside it and took her in his arms and kissed her again and again. Then they held each other close in a warm, bridal-night yearning. "See how it is with us still," he said softly. You know I would do nothing to part us. Lights will show when I get a little closer, and the widow Moen will be up, of that I am sure, and the pastor often reads far into the night."

"That Moen woman!" said Elisabet scornfully. "She is born to weep and wail as I am to love you, Arne!"

Arne drew himself free and called to Gunhild. "Get her back into the house, now." He drew the hawser off the post and stepped nimbly into the boat, drawing up the anchor and lifting the square-ended oars into position and shoved away from the pier. In the faint

He drew the hawse
off the post an...
stepped nimbl...
into the boa...

yellowed darkness Elisabet saw his smile and wave; and as the boat slid away she returned his gesture of farewell with a small re-straining wave. She stood and looked as long as she could see any-thing of him and the boat, and then she allowed Gunhild to lead her toward the shore. There she stopped.

"The sea," she said, with indrawn breath, "has a kind of swelling to it. Can you see it? I thought I felt it shake the pier."

Overawed by the evening's events and still a little piqued over Elisabet's earlier anger, Gunhild said with unaccustomed formality, "Fru Elisabet, I see nothing." The two moved on to the house, where the lamp's light was a puny flame against the encroaching darkness. As they started into the house, something stirred against the back door, whimpering softly.

"Balder!" exclaimed Elisabet. "When did you ever see a boat leave and not bark farewell?" She stroked his head and chided him softly.

"Is that you, Mother?" The back door silhouetted a plump little figure clad in a nightdress.

"Get back to the barn," said Elisabet, giving Balder a little shove. "Yes, who else would it be, Siri?" With troubled eyes the child watched her mother move past her and sit down at the pine table, where a lamp cast its steady flame. Elisabet put her head down upon her arms and began to sob. The child moved toward her grand-mother's rocker. For a while none said a word nor tried to stop Elisabet's tears.

Then Gunhild began to wash the evening's dishes, and Bergit drew Siri to her lap, whispering to her softly. "I'll sing a tune," she said.

Elisabet lifted her head. "Mother, your singing upsets me."

"It upsets me too," said her mother drily. "But it's the only voice I have." She stroked the child's head. "Siri, why don't you wipe dishes for Gunhild?" When the child had joined the girl, the old one said, "Elisabet, surely you are wife enough to know that a man and woman never look at strife through the same window, for a man looks through the bare pane and sees it as it is. A woman wishes to draw a curtain between her and the ugly sight. Your Arne is of a gentler nature than many men—it is this that makes him so easy to live with. Well could such a man grow too gentle, daughter, since he must temper spirit to deal with the young in the schoolroom and a household of mewing women."

"It is easy for you to talk, Mother. He is not your husband."

Bergit did not take offense, but replied calmly, "Light your lamp of faith, Elisabet—so it has been done along these waters since Christian times."

"I wiped the dishes for Gunhild. I thought you were going to tell a story." Bergit felt warm and damp little fingers upon her arm.

"You wiped the dishes, but not your hands," chided Bergit. It was uncommonly difficult to be blind at a time like this; for Elisabet's voice was hard to read, small and even of pitch and concealing rather than revealing.

"The story," said Siri, settling herself down on her grandmother's lap with self-assured finality.

"Yes, the story," agreed the grandmother. "But it is ever well to let a tale move within the mind for a space. Well, once upon these shores somewhere in a time that I cannot name there was a fair maiden who married a farmer of means. She herself came from poor folk. How proud that girl grew, prouder every day of her marriage. Then her parents' humble dowry, the linens that had been spun for her and the wool that had been woven were not fine enough for her. She felt not the slightest pang when she threw these lesser gifts upon a heap back of the barn and bought for herself newer ones: the finest silver and pewter, rugs made by more willing hands than hers."

"Mother, was that the wind?" cried Elisabet.

"I have keen ears, and I heard nothing."

"Well, every day this proud girl looked upon her possessions with more greed and haughtiness, thinking how delicate they were, how they must be saved for finer folk than her neighbors."

"It *is* the wind!" cried Elisabet. Suddenly there was a roar like a descending avalanche; the air within the house pressed warmly; and then the wind was upon them, shrieking, roaring, clattering, and shaking.

"Elisabet! Gunhild! Come here!" commanded Bergit. "Is the light out? Fire would be—"

"I have Elisabet by the hand!" screamed Gunhild into the old one's ear. "The lamp blew out."

"Siri, you sit tight upon my lap." Sometimes it seemed to them that the very sea rode over the house, so thunderous and overwhelming was the roar; sometimes it seemed that the timbers above their heads threatened to fall upon them. Whatever the sound, each one separately or all sounds combined, the roar and the violence struck at their frightened minds like well-aimed blows. They could not measure time, but gradually they became aware of a new steadiness in the storm, fewer thrusts of violence; and soon they discerned the sharp beating of rain on the roof, against the timbers of the house, and upon the black windows. Roused from their individual thoughts of fear and destruction, they heard Siri plead, "Can we have a light, Grandmother? What happened? Please tell me what happened!"

"Light the lamp, Gunhild." Bergit loosened her tight grip on the child and said, "It is a storm." She was aware of Elisabet's grip upon her arm, her head against her shoulder. "Up now," she said, "and help Gunhild with the stove. It has grown sharp and cold. Perhaps a glass of warmed milk would help us all."

Elisabet rose, with a queer unseeing look in her eyes. "I want nothing," she said, going over to the window and standing.

"Look, Grandma, ashes on the floor!" and then Siri put her hands to her mouth and stared with surprise at the old woman's serene face, having forgotten that one did not ask Grandmother to see anything.

"I'll sweep them up," said Gunhild. "The wind has scattered ashes all over the room!"

"Look, Mother, Trina slept safely through the storm and wasn't afraid a bit." She stood by the window, peering uncertainly at her mother's expression. Elisabet did not turn away from the window. "It was Drang, the old man of the sea, that stirred up the storm, wasn't it, Mother?" She tugged at Elisabet's skirts.

"Come, Siri, I'll finish the story."

"At a time like this you can think of a story!" Elisabet whirled from the window, her voice cold and castigating. "It would be more human, I think, if you urged Gunhild to go down to the shore with me."

"There is nothing out there except driving rain and wind and total darkness. Elisabet, I'd bar the door myself before I'd let you stir out of this house." Bergit's voice was a match for her daughter's.

"Is Papa in the village?"

"He could not have made it," said Elisabet, answering her own thoughts more than the child's question.

"Is Papa in the village?" asked Siri, climbing on Bergit's lap.

"Well," began her grandmother, carefully considering a reply, "I shall sit up here and wait for him, but after this story *you* must go to bed."

Elisabet moved away from the window. "How can you sit spinning tales at a time like this? Tell me, Mother, tell me!" She came over to her mother's chair. I do not need eyes, thought Bergit, to see how she looks at this moment—she was like that in childhood sometimes, striking out suddenly at anyone or anything that barred her way, and then afterward the remorse and the self-castigation for her loss of dignity! I thought she had outgrown it; with Arne's coming she has been so gentle. "Mother, I believe now it is not courage that you have. I think you are cold and unfeeling. I would not be like you for anything in the world!" She heard her daughter's steps move into the other room and on into the bedroom.

"Is Mamma angry?" asked Siri, twisting about to look into Bergit's face. "I do not like tonight," she said seriously.

"Let me see," said Bergit, "where did we leave off? Oh yes, she threw the old things on a heap back of the barn."

"It is wicked to throw good things away, isn't it, Grandmother?"

"So it is. Well, this young bride finally grew critical of her husband, too; for what man, busy with the animals outside and the fields to be tilled, can come in without dirt on his boots? First she scowled prettily, in the way of youngest wives, then she began to chide, and finally to scold. Poor boy, it was not long before he felt more comfortable out in the stable than in his own home." Elisabet, now returned to the kitchen, began pacing up and down. Gunhild was warming milk. Siri watched them both, but it was plain that the greater attention was on the tale. Although Bergit seemed somewhat distracted by her daughter's pacing, she resettled her old bones and continued, "Then it came about that the husband stayed in the house as little as possible, for even a duller man than he could easily have discerned what she married him for. Even the plain folk in the parish grew afraid of her airs and did not come for Sunday visits. And now we come to the strangest part of the tale. There were folk who did come, however."

"Who?" The child, who had been gradually slipping down upon her lap, sat up again.

"The little folk. All well known to old and young in Norway."

"You mean the trolls and the goblins?"

"The very ones. Sometimes she would find the prettiest crock upset or broken; and brown streaks, like those made with soiled fingers, came upon her silver pieces. Her woolen skeins grew raveled and twisted. The new house was not so fine any longer. But the greatest pity was that she could not find a living soul to blame for all these misfortunes. She took to dreaming about the rich folk who would come some day, driving across the ice on tinkling sleds, to drink her best wine from goldrimmed glassware and stretch out indolent and pampered hands for her finest cakes served on a silver tray. Yet when she woke up in her lonely bed at night—for her husband had taken to sleeping in the loft—all she could see was a strange and sharp face grinning at her from a leafy branch."

"I feel so sorry for her," said Siri. "Poor woman! Don't you feel sorry for her, Grandma?"

"I would think she had only herself to blame—and such are always to be pitied. So bewitched did the poor girl become by all the faces leering at her that when a beggar woman came tapping at her door one summer evening, she let her in. How glad she was to see another human being! She did not see the old toothless face and the tattered garments; it was another soul she looked upon, for by now the husband had grown so wary of his daft bride that he ate in the tenant cottage. Then the girl fetched the silver with the brown streaks and the goldrimmed goblets and began to make a meal for the old hex."

Elisabet stopped in her pacing. "The tale—I seem to remember it, Mother.

"I told it to you when you were little."

"It is an old one, then."

"A little less old than I. It is one of my own spinning."

"This rain and wind, Mother, I wish it would stop. It goes to my head. I feel miserable." She bent down and whispered softly, "I am sorry I spoke as I did a few minutes ago, but go on, Mother, Siri must get to bed."

"What happened then, Grandma?" Siri tried to conceal a yawn.

"Ah, how the shiny kettles bumped their lids with steam—how the *lefse* baked upon the griddle—how the coffee pot bubbled to its top! The guest, gap-toothed and wondering, gazed at the young woman and thought how things had changed for the better in Norway. Free from his labors in the barn, the husband happened to look toward the house and saw smoke curling cheerfully from his chimney. The inviting smell of soup and hot coffee blew on the air. 'If she has taken to cooking for the trolls whom she sees everywhere,' he said, 'it's time I see a magistrate.' He strode across the yard to his own doorway, where he stood uncertainly until his wife beckoned him in. He did not have the power to withdraw after he smelled *lefse* and soup cooked on a veal bone, but trust her he would not." Bergit shifted the child's weight. "Stir up the fire, Gunhild, for it grows chilly."

"Finish the story," said Siri, who was growing heavy with sleep.

"To make a long story short," complied Bergit, "there the three of them sat at the table: the old woman gnawing upon her gums, the young woman with a smile of joy, and the husband torn between returning love and hunger."

"Am I grown too heavy, Grandmother?"

"No, it is only that I have bones grown too light."

"Then what happened? I'm tired, Grandma."

"Well, it's a good night to be tired. The upshot of it was that the bride put the beggar woman to sleep in her own good bed. 'I'll be off now,' said the husband, 'for by now the dog has warmed my bed in the loft.'

"The girl could not throw off all her pride at a moment's notice, for that is a feat possible only in stories, but she managed to reply with some honesty, 'You think me daft, showering all this upon a beggar; but it came to me, suddenly that the best there is in this world is something human.'

" 'Ah, but I have something even more certain up there in the loft,' he replied. 'The steady love of a good dog.' He was about to leave when he heard her soft weeping. 'You have changed, my girl,' he said. 'Can ordinary folk be good enough for you now?'

" 'The trolls,' she said with a shiver, 'came so thick and fast when I barred the door against human folk that I have learned I must put up with the one to be without the other. If I must choose, it's folk I like better.'

"The young husband sat down on one of the finest chairs in the room and began to unbutton his shoe. 'All I can say is that it is fine to live in a country where we have need of both trolls and humans,' he said. So," said Bergit with a kiss, "the proud girl learned that in this life it's always necessary to have one or the other."

"And never the trolls again," said Siri slipping down from her lap.

"Stay upstairs with her, Gunhild," said Elisabet. "There is nothing to be done here. Kiss us goodnight and say your prayers." The child was almost asleep when Gunhild picked her up. Then the two women sat alone in the room, with the sea washing heavily upon the shore and the sharper sound of the wind-driven rain beating upon the house.

"I suppose we should have prayed together before they went upstairs," said Elisabet sadly.

"It is all we have done all evening," replied Bergit.

CHAPTER 4

Elisabet

On the fifth day after the storm, Pastor Koppen sat in the bedroom where Elisabet reclined somewhat awkwardly against three pillows placed there by the expert ministrations of the widow Moen, who had left them to drink coffee with the pastor's wife and Gunhild. Bergit, sitting in her customary rocker by the table at the window, had declined refreshments.

So far as the pastor was concerned, there was nothing left to do now but take his leave, for he had read to Elisabet from his favorite book of devotions, he had spoken the conventional words of sympathy, and he had read a long prayer written for the comfort of those left widowed and orphaned by the treachery of the sea. Accustomed to the well-expressed, though often blundering, gratitude of his parishioners, he was more than a little exasperated by Elisabet's impassive mien. "Well, Elisabet," he said, rising to offer her his hand, "for now, farewell. When you are strong enough, we shall look for you at services. In the meantime, take comfort in the knowledge that nothing happens which is not the direct will of God." She turned on him at that moment such violet-shadowed eyes of reproach that he was sure he had touched with melting flame the coolness too often exhibited by these two Fjeldstrand women. "It is Mrs. Koppen you will have to thank for bringing Kari Moen over—it was her gracious thought that she would be invaluable to you here, for *she* has tended many a child birth."

Elisabet thanked him again for coming, said goodbye, and turned her face to the wall. As he entered the main room where Bergit sat, still and composed, he hoped that his wife was having an easier time over the coffee cups in the kitchen. At any rate, a few minutes with the old one over there, and they could say farewell.

"Pull up a chair," invited Bergit. "You must forgive me for not being able to wait on you." He picked up the Parisian doll which lay on a chair not far away from Bergit's rocker and set it down firmly on the table. "If you have changed your mind about coffee," said

Elisabet's mother, "Gunhild will be happy to bring you a cup. People have been too kind," she said with a sigh, "for there is much more to eat in the kitchen than we have stomach for."

"Nothing, thanks," he said, his eyes moving back to the table. "That doll over there—certainly it is not Siri's!" he exclaimed.

"It's no one else's," Bergit replied with a smile.

"You understand that I speak out of concern for your welfare here. Now with Arne gone and you women alone to fend for yourself, it will not be an easy task to bring up a child in the fear of the Lord. Such a painted mockery, dressed in satin and lace, how will that influence the child to grow into a sober-minded and thrifty woman? If you cannot throw it out, at least see that Gunhild puts it away, for such frippery has no place in a house of mourning!"

Bergit's grip on her cane was tense, but she said with an even voice, "Then you had no toys when you were about seven? Was it all willow switches, Mr. Koppen, and catechisms?" She did not wait for him to reply, but went on quickly, "This doll was a gift from a couple as childless as you and Mrs. Koppen, and for the joy of their hearts as well as little Siri's, I would not take it away should the bishop himself rant at me!"

It was well that Bergit could not see his look of disdain, a look that said eloquently: It is as I thought, there is no salvation for these women at Fjeldstrand, and the death of Arne must be laid on their shoulders, for what chance did the man have between two women such as these—one cool and unmoved in her pride, the other adamant in rebellion. "Your daughter," he said, "has she not wept? It's strange to find a young widow so self-contained."

"She has wept," said Bergit non-committally.

To make conversation with these Fjeldstrand women was like hunting for a gold toothpick in a straw-filled manger. "Bergit," he said, "she will need much comfort from the Word of God. Isn't it your custom to read the Scriptures daily?"

" 'Twas Arne who read to us." Bergit's sightless eyes looked straight into his face, giving him the illusion that she had a trace of sight.

"I have said, and still say, that had not his death been the will of God, you should have had the sense to prevent his going to the village. Couldn't you have done something, Bergit?"

"Not if, as you say, it was the will of God."

He felt a driving anger at this woman who used her years and blindness as an excuse for a nettled tongue. His hands braced on his knees, he leaned forward and asked in the manner of one tripping up a child, "You do not entirely believe, then, that Arne's death and Elisabet's loss of a child were the will of God?"

Bergit's hands grew white-knuckled on the handle of her cane. "It was only a fortnight ago that Arne and I talked of like matters. I recall his telling me that German theologians once argued whether the blessed in heaven eat both lunch and dinner. I told him then— and I tell you now—that it's something I hope to discover in a few years' time. Until then it is useless speculation." Her voice grew soft and pleading. "Tell me, if you will, why you find it so uncommonly hard to preach the mercy of Christ?"

"We all, and you, too, Bergit, face the final judgment. Therefore, how can you refuse to believe that Arne's death was not the chastening hand of God? Believe me, heresy in the young is bad enough, but with them there is still hope; but pride and heresy in the old can well spell damnation!"

He saw the flash of fire in the old one's eyes and considered it further proof of an unregenerate heart. "You would have us believe here at Fjeldstrand that the entire ocean and all the fjords were stirred into violent storm to cause the destruction of one man—and a good one at that?"

"God works in mysterious ways his wonders to perform."

Remembering the open door to Elisabet's room and the visitors in the adjoining room, she asked more softly, "Then you believe that my blindness is also a judgment upon me—I have heard it said so, never directly, of course—a chastening upon my pride or whatever evils of character I possess?" She loosened her hold upon the cane, sat back in the rocker. "Yes, Mr. Koppen, it is the Lord who put man upon this earth and who established the orderly laws of the universe. But this rolling sphere has both good and evil in it, even as man has." She heard him clear his throat as if to interrupt and said quickly, "Have patience with me a moment, for it's not every day you will find a woman willing to argue with a preacher. The tide below the house here moves by a mysterious law—and whether there is a taint upon the law of tides I cannot say; but there is a taint upon all of us, which we call sin, and it is my belief that it is not only the Ten Commandments which are violated by us, but numberless other laws not well understood."

"But, Bergit—"

"In a moment I'll be through. Ah, I hear we're not alone," she said, nodding to the women whose steps came from the other room. "As I was saying, and with that I shall be done, it was a taint of the flesh, perhaps, or a breaking of some immutable law which struck me down upon the milk house floor." Not without a trace of cunning, she smiled and said, "The doctor in Bergen was a forthright and simple man, for *he* called it a stroke."

She heard her visitor push his chair back. The widow Moen chuckled. "Ah, our Bergit has a head full of ideas if one can get her to talk."

"Bergit, I shall shake your hand and thank you for the coffee," said the pastor's wife in her clipped manner of speaking.

"I am sorry we have no one here to walk down to the boat with you, but if you wish, Gunhild will be glad to call Lars."

"No, no," said the pastor, "for our man will be waiting in our boat. We should have talked of many things," he said. "The parish will want a memorial service for Arne when Elisabet is well enough. In the meantime, may God's blessing be upon all of you."

"I hope so, too," said Bergit. The widow Moen whispered in a flutter of small breathings. "I'll be back in a moment. I'll walk to the shore with them."

"You need not stay!" Bergit caught the widow's hand. "Guro was down this morning, and Anna, Gunnar's wife, tended Elisabet during her confinement and is prepared to come at any time. Gunhild is always here."

"Now, now!" exclaimed Kari Moen. "You think ill of me if you believe that I would walk away from a house of sorrow. I would not for the world's gold stay away from a place where I am needed!" She gave Bergit's shoulder a pat and was off with tripping footsteps.

"Gunhild!" called Bergit when the visitors' tread had faded down the dirt-packed walk to the sea.

"Yes?"

"See whether Elisabet is asleep."

"I was in there a moment ago—she seemed to be resting, but I did not want to get close enough to disturb her."

"And Siri?"

"Out with Lars and my father. You'll be glad to know that the repairs are almost done." Gunhild continued with some hesitancy, "I do not know how to say it, and it is not the work I mind, but—"

"Yes, Gunhild—"

"Bergit, it's a strange custom, serving food to all who come to see you and Elisabet—it's almost as if we have set our minds to forget Arne. And knowing how the sea swallowed him up, Bergit, I could scarcely cross it for the burial service for Elisabet's baby!" The girl's husky voice was choked and broken.

"I am glad you have spoken frankly with me, Gunhild; for when we cannot speak the burden often grows heavier than we can bear. Life is a precious gift, child, which we sustain with food and strengthen with proper care so long as the gift is ours. Yet it is cold fare we eat these days," Bergit said, "with the fire gone out."

Gunhild agreed, her voice more cheerful, yet Bergit knew by the way her words trailed upward that the girl had not caught her meaning.

After the departure of the Koppens, Kari had come in again, tripping about so endlessly that Bergit had suggested she lie down before the evening meal; but Kari said there were things outside she could perhaps tend to. Still Bergit knew that it was not work but curiosity that led her to examine the buildings, some damaged by the storm. Bergit herself lay down, for the afternoon had been trying. By the time the evening meal was over, the rain was back, scraping wind-blown tines upon the window and washing the restless sea on the rocks below. Gunhild and Siri were in the kitchen, Kari Moen with Elisabet. Another evening stretched tautly before them, for with Arne gone it seemed as if the household moved on tiptoe, with a wariness in both thought and word. However, it was not in Bergit to shudder involuntarily as Elisabet had done when the latter spoke of Arne's sea death, as she had done only once. "It's clean, at least, not mouldering," said Bergit. "Do you remember the old sagging houses you saw once in childhood, the houses that had escaped the avalanche of rock and snow that thundered down upon an old farm one spring night? Perhaps you were too small when we sailed by."

"I remember." Elisabet spoke listlessly, but Bergit's spirit rose with her reply, for Elisabet was now more likely to say, "Mother, if you will leave me alone, perhaps I can sleep."

"These old houses, so twisted by the shaken earth—who could even inhabit them again? Only some poor crawling rodent scrabbling in the corners for a morsel of food. So it is with us once the spirit is gone—there's nothing human there to cherish."

"I will never love again, Mother! Never! It would be better to close my heart against Siri, for she, too, will leave it some day."

"You'd rather never have known Arne?"

"That is not what I said." Elisabet turned toward the wall, her words muffled but rebellious. "If I were God, nothing would fade or die or lie in deep shadow—ever!" Recognizing the universality of the cry, Bergit merely shook her head. "Tell me, Mother, how can God be good and still create man for such misery?"

"You have known only misery then?"

Ah, I miss Arne, too, thought Bergit, for more reasons than my heart or mind can name. I, too, know how natural it is for the grieving to arraign their fate; yet when Olaf died I allowed grief its sudden, overwhelming blow, and then I rose against the hooded warrior and fought him into a corner. And now these hurtful days it was comforting to remember how many spoke of missing Arne, expressing their conviction that the memory of Arne's school room would grow dearer with the years. Not a word, though, had Koppen said about the loss to the parish of Arne's teaching! Had he earnestly felt that Arne was leading them astray, or was he envious of Arne's popularity with the young? More than one parent of the confirmands had remarked to Arne how their children dreaded the minister's instruction, for he was all Law and little Gospel.

Kari was in the bedroom preparing Elisabet for sleep, while Siri wiped the evening dishes for Gunhild. She had seen little of the child since the premature birth of Elisabet's little boy, for Guro had kept her at Ørnheim for two days; and then when Lars and Gunnar began the repairs on the battered buildings, she had spent much time there. It was difficult to know how much the child wept inwardly. She had had one frightening nightmare; and since then Bergit had kept her in the little room in which she slept, although Siri still begged to crawl in with Elisabet. Except for Kari's willing but somewhat exhausting company, this was the first night they were alone since the storm—Nels, Guro, Olaf's cousin in the village, all had stayed one night or another.

Her hand began to search for the knitting basket on the table— perhaps work would quell her uneasiness. As her fingers touched the wool she was aware of the uselessness now of knitting, for these were the socks she had been making for Arne's Christmas. Suddenly the burden that she bore—and had been bearing for almost five years—and the pain and grief of the past week became millstones crushing every kernel of faith and hope. Ah, she had been brave enough when Arne was alive, so independent of spirit, so unwilling to bow to the scourge of blindness. Scourge it was, never to walk uprightly, step steady and firm; never to know what one's face spoke to the world, nor whether there were stains on one's dress; never to see Siri and Elisabet again, one skipping into girlhood, the other walking into the full bloom of womanhood. What *had* the pastor seen when he stood looking at her? A noisy old churn beating out words of dubious wisdom? Yet what did he want from his flock—smiling and obsequious compliance?

Light steps danced across the floor; a warm, kitchen-damp hand was thrust into hers. "*Grandma, I love you!*"

"And why do you love me?" she asked with playful hunger.

"Because you smell good."

"And what does *good* smell like?"

"Oh—like soap and lavender. But Kari doesn't smell like you. She smells *oof.*"

"Hush. She smells of camphor, which she keeps on a string around her neck, for she tends so many sick." Bergit felt a rise of spirit in the presence of childhood's forthrightness and simplicity. She felt now that her disquietude after the pastor's visit had more anger in it than anything else. Well, if he had upset Elisabet, let him remember that for every passage of judgment he knew, she could quote two of love and mercy! Siri's mention of lavender brought to mind Elisabet's tenderness. Shortly after her blindness, when the first sightless days were searching and bitter, Elisabet had said, "Mother, if you are afraid you will grow as foul smelling and neglected as old Torbjørn, whom sitting next to in church is like a papal penance, that will never happen to you. Our goat will eat up the garden before we let *you* go untended." Until Bergit had learned to care adequately for herself, Elisabet had been as good as her word, for comb and basin and cloth were always handy, and fresh clothing in undiminished lavender-scented piles lay in the drawers of her old chest.

Siri, nestled against her bosom and her warm breath coming softly through the old one's starched shirtwaist and undergarments, said in a muffled and guarded voice, "How can Father be down in the water and up in heaven too?" Ah, thought Bergit, it is the littlest ones of the earth who ask the hardest questions! The little stream runs meandering through thicket and woods, twisted with curiosity, effervescent with the joy of searching; but the old stream flows heavily toward the sea, taking in its deep course all that hinders its well-marked progress—dam it, and it only gathers its waters for the ultimate and roaring leap downward. Arne had once said that about the religions of the world—how pristinely fresh they often were in their origins, how burdened with the clogging debris of custom and cant in their swollen strength. So, she thought, collecting her wits, it behooves the keepers of the young to be, above all, honest.

"*Grandma*," persisted Siri, sitting upright, "don't you know?"

"We *believe* we know—we who call ourselves Christians."

"Know what, Grandma?"

"We believe that your father is with God in heaven."

"But—"

"You just said, Siri, that you love me because I smell good. What makes me smell good?"

"Mamma's lavender?"

"Yes. Where is the lavender she grows, now that winter has come and the long rains and snows set in?"

"It's dead. You know that, Grandma!"

"If it's dead, how can it make me smell good?"

"Because Mamma crushed it and put it into sachets." Her voice grew eager with disclosure. "I sewed two of the sachets in your drawer myself!"

"*Many thanks!*" Bergit said with pretended surprise. "Even if the old plants, Siri, are dead, they had seeds to grow lovely new ones and flowers, leaves, and stalks to live on more sweetly than the plants themselves. So, we believe, it is with us—like old stalks, we, too, some day will die, but we as persons, like the living fragrance of your lavender sachets, will live on.

"Oh. Will you be blind in heaven?"

"My no! I expect to see better than you can imagine, little one!"

"Why can't I go in the bedroom when Kari bathes Mother? Will Mamma have another baby someday that won't die?" Bergit set herself the task of answering childhood's ubiquitous questions, but her mind was largely on Elisabet and Kari, the latter's voice coming to her with pounding regularity. Was Kari going to be more of a trial than a help? How long would Kari expect to stay? Why were the well-doers of this world often such consummate bores, prattlers, and newsmongers?

Meanwhile Kari was maintaining her redoubtable reputation. "It's a pity, Elisabet, that you had Anna's rough hands tending you when you lost that little angel child. But as you well know, I had my sorrow at that time, too." She rubbed Elisabet's back with brisk, circular strokes, her movements automatic, her own voice of primary interest. "Elisabet, if I were a talker, I could tell you about many a confinement along these shores. I could tell you about women too proud to have poor Kari Moen at their birthings; but, let me tell you, when their daughters carried on something terrible down in the hay meadows, then I was good enough for them and turned out to be a Kari-come-quickly!"

"Must these bindings be so tight, Kari?"

"Of course, poor lamb. A little thing like you would look fine, wouldn't you, all pouched out the rest of your life? As I was saying,

I could tell you about folk—but I'll never name them—who are so stingy that they starve a person on mush and flatbread, but they do not fool Kari, for they're likely to have a pile of money stuffed in a box under a creaking floor board."

Her voice threatened into oblivion by the many folds of nightgown thrust over her head, Elisabet said with a small return of her usual good nature, "You are starving here, Kari?"

"No! No!" Kari gave a final tug to the gown and extricated Elisabet from its folds. "You're lucky at Fjeldstrand, for you have not known the empty cupboards of the Moens. "Oh, I could weep when I think of my boy! It is sad for you, but sadder still for me these days."

"But he will write—"

"Perhaps," said the widow. "If he lives to cross the sea." She stabbed at one of the pillows behind Elisabet's back. "There you are now—that will rest your back. It is possible, though, to cross the sea and still be eaten by savages in America."

"I have never heard that there are cannibals among the Indians!" exclaimed Elisabet.

"Well, one might just as well be eaten as to be scalped alive!" replied Kari with good cheer. In spite of herself, Elisabet smiled slowly, for she should have remembered that, above all, Kari must chew on trouble—her troubles, others' troubles, anyone's troubles— as if they were a tantalizing tidbit. Spying Siri, she clapped her hands. "There you are! Come to see Mother, aren't you, and just in time!" With a shy, sidelong glance for the effusive visitor, Siri settled on the foot of the bed, overcome—even as many adults—by the strangeness of a sickroom, and most of all by the wellpadded nurse who was always adjusting the underbedding and the overbedding, pulling a rug one way, a scarf another. There was always a flurry of moving objects: something being carried, something being set down, something waving in midair, all to the accompaniment of a bagpipe voice, varying yet essentially monotonous.

"Yes, Elisabet, the Lord has been kind to you, giving you this round-eyed little girl—and who knows? There may be others." Although Kari was blissfully unaware of it, the child was not, for she saw the quick tightening about her mother's mouth, as though she held both thought and speech in rigid check. As time passed, she would grow used to this in her mother, but never wholly forgetting the gentler smile of the earliest years.

"You must be good to Grandma," said Elisabet, "and wait on her all you can.. I have been told that you have been helping Gunhild and Lars too. When I feel better, perhaps we can have some lessons—"

"She'll soon be in school!" exclaimed Kari. "Just think, it won't be long before you can read all these pretty books in the cupboard here!" The widow indicated Arne's little library with a sweep of her plump arm.

"I can read now," replied Siri with great seriousness.

"Not really—surely not a little thing like you!" The widow studied her with narrowed, unbelieving eyes. "You're only six."

"I shall be seven in November. I can read some American words too. Papa taught me." Her little hand flew to the open mouth, for Bergit had told her not to talk about Papa unless Mamma mentioned him first, Mother being too tired for much conversation. "I'm sorry, I'm sorry," she began, tears spilling on her cheeks.

Elisabet longed to sweep her into her arms, even to weep with her in a rush of relieving tears, but the hovering widow, and, even more, something in herself held her taut with restraint, even as Kari's strips of binding held her body firm and rigid.

"Come, come.." Kari's hand grasped the child firmly. "We mustn't tire your mother."

"A kiss," said Elisabet. As the little mouth puckered to touch her cheek, Elisabet felt delight stirring; but she kissed Siri briefly in return and bade her prepare for bed. When Kari had blown out the lamp, Elisabet lay staring at the ceiling, dimly lit by the lamp in the other room. When the pastor had brought Kari along, she was certain that she could never bear to look at the woman again, the poor prattling old soul for whom Arne had shown so much pity, yet she found it bittersweet to endure her; but those who were left among her loved ones, it was with them she felt on guard, for they had the power to hurt.

In the next room Siri, still unnoticed by Gunhild and Bergit, had won a temporary victory over bedtime. The widow was searching in her bosom for a handkerchief; in the other hand she held an apple which she munched from time to time. Bergit's task was chiefly to say *yes, yes* at appropriate intervals. At the moment Kari was wailing her son's secretiveness. Bergit reached for the knitting basket.

"For whom are you knitting now?" asked the wide-eyed Gunhild.

"It came to me this afternoon," said Bergit evenly, "that Siri's uncle Roald, who lives in America, might enjoy the work of my hands. I put stockings in a box we sent over last year."

"I have heard of him before," said Kari. "No doubt he has money?"

"It's something he has never written about to us," replied Bergit sagely.

"Money is the root of all evil," said Kari. "Gunhild, would you be so kind as to pass the basket of apples?" When Gunhild had complied, she continued with, "My greatest worry is that poor Mikjell will get into bad company—it's hard for youth to remain untouched by the evils of the world."

"The village is not without *its* temptations," remarked Bergit. "I have been told that it is easy enough to drink and gamble away one's earnings even here."

"Not to my knowledge," said Kari stubbornly. "In truth, I have little time for talk, though, and when I have a day or so of freedom, I like best the company of our pastor's wife for it is rare to hear evil in the home of the Koppens."

"Siri, where are you sitting?" asked Bergit.

"With the cat, Grandma."

"Gunhild, get her to bed. Say your prayers by yourself, now."

When the child had said goodnight, the two women sat in a rare moment of silence. Kari looked about uncomfortably. "The quiet here at Fjeldstrand, does it not disturb you, Bergit?" Not waiting for an answer, Kari said with genuine wonder, "How can you knit?"

"I see with my hands."

When Gunhild returned Kari asked, "Would there by any chance be some cold coffee left in the pot? I do not wish to disturb you at your sewing, Gunhild, but the apples sit a little heavy on my stomach. It's no doubt worries that press on us all. I feel so deeply."

"Heat the coffee," said Bergit. "I myself will join you in a cup, for the cold rain makes my bones ache. No, Kari, it is not strange to see with one's fingers, not any stranger than it is to see loved ones in your mind's eye or remember how the mountains look on a spring morning."

Kari's mind had quickly disposed of this problem. "I have not wished to question Elisabet much, for clearly she does not like to talk." She lowered her voice. "When did the pains first come upon her?"

"The morning after the storm we found Balder wounded, a gash on the side of his head—it was shortly after that, I think."

"Yes, there is no doubt that the storm struck most violently on this side of the water. I expect you will have to pay Lars and Gunnar for all the repair work. Is that not so?"

"It will not hurt to offer," replied Bergit blandly.

"Gunhild, here—will she stay with you?"

"It's certain, Kari, that you have more questions than I have answers." With a feeling of reprieve, Bergit said, "Ah, we'll soon have our coffee. Gunhild, bring Kari some food." As Bergit suspected, only food could take precedence over talk, and for some minutes Kari was happily engaged in a whirlwind inspection of a hand-scrolled tray on which lay the best bakings of many of the folk along the fjord, as well as offerings from Guro's and Elisabet's ovens. Unaware that many eat not for the pangs of the stomach but for the pangs of the mind as well, Siri, enchanted, had crept out of bed and watched from the shadows until Gunhild spied her and waved her back to bed. Kari in the meantime surveyed the gustatory battle-field which she had vanquished into crumbs, and now she gave Gunhild her cup, suggesting that she would be glad to help empty the pot so that it could be rinsed out for the morning.

"No doubt your brother will come down to live with you, for certainly you will need a man about the farm, Bergit."

"We have given it no thought, Kari."

"I have been told that Guro's aunt in Bergen left her a little money. It's good to have a little put away!" sighed Kari.

"But not too much," said Bergit with a sly smile.

"How so?" Kari drained the coffee cup.

"One might grow to love it. It's the *love* of money that is the root of all evil, Kari." Bergit searched for the cane which always hung on the arm of the chair. "I am tired, as I suspect you are. It's comforting to know that you will be with Elisabet." She said her goodnights.

"I promised the pastor I would read the devotions."

"Not tonight. Tomorrow when I am not so tired, I shall welcome your reading, Kari."

When Bergit had tapped out of the room, the widow turned to Gunhild, who was tidying the room. "This is an eerie place. I would not live on this lonely shelf of land for anything. Come sit for a moment, girl, and we'll have a cozy little chat." Gunhild, however, said it was necessary for her to rise early for the milking and other chores, but she would leave the lamp on the table. None would object to her sitting up longer, if that was what Kari wished to do. "No, I have no wish to sit stared at by those black windows and wonder where Mikjell is tonight."

In her room, beside the sleeping Siri, Bergit heard Kari move on into Elisabet's room and Gunhild's quick steps climb to her bed upstairs. For all her tiredness, Bergit found it impossible to go to sleep. *Sjø-en, Sjø-en, Sjø-en!* whispered the waters. The sea, the sea, the sea! Beside her, Arne's own slept, her hair damp at the temples, one arm flung upon Bergit's pillow.

CHAPTER 5

Siri

Spring had come like a shy visitor, one foot set timidly upon the threshold, the other prepared for escape at the first clouding frown. It was late morning, with no curling fog to shroud the mountains or sea. Lars had left for the village early in the day on an errand for Gunnar; and at Bergit's insistence Elisabet had gone along to purchase depleted supplies and have a coffee chat with the Engs. "Stay a day or more," urged Bergit. "They have begged you to come often enough." Evasive as Elisabet had become this past winter, she gave no certain reply. Seven-year-old Siri had begged to accompany them, but Bergit remained firm: Elisabet was to go alone; there would be other visits to the village, and Elisabet needed an expanded scene and time to be herself. Usually amenable, the child had pouted, following the course of the boat with tearful eyes and returning to the house to trail her discontent like a sorry entangling vine. "No more sniveling!" commanded Bergit. "This afternoon we shall walk together. In the meantime, you might help Gunhild pick over potatoes for *lefse*. It is a slow task these days, with the potatoes so old they're nothing but eyes."

Even Gunhild, impatient with the many tasks left undone, did not want Siri's petulance. "Go play with that fine doll of yours!" she suggested, tossing her red hair in an impatient gesture.

It was scarcely the morning for peevishness, thought Bergit, beginning to doze in her rocking chair. Smelling heavily of sea and earth and plants, the air came sun-warmed through the doorway. On the stove a kettle of veal and mutton was boiling. Slurp! Slurp! sang Gunhild's churn and the kettle bubbled.

"I'll churn," said Siri, making tentative peace.

"No, no," replied Gunhild, with equal stubbornness.

"Then I shall sew."

Gunhild was silent for a while. "And what are you sewing now?"

"The coverlet for Lars. *You* know that, Gunhild!"

54

"It will have to grow bigger than the henhouse door to cover the long shanks of Lars!"

"One may not do it," said Siri primly, "but I can sew many small ones together."

"And then some day Lars will fetch home a bride and together they will sleep under a coverlet *you* have made!" taunted Gunhild.

"He will not. We are betrothed."

"You betrothed to Lars!" Gunhild laughed. "He will have gray hair before you make your confirmation vows."

"And I will love him still!" wailed Siri, throwing down the patchwork and rushing to the open doorway. She rushed out into the sunlight and then stopped long enough to give the hired girl a withering glance.

Bergit awakened suddenly. "What goes on?"

"It's Siri again. Piqued over nothing."

Bergit rose stiffly to her feet, reaching for her cane. "You teased her?"

"Only about Lars. But she is so touchy this morning."

"Sometimes it is a sign of growth. Who knows, Gunhild, what is in a small one's mind? Children do not understand the sudden unraveling of the fabric of their lives. One must catch at escaping threads and keep some sheltering garment for them. Let her run outdoors for a while. This has, in truth, been a long and difficult winter for all of us." She tapped her way to the sun-filled stoop. "Do you need help, Gunhild? No? Then I shall go out and sit in the sun."

Watching her go, Gunhild observed that even Bergit had bent somewhat in the long winter's darkness, and what would any of them do without Bergit, despite the occasional chopping-block quality of her words? Elisabet she found hard to understand at times; and on some days she could please her neither by doing nor undoing. Often she said in a fretful voice, "Leave the baking dishes, Gunhild. I'll do them." Then two hours later the dishes were still standing on the work table, batter hardening along the edges, and the burden of cleaning them having grown twice as hard. Perhaps Bergit was right: there was much to upset Siri, especially with her mother grown detached and cool. At Christmas both she and Bergit

had commented happily about Elisabet's decision to let Siri sleep
in her room, although the child's legs had grown so long for the
old trundle bed that Lars said they would have to fold her like a
book to fit her in. Still, Gunhild doubted that the child had regained
her secure place in Elisabet's heart. It was always, "I'll read to you
tomorrow, I'll hold you later, I'll tell you about it some day." Even
Bergit, Gunhild recalled, had said in piqued candor, "There comes
a time when one discovers, Elisabet, that a child can travel upon
one path, you another, for nothing human is long content to remain
where you leave it."

Gunhild molded the butter and set it carefully in a blue-edged
stone crock. She loved them all at Fjeldstrand—Elisabet like an
older sister, Siri like a younger one, and old Bergit like a mother
she might have had. Gunhild remembered the day, for instance,
when she had inadvertently sent the widow Moen packing! It was
a day in early December, when clearing skies and a drying wind
sent the household into a flurry of pre-Christmas washing and airing. She had accepted Kari's laundry along with the mountain of
soiled clothes lying beside the tubs at the back of the house. When
Kari had come mincing along with, "Mark you now, Gunhild, this
is not to be put in the regular wash, but you must wash this by
hand. Surely Elisabet has some fine soap put away?" Gunhild recalled how she had drawn her reddened hands from the tub and
dried them on the apron which covered the front of her brown
work dress.

"I shall give you a basin and a cake of Elisabet's best soap, but
you will have to wash your own finery. It's hard enough to finish
what I have here. The days are so black most of this will have to
dry in the sheds."

Kari's retrousse nose had climbed higher, her small black eyes
sharp and pinched. "Well, it is a lady who serves the folk here at
Fjeldstrand, I see. If I were poor Elisabet, I'd soon send you packing
to your father's hut beside the rocks!" Gunhild recalled her own
sudden fear and awkward blushes. "Had I not come to tend Elisabet,"
said Kari, rising on her stubby feet, "there would have been twice
as much work for you here, girl. Had you thought of that?"

Yet she had retorted, "Were it not for you, Kari, and your mewling,

Elisabet might not be a widow.. It was your howling and yammering that sent Arne out that night!" The widow had not made a single reply, but turned on her heels and waddled toward the house. Gunhild recalled her fright afterward, for Bergit had always been firm about showing politeness to guests; and hadn't poor Elisabet herself put up with Kari's gabble and gobble for at least three uncomplaining weeks?

Gunhild smiled to herself as she recalled Kari's amusing little tussle with Siri, as told by Guro. The widow had cornered Siri out at play and was tossing questions at her like feathers flying out of a pillow. Had Mamma and Papa quarreled on the night he left? Had Papa said why he wanted to go when it was already growing dark? Had Bergit tried to keep him at home? When the child did not respond to these interrogations, Kari had wagged her finger and said that of course Siri understood that she really didn't mean that Papa and Mamma had quarreled—but perhaps there had been a teensy argument, maybe some words? Wasn't that so? Guro reported that Siri had dragged a foot in the dirt, pretending not to hear; but when Kari's wagging finger came uncomfortably close to the child's nose, she had said, "Fru Moen, I am so small, I can know only so little." How Guro and Bergit had laughed over that, and even Elisabet had smiled! Yet it was a different matter when a servant gave tongue, and Gunhild recalled that she had worried, particularly when Bergit came out later.

"When Lars crosses to the village in the morning," said Bergit, "Kari plans to go home."

"I suppose I should be sorry—" began Gunhild.

"You need not be," replied Bergit. "Kari never has been known to leave a household without a well-stated reason. But I am sure I am like the man with one ear: I have heard only one side of this tale." When Bergit had heard Gunhild's side, she said, "I left Kari quite contented with herself, for, as she said, a lonely place like this was hardly the location for news from the great world; Mikjell could be lying in a pest house somewhere, and word would never reach this lonely spot. "No," concluded Bergit "she needed but a push, and that you gave her."

With the kitchen to herself, Gunhild began singing the lonely plaintive song of a shepherd girl listening to church bells in the valley. Soon the love song inspired romantic thoughts, and Gunhild began to speculate about her own future. It would be a brawny man for her, she thought, one built like the oldest Eng boy perhaps. And though she tried to shake the picture from her mind, she seemed always to be visualizing the eyes of the merchant, for he had a way of holding her glance until she became weak and confused.

As Gunhild worked, Bergit heard the girl singing to herself and hoped that with the passing of winter, they had weathered the worst. Good that she sang, this redhaired helper, for she had shown a worth none had expected. When the first pains had knifed into Elisabet, it was Gunhild who tended her until Lars could fetch Anna, and it was Gunhild who did Anna's bidding so well that the taciturn, bony woman, sparing of praise for anyone—and especially for the child of Gunnar's adventuring—had spoken generously of her step-daughter's good sense. Although the girl was coltish at times, she was also generous and loving, and Bergit hoped they could keep her with them as long as she or they had need for it. Yet, thought Bergit with a knowing smile, let the right man say "come" to such as she, and Gunhild would be yoked and led soon enough.

Where was Siri now? Did she hear her prattling down by the stream, or was it the stream itself chatting along its course to the sea? "Gunhild," she called, "is it not near noon?" When the girl's steps came out of the house she asked, "How would you like to set a cloth on Olaf's old work table by the big tree?" As Gunhild started into the house, she admonished, "Wash the table well; it's certain to be full of winter's grime." Siri would like that, she thought, and by now she most certainly would be over her morning's pique. Elisabet, she knew, spoke of the child's moods as unbecoming stubbornness, whereas Gunhild pronounced them as a bit of sass, but Bergit recognized in the child some of her own independent spirit, a search for the rightness of things, a guarding of some inward truth or justice one held inviolate. Even when one learned to take it day by day, life could be unbelievably harsh, she reflected, so it was comforting to know that this little one had something rebellious enough in her nature to fight openly and not as Elisabet was doing, turning in upon herself until the wounds refused to heal.

Down in the bare-limbed orchard where Siri sat on a great rock, Balder beside her, the child did not know that this was a day to be photographed in her memory. At age seven she could not know that days of great decision and success and defeat are not necessarily those preserved in the frame of memory. It was in this seventh year that Siri became aware of herself as a person, as singular and individual as any in the household. True, she had long ago learned to say *I* want, *I* wish, *I* am—but never before had she seemed to stand off with detachment to regard the differences between herself and others. Every day had moved surely toward night, night had paled into day, and what was seemed always to have been and thus might appear to go on forever. Perhaps her father's sudden disappearance had lent emphasis to emotion and perception; but whatever it was, she seemed to stand guard as if to say, "Here I stand in my own circle, and I will draw into it what I want, push away what I do not want. I will throw my arms upon this rock and taste its dusty sweetness. Those trees hugging the sky are mine; that sad, lop-sided building is mine because I love it; today the sea is not mine, for it gave me an ugly dream—and even Duppa, our own lovely stream, is being swallowed by it."

Long after the others had arisen that morning, she had awakened to fight off the choking memory of a dream, a dream in which she had struggled vainly to leave a cavern deep in the recesses of the sea, where dancing prisms of light played upon a mass of seaweed and the fish circled and circled. Even as she sought to flee with feet suddenly turned to stone, she saw the gently oscillating weeds shape into Papa's face, then move back to weeds again. After she had dressed, she came into the kitchen to find Mamma ready to go to the village, while Grandmother was preoccupied with messages and comments, and Gunhild teasing Lars about his new cap and jacket, which, she said, would catch him a girl in the village. The more the family laughed and called endless farewells, the more obdurate grew Siri. Even Gunhild's badinage, she knew, was not innocent, for Siri felt a stab of superiority in her thrusts and her watchful smiles.

Stinging with tears of anger, she had called to Balder lying in the sun beside the barn; together they had run down through the orchard to the tumbling stream, picking their way across the wobbly stones up to the great flat rock where the curling edges of the stream swirled about them. She had hidden her face in the dog's fur and wept and wept—wept for Mamma grown so still and strange, for Bergit's sudden denial of her needs, and for Gunhild's teasing. Most of all she had wept for Papa. Her life now seemed like the first square of weaving she had attempted on Mamma's loom: there was no proper design, no harmonious blending threads, only tangled confusion. She wept until she took a kind of pleasure in it, listening to her own sobs; finally she took her hands off the dog's neck and sat up to look about her. Balder moved warily to one side of the rock, where he settled down to the freedom of his own thoughts. The stream swooshed and rattled, the breeze cooled her face. Suddenly the farm and the sea, the mountains and the sky seemed unbelievably beautiful; the great falls far across the fjord leaped in a silvery arch to the sea; and above it, on the very crest of the ranges, a froth of white clouds rested.

She heard Gunhild's call. "I see you, Siri. Why can't you answer?"

"I'm coming." Balder leaped across the stream, then stood waiting as though to assure himself of her safety. When she had teetered across the last water-encircled rock she still did not hurry, but took a mildly perverse pride in observing Gunhild, arms akimbo, watch her slow progress. When she spied the old outdoor table fluttering a white tablecloth, the pewter milk pitcher and the plates upon it, she would have run except for her newly found dignity. Yet when she saw Bergit, face uplifted, listening to her footfalls, she ran across the lot and threw her arms about her grandmother.

"Do you like our surprise? We eat outdoors today."

"Like the people in Papa's story?"

"In the story about Paris? Is that what you mean, Siri?"

"Then I must fetch Trina." She almost upset Gunhild coming through the door with a platter of cold meats and cheese.

"Now, what is the matter with her?"

"It is well to warn you," smiled Bergit, "that this table has flown to Paris—and Trina, being a Parisian doll, is to dine with us." She hung her cane over the back of the chair. "Did you ever think, Gun-

hild, that our child has led a lonely life? At least *I* had Nels to play
with, up there on the mountain."

"Well, she's had it easier than I—"

"Hush! Here she comes," warned Bergit.

Gunhild watched the child's earnest and somewhat unsteady progress through the back door and across the lot to the table, a chair
held awkwardly in one hand, Trina held carefully in the other. Bergit
waited with patient amusement, her hands lying in her lap. "If
you're ready now, Siri, we shall say grace."

"Do they say grace in Paris?"

"*We* do when we visit in Paris." Bergit bent her head and thanked
God for the pleasant weather, the spring herring run, for the family's health, and for the food in the larder and on the table.

When she had finished, Siri said, "Have you forgotten our family
prayers?"

"No, indeed," she replied, accepting the plate Gunhild had prepared for her, "but God made no two of us alike. Must we always
sound alike?"

Returning to the matter at hand, Siri asked, "If we are fine folk in
Paris, how do we talk, Grandma?"

Bergit set her cup carefully on the table. "Well, it's certain I know
little of the great world, but it seems to me that the higher folks'
station in life becomes, the smaller grows their talk."

Gunhild giggled. "But I don't understand," said Siri.

"Nor do I. But we shall try it, at any rate. It will be necessary to
look about the farmyard with a sharp and critical eye—yet seem lan-
guid, as though what you see is of no great importance. But prattle
about it all you must, for silence may be considered a great social
evil."

Siri pursed her lips, gave her grandmother a sagacious look. "That
goat up there among the rocks and bushes, don't you think he is
lightheaded and silly for one scarcely able to stand on his old legs?"

"That he is," said Bergit, entering into the game, lowering her
voice to a confidential whisper, "for only yesterday I found him
chewing the lady Siri's petticoat which hung on the line."

Siri glanced with amusement at the openmouthed Gunhild. "Fru

Bjørnsdatter," she began, bending toward her grandmother, "did you know that the cat is with kittens again?"

"Are you sure?" exclaimed Bergit, tossing her hands upward in a pretty little gesture. "Who told you that, Fru Arnesdatter?"

"The cat herself!" exclaimed Siri proudly.

Gunhild put her cup on her plate with unnecessary firmness. "You surprise me, Fru Bergit—you of all people! Sitting here and encouraging such silly prattle, when it is you yourself who grow most angry when a light and silly tale is carried from one person to another!" She gathered her dishes with great dignity and moved slowly toward the house.

"What is the matter with her?" whispered Siri.

"She felt left out, I suppose," said Bergit. "We weren't such fine folk, you and I, if we forgot to include her in our pleasures. Have you finished, Siri? Take in our plates for Gunhild, and then we shall walk down to the sea. Perhaps Elisabet and Lars will be along soon."

When Siri came out again, her grandmother stood at the corner of the house, her hand resting upon the back of an ancient bole chair. "Here, I'll take your hand," said the child.

"I can smell the greening earth, and it's good to hear the gulls mewing again—we have been shut in so long," said Bergit, shuffling slowly down the path with the patient child. Down near the little pier she stopped. "The snow, Siri, how low does it lie upon the mountains across the fjord?"

"Down to the troll crag where the trees begin to climb upward."

"Lead me to the great rock at the water's edge—it's there I have often sat, long before I grew to be like a gnarled limb cast up by the waters."

"You are handsome still. So I have heard folk say," remonstrated Siri.

"Ah, Balder, you are here, too," said Bergit, stroking his head with long thin fingers. "Are you content to sit here a while? Or would you like to play along the water's edge, Siri?"

But the child did not hear her, for she was down beside the sea. With a little wail she cried, "It's a bird. It's a bird with a broken wing!" The old one sat still, listening. "It's a bird washed against the rocks. "Oh, no!" she cried.

"What is it?"

"It's dead," lamented the child.

"Drop it then," commanded Bergit, "for it is now beyond sorrow. Drop it!" she commanded, rapping her cane sharply against the rock.

"I have dropped it, Grandma, I have!" Balder talked with imploring whine.

"Come here," said Bergit impatiently.

"I'm coming."

For a while the old one spoke not a word, but sat and stroked the child's head gently, and then she began, "Mercy and pity are the finest of human qualities and must bring even the angels to one's side. Still, when there is no help for something, no remedy save forgetting, it is as useless to lament as it was for this bird to beat its wings against the sudden spring storm. Such accidents are the inevitabilities of life, like labor before birth, struggle before knowledge. It is a mistake, as your own father used to say, to teach the young that life is all sweet puddings and fairy stories."

"I used to love the sea, Grandma, but now I think it is wicked!"

"You love it still, Siri," she said fondly. "You are the first to run to the window in the morning and say, 'The sea is blue, the sea is green, the sea is gray.' It was not the sea that killed this bird—it was a storm." She placed her arm about the little one. "And the sea is cruel because in it lies one so dear to us. Is that not so, Siri? I knew your Papa very, very well; and he would have no quarrel with his resting place, only that he had to leave you and your mother while you were all so young. He rests with many an ancient king about whom he used to read to us. The sea, child, is like a mother to us in Norway; it feeds and sustains us—we would all be miserably poor without it. When your Uncle Roald in America wrote to us, grieving for the loss of his only brother, and offered us all a home across the sea, what did you and your mother cry? We'll never leave our home beside the sea! Now, were not these your words?"

"I think so," answered the child, "but I miss him so!"

"That is because you love him. And as long as you live, Siri, he lives in your love." The child was so quiet that Bergit said with a sigh, "It may sound like nonsense now; but when the time comes, you will understand."

"Shall we go up to the house again, Grandma?" The child steadied Bergit as she rose stiffly to her feet. Balder, who had been nosing along the wet sand, joined them.

"It has been a good day," said Bergit, "the kind of day one keeps in mind and takes out now and then for comfort."

As they approached the house, Siri saw Gunhild waving excitedly. "A boat! I see a boat coming," she called, shading her eyes. "But it is not our sail, and it is not Lars."

"But it *is* Mother!" said Siri.

"Ah, I know who it is," said Gunhild with assurance. "It is Tosten Vegg, the man who left us the new copper skillet last fall. You remember him, Bergit?"

"I remember him well. Had he filled the skillet to overflowing with honey, he could not have dripped more sweetness. Ah, well," she sighed, staring in the direction of the landing.

Siri's small hand sought Bergit's wrinkled one. "They're here now. But I will not go down to the sea."

"Go if you like," said her grandmother. But the child moved closer. Watchful and wondering, she saw the stranger assist her mother to the pier, saw his little bow when Elisabet gave her thanks. Though she had never met him, she remembered him well, and her remembrance brought a sharp feeling of animosity that *he* should be here and Papa gone. Down at the little landing Elisabet waved cheerfully and called a greeting. The broadshouldered stranger pulled a smart cap off his sunburned mop of hair and bowed to the three of them. Had she wanted to, the child could not have lifted her hand in return, but buried her head in her grandmother's skirt. The old woman stood impassive but welcoming, one hand resting upon the knobby handle of the cane, the other holding on tightly to the child beside her.

"So you do not want to go down," she said, patting the child lightly, where soft curling hair tumbled upon the little shoulders. "You have nothing to fear, little one, for when spring comes, such folk as he come selling their wares to folk like us who have sat upon their farms the winter long." Even so, she did not believe her own words.

CHAPTER 6

The Letter

The summer had proved as mild and fruitful as any Bergit could remember. Even the rains, always so prolific in the western fjord country, had not been too lingering or burdensome. The sun encouraged both fields and orchard; and Gunnar, who worked the farm on shares, found that he and Lars were hard put to find time for harvesting the land and fishing the sea.

Remembering the severity of the winter and the Sundays when none on the lonelier side of the fjord attempted to cross to church, Guro scarcely let a Sunday pass when she did not come down the mountainside, sometimes with Nels and sometimes alone. Even Nels had attended services once; and whether the old bishop's encompassing love for all folk along the fjord—and especially for Arne for whose appointment to the school he was largely responsible—had weakened the battlements of Koppen's arid theology, none knew. But even Nels had come away with the feeling that he might eventually reacquaint himself with the old stone church of his childhood.

Yet on this late August morning both he and Bergit remained home, while Guro's two roasting hens, brought down from the mountain ready for the oven, teased their appetites with rich promise when Nels's strong pipe or the heady odor of drying hay did not vie for ascendency.

"Elisabet has read Roald's letter to me twice," said Bergit, "but when I wished to hear it again yesterday, she said I was foolish if I thought that anything said today could ease the pain of yesterday."

"Poor little one!" said Nels. "She is much like our own mother, Bergit. No wound to her spirit ever really healed." He rattled the crisp pages of the letter. "Want me to read it aloud?"

"Naturally."

"My dear folk at Fjeldstrand," he began. "Arne's frequent letters, as I wrote you last winter, have made me feel heart-close to all of you. I look for the day that all or some of us may meet—Elisabet, our little Siri, and Bergit, who, Arne often said, was the keel of the household ship."

"Ah, I shall never meet them," said Bergit.

Nels made no reply. "For a long time here in Minnesota we have thought of ourselves as frontier people; but unless you could see this country, you might find it hard to believe how America is changing. Not a day passes but we see the country on the move—the hopeful, the too hopeful, the hopeless. Some travel singly, some with their families. Most of them are headed for the great treeless plains to the west of us." Nels paused to fill his pipe. "Wonder if the Moen boy is among them?"

"Who knows?" replied Bergit.

Nels took a few drags, and then he picked up the letter and resumed with, "There is more black earth waiting for plows than Norway has water! Our winters here in Minnesota are cold enough, but not so cold as theirs will be, with few trees available for firewood and nothing but sod huts for shelter. Courage they have, if not always the best judgment. Full half of them, I think, you could talk with, for often as not they are Norwegians, Swedes, and Danes."

"Such a thing cannot be stopped," said Bergit.

"What?" asked Nels.

"Emigration."

"A good thing, too," said Nels, "for would Koppen and his kind be willing to feed all those who cannot make a living here?"

Now that she had a man to visit with, Bergit was enjoying herself immensely. "Of course, it *is* true that some do not leave Norway out of need, at least the kind of need that is apparent to the eye. Some may even be scamps the country is well rid of."

"Yet if they want to go, it's *their* business," said Nels. "Do you want to hear the rest of the letter?"

"Of course," she agreed with alacrity.

"Our little community is growing at a fast pace. A stranger, a man from Valders, came by in his wagon today, stopping on the road at the outskirts of town, where I am building a house for our new mayor."

"He must be doing well," said Bergit.

Nels smiled at her with amusement. "He was a carpenter by trade and showed the curiosity a tradesman shows for one of his kind. I offered him a job, for the summer at least. But though his eyes lingered on my men hammering on the roof, he set his team westward, as so many do, mumbling that a man cannot afford a golden chance at free land. I felt pity for them, however, and could not shake them from my mind. The wife, I think, would gladly have clambered down from the hard seat beside her husband, for she had a small ailing child on her lap and would certainly soon have another babe; and there were three others in the back of the wagon, sitting on the extent of their worldly belongings. Yet when such folk set their minds to such an undertaking, the tongue of an ordinary man cannot prevail against the adventure."

"He writes wisely," interpolated Bergit.

"As Arne would have said it," said Nels.

"Our household is all well. Joanna keeps busy, both at home and with her church work."

"I cannot think what he means by her 'church work,'" said Bergit.

"We had a young sailor once who had lived in America. I recall his telling that many of the frontier churches have been helped along by the womenfolk, who bake and sew and raise money."

"So!" Bergit laughed with a deep chuckle. "How Koppen would storm over that!"

"Johan, whom we in America call *John*," continued Nels, "is now thirteen and 'reading for the minister.' It is too early to say for certain, but we may have a doctor in this family some day, like Joanna's brother. Brun is now eleven and eats up the garden before it can grow. Tommy, who is like to the age of your Siri, is the liveliest of all.

"If it is not too much trouble, both Joanna and I should like to hear from Elisabet herself. However, please tell Guro that her letters on Bergit's behalf have been very welcome and we would be loath to see them cease.

"It was heartwarming to know that the bishop himself gave a tribute to Arne when he occupied the pulpit last winter. It is my belief that some of us shall meet before our lives are over, and anything we can do to further that hope, we shall certainly undertake.

May our merciful Lord continue to bless all of you at Fjeldstrand. Heartiest greetings from us all.. Roald Gabrielson."

Bergit picked up the border of her apron and wiped her eyes. "I must see that Elisabet writes. Nels, would you take a look at that stove? I promised the cooks that we would keep the hens roasting." When he had finished enlivening the fire she heard him moving to the little kitchen window that overlooked the sea. "Have you wondered, Nels," she asked, "how far Arne got on that fateful night?"

He began to walk the floor. "Ah, yes I have. Many a time I have come down here on the pretext of taking my boat to the village or trolling for a catch of fish. I have been up and down these shores, Bergit, but not a plank or fragment have I found of that boat. Yet I suppose it is far better that way." He paused in his pacing and turned to Bergit. "Can you tell me how you ever let him go on such a threatening night—you of all people, Bergit, could certainly know the look of a threatening sea!"

"Yes, *feel* it I certainly could," said Bergit sadly, "but *see* it Nels, no."

He was beside her chair instantly, his muscular hand upon her shoulder. "I am sorry, Bergit.. You are so self-sufficient, so little changed from childhood days, I often forget that you are blind."

Her hand drew up to meet his own. "One thing you could do today," she said, smiling up at him, "is take Siri for a boat ride. Lars and Gunnar have been so busy that the child has been lonely. She grows beyond my reach at times, and when her mother tries to read with her, there is often a kind of crispness in Elisabet that goes down the throat like dry grain. I have tried to persuade her to let Siri go over to the village and play with the younger Engs—but I get nowhere."

"You will be sending Siri across to school, won't you?"

"We cannot do anything else," replied Bergit. "Learning was the one thing Arne desired most earnestly for her. The sexton is still taking Arne's place until another teacher can be found."

"Ah, old Tvet has a salted-herring kind of mind. Koppen won't have to look any further."

"There is something that has been bothering me a little, Nels.. Do you know this Tosten Vegg?"

"Guro has mentioned him. He has been here once or twice, hasn't he?"

"Twice this summer. And both times Elisabet has been more like herself than at any other time. He brought her back when Lars was detained in the village helping Gunnar unload some fish. My, how he had both Elisabet and Gunhild laughing! Apparently he is the soul of mimicry."

"How old is he?"

"Judging from what Elisabet and Gunhild said, I should imagine that he is about thirty-five. Of course, they could not agree after he left, Gunhild believing him to be about twenty-eight, Elisabet about thirty-three; yet from some words he let fall about his childhood in Bergen, I should judge him to be about thirty-five. He had a coaxing, boyish voice and a hand like a chine of pork. My fingers ached afterward! He is not so tall as you, Nels, for his voice came straight at me when I stood beside him; he is about as heavy as you, for the floor had a shake to it, as when you tread across the kitchen."

"Ah, Bergit!" Nels laughed. "The women are safe with you!"

"But it's not so," said Bergit. "Poor Kari once said a true thing: it takes but the sweep of a clock's hand for a man and woman to start a matter that even a lifetime cannot undo."

"The second time—what did he come for then?"

"To tell us that the shoemaker from Bergen would be by at the end of the week. I told him we could well have waited without going barefoot. In truth, he came with gifts for both of them—a bit of dye for Elisabet, who has taken to working at the loom again. For Gunhild he had a silver circlet for the wrist, a thing shaped like a sea serpent. Let me tell you that there was no living with Gunhild for a week afterward!"

"And for Siri?"

"Strangely, not a thing. 'Smile at me just once, little one,' he said, 'and I'll bring you something pretty next time.' But she only clung to my chair. Elisabet seemed not to like our coolness toward him. She said we had more smiles for poor half-witted Per when he came gathering sea shells than we had for the merchant."

"Then he is not married?"

"I do not know where all their wisdom comes from," said Bergit, "but these two girls of mine know that he lost wife and child at confinement." Bergit shook her head ruefully. "I asked Elisabet after he had left if she had given him a glass of berry wine—how angry she became! When had I taken to measuring out hospitality with parsimonious questions, she asked, and would give me neither yes nor no."

"Well, why *did* you ask her?" teased Nels.

"When he shook my hand and said goodbye, I thought I caught a whiff of something stronger than clabber. Siri would not say goodbye at all, but fled to Gunhild's room upstairs. I could tell he did not like that, but then," said Bergit with a waggish smile, "his charms are evidently not apparent either to the very young or the very old."

Nels said, "I see Gunnar's boat. Would you like a little exercise?" At her nod, he fetched her shawl and took her arm as she prepared to rise. Slowly they walked down to the little wharf and boat house. The family had gone to church in Gunnar's larger boat; and when it was tied to the wharf, and Bergit heard Siri's light steps on the plank she said to Nels, "Anna is there, is she not? Well, then, I shall ask them to stay for a meal."

"Many thanks," said Anna after Bergit's invitation, "but we must go on." Though Bergit could not see the tight-lipped look on the woman's sunburned face, she heard the taut strings of her voice. Never, according to talk along the fjord, had Anna eaten in any other's home except when her rough hands had gently tended Elisabet.

"But Lars can stay!" said Siri, nudging shyly up to the boy, who stood with his black wide-brimmed hat in his hands, awkward in his Sunday clothes. But Lars said it was better that he go home with his family and change to workday clothes. He could come over later, perhaps. Guro, with her mind on the roasting hens, had drawn Elisabet and Gunhild up to the house with her. Bergit called her thanks to Gunnar, and Lars freed the rope and jumped in nimbly. "I wish he could have stayed!" said Siri.

"You and I are going to take a boat ride this afternoon," Nels promised. When they sat at the table, however, it was another boat ride that was talked about.

"Elisabet," said Guro, picking delicately at her small piece of chicken, "don't you think you would enjoy a little trip? It has been much over a year since you have gone anywhere except to the village. I myself have sat up on that mountainside like a rooted tree." She watched Elisabet's face covertly and was pleased at the young woman's wide-eyed look of surprise. "The steamboat," she continued, "comes to the village next Wednesday. Can you be ready for a little trip to Bergen? It will do us both good."

"And *I* do not go?" whispered Siri to Bergit.

Guro, who missed little, said in her sprightly way, "This time, of course, we'll be unable to take Siri, for we cannot have her with us when we find packages for the tree which we shall have on Christmas Eve. But believe me," she said looking earnestly at Nels, "one of these times you are going to sit alone up there in your eagle's nest, for Siri and I shall go on our very own tour!"

"That will indeed be great fun," said Bergit, seeking the child's hand at her side. "I could almost wish to go along with the two of you, but of course I shall remain home to take care of Lars."

As Gunhild brought in the baked rice pudding and cream, Nels asked, "And what was the sermon this Sunday?"

"Don't tell him." said Guro. "He can always find out for himself."

"I almost feel," said Elisabet, pursuing her own thoughts, "that he preaches at *me*, for who else here has been chastened as bitterly as I?"

"That again!" exclaimed Nels.

"So much that happens to folk in life comes without any understandable reason, so I think it is better not to line up our deeds and misdeeds, as one does with children in a schoolroom, for praise or chiding. I have heard like talk about my blindness. Fie!" exclaimed Bergit. "It was the devil's own work, if anything! What pleasure would the good Lord have in knocking me to the milkhouse floor when I was making such good cheese?"

Later when Nels and Siri went down to the wharf, Nels said companionably, "I do not think we shall hoist a sail, skipper, for it's such a still, warm day. Here, let me give you a hand. In we go!"

"Do you miss the sea?" She pursed her lips as Mamma did when she visited the minister's wife.

"Yes, yes, I do," said Nels with equal dignity. "My vessel is beached up on the mountain there, like the ark on Mount Ararat."

"Did you ever see Mount Ararat?"

Nels pulled rhythmically on the oars. "No, little chicken, but I have been in the harbors of Madras and Hong Kong; I have been stranded at the tip of South America. I have seen the brown-eyed beauties of Brazil and the veiled maidens of Turkey, but never have I been in a boat with a lovelier lass."

Siri straightened the small pointed cap which sat on her yellow-brown hair. "Which way are we going, Uncle Nels?"

"If you mean," he said with a big wink, "are we going sea-ward or Lars-ward, we are going sea-ward. Today I will share my girl with no other man." The child trailed her fingers in the water and tried to hide the delight of her new status. When he spoke of strange harbors, his words had a shine, like a silver fin glistening for a moment in the green depths of the sea. "Some are content with a churchyard kind of life," he went on, glancing toward the shoulders of the great mountain mass crowned with unchanging white, "but I have liked the sea, child, because on it one is always going somewhere; for even when one drops anchor, the sea pushes and strains." He smiled, blinking in the bright sunlight, his face furrowed and tan. "Here in Norway, the sea is our keeper, the very cupboard of our nation and the air in our lungs."

Siri drew her fingers from the water and brushed them briefly on her red skirt. "I like it, too—now." Her shining brown eyes looked directly into his, confiding, yet shy.

"This cannot always be said of humans, but the sea has no malevolence in it. It does not scheme and plot; the beggar with his well-baited hook has an equal chance with our king. On a quiet moonlight night it whispers as sweetly beside the fisherman's cottage as it does below the home of the rich."

With the forthright curiosity of childhood, she asked, "Then why do you live way up there?"

"It's Aunt Guro who likes it," he said. "We have not always been together as we are now, child. She has tethered me safely to that nut-brown cottage up there like an old billygoat."

"But you *like* it, Uncle Nels!"

"Ah, yes, I like it—but that's the saddest part of all, that I should like it. For when she put her little arms about my neck and wept because I must leave, it was then we were young; and though parting stabbed our hearts, she would not have kept me home, nor would I have stayed." He rested the oars for a moment and looked about. "Ah, we have come a longer way than I thought!"

"Yes, there's the falls that spills the stream that runs beside Ørnheim!" she said happily, gesturing toward the granite wall that rose straight from the sea. "How long was it since these waters went under your bridge, Uncle Nels?" she asked thoughtfully, her eyes dreaming.

"There's only one way to tell, and I am not foolhardy enough for that!" He laughed. "We must turn back," he said, "for Guro will be fretting about milking time." He swung the boat around in a long, sweeping arc that left a glassy path upon the sea. He rowed in silence for a while and then said, "You must not be sad that your mother and Guro leave you at home. It has been a hurtful year for that little mother of yours." He suddenly brightened, "If they allow it, would you like to come up and keep house for me when they are gone?"

She looked at him with sudden interest, quickly measuring his seriousness; and then her glance was upon the half moon of fertile land and orchard on which Fjeldstrand lay, the clustered buildings on the slope of their own little hill. "I thank you just the same," she said seriously, "but Grandma will need me, for I am often her eyes and feet." When they were almost in at the shore, she leaned toward him and said, "Uncle Nels, you're just as nice as Lars!"

CHAPTER 7

Christmas

The women at Fjeldstrand would have found the preparations for Christmas somewhat onerous had they not been so customary and traditional. Elisabet discovered, as many do, that the acceptance of human mortality was an affront to the spirit—that a pipe on a rack, a coat on a peg, and paper with flowing script claimed a survival beyond that of flesh and blood. The room had been left as it was in Arne's time; and though she grew accustomed to the reminding presence of his books, his papers, and his intimate possessions, she was often more rebellious than resigned.

In gathering their handmade decorations for the Christmas tree, she found those which Arne and she had made for Siri's earliest Christmases. The day, for example, when he had cut out a four-sided silver angel came back to her with poignant clarity. Bergit had gone across to the village, for she was not blind then; and the two of them had laughed and cavorted like merry children. Finally Arne had caught her in his arms and kissed her again and again, pushing her playfully to the settee under the window, where they had lain in loving embrace in the winter's half light. The pressure of his lips, the fresh sweetness of his breath, and the soft cadence of his words came back with startling reality, as did the swish-a-swish-a-swish of the sea below and the humming and crackling sound of firewood and the wheaty smell of fruited bread baking in the oven. Now why would a merciful God, she thought rebelliously, concern himself over the fall of a sparrow and not intervene to prevent human disaster? To hold to the conventional Christian thoughts was a road to madness—better to be a pagan when such senseless grief struck, for then you could put conscienceless blame upon an agent, some malevolence from above, and seek to appease it. It was no wonder, she thought, as she sorted out the Christmas decorations, that she must daily cry to the watching angels above—if indeed they watched—why, why, why! Or had the angels fled from her and were the devil's own swiftfooted sprites nipping at her heels?

74

It was in this mood that she also had to endure one of Bergit's rare questioning sessions. Elisabet was busy with the rolling pin, preparing the last batch of *lefse* for the *lutefisk*, Bergit sitting beside the table coring apples for baking. "Will you have Siri's dress sewed by Christmas?" asked her mother. "And how will you trim it?"

"With the velvet I bought in Bergen," replied Elisabet, wiping the huge iron griddle on the stove.

Though she regretted the words before they were all spoken, Bergit asked, but not unkindly, "Elisabet, why did you not tell me that you spent a day seeing the sights of Bergen with Tosten Vegg?"

Elisabet replied crisply, "What need to tell you? Wagging tongues will do that!" Yet as she glanced toward the table she saw her mother's hands shaking as she held apple and coring knife. "Better let me do that," she said gently, but when Bergit shook her head, she resumed with a kinder tone, "Anyway, it was only an afternoon we strolled together. Guro was making a call on a tiresome old acquaintance, and I went strolling through the streets. Was not that the purpose of the journey, to give me a holiday? I had stopped to look in a shop window when a man came swinging out of the door, a parcel under his arm, and there stood Tosten, as surprised to see me as I him. I had not eaten, and it was only natural that he offered to take me to dinner. How could there be harm in that, Mother?"

Once a fire had been built, thought Bergit, one might as well get warmth from it. "Do you like the man?" she pursued.

"He is a *man*," said Elisabet, turning over the *lefse* on the griddle. When Bergit finished with the apples, she pushed the pan toward the center of the table and sat with intertwined fingers. "One gets tired of a household of women, that's all. It is neither warp nor woof whether I *like* him. It is the chance to be human that I want most of all. You know that you yourself have always taught me to try to understand myself."

"Good," said Bergit, "but sometimes we are so bedeviled and upset we are not certain what we want. Then it takes time. A better daughter no one has," continued Bergit, "affectionate and dutiful."

Elisabet laughed coldly. "See where it has gotten me!"

"For every stone in the churchyard there has been a house full of grief. I lost your father, and twice I miscarried." Even to herself,

the words had a hollow sound, for what person ever knew the deep-
est needs of another, and when had the young truly believed that
the old had once kissed with passion and known the secrets of love?
She longed to catch Elisabet by the skirt and pull her into her
arms, but even such a natural impulse would effect more harm than
good. "What else is there for me to do?" she asked when Elisabet
took the pan of apples.

So they spoke only of ordinary things, Elisabet lamenting that
neither lamp nor daylight gave her enough light for her tasks; and
Bergit thinking that she would give up five years of her life to come,
were they to be had, if she could have but one year of even the
dimmest daylight.

Toward afternoon Lars, Gunhild, and Siri came into the kitchen
smelling freshly of cold and the sea, for they had been to the village
to fetch Siri from school. As Lars went out to do the chores, Gunhild put on an apron and prepared to set the table, exclaiming over
all the baking and cooking Elisabet had accomplished during her
absence. "See here, Grandma, how cold my cheeks are. They're fairly
frozen!" exclaimed Siri with pride. As the child knelt by the rocker,
her grandmother's fingers stroked the upturned cheeks, caressed the
temples and the forehead, patted the braided hair. The pleasure such
physical contact gave the old one, none there could know. Sometimes
she longed to put her hand upon all visitors, those disembodied
voices that spoke from one end of the room or another. She even
thought facetiously that could she search the geography of Pastor
Koppen's face, she would know him better and discover whether the
lines on his face matched the craggy voice.

Siri's attendance at school became a source of deep pleasure to
the grandmother, for the child had an exuberance of spirit for learning, and like her father she cherished not only the contents of a
good book, but spoke wonderingly about the very fact of its existence. "Who, Grandmother, had the thoughts to put it together?" or
"Is it not strange that all these words lie here waiting to be read?"
Perhaps the sexton might not be versed in pedagogy, thought Bergit,
but she gave him thanks for his devoted attendance to duty and for
something else besides: his ability to arouse patriotism in his charges,
for often, she heard, he spoke with deep feeling of Norway's need

for dedicated countrymen in the intransigent struggle between King Oscar II and the *Storting*. For Siri, too, he had a special regard and spoke gently to her of her father's influence on the young. When she heard this, Bergit felt her own private conviction had been vindicated, that Arne had been misunderstood by only a handful, at best—and who could move through life not being misunderstood by at least a few?

She had been anticipating the hours when Siri would be able to read to her as Arne had. Otherwise she would have to sit witless and uninformed, for Guro was not down often enough; and when Elisabet consented to read she read with a distracted mind. Gunhild did not read with ease and could undoubtedly profit from practice, but Elisabet always complained afterward about the waste of Gunhild's valuable time! With a lift of spirit she dreamed about the time Siri would be able to reopen her father's treasured books and share them with her—and thus Arne would live again, recreated, so to speak, in the mind of another.

As her school holiday moved into the very heart of Christmas, Siri began to worry about the weather. What if Guro and Nels were unable to come down for Christmas Eve? Who would help her wrap packages and prepare the dish of rice for the Christmas goblin? The weather continued clear, however, and on Christmas Eve morning the watched path revealed a large and a small figure moving through the barelimbed trees that bordered the icy stream, the large figure grumbling pleasantly under the burden of many packages, the small one struggling valiantly with a basket of food. In the pale winter light they looked like creatures stumbling out of a fairytale; but Siri, capless and shawlless, streaked out of the kitchen door and met them with a shouted Merry Christmas.

All morning and well into the afternoon plots and counterplots prevailed in the miniature kingdom of Fjeldstrand; a closed door was held to be inviolate, and crossing a threshold under such circumstances an act of aggression. Nels was the benign monarch, Guro the queen, Bergit the dowager. Once Elisabet lifted her hand to Nels's neck and gave him a swift kiss upon the cheek, whispering shyly, "Oh, it's good to have a man in the house again!"

By the time early night had pushed timid day over the shoulders of the mountains, Siri's stomach had coiled into a hard knot of anticipation, but the waiting proved well worth the strain, for Guro's talent had transformed the supper table in the main room into red berries, greenery, and candles. Glass sparkled and silver shone. The fire in the corner hearth snapped and hummed. Bergit said a conventional grace, and Elisabet began to pass the *lutefisk*, *lefse*, and potatoes. Nels remarked that they had better not eat too much at this meal, for they planned to remain through the greater part of second Christmas Day, their neighbor, Old Mons, having agreed to tend to the animals. The family met this news with increased joy, Siri most of all. Two recurring thoughts, however, nibbled at the edges of the evening's perfection: one, Siri's feeling that somewhere outside the black windows where a small wind scraped sharp branches against the panes, Papa watched and wondered how he could be so easily forgotten; the other, her disappointment over Lars's decision to remain with his own family, although Bergit and Guro had patiently explained that one does not desert his own family at Christmas. As the family ate they kept the Christmas peace and visited only about pleasant events; but once in a while conversation came slowly to a halt, and it was Bergit whose low voice bridged the stream of lonely thoughts with, "Do you remember the time," and Nels's reply that yes, indeed, they recalled such and such a time or event.

Finally Gunhild brought in the rice pudding and the cream. "My!" exclaimed Guro, blinking rapidly at her dish. "I hope I do not find an almond in *mine,* for I am quite too old to break in another man!" Of course Gunhild had intended Siri to get the desert dish containing the almond, but it was Elisabet's spoon which struck it. She would have pushed it into the pudding again, but Siri's quick eye discovered its presence; and her surprised cry, "Mother has it! Mother has it!" left them all sitting in surprised silence. Guro leaped over the impasse by saying she heard something rattling around outside which sounded suspiciously like the yule goat. Therefore mustn't they clear the table quickly and proceed with their celebration?

Naturally one fabrication called for a more intricate one, and Guro was kept busy assuring Siri that while Nels read the Christmas story out of the Bible, the yule goat—if it were he she actually heard

—would not flee and ruin their Christmas; the important thing, she declared, was for everything to proceed with traditional order, for this, too, was even the expectation of the Christmas goat. At Siri's pleading to step outside with her to see whether the yule goblin had actually eaten his rice pudding, Guro was called upon for more resources, and finally the little aunt began to conclude that Christmas was slowly weaving a silver net to entrap her best intentions.

Finally, however, the table was cleared and the candles placed at one end beside the brassbound family Bible. Nels then began to read the first chapter of the Gospel According to Luke, not without some embarrassment, for never in his seventy-two years had he been called upon to read the Christmas Gospel. Soon, however, his attention was wholly given to the narrative itself, its force and directness, to Gabriel's majestic poetry and Mary's dedicated reply. The room grew so quiet that the hum of the fire seemed an intrusion and the sea a visitor pushing, pushing against a closed gate.

When he had finished and had closed the Bible with his work-bitten hands, none stirred until Bergit said, "Let us all join in the Lord's Prayer."

When their heads were raised again, Siri said expectantly, "We used to sing."

"*Used* to sing!" scoffed Guro brightly, and then she led the child in an old favorite, "Thy little ones, dear Lord, are we." Nels smiled at them and said that he felt like having a smoke out in the starlight, and Gunhild followed him to the door, where both became engaged in suspicious whispers. Though Siri did not miss a note, she also did not miss the tête-à-tête at the kitchen door. Finally both the smoke in the crisp cold and the song in the warm house were finished, and Nels was appointed to light the tree. The white candles with their golden flames lit up paper cones and paper swirls, four-sided angels and gilded sea shells. Siri heard a sudden sharp scratching on the windowpane and then a loud stamping at the front door.

"See who it is!" commanded Elisabet, giving her daughter an encouraging push.

"Come, come," said Nels, rising to give Siri his hand, and together they opened the door to a grotesque creature with a sack slung upon his shoulder, a creature that seemed neither human nor goblin, neither sprite nor goat—though perhaps goat more than anything else. It danced and muttered its way into the room and shook out a sack of packages beside the tree. When it would have fled out the door through which it had come, Nels grabbed it roughly and shook the horned cap off its head; and suddenly there was Lars, red with blushes and smiling sheepishly. Siri flung herself at his padded stomach. "I don't care that you're not a real yule goat! I don't care, because you're Lars!" she cried, hanging on to his midriff tightly. "I knew you'd come! I knew you'd come!"

Christmas morning was as black as the mountain cave above Ørnheim, but Guro prodded the lazy ones out of bed, carrying steaming cups of coffee for Bergit, Elisabet, and Nels. Later they sat like pale automatons eating yule bread and sipping more coffee.

Eventually they heard Gunnar's shout to Lars, and soon they were bundled up for the ride across the fjord to church. As the boys set to rowing, Siri saw that the early morning sea was like black glass, and the stars blinked frostily above. Where was Jesus now, she wondered—Jesus who had come to them as a child? Where had he put Papa? In which of the twinkling stars above? *"Far min!* My Daddy!" she whispered softly, and the ache of her longing set her to shivering.

"What did you say, dear?" asked Guro, sheltering her against the morning's frostiness. The child did not reply, but shook her head, blinking at the tears which lay in cold droplets upon her cheeks. Ahead of her sat Nels, with his big arm around Bergit's shoulders. Although it had been scrubbed for the Christmas Day crossing, the boat still carried the smell of fish and seaweed. Lights began to blink along the shore and soon Siri could make out the tall church steeple and the faint ghostly slabs of stone in the churchyard, where the folk lay who had crossed the fjord for all the Christmases of their lives. As the boat docked and they went ashore, they moved slowly toward the lighted stone church, exchanging friendly but subdued Christmas greetings with other church-goers. As they moved down the long aisle to the women's side of the church, Siri held tightly to Guro's hand. Ahead of them moved Elisabet, guiding Bergit slowly up to their pew. Back of them came Gunhild and her stepmother. The air had a damp chill and carried waves of mustiness, as though the sea had once moved in and left a moistness. The suspended lamps flickered in yellow tongues of flame. The child glanced covertly across the aisle where Nels sat with Gunnar and Lars; but before she had turned back to the hymnbook on her lap, her attention was caught by a man who sat two seats back of Nels, his eyes fixed on her mother's face, bold, admiring, unashamed.

The long service began. "From fjord and beach, from mount and dale—" sang the congregation, young and old joining in with earnest voices. Although the service swept her along with zealous reverence, Siri could not command her mind to complete attention, so acute was her awareness of people, individual and congregated. The minister's face seemed to rise out of his stiff, spiny collar like a picture of a head carried on a pike in one of the history books on her father's shelves. Beside her stood Bergit with closed eyes, tiny blue veins delicately traced upon the heavy lids.

The minister finally ascended to the ornately carved pulpit raised well above the congregation, and although Siri could not follow all his words, she gave him steady attention, the sexton having warned his charges that the pastor was aware of the slightest childhood defection in this respect. Siri drew closer to her aunt, who gave her a wisp of a smile. She yearned to lay her head against Guro's arm, close her eyes, and surrender to the pulling waves of sleep that drew her downward. Guro nudged her gently, so that the child's eyes flew open. In the instant of awakening she had thought herself at home, but the same shoulders and heads confronted her and the same voice cajoled and threatened. She wriggled her toes and flexed her fingers, and then she counted the posts in the altar railing and studied the familiar paintings on the roof above the altar. A gust of wind outdoors penetrated the ancient walls of the church like a hushed whisper, the lights danced and flickered. The voice in the pulpit came to a whispering stop, and the congregation rose stiffly for the Gloria Patri.

Out in the churchyard Siri stood with the smaller Eng children and listened to their mother entreat them all to stop for a cup of coffee. Gunnar looked hopefully at his wife, but Anna shook her head and when Elisabet thanked them, Sara Eng said, "If the weather holds, we shall be over to see you tomorrow then." Anna had moved down the pathway with Bergit on her arm, but Elisabet had stopped

to greet Mrs. Koppen; and before she rejoined the family, Tosten
Vegg was at her side, his hand extended.

When they were all at the shore again, Gunnar and the boys
hoisted a sail, and soon they were skimming across the fjord. Gray
clouds had moved in from the peaks, and the gulls sailed over the
slate-colored sea.

"Do you think it will rain?" shouted Nels.

"Not for a day or so," said Gunnar, his hand upon the tiller, "and
then I think we'll have snow," he finished with conviction. At the
little wharf below the house Elisabet did not invite Gunnar's family
in, knowing that an invitation would be futile and recognizing as
well the custom of spending the day quietly with one's own folk.
Even Siri, heavy-lidded with sleep, did not protest Lars's going. By
early afternoon a short rest and another pot of coffee had overcome
the morning's lassitude, and soon the womenfolk busied themselves
preparing the Christmas dinner. By the time early darkness closed
in again, the house was fragrant with cooking and warm from oven
and hearth. The ancient stone fireplace, unused for generations, had
been rebuilt in Bergit's younger years. Never had she regretted her
insistence to save and employ it, for it gave color and fragrance to
the old room, as well as considerable warmth. But now, in her blindness, it gave her even more—a tangible evidence of light and warmth,
something toward which she could stretch her hands, something
alive with changing sounds, something that spoke even more deeply
of man's immutable link with earth and its unalterable cycle of
decay and growth in leafmold and tree. She and Nels sat before it
now, and along with him she had accepted a small glass of wine. "I
have always been grateful," she said, "that neither in ours nor in
Olaf's family has drunkenness ever been a source of worry."

"It was that, you know, in Guro's family that sent her out so early
to earn her living in others' homes."

"Talking about me?" asked Guro pleasantly, coming in with a platter of roast pork. "Better finish your wine, Bergit, for Elisabet will
be calling us to the table any minute now." When they were all
seated and Bergit had said grace, Guro indicated to her sister-in-law
what was on each plate she held, for the latter often liked to help
herself and had become adept at remembering the variety and loca-

tion of foods on her plate. She always took great pleasure in being reminded of the visitors who came to the house at mealtime and did not discover that Bergit was blind until a chance remark made as they rose to leave the table informed them.

Almost everything that had been baked and broiled and roasted in the two households for the past weeks found its way to the loaded Christmas table, and each person enjoyed the meal in his own way, Nels remembering lonely Christmases at sea and the sailors' makeshift attempts to capture a fragment of the joys they remembered, Bergit cherishing the loving labors which had filled her plate but tasting as well the bitter flavor of her uselessness. Although Elisabet had returned home from worship with a steady resolve to hide her feelings, she had come home wearied by the sermon and the crossings, plagued by feelings of futility, and exasperated by the attempts of people to be kind. She sometimes felt an almost overwhelming desire to break into their conversations with a shouted, "How foolish you are with your constant feigned cheerfulness! How empty the rattle of human words! How deep the pit that lies before us!" Neither Guro nor Siri was unaware of Elisabet's black moments, and even Gunhild had been stung a time or two by her sudden lashing out after some domestic misdeed, like upsetting a glass or spilling ground coffee.

When they were finishing their meal with a traditional cream pudding called *rømmegrøt*, Nels began to laugh heartily. Directing his glance to Bergit, he asked, "Do you remember the time when you and Sara Eng slept together in your bed at Ørnheim?"

"I fancy there was many a time we did that," replied Bergit with a chuckle.

"Well, this time I speak of you had been to a dance that followed one of the weddings down in the village and whether you had danced too many steps or drunk too much ale, I do not know. At any rate, Mother could not awaken you for breakfast, so I slipped into the room and tied your braids together, one as black as coal and the other the color of honey, and then I stood outside the door and cried "Fire!" at the top of my lungs.. Each of you sprang out on her own side of the bed. Never did you hear such hair pulling and weeping and wailing in your life!" Siri thought it cruel, but Bergit laughed and Elisabet smiled, whereas Guro said it was probably the reason Bergit had such a good head of hair, even to this day.

So unwittingly Nels had begun an evening of recollections. Gunhild hovered between the kitchen and the main room, afraid to miss a word, until Guro said, "Oh, come sit down. I'll help you wash dishes later." Siri sat by the window seat, half-hidden in the crook of Nels's big arm. Sometimes she squirmed from under the protecting muscles and turned to peer out the window, cupping her hand over her eyes and straining to see the fjord below and the dark mass of mountains on the other side with their soft glimmering snowfields. The *Christmas* stars—for such they seemed to her—twinkled icily, and there was a silver shimmer upon the sea, though she could see no moon. She took a strange pleasure in turning away from the warmth and brightness within to the darkling world without.

"If one lives long enough," Bergit was saying, "much happens that cannot always be explained." In spite of Elisabet's protest that Christmas Day was no time for such goings on, Bergit had picked up her pipe which Nels had risen to light. When she had taken a few puffs and Elisabet had begun to fan the air with impatient thrusts, she said slowly, "I recall the time when I was just a few years older than Siri there and Mother had been making soap out in a nearby shed. She had hung a hot bubbling kettle on a long hook fastened to a rafter above, so that the kettle would cool out of reach of forgetful human or curious animal, for night was falling and the soap makings would remain there until morning. I was left to clean up the table under which the kettle hung. The hens had gone to roost and the animals were bedded, and down the hillside I could see Mother and Father already at the table."

"Mother," scolded Elisabet, "you dropped a spark on the floor from that old pipe of yours. You can see," she said in an aside to Guro, "why I do not like to have her smoke. Apart from the fact that I think it is very unsightly."

Bergit heard well enough but ignored the issue and went on. "As I was saying, I was in a hurry to join them at supper and had just gone back to the table to fetch some forgotten item. I had my fingers upon it when I heard someone calling 'Bergit! Bergit!' in a sweet but urgent voice, so I ran out into the twilight. At that very moment

I heard a loud ripping crash in the shed behind me, and when I turned back in some confusion, I saw that the kettle had fallen and spilled the hot soap makings all over the place where I had stood only a moment before."

"Who called you, Grandma?" Siri's hold on Uncle Nels grew tight.

"Well, it was neither my father nor my mother, and we three were alone on the farm, for you had gone to sea then, Nels."

"It was an angel," said Siri with strong conviction, though she glanced briefly at the dark window behind her and moved even closer to her uncle Nels.

"You must go to bed now," said Elisabet, thinking of the Eng children who would be over in the morning.. But Guro, who had never forgotten what it was like to be a child, knew that Bergit's recital had cast its spell upon the girl, nor had she missed Siri's quick glance toward the darkness that pushed at the windows and the other darkness that lay in the waiting bedroom. "Come," she said, calling forth a yawn, "and I'll help you get ready and maybe even lie down and visit with you for a moment."

"You spoil her," said Elisabet, though she was not displeased.

"As I spoiled *you*," said Guro.

The next morning everyone arose early, the women thinking that company might arrive with the first glimmering upon the sea and Nels insisting that they must start for home early in the afternoon. By noon the Engs had arrived with the two youngest children, age twelve and fourteen. Sara's last two children had come when all thought of child-bearing had been over—Klara, the twelve-year-old, having come when Sara was fifty-five. Although Sara was almost Bergit's age, the casual observer found it hard to determine whether Sara's hair was yellow or white, and she still had a fresh bloom in her cheeks. Sara sat in the kitchen now, stirring sugar into her coffee cup. "You'll have more visitors, Bergit," she said, "unless something unexpected prevents their coming. The Koppens and Kari Moen. Can you believe it, Kari had a letter from that poor boy of hers! No. I will tell you no more, for she is sure to be carrying that envelope in her bosom, and you will hear every jot and tittle of it, I am sure."

"He is well, then?" asked Bergit.

"Oh, my!" exclaimed Sara. "He is likely to be the president of the entire country, to hear her tell it!" Sara buttered the coffee cake which lay on her plate, and asked Elisabet in her forthright way, "And how are you feeling? I am thinking that you look a little hollow under the eyes. I sure it would do you good to—" She did not finish her sentence, having observed Elisabet's strange look as she glanced out the kitchen window. Sara noticed then that the Koppens and Kari had arrived, and with them, Tosten Vegg. She remarked to Bergit about Mr. Vegg's appearance, noticing at the same time that Elisabet had paled. "He's well acquainted with the pastor's wife," she said chattily to Bergit, "for their families knew each other in Bergen." Sara helped Bergit rise so that she might be in the living-room when the guests came up; and when she looked about the room for Elisabet, the latter was nowhere to be seen. At the front door Nels and Harald Eng came in with the visitors, and Guro looked for Elisabet to do the ceremonies of welcome, but in the end was obliged to perform them herself. As she began to find chairs for them, she noticed that Mrs. Koppen had taken a small birch-wood chair not far from the stairway to the balcony, where she leaned primly forward, her hands clasped upon her lap. The pastor accepted a high-backed chair near Bergit's rocker and was soon engaged in polite inquiries about the old one's health. At this moment Guro was unsuccessfully endeavoring to seat Tosten Vegg in a similar chair close to the front doorway, whereas Tosten, nodding and smiling, was equally insistent upon Guro's taking this particular chair. In the moment of interested silence which accompanied this stalemate the two children up on the balcony snickered foolishly and were rewarded by a sly wink from Uncle Nels. With an amiable grin and a mumbled thanks, Guro finally acceded to Tosten's wishes and observed him finding a chair as close as possible to the kitchen door. At that moment Kari emerged from the little hall leading to the downstairs bedrooms, leading Elisabet by the hand like a recalcitrant child. "Look what I found combing her hair!" she said. "My very own little pet whom I nursed with such loving care!" Elisabet was clearly embarrassed by her undignified entrance and readily took a chair held out for her by Uncle Nels.

Kari, in the meantime, was fully aware of her captive audience. She stood in the center of the room holding a letter which still carried traces of warmth from its home in her bosom. "I know you will wish to hear the good news," she said dramatically. When she discovered Nels and Harald still talking, she reprimanded them to silence with a rap of her fingers upon a small table and several well-aimed looks of mortal injury. "Those who have already heard this letter from America will pardon me if I read it again." At this juncture she nodded stiffly to Mrs. Koppen, who nodded stiffly in return.

"My dearest Mother," she began, "You will undoubtedly be glad to hear from me at last; for it is your very own son Mikjell who now sits with pen in hand to let you know that he is both alive and well, though thousands of miles away from the two mothers of my youth, the one my fleshly mother, the other old Norway."

"That is well said," remarked the pastor.

"I will continue," said Kari, rocking a little upon her heels. "I shall not tell the tedious tale of my journey across the sea and how hard I labored to pay my passage. Nor would I have you weep, Mother, over the story of my burdensome travels across a land so big that you cannot conceive of its size. In one of the sections of the country which they call Illinois (Kari pronounced it Ill-i-no-iss), I became so ill that I lay upon death's doorstep, and had it not been for the kindness of a Swedish family, this pen would now lie idle." Kari extracted a handkerchief from her waistband and dabbed at moist eyes.

"I suppose over there even a Swede looks good to a Norwegian," said Harald Eng.

"Had I but known what Mikjell was going through," said Kari, returning the handerchief to its tight repository, "this heart would now lie broken and the letter unread." At this point Elisabet looked nervously toward the kitchen, where her duties lay, and met Tosten's brown-flecked glance. She had a swift impulse to leave, but knew that Kari would miss her instantly and embarrass her further by demanding her immediate return to hear the rest of the letter. Kari turned the sheet of lined paper and continued, "When I was well enough to travel, I continued westward, for I had been told frequently that the farther west I traveled, the better would the climate be for this affliction which, as you know, has often plagued our family." Kari put the letter down for a moment and said, "In *that* remark the poor boy is not entirely correct. It is an affliction that

comes from his *father's* side of the family, the Moens." She turned
to Bergit, who sat with her eyes closed, her head resting on the back
of the chair. "Bergit, you remember Torgill, Mikjell's grandfather,
who had the mill where the stream turns westward—you know well
how *he* suffered."

"Kari, get on with the letter," said Fru Koppen suddenly. "We
cannot stay long, you know."

Kari, who was nearsighted but extremely proud of her ability to
read without glasses, moved the letter up close to her face, searching intently for her place. "I will not burden you with the tale of
my travels to the city where I now live. It is enough to know that
here in Denver I am blessed with returning health. I am outdoors
most of the time, working for a Dane who is in the building trade.
I have hope to prosper, and then, you may be sure, I shall not forget
that little mother of mine. Convey my greetings to all who name me
friend and in particular to our pastor and Arne Gabrielson. Your devoted son, Mikjell Moen."

In the short silence that ensued, Elisabet escaped to the kitchen, to
find Gunhild sitting in a chair by the doorway, wiping her eyes with
her fingers. "We went to school together, Mikjell and I," she said
mournfully.

"I don't care what you did together," said Elisabet tersely. "Have
you forgotten the house is full of guests? Is the coffee water hot?
You have taken no plates and cups out of the cupboard!"

"What is the matter?" asked Guro, coming up silently.

"She has not ground the coffee!"

"I could not grind it while the widow was reading!" said Gunhild,
fleeing to the back stoop with a sack of coffee and the grinder.

"To grind the coffee, she had the shed and the whole world outdoors, besides," said Elisabet with considerable exasperation.

"Fru Elisabet, may I have a drink of water?" She turned to find
herself looking up at Tosten's broad face and the grin which curled
slightly upward, giving him an air of mild ridicule. He had a way
of holding her with his glance, but she broke away, and when she
returned with the drink, she found that Guro had gone into the next
room with a tray of dishes and that they were quite alone. "Thanks,"
he said. "Something has made me thirsty—Mrs. Koppen's smoked her-

ring no doubt." He emptied the drinking cup and placed it on the table.. "But you have not given me a word, only the smallest nod when you came into that room some time ago." Seeing that they still had the kitchen to themselves, he said, "Have you forgotten the afternoon we walked around Bergen together, and you had that little hand of yours in the crook of my arm?"

"Only because it was raining and the streets were slippery," she said pertly.

"My, what have we here?" exclaimed Kari. "Tosten, they want you in the next room to give an imitation of the steamship runners in Bergen. Come, Elisabet, you should hear this!" But Elisabet said that they were already late with their refreshments, and as the laughter came in little bursts from the other room, she and Guro worked with rapidity to prepare a meal that would not shame either Fjeldstrand or Ørnheim. Gunhild returned with an ample supply of ground coffee, and though it was evident she would have liked to stand in the doorway and gape at the entertainment, she continued working with an air of affronted petulance. Karl, Sara's boy, appeared timidly at the back door, and Elisabet bade him fetch Lars, for the table was almost ready.

"Can you believe it—Nels has forgotten all about the time?" whispered Guro. "I'm afraid you'll have us sleeping in your beds again tonight. But old Mons will take care of the animals and keep a small fire going. There is no need for Nels to rush up there, only to sit staring at treetops and barren rocks."

"The pastor has not forgotten the time," said Elisabet, "for every time I have gone in with a plate, he has been pulling out that gold watch of his and frowning at Mrs. Koppen."

The meal, however, was eaten more quickly than it had been prepared, and soon there were many handshakings and farewells. When the last guest had moved downward to the waters, Bergit rose stiffly, unable to conceal a yawn. "If someone will be so kind as to move all the chairs to their customary places, I should like to walk a little."

"I'll do it, Grandma, and I'll walk with you, too."

"It was rather a pleasant afternoon, after all," said Elisabet, sitting down to join Guro and Gunhild at one end of the table, which had been cleared for their eating.

"Now that Tosten *is* rather a strange fellow," said Nels, "but rather likable too. Wonder if he has given up his merchant's trade?"

Elisabet did not enlighten him, although she could have told him, for when she had gone to fetch some of her baking to send home with Kari, he had met her in the doorway of the little storage shed. She could still feel the tingling pressure of his hand and the surrendering weakness that rushed over her when he said, "I hope to see a great deal of you, Elisabet, for I have sold out my merchandise and plan to remain in this vicinity."

As she picked up her coffee cup and refused the plate of sweets Guro held before her, she heard her child commenting to Bergit, "Do you like Tosten Vegg, Grandma? I do not like him myself—not really."

Tosten

Sense, experience, and imagination are not always guarantees against the perversity of the heart, thought Bergit. Shortly after the Christmas visit, it became apparent to her, as well as any others who concerned themselves with Fjeldstrand affairs, that Elisabet had a suitor.

Elisabet was reluctant to admit, even to herself, that Tosten had a serious intent. He flattered Bergit, tormented Gunhild, and teased Elisabet—with Siri alone he seemed ill at ease. In the first of his regular visits he had experimented with a few humorous sallies in her direction, most of them centered about her love for Lars; but he was to discover—and finally not to care—that Siri could be teased into shared laughter only by those for whom she had a regard. Tosten, too, was not without his own reservations: he could scarcely endure anyone who did not like *him!*

Had Mrs. Koppen been disposed to talk, she could have told them that Tosten came by this trait early in life, for she had known him since he was a little boy. His widowed mother had doted on his golden curls and flashing smile and had exploited them shamelessly. There was not a parlor in an upper-class section of Bergen that had not known a little visitor clad in plum-colored breeches and a white ruffled shirt reciting portions of the poem "Terje Viken."

> *There lived a curious gray-haired man*
> *On the outermost naked isle.*

When Bergit observed the frequency of his visits and the return of most of Elisabet's good nature, she ventured to question her daughter about Tosten's prospects, since it was common knowledge that he had sold his merchandise and was without any apparent source of income. Although Elisabet did not openly resent her query, her daughter replied airily that he had means enough, she supposed, and might well come into more. "I did not know it was our custom, Mother, to question our visitors about their income and their outgo."

Elisabet spoke with an attempt at levity, but her mother sensed the tindery quality of her daughter's voice and had no intention of allowing the subject to flame into argument.

Sometimes as Bergit sat in her familiar worn chair she felt that the old clock alone remained unchanged—it ticked and gonged in its unfailing and steady way. Siri's voice and body were no longer the voice and body of wonder-caught innocence; for circumstance, learning, and inevitable growth had washed over her like a heavy, importunate sea and what had once lain open to the light of day flowered in the deep recesses of her mind. To Bergit, Elisabet had become somewhat of a riddle, a riddle not without clues, however, for she remembered how permissive Olaf had been with the child, never liking to hear her cry from her earliest cradle days. The truth of the matter, thought Bergit, was that Elisabet was Olaf's child, reflecting light and shadow like a mirror.

Long ago Bergit had learned to look at herself critically, and in her own rock-ribbed nature had learned to endure the unalterable. Even so she could understand how Elisabet's malleable nature had expanded and grown in Arne's love and shrunk and dimmed during months of grief. And this was what tormented her about Tosten's courtship—what would it cause Elisabet to become and at what cost would Siri remain herself?

Clearly Tosten was not the kind of man who inspired indifference. Whereas Gunhild looked forward to his visits and tittered foolishly whenever he was about, Lars appeared to avoid him. Bergit mistrusted his superficiality, for he could praise a moral quality as glibly as he praised the delicate stitches in Elisabet's sewing. Although she had kept her qualms to herself, Bergit was troubled over the changes such a marriage might bring to the household itself. Would Guro and Nels continue to be as welcome when they came down from their farm? Would her rocking chair always sit as if rooted to the wooden floor so that her hands could easily find its satin wood? Could she continue to eat from plate and bowl and cup without giving offense day after day? Would Tosten be willing to forego the pleasure of warm little rugs everywhere upon the floors so that an old blind woman could tread safely? Yes, even more, could he welcome daily—or at least endure—the intruding presence of an old woman and a young child not his own? Would he have the patience and the grace to discover that sometimes the most rewarding and faithful child is not always won over easily? Or was she like old Per, collecting useless seashells of worry to encumber her mind?

One day early in spring, however, when Elisabet had gone over to the village early in the morning with Lars and Siri, Gunhild came into the living room to tell her that the pastor was coming up the pathway from the sea. Some intuitive sense warned Bergit that such an unexpected visit was not an ordinary one, so she suggested to Gunhild that she put water on the stove for coffee and leave them alone for a short while. Once the amenities of greeting were over, Mr. Koppen came quickly to the purpose of his visit. "Elisabet and Tosten were in to see me a few days ago, and, as you know, they plan to be married." Bergit felt a loss of stability, a sinking, as though the rocker had melted away, but she allowed herself no admission of ignorance and merely nodded. "After the customary banns, they wish to be quietly wed, here or in the parsonage. In that," he continued, "they show good taste, since each has been married before." Still unable to find the proper words, Bergit merely nodded. "I could not agree to marrying them," continued the pastor, "until I had talked with you." He hesitated, waiting, apparently, for an approving comment. "How well acquainted are you with Tosten Vegg?" he asked, after a pause so long that Bergit was aware of all the sounds upon the farm, Gunhild's voice by the pier, the bleat of a lamb, and the crowing of a rooster.

"I was going to ask you that question myself," she said.

"I did not know him before he came to this district, but Mrs. Koppen was well acquainted with his mother and his uncle with whom they lived."

"I can't like a man who does not work," said Bergit positively.

"I am afraid he has been spoiled by the prospect of an inheritance," said the minister drily.

"After Arne," sighed Bergit, "it would be difficult to welcome any other son-in-law. Still it is Elisabet herself who must live with such remembering."

"Elisabet," said the pastor, "spoke with some concern about Siri's acceptance of a stepfather. I have warned them that the problems of an individual are not only doubled by marriage, but sometimes compounded."

"And sometimes made lighter," said Bergit thoughtfully, "for so it was with Arne and Elisabet."

"So it has been for my wife and me," said the pastor. His apparent sincerity warmed Bergit, although she wished that she could see his face. Yet much was to be learned from the human voice if one learned to listen. Apparently the man was not without tenderness, she thought. "I have not had the opportunity of knowing you well," he began, clearing his throat, "but this I know, that there is no river that runs between your ears and mouth, for you are well known for keeping your own counsel. I feel free to tell you that I had a sweetheart once and lost her. I will not go into that—it was long ago, but we would have been two such as Arne and Elisabet were. Never did I see those two together but I thought of that! And when I met Mrs. Koppen I had no thought of marriage; but in matters of the heart women are often wiser than men, and soon I discovered that I had need of her and she of me. So it may be with these two, though I am a little afraid that Elisabet is getting more boy than man if she marries Tosten."

"Such has been my thought," agreed Bergit, fingering the corner of her apron. "You will drink a cup of coffee with me? Gunhild!" she called.

"I had not thought to stay," admitted the pastor, "but I will drink a cup with you." He lowered his voice. "There is something else about Tosten that perhaps I should mention: he does not always keep the best company, but that weakness can perhaps be remedied by a good marriage."

"If Elisabet were not so unhappy at times, I could wish to keep things at Fjeldstrand as they are. But my years are almost over and Elisabet must move in her own way, even as I have done since earliest years." She accepted the cup of coffee which Gunhild placed in her hands. "But this I can tell you, Mr. Koppen, as long as I have the wit to know I shall have the will to see that no harm comes to my grandchild; for if something of me endures after I have been put to rest between the sea and the white stone church, it will live in in Siri."

The minister appeared strangely moved by the old one's words and did not make an empty reply. As he sat sipping his coffee, he thought in his cold honesty how much he had learned from the old folk along the fjords of his parish. Since there was nothing more to be said, he finished his coffee, thanked her for the visit, and went out to have a few words with Gunhild.

After he had left Bergit sat for a long time with the empty cup in her hands. She would not chide Elisabet for not confiding in her, for there must be some quality in herself that had made such confidence impossible. Yes, she who could do so little could do two things well: she could accept with grace what must come and she could help prepare Siri for it, and she knew it would be easier for her than it would be for the child.

* * *

So it came about that on a morning some time later when the fruit trees were a froth of white upon the little slope beside the sea and the gulls swept tirelessly in graceful arcs, Elisabet was dressing for the vows which were to hold her for many years. Bergit had done the weeping which had to be done before the first birds chittered her to wakefulness; and now she sat on a chair in Elisabet's room and helped to keep up the small chatter that would lend cheer to her daughter's wedding day. Guro had come almost with the first chirping birds and was lending a hand with the pale-blue dress Elisabet and Sara had made, for the latter had an English sewing machine. For Arne's and her wedding Elisabet had worn the costume of the locality, the festive peasant dress with its ornate embroidery and the bridal crown upon her loosely flowing hair. Now as widow once and bride twice, she wore a dress of her own choosing, simply made but accentuating the girlishness of her small figure, a gently hooped skirt, a bodice with three rows of tucks at the waistline, and a soft draped effect rising from the uppermost rows of tucking to give a fullness at the bosom. The sleeves were long and full but caught tightly at the wrist with a band of white cutwork. A small white collar was pinned together with an ornate bridal pin called a *sølje*, and a dozen small buttons closed the front of the waist.

Siri sat on a chair beside her father's desk and yawned widely.

"Go over to your mo[...]
suggested the [...]
"and let he[...]
the fit and ma[...]
of this d[...]

"Now! Now! You mustn't do that!" exclaimed Guro, standing off to examine the full effect of the dress. "We cannot have your mother catching your yawns at her own wedding!"

"It's excitement which causes that," explained Bergit. "Do you remember, Elisabet, how Sara's oldest girl hiccupped through her own wedding?" Changing the subject, she said, "Tell me, Guro, how does Elisabet look?"

"Go over to your mother," suggested the aunt, "and let her feel the fit and material of this dress." As Elisabet stood beside the old one's chair, Bergit put out her hands and rested them on her daughter's hips. "You are still as slender as a school girl. Tell me," she said softly, "do you have money with you for your journey?"

"Oh, Mother," said Elisabet, "Tosten will take care of that!"

"Even so," she said, "a woman likes to have a little of her own along." She reached into a pocket of her skirt and put a small packet into Elisabet's hand.

"Mother," she said tenderly, her voice on the edge of revealing tears.

"Where will you sleep tonight?" asked Siri suddenly.

Guro was straightening the handwoven coverlet on Elisabet's bed. The explosive manner in which the question was thrown bothered her, for she was fully aware of the child's inner turmoil. A posh with wrinkles she thought, going over to the desk where the child sat and putting her arms about her. "The steamer for Bergen gets in there before nightfall. Rather you should ask, Siri, where *you* will sleep! And I shall tell you! Right here in your mother's bed, and little sleep you'll get, for I shall tell you one story after another about trolls and bears and goblins." Nevertheless, Guro's own heart was not as light as her voice, for she saw the child's eyes brimming with tears and her lips trembling.

There was a quick tap on the bedroom door and Gunhild's flushed face appeared in the entrance. "They're coming! I was upstairs, and I saw them. They're coming!"

"Well, God go with you, Elisabet!" said Bergit, putting out her arms to embrace her. "Come, Siri, kiss your mother, and then we shall go in and greet the pastor and his wife and the Engs."

For a moment Elisabet thought that the child would brush by her without stopping, but suddenly Siri threw out her hands and said in a tight and anguished voice, "Mother! Mother!" Elisabet bent down to embrace her. "I'll be so unhappy if you cry," she said. "You know that I'll be back in a few days, Siri."

Guro took matters in her own hands and led the grandmother and child out of the room. When she came back into the bedroom she found Elisabet sitting on the coverlet, as one might sit alone musing on a rainy day. "Come, come!" she said, "Kari will be upon you in a moment. Here, let me straighten your skirt. Your hair is lovely, Elisabet—there's nothing like eggs to bring out the sheen; but you *are* a little pale." Guro heard Kari's overwhelming voice in the next room and Sara's sweet-voiced laughter. But when she heard Tosten's proud and confident voice, she turned her little wrinkled face away to hide her own tears.

*   *   *

Guro stayed down at Fjeldstrand the entire week, though Nels walked down and grumbled every other day that "that fool Tosten is upsetting everyone's life." They fed Nels well and pampered him with attention until he appeared glad to escape to Ørnheim again, where no women were performing the mysterious rites of housecleaning. The women themselves seemed content enough, except that occasional conversations revealed how often their minds were on Elisabet and her marriage journey. It was their task to clean the bridal chamber and make disposition of Arne's clothes and the contents of his book shelves and the desk.

"We could leave the books," speculated Guro. But Bergit remained adamant and insisted that all of Arne's possessions must be taken out of the room. "But how empty it will look!"

"There are other books around the house besides Arne's. And this book wall has the morning sun—why not house plants?" suggested Bergit. "Speaking of others' treasures," she went on, "I have a few mementoes for Siri. It may amuse her at this time to be given something."

"You don't want to surprise her?"

"Now why should I do that?" asked Bergit. "How could I enjoy giving them to her when I am dead?"

When Siri had joined them, and Gunhild too, at the child's insistence, Bergit made a little ceremony out of the presentation. "Now what is a treasure to one is not always a treasure to another," she said somewhat sententiously. "Now what is that you have in your hand, child?"

"A letter."

"A letter from your father asking if he might come to see Elisabet, your mother, whom he had met when we attended a meeting in Bergen." She paused. "Well, put it down beside you. Some day you may wish to read it. What's next?"

"A picture," said Siri. "It's a picture of Mother. I can tell."

"When she was a little younger than you are now a traveling photographer came to the village. I put that in with the other things, so that when your lovely mother grows old some day, you will see her as she once was. The child should not be lost in any of us— sometimes I think it is the only thing worth saving, after all."

"What is next, Siri?" asked Bergit, enjoying the ceremony of presentation.

"I don't know," the child said seriously. "It's just a paper with a lot of names."

"A family tree, Siri."

"Now *that* is a paper with both good and evil in it. It will serve you well if you remember that were it not for all those ancient names, you yourself would not be here; but it will serve you only ill if pride roots upon these names and grows a thistle."

Gunhild began to wipe at her eyes. "What is the matter with you?" asked Guro with more amusement than concern.

"I shall never know who my mother was!"

"Hush," said Guro. "Remember who is sitting with us."

"Better is it," said Bergit, repeating one of her favorite sayings, "for little ones to meet small mice before they are thrust out into the world of big rats."

"Well, if I must say it then," said Guro, "I have worked out in the world in my younger days, and I have observed that it is not necessarily the poor and the humble girl who has been led into a misadventure. Who knows, you may have a lineage that could put you in a carriage." She observed that Gunhild's mercurial nature brightened considerably.

"Let's go on with this," said Bergit, growing impatient for a cup of coffee. "What do you have now, Siri?"

"A *sølje!*"

"One of the prettiest pins I have ever seen," said Guro.

"I wore it as a bride when Olaf took me—and how many had worn it before me, I cannot say."

"I shall show it to Lars."

Bergit laughed. "Do that and you will lose him. You must remember when you get a little older to put on your prettiest gown with this pin at your throat; and when Lars stares at you, you look the other way—only then will he come running." She grew a little serious and said, "But I should like to have you wear this on your wedding day, Siri, though if you press me for a reason, I am hard put to find a good one—for how can it matter to me when I am gone?" She sat there, seeming to search for the right words. "I would like you to wear it because wearing it may mean something to you—and if at the time wearing it should mean nothing to you, then the pin itself is nothing but dross."

Siri had been listening to her cryptic words with a little frown and said, pursing her lips and looking at her seriously, "You mean wear it if I like, don't you?"

"I suspect that is what I mean," said Bergit drily.

"This is heavy, Grandma," said Siri, shaking a little hand-carved wooden box.

"For some it has been a heavy burden," said Bergit.

"Why, it's money!"

"Just something to put away, child. It is not much—just a little for what may be a great need some day." Bergit began feeling for her cane, and as she hobbled out to find her chair in the kitchen, she reached into an apron pocket for a handkerchief.

        *   *   *

No one at Fjeldstrand ever learned from Elisabet the full story of her wedding journey. Bergit was aware of a miscarriage of their original plans, and Elisabet's reluctance to discuss places they had visited lent credence to her suspicion that all had not gone well.

After the short wedding ceremony at Fjeldstrand, the bridal couple had gone across to the village with the pastor, the Engs, and Kari—the latter having provided herself with a nightgown, thinking that she might be invited to stay the week with Bergit. The only satisfaction afforded by her disappointment was the opportunity to observe the bridal pair closely as they journeyed together across the fjord. The steamer came shortly afterward, and soon Elisabet and Tosten were waving goodbye to the Engs and other well-wishers gathered at the pier. It was at this moment of farewell, when the white stone church and the scattering of houses that comprised the village began to recede into the compactness of a painting, that Elisabet became fully aware of the break she had made with her past and the pact she had made with the future. As the small steamer moved into the deeper waters of the fjord and Tosten went on to have a few words with the captain, she stood alone at the railing. Back to her right the village was swiftly disappearing; forward to her left lay the little slope of land which had nurtured her flesh and spirit. Were the family at Fjeldstrand watching the smoke of the steamer and telling Grandma of its progress? Had Siri commenced to smile again? Shading her eyes and staring intently at the distant farm, she saw the white patch of the flowering orchard and a dark strip of land above it on which two figures moved—that would be Lars with the dun, harrowing the upper field that lay below the green drifts of timber.

"Come, dearest," said Tosten, slipping his arm around her waist. "The captain wishes to drink a toast to us." At first she demurred, but finally she allowed herself to be led to the captain's small quarters. He greeted her graciously and said that he had known her father well; in fact, it was her own father that had inspired his son to enter the university at Kristiania.

"Did your mother ever regain her sight?" he inquired. "Such a pity. I always enjoyed a chat with her." Although he smiled at Elisabet openly and admiringly, several times she caught him studying Tosten and her with a speculative frown. It was a look she was to see often on this bridal journey.

In Bergen, Tosten found a room for them in one of the best hotels, one which Guro and she had considered too dear for their expedition; but this was a wedding trip, after all, she thought, and in all

probability she would have been disappointed had Tosten provided
different quarters. After they had been settled in their room, she
was overwhelmed with shyness every time Tosten put his arms
around her and pressed her for more kisses. They had kissed often
enough the past month: in the boat on moonlight sails, in the
orchard; and once when they had taken the old path that wound
close to Ørnheim, their lovemaking had grown warm and tempes-
tuous, until she had suddenly pushed him away and run down the
pathway. She had expected him to be angry at her sudden change
of mind, but when he caught up with her he had merely laughed,
remarking with his big teasing smile that the next chase would be the
merrier for this one. She enjoyed his air of mastery, for this she
needed, having grown almost insane over the directionless monotony
of their womanly life at Fjeldstrand.

Now she tried to meet his kisses with answering ardor, but she had
no taste for lovemaking now, not with the sun glistening off the
steep-pitched rooftops of the city and the clop-clop of horses' hooves
in the street below. "Eat or rest?" asked Tosten, suddenly releasing
her, his flecked eyes sharp with teasing humor.

"I think I should like to eat," she replied, putting up a hand to
straighten her hair. So with Tosten sitting in a chair—one leg thrown
over its arm—she poured water into a china bowl and washed her
hands and face.

"You know there's something virginal about you!" he laughed. "It
would be easy to believe that you have never had a child—except
that I cannot forget the accusing eyes of that little one of yours at
Fjeldstrand."

"They're not *accusing!*" defended Elisabet, with a rush of desire
for the sight of Siri's little-girl face and the unforgettable directness
of her large, well-spaced brown eyes. "She's not accusing *you*," she
reiterated. "It's only that she's so like Mother—everything must be
placed on the scales of reason."

"It's no way to live!" exclaimed Tosten, rising to fill the basin for
his own washing. She could hardly make out his words as he bent
down to rinse his face, but she heard him finish with—"at least *we're*
not going to live that way!"

Downstairs in the diningroom Elisabet felt insufferably conspicuous and provincial in a setting where fashionable women moved with complacent ease and caused her simple dress to appear like a morning garment. It might just as well be Gunhild who sat here with Tosten, for she wore her braids wound around her head in coronet fashion even as their serving girl did, and she had come with a *shawl* for her shoulders in case they would stroll later! All the women whom she had covertly noticed wore velvet or silk wraps, beautifully fringed or ruffled, with great capelike sleeves. How she must have embarrassed Tosten as he drew the shawl from her shoulders and placed it on the back of a chair! She blushed deeply and wished at the moment that he had chosen the most inconspicuous hotel or the humblest boarding house. Soon, however, her better sense prevailed. What was it that Arne had said? "We Norwegians cannot clamor for our independence from Sweden until every man, woman, and child in Norway is calmly aware of his own unique worth to the cause of freedom." How strange, she thought, that at this moment—on the eve of her union with Tosten—she would hear *his* voice again in her ear. She glanced across the table to find Tosten staring at her with frank delight. "Elisabet," he said, putting down his napkin, "put down that spoon and admit that you have finished. I have no intention of sitting *here* the entire night." She felt herself blushing deeply and quickly acquiesced. Instead of going upstairs to their room, he took her arm and led her through the lobby toward the entrance.

"Tosten Vegg! Just a moment!" They turned to discover who was hailing them. A well-dressed gentleman bore down upon them, his hand extended. Tosten introduced Elisabet. "I know your district well," the man said kindly. "In fact, I was scouting it this summer as a possible site for a tourist hotel. The English, you know, are fond of this area for fishing and hunting." He turned his glance toward Elisabet again. "Your husband and I were schoolmates, and I can say, Mrs. Vegg, that it is about time this man of yours took on a settling influence." He extended his hand and suggested that if they planned to remain, his wife and he would welcome a call.

"Thank you," said Elisabet. "But we're bound for a small journey to the south." When he had left, they moved through the remainder

of the lobby and out to the street. "I am sorry," said Elisabet, "I
have forgotten his name."

"Paul Johann Blekstad. Not that it matters," he said, "for I don't
intend to spend this week bowing to the snobbery of the newly rich."

In the morning Elisabet was awakened by Tosten, who stood
above her, fully dressed. "It's a shame to awaken you," he said
soothingly, sitting down on the bed beside her and running his
fingers through her loose hair (she remembered how he had un-
braided it during the night), but I didn't want to leave this heart
of my heart—" here he kissed her—"until I told her where I am
going."

"You want me to dress quickly and go along?"

"Oh, no—it's sure to be an unpleasant visit. You remember I told
you about my father's brother? The one who is sick in a nursing
home? I must call on the poor fellow—he's been dying for a year."
Elisabet reached toward a chair, across which she had thrown her
nightrobe. "No, you don't—stay just as you are! Elisabet! Elisabet!"
he whispered wildly. "I could—"

"No, you don't," she said, sliding out of his arms. "You go on and
see your uncle. I feel so—so disheveled," she finished quickly. "Please,
Tosten, let me wash my face and comb my hair!"

"And wash off all my kisses!"

"Well, think what fun you'll have putting them back again!" she
said, eluding him.

"All right, Elisabet," he said finally. "But in the meantime you
dress and get downstairs for your breakfast—you might pack, too,
for we shall be leaving this afternoon. Since you'll only wash them
off again, you'll go kissless this time."

When he had closed the door, Elisabet pushed her feet into the
slippers Guro had knit for her and went over to the mirror above
the washstand. What a sight she was! But she supposed a man like
Tosten liked her better that way—it was a sign of his mastery. How
childish (but, oh, how sweet) had Arne's and her union been in comparison! The fjord and the house at Fjeldstrand seemed a thousand
miles away and a decade ago. The stormy abandon of the night
seemed to draw a heavy curtain between what she had been and
what she might become; it was as though she were two persons: the

Elisabet whose gentle hands had held a ewe at lambing and tended her mother with patient devotion after her stroke, and the Elisabet who had spent herself so completely that she had been washed free of the venom of grief, fear, and frustration. She dressed slowly, packing her toilet articles into the valise and moving to the window from time to time to glance down upon the busy street still wet from the night's rain. The sky was overcast, and she smiled, remembering how her father often said babies in Bergen were born with web feet. *Babies,* she thought. Was the doctor she and Guro had visited here right in his speculation that she would never bear another child? How she had often wanted children in her previous marriage, even as Arne had! Although she knew much about Tosten now, she did not know how he felt about children, except that he had been unable to strike up a friendship with Siri. Yet she was not surprised, for mixed relationships always posed problems—one had only to observe how it had been with Anna and Gunhild! She opened the window to ascertain the temperature outside and discovered that it was cool enough for a shawl. One thing she would *not* do was to eat breakfast in the diningroom. She would find a place where her white fringed shawl did not look unsuitable.

When she had left the hotel and was strolling down the street, she enjoyed a feeling of release; for after Tosten had left, the objects in the room seemed to close in upon her—the rumpled bed (she had put it in order almost immediately), the valises standing side by side. After she had opened the window and smelled the rain and the sea, she had had a moment when she wanted to lay her head on her arms and weep. Weep for what? Weep for the loss of a perfection she had once known, she supposed, and—even worse—weep because she had not known it to be perfection. She pressed against a shop front to let a family of emigrants pass by, a mother, a father, six children. Between them, the father and the oldest boy carried a chest, the mother had a babe in arms, and the remainder of the family carried bundles of varying sizes. Doggedly, serious, frowning, and tired looking, they did not appear like pilgrims going to a promised land. Perhaps their pastor was right: of what use was it to exchange one misery for another in this world? She stood for a long time watching their retreating backs and was reminded of Landstad's familiar

poem about an emigrant mother who watched her baby's burial at
sea and thought longingly of the hallowed ground of the churchyard, where the infant might have been buried had they remained
home.

As she turned to go on, she was aware that she had been standing
beside a bookseller's shop. On impulse she moved to the doorway
and stood hesitantly, debating whether to surprise Siri with a new
book or material for a new dress. "Come in, Mrs. Gabrielsen," said
a pleasant voice. For a moment she could not locate the speaker,
but soon discovered him descending a short ladder at the rear of
the shop. She was sure she had known him at one time—at any
rate, he knew who *she* was. The short, stubby little fellow advanced
toward her with his hand extended. "I have not seen you since the
death of your husband."

"You are Johannes Monson!" she exclaimed with pleasure.

"Your Arne was one of my favorite customers," he replied, "though
we frequently did our business by mail. I was indeed sorry to hear
of your loss." He had an amazing memory, she thought, for he inquired about her mother and Siri. "You are not here alone?" he
inquired.

"No, I came with someone," she said, wondering immediately what
caused her evasion. "I know so little about books," she said, seeking
to cover her confusion, "but I wondered if you have something Siri
might enjoy."

"She is in school now?"

"Oh, yes!" said Elisabet. "This fall she will be eight," she boasted.

"One of our new writers, then?"

"I am afraid," she admitted, "that I have done little reading myself
of late. I want something entertaining, for the sexton—you know he
took Arne's place, don't you?—gives them ample religious material.
Perhaps something of Bjørnson she might cherish. I recall Arne's
saying to my mother that he had never owned *Sigurd Slembe,*
though he had read it."

"Well, it *is* a play," said the bookseller thoughtfully, "but its setting
is exciting—the twelfth century, you know. Still it is challenging,"
he said, "for a good reader to possess a book beyond his capabilities."
He moved down the aisle and bent down to extract a book from

a shelf. Going over to a cluttered desk, he sat down for a moment, dipping a pen into an inkwell. "There!" he exclaimed, blowing upon the flyleaf to dry the inscription. "My compliments to the little one, Mrs. Gabrielson."

"Oh, but you mustn't," she protested, blushing with embarrassment. He wrapped it in a paper and presented it to her with a little bow. She thanked him several times, and when a customer came in, she said goodbye.

"Bring the child in," he said, shaking her hand again. Outside in the street, now grown sunny, Elisabet hesitated for a moment. She still had not found a place for breakfast, and Tosten could well be waiting for her, alarmed at her absence. She retraced her steps to the hotel.

The room was unlocked, and Tosten stood at the window, his back to her. "Where have *you* been, then?" When he turned around she saw that his face was flushed, his eyes hot with excitement or anger.

"I started out for breakfast," she exclaimed lamely, "but I got no farther than the booksellers, where—"

"Never mind about that!" he said, advancing into the center of the room, his hands jammed into his pockets. "Elisabet, how much money do you have with you?"

"Why do you ask?" She threw her shawl on the chair. "Has something happened?"

"If something had not happened, would I ask you?"

"Is your uncle—"

"My uncle is a vindictive old fool."

"I thought he was near death," she began.

"Not close enough to it to have a civil tongue in his head. 'What have you come for this time, Tosten?' he asks me. 'Do you want some more money, or do you want to see how slowly an old man dies!' "

"You have never really told me anything, Tosten," she said, sinking upon the edge of the bed. "I can't understand what this is all about."

"First he takes my boat and merchandise away—he said I wasn't making any profit. He said he'd settle with me when he went through his books, and now he tells me I haven't a cent coming. My father's own brother!" he exclaimed, pacing up and down on the flowered carpet.

"Was that what we were planning to take our wedding trip on—the money you expected?" asked Elisabet.

"I had it coming. It was he himself who talked me into selling out the old merchandise he carried in his shop. I can tell you that if Mother were alive, this never would have happened!"

Elisabet reached into the little reticule she carried. "I have some money with me. But not enough for that trip South that we planned."

"I am sorry, dearest," he said, sitting down beside her, pulling her into his arms, "I am very sorry my little sweetheart must suffer for an old man's parsimony."

"We could go home again," suggested Elisabet, drawing away.

"*That* we'll not do!" said Tosten emphatically.

"Well then, we can stay here, but in a cheaper lodging." She waited for his reply.

"My little Elisabet must let *me* worry about what we do," he said, pocketing the money. "I think I have an excellent plan."

Although Paul Johann Blekstad was unaware of it at the moment, he figured in the week's plans. For the use of one of his boats, Blekstad was assured that Fjeldstrand lay waiting to be surveyed as a possible site for a tourist hotel. The new Mrs. Vegg, quiet and ladylike, so impressed the Blekstads that they pressed the keys to their summer lodge upon the newlyweds. None of this Elisabet was really aware of, for the former achievement took place when Tosten and Blekstad were in the cellar sampling ale; the latter favor came as a result of Elisabet's being left with Mrs. Blekstad, who told Paul as they waved goodbye to the couple, "I didn't offer our lodge to them because I care for *your* friend Tosten. I fell in love with that little wife of his." She took her husband's arm as they moved up the graveled walk from the boathouse. "I am not sure it was so wise, Paul, to leave her alone with him in such a lonely place."

"There is nothing he can do that will surprise her," the husband answered drily. "She is a widow with a child."

"Oh, I know all that!" she said impatiently. "But her first husband was an educated man." She turned back to watch the progress of their sailboat. "What ever will those two find to talk about!"

CHAPTER 9

Cross Currents

On the morning after her mother's return from the wedding journey, Siri—by design—awakened early. She felt an embarrassment at being a spectator to her mother's and stepfather's arrival for breakfast. Gunhild, who had been awakened by the child's movements, sat up in bed with curl papers at her temples and warned Siri not to awaken the sleepers below. Foolish Gunhild! It was the last thing she *wanted* to do, awaken this stranger behind her mother's closed door.

She remembered how it used to be when Papa was alive, how often she had crept into their bedroom to find both parents lying side by side asleep. Because she felt closer to them at such an unguarded hour than at any time afterwards, she often shook the bed slightly as she watched them, knowing that the small tremors could be construed as accident should they awaken. Oh, there had been many advantages to being present at Papa's awakening: promises could be exacted, plans formed, and the entire affairs of the farm turned topsy-turvy before Papa knew what he was saying. Mamma, however, could be awakened in the middle of the night and come up with a clear answer about where the trolls slept when the mountains were packed with snow.

Now she was aware that the new state of affairs in the household would require careful thought before her compromised acceptance, for even at this age the child had well-established patterns for her psychological survival. One of these was to examine all significant relationships as carefully and as logically as time and her own understanding permitted.

The overwhelming problems of her father's death and her mother's seeming indifference to her needs she had in earlier days taken down beside the purling creek. Now she roamed more widely, sometimes to the higher levels of their stream, where traces of an old millwheel lined the plunging creek and lay moss-grown along its edges. Just as often she went down to her grandmother's favorite rock at the sea's edge, a place she had formerly shunned after the raw shock of her father's drowning. Now the place afforded an odd kind of comfort, a preliminary in a sense to her innocent and whispered communication with Papa himself, for she did not doubt that he heard her. How could anyone as loving and concerned as he had been disappear without even an attempt at return, particularly when angels bent on various errands of duty and mercy (so the sexton informed them) flew ceaselessly over mountain and dale and fjord?

Now as she lay upon the cold rock, where the morning sun had not yet appeared, she listened to the cry of the birds above the sea and Lar's gee and haw to the dun on the small slope above the house. The sun struck the snowy summits of the mountains until they shone with almost blinding radiance; at the foot of the slopes and in the narrows of the fjord a blue haze added mystery and depth to the distance.

"*Father, Father!*" she called softly. "I still love you." She put her hands to her throat. "See, I carry the silver locket you gave me and keep most of your books in my room. I lead Grandma about as you asked me—" She sat up and looked toward the house, putting her hand to her cheek. "Only I forgot I am to help her dress whenever there is company—but, Papa, I can't go in this morning. I can't because *he* is there." She blinked in the sudden light that shone upon the farmstead, for the sun had risen over the summit of the eastern peaks. "And you can't go in there either," she said slowly, "for Mamma has let someone take your place—but not really, Grandma says, and never at all with me, Father."

"Come, Siri, breakfast!" She saw Gunhild at the back door, her golden-red hair frizzed under her heavy crown of braids. She had on her "in-between" dress and a heavily starched apron at her waist. "Hurry!" she called.

At the back door Mamma met her, scolding softly because Siri had forgotten to put a clean dress on, and, "What ever were you thinking of? Without shoes!" She washed her face and hands at the back door and would have slipped upstairs to change, but her mother took her firmly by the arm and directed her to the table. Bergit was already seated, and Tosten helped Elisabet to her chair.

"You haven't said good morning, Siri," he chided, eyeing her with playful disapproval.

"Good morning," she said dutifully.

"You see," he said, turning to Elisabet, "I can't ever bring the child a thing until she likes me. I do so much for children who *like* me!" he teased, pouring milk on his porridge. "In fact, I was just telling your grandmother here that when I inherit some money which I expect soon, I plan to buy an organ for the parlor. Think how fine that would be for Grandmother if a little girl learned to amuse her by playing an organ!" She stole a glance at Bergit, who was carefully wiping crumbs from her mouth, her head lowered. "Maybe *you* would like to learn to play the organ, Gunhild!" he said, as she set a cup of coffee at his place.

"You are so kind!" said Gunhild, as though the organ sat in the parlor, an impressive, accomplished fact. "I'm afraid I'll be too slow to learn."

"Is your uncle then so near death?" asked Bergit.

"Yes, poor man, I am afraid I shall lose him." After the meal was over, Siri led Bergit for a walk, for the night's small rain had left the ground somewhat slippery. In the meantime, Tosten and Elisabet had gone to the parlor, where he was measuring the room. "Be sure to put Mother's chair back in the same spot," warned Elisabet, going on into the bedroom.

"Just a minute!" called Tosten. "Your mother is an enviable old character. I do not doubt that, sweetheart. But there *is* a limit to what the young must endure to please the old. I have only to look at her to know that in her time she was the one to be pleased—isn't it time, Elisabet, that you thought of yourself occasionally, or of *us?*"

"She asks so little," argued Elisabet, on the defensive, "Anyway, this is *her* home, Tosten." She turned on her heels and returned to the bedroom, where she began to shake the pillows with unnecessary energy. He came up beside her, removing the pillow from her hand. "You see," he said, "I cannot even take you in my arms at this moment because of prying eyes and stealthy footsteps." He forced her to look into his pleading eyes, tilting her chin upward with the palm of his hand. "Promise me, little wife, that you will take a firm hand in the running of this household. Or I shall move you out and let them see how they fare if we leave them."

"O Tosten," sighed Elisabet, weakening under his steady glance, "you're jealous—that's all." She eluded his grasp and resumed her bedmaking, "Anyway, where would we go and what would you do?"

"I wouldn't sit on the slope of a hill the rest of my life, I can assure you of that—not when I know men of wealth and influence like my friend Blekstad."

"Tosten," said Elisabet, unconsciously using the tone of a mother with a child, "why don't you take a look about the farm? I am sure you will find Lars up on the hill somewhere."

On his way out, he stopped in the kitchen for a moment to ask Gunhild for a drink of water, though the bucket was almost under his hand. "Do you like it here, Gunhild?" he asked, sipping slowly from the glass she had offered him. "If there is any way we can make the work more pleasant for you, be sure to let me know, girl." With considerable blushing and a little tittering Gunhild continued washing the breakfast dishes, assuring him several times—always with thanks—that she found everything to her liking at Fjeldstrand.

"Much better than at home," she finished quickly.

Tosten scented an interesting trail. "Why do you say that?" he asked.

"Oh, I can't say," she said with embarrassed honesty. Tosten, however, mistook her answer for a further invitation to inquiry and would have continued the badinage except for the sudden arrival of her brother Lars.

"Gunhild," said Lars, drawing the battered yellow cap from his yellow head and wiping perspiration off his forehead, "has Elisabet an errand to the village?" He nodded briefly to Tosten. "If not, I'll go home and help Father with his nets."

"My dear boy," said Tosten, setting down his water glass, "you'll do nothing of the kind right now. My wife has requested that you show me about the farm. After that I think we can give you permission to go." Lars raised a questioning eyebrow in his sister's direction, but the latter was too confused or flattered by the recent conversation to notice her brother's look of critical inquiry.

"Some of these farms are a bit primitive," said Tosten, following Lars to the cowshed. "The farther back you go, the worse they are. Believe me, I know—I have touched at all of them when I was in business." Lars made no reply. "Now this old storage building should have been torn down years ago, a useless relic of the long-ago past."

"Old Bergit is very fond of the old building," said Lars in a noncommittal voice

Tosten moved back a few steps, squinting in the bright sunlight. "Still, it is a quaint touch and my friend Paul might be charmed by it. Yes, Lars, I think we'll let it stand!"

"I am glad to hear that," said Lars, thinking to humor him if he could not understand him.

"How far does our farm reach?" asked Tosten.

"Oh, I have cut wood way up above the old mill-race," said Lars. Tosten chose to ignore the lad's oblique humor.

"What's this to be?" he asked, indicating a small field to the right.

"Barley, God willing."

"Your sister down there," began Tosten, "really bears little resemblance to you." When Lars made no comment, he said with some irascibility, "Oh, go on, boy, I'll walk around by myself." Lars left with the speed of a youngster escaping the sexton's catechization.

"What's he doing up there?" asked Gunhild, waiting for her brother at the back door.

"He's as crazy as Per," commented Lars, attempting to dismiss the entire walk from his mind.

"Elisabet said you can leave, Lars. *I* think he is a wonderful man," argued Gunhild. "The trouble with you, Lars, is that you have never done anything but fish and farm."

"And what remarkable things have you done in life, sister?" asked her brother with an amused smile. He patted her playfully on the shoulder and headed down the pathway for the beach.

Guro, who lived two lives—one up at Ørnheim and the other in Fjeldstrand—had arrived to greet Elisabet and Tosten by the time the latter had completed his tour of the farm. Of all Elisabet's kin, Tosten felt most at ease with Guro, who had led a busy, if not a significant, life out in the world. Her arrival called for the usual *kaffee kalas*, and soon they were all around the table in the parlor. "It's good to have a man here again," said Guro kindly. "It's a wonder that things have gone as well as they have, but Gunnar and Lars are a godsend." She turned to Gunhild and said, "I suppose conscription will be taking that young brother of yours one of these days."

"He looks a little young for that," Tosten put in.

"I have heard this is one reason many of our men leave for America," remarked Bergit. "It is one thing to put on a uniform and fight for one's own country, but it is another story if one must fight for something he does not want, another's heel upon one's neck."

"I cannot see that it matters who rules us," argued Tosten, "as long as we can live in peace and be free to pursue our own desires."

Bergit's hand shook as she put down her coffee cup. "If you truly think that, and many others think in a like manner, our desire for freedom will die."

"You know," said Guro, changing the subject, "I think we'll have to give up our little farm one of these days. I am getting a little old for that up-and-down-hill journey."

"I have told you many times," said Bergit, "that you and Nels can come down and live with us."

"You really mean that, Grandma?" asked Siri.

"There are some changes I have in mind for Fjeldstrand," said Tosten, ignoring the child's question. "I think such changes could well be an advantage to you should you decide to come down."

"O Tosten!" said Elisabet, scowling at him prettily. "You must not be carried away by your daydreams."

Bergit said crisply, "I should be interested in hearing them."

"At the moment all I can say is that they depend on my inheritance."

"In that you are mistaken," said Bergit, putting her hand upon her cane and rising, "for I am not in the churchyard yet; and any major changes made in this house will be instituted by me. I am a blunt old woman, perhaps, and it may be I might even like what you propose, but first I must know your proposal."

"I am so tired," said Guro placatingly, "I think I shall spend the night here. Nels is really not expecting me back until tomorrow." As Guro spoke, she saw a whispered consultation between the newlyweds, who soon remarked that they were crossing to the village, for Tosten was eager for his mail.

Guro's intention to remain over night had been inspired chiefly by her desire to have a long talk with Bergit, so the departure of the two gave Bergit and her ample time for visiting. "I wrote Roald of

Tosten's courtship. At the time, of course, I did not know how serious Elisabet was." She sat in a straight chair near her sister-in-law's rocking chair and observed that Bergit had aged rapidly in the past month, the eyes more hollowed, her bearing less assured. "Have you wondered what our Elisabet sees in the man?"

"Until now," replied Bergit, "I have accepted blindness as something to be endured patiently. But you cannot know, Guro, how I chafe against this blackness now that a stranger sleeps under our roof. I should like to match his glance and voice, for I think that one does not always belong with the other. On the night of Arne's death my daughter said she would not be like me for anything in the world. I have often heard it said that words spoken in anger should be regarded lightly, if at all, but I am of a mind to believe that they are often rooted in a conviction so deep that only anger can unearth them."

"Things may turn out much better than you think," said Guro. "The man has some charm, though I wouldn't want to take it to bed with *me*." Guro laughed, in an attempt to lighten their mood.

"He must have something for the eye, at any rate." Bergit smiled. "Kari has always been full of praises for him, and poor Gunhild titters every time he is near. But my Elisabet," she said thoughtfully, "who was of such a oneness with Arne, what can she see in a man so different?"

"A man who would never strive to take his place, I think. A man who skitters lightly over the surface and never gives her time to see what is below."

"But enough of that," said Bergit. "How would you like to take Siri up to Ørnheim with you for a few days?"

"I was going to suggest that myself."

Bergit's visit with her sister-in-law cast a brighter light upon the week of her daughter's return. Still they had not touched upon a problem that worried her. How did Tosten plan to provide for his wife? Would he be willing to accept the burdens of the farm or did he plan to resume a merchant's trade, the latter at best a doubtful kind of living with the steamer plying regularly between one village and another.

In the coming weeks she sought to understand better this man who had bewitched her daughter into marriage. The night of their visit to the village he had come in a little merrier for ale, but nothing vexatious had come of it except a long morning's sleep. Stopping Tosten's progress past her chair, she remarked pleasantly, "Lars tells me you have taken much interest in surveying the farm. Perhaps you have in mind to try something new?"

He stopped with some surprise, for the truth of it was that he was a little afraid of this old woman, who stared so directly at one when she spoke that it was difficult to believe she had no sight, only the insight of an alert mind. Furthermore, he had never had much patience with the aged—and much less lately, for his uncle had irked him because of his obdurate parsimony. "I am not a farmer," he said, "and I suspect I shall never be one."

"Sit down, Tosten" she invited. "Our acquaintance comes slowly, and I am afraid it is much my doing."

"I wouldn't say that," he replied politely.

"Perhaps you see some things that might be bettered," she said, "even though you do not like farming."

She heard again the low, teasing timbre of his voice as he answered, "It would not do any good, for it is not my right to say."

"Say it," she urged.

"It's only that you are so content with herring and boiled potatoes here, when you could fare on finer diet, so to speak." He drawled, "It is a small use you have here of a big thing, but I can understand how in your blindness you are unable to see the great changes that have come everywhere. Much money can be made from visitors who like to fish our streams and hunt the upper reaches of our mountains. The English—"

"I know," she said, striving to keep her temper. "I have not always sat like a hex in a black cave. The tourists I myself have seen, and as to the changes which have come, I have observed some and have read of others—for if one reads and observes, Tosten, one can learn much of this world, even at one's own doorstep."

"Of course it is necessary for others to read for you these days. So it has been for my uncle, whose sight is failing."

"Your uncle—" she bgan kindly, striving to detain him, for she had heard him rise, "your uncle, is he better now?"

"I wait daily to hear," he replied.

"You are his only heir?" she asked frankly, disdaining subterfuge, since profit, clearly, was in his own mind concerning her property.

"Poor man," he said unctuously, "he is of a mind to make me his heir on Monday, the bookseller on Tuesday, and the church the rest of the week.

She smiled at his caustic humor. "Have you told him of your marriage? Elisabet said he was too ill for her to meet him."

"Oh, yes, I told him. All he had to say was that he was glad I had made a better marriage than the first, for uncle thought my first marriage even the bishop could not have blessed. But let me tell you, my uncle wasn't above looking down the front of her dress when she bent down to pick up wood for the fire!"

*　*　*

During the following weeks Tosten was in and out of the house so much that Bergit wondered what was afoot. Sometimes he stopped for a small chat, and once he brought Bergit an old cherished Fjeldstrand clock, long out of repair, which he had put in working order, for he was clever with his hands. Not a day passed that Tosten did not go to the village; and though it was true that he came back in higher spirits than he had been in when he left, Bergit would not quarrel with that so long as he was sensible, and kind to Elisabet and the child.

Still it worried her that the child and he had made no progress in friendship. "Is the girl unfriendly to him in looks or actions?" she asked Guro once.

"No," said Guro thoughtfully, "she only looks at him with those big brown eyes of hers. Indeed, her look is somewhat like your own when I met you years ago, for do you know, Bergit, that when I first met you I was afraid of your steady, thoughtful look. Poor me," she laughed, "I used to wonder what awful thing I had done."

Shortly after this conversation Tosten came scurrying into the house to say that he had been summoned to Bergen, for a letter said that Uncle Andreas would undoubtedly be gone within the next few days. While Elisabet packed, Tosten stormed over the stupidity of the writer. "Why couldn't he have let me know sooner! I tell you,

I'll have it out with that Johannes one of these days! Lifelong friends these two, but what's a friend, lifelong or week-long, compared to kin at a time like this!" Elisabet purred him into good temper, bringing him warm water for shaving and calling Siri to put a shine on his shoes. At last he was ready, with Lars called upon to row him across the village, though the latter could see no sense in all this flurry because the steamer would not arrive any sooner for the wish. Tosten shook hands with Bergit and told her that it was quite possible there would be affairs of some moment for them to discuss when he returned. Bergit, however, ignored his implications and wished him a safe journey and his uncle peace in Jesus' name. Elisabet clung to his hand and went down to the shore with him, while Siri sat on a chair and watched Gunhild cope with misted eyes.

The women spent a busy week while he was gone, for Elisabet said that he might be bringing some things back with him and the rooms needed cleaning and arranging. "Surely he will come today!" exclaimed Elisabet eight or nine days following his departure. And though they sat outside in the long blue twilight of the summer night, not a boat could be discerned coming across the waters. The faint lights in the village went out one by one, and the women brought in the chairs from beside the house.

Sometime during the same night, however, they were all awakened by a furious banging of doors and the crash of crockery in the kitchen. Elisabet sat up in bed trying to shake off the confusion of interrupted sleep. Had a wind suddenly arisen, she wondered, or had she awakened from a nightmare? She heard the dragging footsteps of some intruder coming across the floor in the parlor and the sound of falling furniture. She remembered tales of wandering bears, but surely they had closed the doors! And old Per, crazy as he was, had never once intruded in anyone's home.

"Elisabet! Elisabet!" Strange and loose-jawed as the voice sounded, she recognized it at once, threw back the covers, and moved swiftly to the bedroom doorway. In the pale light of summer night she saw him standing with a hand upon a table, bent forward, as if in pain.

"Tosten, you are hurt!" She hastened across the room and threw her arms around him; but at her first touch, he pushed her roughly away so that she had to struggle to retain her balance. She was aware of Gunhild's lamp on the balcony and a cry of "Mother!" from Siri. He came toward her slowly, almost catlike, despite his unsteadiness

"You're the sly one, Elisabet. You're the sly one. Knowing Johannes all this time and never letting on. You're the sly one, Elisabet!"

"Leave her alone!" Bergit's cane slammed against the doorjamb. "I'll break this on your head, you drunken fool, if you don't get out in the hayloft and sleep off the poison of your addled mind!"

"And there she stands," said Tosten, acknowledging Bergit's presence with a derisive smile, "the sunken-eyed captain of this female schooner. I spit on you all, you fish-eating peasants!"

Bergit's cane began to tap toward him with ominous speed. "Mother, leave him alone!" interceded Elisabet. "He'll sleep it off. He's had one drink too many, that's all." She stood between the two, venturing for the moment neither to restrain her mother nor assist her husband. "Mother," she said pleadingly, "if you come between us now, I'll never forgive you. Never!" Then she moved swiftly to Tosten's side, cradling her arm in his, "And you two up there," she called, perceiving Gunhild and Siri, "what are *you* staring at? Get to bed, both of you!"

Bergit shook her head and moved slowly back into her own room. She could hear Tosten's plaintive tones and Elisabet's soothing voice. She could scarcely restrain the flood of anger that wanted to wash itself away in action. How she would like to go out there and thrash him soundly with her cane, for coward he was, had been, and no doubt would be unless someone took him in hand! And while she was at it, she would like to shake a little sense into Elisabet too. Yet what was the use? She knew only too well her daughter's stubbornness and the tenacious defenses of her heart. By now, she supposed, the entire village had heard his ravings if he had come by steamer. On the other hand, there was a chance some fisherman or farmer, returning from an errand, had left him at their shore. Even so, there would be talk.

The worst of it all, she thought, as she lay down on the bed again, was that Siri had to see such a shameful performance. Now she was glad that the child had never given him her heart. She heard his groaning snores in the adjacent room and her daughter's pattering footsteps and the opening of a window. Pity rose in her for the daughter-wife in that acrid and sour room; and as she lay upon her back with folded hands, she prayed that Elisabet would soon learn to strengthen mercy with wisdom.

During the night Bergit awakened again, not knowing whether she had slept for an hour or two or only for a moment. A small wind scratched a twig against her window pane; damp sea air moved gustily through the room. She sat up in bed and felt for her cane. She recalled that no one had looked to see whether the doors were closed after Tosten's precipitate arrival, and any creature of the night would be able to wander in. Not a sound came from the bedroom beside hers. Softly, her cane a whisper upon the floor, she moved slowly across the parlor. Cold night air came in a rush from the kitchen. Her cane extended for the next step, she suddenly found herself without balance as the stick caught in the ladder back of a fallen chair. Arms flailing, she struggled for balance; and then she fell heavily upon the sharp edge of the upturned seat.

CHAPTER 10

The Running Stream

There was not a single moment to which any of them might point and say, "This is the moment of our deciding upon America." Each of them was, in a sense, a contributor, and each event contributing. How could they know that Old Mons would leave his pipe on the table edge and that Lubbe, his black cat, would playfully brush its bowl of aromatic embers into a basket of dry shavings? How could they know that Bergit's fall—in breaking for a while the methodical sequence of her days—would lend new sharpness to her thinking? How could they further know that two men in Bergen, friends for a half century, would scheme to take a small inheritance from one and give it to another, thus sending a child across the sea?

It was this last circumstance that had so enraged Tosten upon his return to Fjeldstrand, though Elisabet was not to know the cause of his ire for several days. With Siri helping, Gunhild and Elisabet had entwined their arms and made a seat to carry Bergit to bed; and the doctor, from a village halfway between Fjeldstrand and the seaport, had come and gone before Tosten awakened. Nels, in the meantime, had come to take his boat across to the village. It did not take him long to arouse the furry-tongued lie-abed, although Elisabet had coaxed Nels entreatingly, until, alarmed at her uncle's taut fury, she had finally but tearfully allowed the door to close on her, while Nels (she listened, white and shaking, at the door) thundered at Tosten to awaken or, by God, he would throw both him and the bed into the North Sea. Once she put her hand upon the door to intercede, but drew back with alarm at the sound of a dull smack like a fist against a man's flesh. Then she put her head into her arms and stood weeping. Siri had been sent out to Lars, while Gunhild, at Nels's command, was brewing coffee. Bergit was asleep, for the doctor had given her opiates for bruises of both the heart and the body.

Gunhild, in her excitement, had built a roaring fire, hardly commensurate with the brewing of a pot of coffee, and stood salting the brew with her tears. She could not have said exactly why she wept, but she was aware of a great weariness, for none but Tosten had slept that night. Perhaps she wept for her own deliverance, remembering a moment some weeks ago when Tosten had surprised her as she was picking berries by the old mill site. "Afraid of me, Gunhild?" He had put his arm about her and drawn her toward him, teasing her with his low-pitched voice and his provocative smile. Though she had pulled away and resumed her berry-picking with shaking hands, she had not escaped so easily in her dreams. On the night of Tosten's return, their shocked observation from the balcony had served to complete Gunhild's disenchantment; for in Siri's reiterated, "I am afraid! I am afraid!" Gunhild had traveled backward in her own memory to unlock a shadowy door in her own childhood and give the child a sister's ear and a sister's counsel. When Siri's sobs had subsided Gunhild asked the child why she had kept these fears to herself. "Mamma wouldn't care, and Grandma would care too much," she replied, with an acumen that surprised Gunhild into unaccustomed reflections, while she held the child fast with one arm and stroked the hot, damp forehead with her free hand. Thus the two lay, moving slowly into a turbid stream of sleep. It was at the very moment of their dropping off into a maelstrom of whirling slumber that they were rashly awakened by Bergit's sudden fall and the sharp crack of her flying cane as it hit the stones of the hearth.

In the days that followed, Bergit's bruises healed slowly and Tosten picked up his soiled garments of shame, edulcorating them in the fresh waters of rationalization, until he almost convinced Elisabet that he had found the door wide open when he returned. For if the door had been locked, how had he got in? If he had overturned the chair by the doorway, wouldn't they have seen it? Guro, who had come down to nurse Bergit, had said with rare sharpness, "Be still, Tosten! You know that few draw a latch on their doors here, for against whom would we lock them? Close them we do—bolt them we do not—yet perhaps we too have learned our lesson."

Tosten set down his coffee cup, arose, and signaled to Elisabet to follow him. She fetched a shawl from a peg and without looking back slipped outdoors to join him in the remaining twilight. They walked hand in hand, but she was aware of his punishing coolness and sighed to herself remembering how bitterly peace had recently been won and at what cost to her own sleep and composure. Few had been the times when Arne and she had misunderstood each other, and never had he accepted pique as a bed fellow. How could she put into clear and lucid thoughts what Tosten was able to do to her—how he could use her womanhood to elevate and degrade her spirit, to illumine and extinguish the flame within, which she regarded as her soul? "You are not listening, Elisabet." She turned her face upward, afraid as she did so that he would read into her glance perplexity and unspoken criticism. "You must have told them, Elisabet," he said, stopping abruptly on the path that led down to the sea. "You promised not to tell them about the inheritance."

"Please don't press so on my arm. I have not told them, Tosten."

"They're scornful, all of them. Even Guro. And that Gunhild—like a cat that has fallen into a bowl of cream! And Lars, never have I seen such rectitude in a ploughboy!" They came to the water's edge. He dropped her arm and moved toward a rock, placing one foot upon it and resting his hand on his knee, looking out toward the sea and Gunnar's fishing boat, barely discernible in the fading light. "When my first money comes—our money, you will not be niggardly with it, Elisabet?"

"Why do you torment yourself, Tosten?" She moved up beside him, hugging the shawl closely. "It is only that he was so against drinking—your uncle—and that you have a *family* now." She loosened her shivering hold on the shawl and moved up against him, slipping her cold hand into the crook of his arm. Would he ever believe her, she wondered, when she told him again and again that she had known old Monson only as Arne's bookseller and that her wandering in to buy a book was not an act of complicity, but merely an accident? That it was Tosten's uncle, in one of his many visits with the bookseller, who had learned details about the family Tosten had married into? Alone, in the privacy of her room, she had read the letter from Johannes Monson again and again, until she knew it from memory.

He spoke of the enduring friendship between him and Andreas Vegg and how the latter had always conducted himself with the highest principles, though "perhaps a little too unyielding by today's standards." Therefore the little money he had invested in a British colonial firm he wanted used for wholesome purposes, not for the gain of those Andreas had termed "weak in morality and unrestrained in appetite." Monson had gone on to write that Andreas had been gladdened by the quality of his last marriage, but saddened by the thought of how the innocent might suffer unless Tosten met his future obligations with more zeal and character than his past. She had never shown the letter to anyone, and none at home knew of its existence, for Lars had brought it over with him in Tosten's temporary absence. As if reading her mind, Tosten pulled his foot down from the rock and turned to face her. "We will no doubt hear from that weasel Johannes soon—or perhaps *you* will hear, dear wife." His tone had a touch of acid, though he kept his voice purringly soft and curdled the composure for which she strove, like vinegar upon sweet milk.

"Please, Tosten, no quarreling."

"You love me, then?"

"Of course." She moved to him swiftly, nestling her head against his jacket. She had had the strangest feeling in childhood when she had disobeyed her father and roused his momentary ire, so that it was necessary to snuggle against him and regain his approval by wily sweetness. If only it were so simple now! Even now as his lips brushed her eyelashes and the tip of her nose and rested demandingly upon her mouth, she felt the trembling weakness of surrender—if such was his power, why did she in the very moment of complete yielding allow herself the flash of pretense that it was Arne to whom she surrendered?

A few mornings later the family awakened to Lars's pounding on the door. Bergit was the first to hear him knock and call and reached for her new cane to pound on the floor and awaken Elisabet. When the latter opened the door to Lars, she smelled the sharp-sweet odor of burning timber. "It's up toward Ørnheim," said Lars. "I wanted you to know I am running up there, so that Bergit would not grow too much alarmed. Perhaps you better get Tosten up, too."

"Oh, Lars! Lars!" cried Elisabet, clutching at a wrap she had hastily drawn over her nightclothes. "If anything happens to those two up there!"

"I don't think it's Ørnheim!" he called back. "It looks a little farther to the north and east." She watched him sprint between the buildings and head in the direction of the pathway. As she turned back into the kitchen, she heard Bergit's call. Elisabet stopped long enough to tell her mother that she was coming, and then she awakened Tosten and Gunhild, ordering the latter to get the fire going for coffee and a hasty breakfast. When Tosten was ready at last, she joined him on the trek up the mountain, dissuading Siri from following, for someone must tend to Bergit. Characteristically, it was Bergit who remained the most level-headed, assuring them that if it was, as they said, over in the direction of the rocky plateau which lay above and to the northeast of Ørnheim, it was not Nels's place. "Anyway, it rained heavily during the night. The fire could not spread far. Mark my word," she said, trying to raise herself upon her pillows and wincing with the effort, "it will be Mons's old shack that is burning or one of his outbuildings."

As usual, Bergit was right. By late midmorning Lars was back, assuring them that there was no loss of life at Mons's place except for Lubben, but that Mons was inconsolable over the loss of his cat. He had built no fire in the house, Lars reported, but remembered leaving his pipe on the edge of a table next to the wood basket when he heard a wild squawking in the chicken pens and had run out to frighten off a predatory animal. "Poor Mons!" said Lars, sipping coffee in the kitchen. "He said he had spoiled Lubben by letting her lie on the table. It was sad to see the tears running down the old fellow's cheeks."

"What will become of him?" asked Gunhild.

"Guro has invited him to make a home with them. He shouldn't be alone, anyway, in that old house of his. He is ninety years old," finished Lars, setting down his empty cup. "Did you finish the chores, Gunhild?"

"Well, of course. Why don't you go in and assure Bergit that everything is all right?" So Lars, cap in hand, and followed by Siri, went in for a reassuring visit with the grandmother.

It happened that Gunnar, out in his smaller boat to get a catch for the family, had also spied the flame and curling smoke and had run in at the closest shore. An ancient, rarely used trail led up to the old chalet, a path so familiar to the folk at Fjeldstrand. Beside this almost obliterated trail old Per had built himself a shack out of remnants of timber and his scavenging visits to farm and *saeter*. When he perceived Gunnar's headlong dash past his shack, he intercepted him with muddled questions about his destination, although he could not grasp or retain even the simplest explanations. At that moment Gunnar could not have told why he did not break away from Per's restraining clutch unless it was that a familiar plank nailed to the side of Per's shack had caught his eye. He threw off Per's grasp at last and strode toward the hut, with Per following and blabbering a torrent of innocent idiocies. "Per, where did you get this?" Per only nodded happily, smiling broadly with his jagged-toothed and slack grin.

Gunnar turned his head sideways to read the remnants of brown lettering upon the faded blue plank. "Great God!" exclaimed the brawny fisherman. "Where did you find this, Per?" He scrutinized the lettering more closely. "This is a piece of Arne's boat!"

Per let go of his hold on Gunnar's shirt and scuttled into the dark entrance. "More! More!" he cried, but when he emerged, he carried only a handful of sea shells. Gunnar replied with a few sharply ejaculated oaths and peered into the shack, emerging to shake his head.

"You're crazy, Per!"

"*Ja, Ja!*" said Per happily. But Per had lost all interest in Gunnar's visit and settled himself upon a heap of rotting sailcloth, staring disconsolately out toward sea. Gunnar shook his head with exasperation; but before he resumed his flight mountainward, he circled the shack to ascertain whether more portions of the boat remained.

By nightfall the entire village and many of the small farms were aware of the day's events. Some who had planned to visit Bergit since her fall but had been restrained by either work or procrastination decided to make a call. The doctor himself came by with a wheelchair which he had obtained from his own village, and which Bergit might use until she could safely resume walking.

Undressing for bed that night, Tosten was aware of Elisabet's constraint as she postponed the usual rites of taking down her hair and fetching her nightclothes. She evaded a glance-to-glance encounter, puttering about the clothes press and arranging some under-wear in a drawer. "Come, Elisabet," he said, seating himself on the edge of the bed. She turned her back to him and fumbled with a handkerchief. "You're thinking about Arne," he said, his round eyes narrowed with anger. When she began to snuffle, Tosten threw his shoe halfway across the room and remarked scarifyingly, "Great God, woman! No matter how many rotten timbers they find, that school-master of yours is still a heap of whitened bones!"

❀   ❀   ❀

Another autumn had come, with rains closing in upon sea and mountains, so that Bergit could not take the customary delight in her wheelchair. Siri was in school, sometimes remaining with the Engs, sometimes returning home if occasion or opportunity war-ranted it. Lars spoke frequently of conscription, so that Elisabet, at Tosten's urging, had spoken to one of Gunnar's other sons to gain his help in the event of Lars's leaving.

"So many changes!" thought Bergit. There had been a time when one day appeared to move into the next with only a change in its texture, not in its pattern. Sometimes it seemed that the one and only constant in her dark world was the sea, despite its changing voice. Elisabet's singing in the kitchen, the sound of snapping fire-wood, and the humming of the teakettle on the back of the stove were small domestic sounds this morning that could not drown out the greater sound of the sea, roiled and sullen after last night's storm. Its moaning voice said to her, "Beat upon me, wind, and hurl my waters to the sky, but I am the sea, the sea, the sea. While you whine and whistle and scream down the crevasses, I hide moun-tains in my depth and forests of moving sea grass, working my un-hurried will upon all that you have driven down to me." Elisabet could not get Arne out of her mind and felt a deep ire at the frequent senselessness of Tosten's behavior—how unlike the Fjeld-strand of Arne's time was the Fjeldstrand of today!

And Elisabet was the most changeable of changeable humans, she thought: one minute singing, the next so self-contained that none could get a word from her. In a moment of unusual confidence she had told Bergit that Tosten's uncle had left her a small annuity, feeling that she could handle money better than her husband—and the next day when she had grown a little peevish after their small argument over boiling cream for the pudding, she had said that the money had really been left to Tosten, but since they were married, she supposed it was as much hers as it was his. "And I will never tell you how much it is, Mother, for it is none of your concern."

"I will never ask you," she had replied, "for there is enough for Siri and me to live on here, as long as Gunnar or his boys can spare time enough to seed a plot of ground and there is a lonely cow on the place to give us milk and cream." Yet she could not grow angry with her daughter, for certainly she had been upset by the sudden discovery of Arne's boat, or what was left of it, and she had heard enough to know that Elisabet must also endure Tosten's sudden and angry jealousy.

As for herself, she had learned to tolerate the man, treating him with indifference, kindness, and humor—whatever the occasion dictated. It was Siri, with the idealism of the young, who continued to feel him an intruder, a dark shadow upon the shining father-image of Arne. Bergit recalled that she had heard from Sara Eng that some of the children in school had taunted Siri about her new "father"— the very children, said Sara, whose fathers willingly drank the ale that Tosten's money provided and won even more from him at cards. She supposed Guro was right: the child deserved something better than she was getting, for if Elisabet had to choose between the issue of her flesh and the possessor of it, Bergit felt she would choose the latter. Yet, she reflected, the world had always been an arena of violent struggle and the child must learn this sooner or later (had Elisabet ever learned it, she wondered), saying as she often did, that it was better for a kitten to play with small mice before he tried to vanquish a rat.

"Had you ever thought," finished Guro during one of their discussions, "that both you and the child could go to America, for Roald has written often enough that you would be welcome?"

"Never!" she had scoffed. "Am I who cannot lead the child safely across the wood lot suddenly presumed able to guide her across a great sea and a wide land?"

Nels at that point put down a week-old paper and interposed his comment. "If it comes to that, I'd see her across—old Mons can tend to our farm—and have it, for that matter, and Guro can stay with you."

"Never!" the latter had retorted, though Bergit was never aware of which of Nels's proposals had aroused Guro's spirited rejection.

The chilly fall day seemed interminable to Bergit, who was growing increasingly restless. Gunhild had left shortly before breakfast to spend the day with her stepmother and help her with butchering. The rawness in the air made the pain in Bergit's hip almost intolerable. Finally she put her hand on the cane and struggled out of the wheelchair to her feet, hobbling slowly to the kitchen.

"What are you doing now, Mother?" Her daughter replaced a stove lid with clattering impatience. "I thought you were told to be careful about walking."

"I am restless, that's all. It's one of those days which seems to have a burden upon it."

"You're lonely, Mother." Her mother did not reply, and Elisabet busied herself between the cupboard and the stove.

At that moment Elisabet looked out the window toward the boat landing. "There's Lars with Siri!" she cried. "Now what can be wrong?" Bergit heard Elisabet move toward the door and felt the damp air swirl about her shoulders and chill her feet. In all her years of blindness, Bergit had never allowed herself the dubious comfort of ascertaining, in her own mind at least, the cause of her affliction. For she had observed that those who ascribed others' troubles to the chastening of God were often resolutely averse to assigning their own afflictions to the same cause.

At this moment, however, she ached to possess the full perceptions of the sighted. Yet her keen ears heard the hastening steps, the choked sobbing, and the gentle chiding of Elisabet. "Take Siri to my room!" cried Elisabet. Although Bergit put out her hand and called to the child, none paid her the slightest attention. She struggled to her feet, attempting to follow them.

She felt a strong hand on her shoulder. "It's all right," said Lars, directing her to a chair. "Sit down, if you will, and I will tell you what happened."

"The child is not injured, is she, Lars?"

"Not really," he said. "It's Tosten again." Lars cleared his throat, then continued, "The poor thing was so wet and frightened when I picked her up, I could scarcely get the story out of her."

"Picked her up? Where? In school?" Bergit's hands were rigid on her cane.

"On the sea," said Lars bluntly, not knowing how to relate the events and still spare Bergit. Once started with the tale he related how he had been sent on an errand to the village, and when he was about half-way between the village and Fjeldstrand, he saw a boat circling about crazily. He rowed vigorously toward it, and soon saw its occupants, a man and a child.

"Tosten?"

"Tosten," replied Lars. "He had lost an oar and was as drunk as an eel in a wine keg. I set myself to rowing as fast as I could, for I recognized the red wool scarf Siri wears on her head when I take her across to school. As I came closer, I heard him yelling and cursing. He saw me, then, and began slapping at the water with his remaining oar so that the two of them were drenched with spray."

"Poor child," sighed Bergit.

"Ah, but she sat there, her little back so straight, her books on her lap! Once in a while she sent me an appealing glance but most of the time she stared at Tosten as if she dared not take her eyes from him."

"The child is impossible! I cannot get a word from her!" interrupted Elisabet.

"Well, Lars has a word or two I think you should hear," said Bergit. When the lad seemed doubtful about proceeding, Bergit prodded him sharply.

"I am sorry to have to speak so frankly about your husband, Elisabet. But you will understand he did not know what he was doing, for someone must have given him too much to drink in the village."

"Go on!" said Bergit impatiently.

"The closer I came, the more enraged he grew, standing up in the boat and lurching at me with the oar, until the boat threatened to capsize several times. I had all I could do to outwit him. But when I was able to approach close enough, I picked up an oar and slapped him sharply upon the back of the head." He heard Elisabet's soft groan, but continued steadily, though with a small apology, "I am sorry it had to be done—but at that he was lucky, for I was angry enough to have killed him."

"How foolish you talk!" scoffed Elisabet.

"I towed him in," said Lars. "He's in the boat house sleeping off both his misfortunes." He did not resume until Elisabet had slammed the door and pattered down the pathway to the sea.

"There is a weakness in both of them, Lars," said Bergit. "And with Elisabet, perhaps I am somewhat to blame. You did well, Lars, and have my thanks."

"It's growing late.. I'll tend to the chores and then fetch Gunhild." He stood above her uncertainly, then drew his hand softly against her wrinkled cheek. "The child—you should know, Bergit, how sweet she was. First she would hand me her books, wiping the salt water off them carefully, and then she helped me with Tosten. It was not until I had begun to row again that she began to weep. I asked her why she wept when it was all over. "I weep because I hate him so!" she sobbed.

Bergit sat still, his words seeming to shed a veil of quietness upon her. "Lars," she said softly, "it is given us in this life the power to inspirit other lives—and there's not much that I have done, nor is there much left for me to do. But the child is mine in spirit, and has been since cradle days. Elisabet sews for her and mends her clothes, but their minds must seek to meet with words. For the child and me no words are needed; we are often as one. This I know, Lars, and this I cannot help." Lars put his hand on her shoulder and then moved softly out to tend the waiting animals.

In the days that followed Bergit learned from Nels, who made it a point to inquire, how Tosten had come to have the child out to sea with him. As he later told Nels, he had been drinking with some friends who frequently gathered in a bachelor's hut some distance from the village. His losses weighing heavily upon him, he had left to make his way back to the wharf, a course that took him past the school, where the children were outdoors playing during a short recess. He became aware of Siri's red scarf and her ringing laughter as she joined hands with a circle of playmates. With grim bitterness he told Nels, "I saw her and she saw me, but she pretended to look the other way. I grew angry then, for was I not the child's father now, and had she ever shown me any affection, any concern? This was once she could not run to her grandmother—and safe beside the old woman's wheelchair, stare at me with round, accusing eyes." He had related to Nels how he wished only to teach her obedience. He had sidled up to the sexton and told him that the child was needed at home.

From the sexton Nels had learned how loath the former was to allow the child to leave with Tosten. "Even as nearsighted as I am," he told Nels, "I could see that the man's gait was unsteady. I assure you, though, I exacted a promise from that fellow that he would stop by the Engs, and let them know, and this he assured me he would do, with many smiles and confirmations."

"And the child?" asked Nels, who felt only pity for the old school-master.

"Several times she asked him in that clear, low voice of hers, "But who wants me at home, Tosten? Is it Grandma who is ill?""

After Nels's unpleasant interrogation of Tosten, he had walked up to the cottage and talked long into the night with Guro. A few days later both of them were down for an afternoon's visit with Bergit, Elisabet and her husband having left for the village.

"I think the child should come up and live with us."

"Never," said Bergit.

"Well, there's scarcely enough room for us, now that Mons is there," commented Guro. "But tell her what you really think, Nels."

Nels studied his sister for a few moments and thought how old she had grown since her fall, her eyes more hollowed, her skin almost translucent. Straight of back, she sat in the wheelchair, only the restless fingering of her black skirt betraying her well-concealed emotions. "Then let me say it," he said abruptly. "We're old—the three of us—and I think the child belongs in America. She is Arne's child, too, and we must never forget that. You have always been one to keep family affairs to yourself, Bergit, and must not grow angry when I tell you that Guro has written Roald about Elisabet's marriage." It was so unlike his sister not to have a spirited reply that Nels was at a loss how to go on.

Finally Bergit gave a long sigh and said, "I have thought so myself —I have known it myself. I am glad you have said it, Nels."

Guro rose and put a wrinkled little arm about her sister-in-law's shoulder. "Still it is cruelly hard, Bergit."

"I have often said there is not a hand we grasp in greeting that doesn't need to be relinquished in farewell."

"Well, it need not be done today," said Nels, rising to empty his pipe in the fireplace.

"Nor need it be left until I die," remarked Bergit with a return of her old crispness. "Yet it will be hardest on Elisabet."

Nels stopped abruptly as he was lighting his pipe and asked tersely, "Why do you say that?"

"Because she will never believe that it has to be."

"Nonsense," said Nels.

"None of this would have to be if Elisabet could ever have believed it possible."

"Still nonsense," reiterated Nels.

In the course of time Roald's warm reply to their letter of decision came to Fjeldstrand. In the following weeks Elisabet had been convinced, only to weep and need convincing again. "What will they say of me?" she often asked. "Everyone will say it is a poor mother whose own child must seek another home."

Bergit had grown frail in the dark days of winter, but she hung on tenaciously to the self-image of her former strength and countered with her usual asperity, "That they'll never say, that you have been a poor mother. Nels and Guro speak of it only as a visit. They may all be back in a year's time." Bergit's voice betrayed the hope which lay as a bright thread among her skein of thoughts.

"And poor Kari, she weeps her eyes out because she cannot go with them. I have a little money," Elisabet said tentatively, "and Roald was far too generous with passage money—can we not make a purse to send Kari too?"

"I think not," said Bergit. "There may be a reason she has not heard from Mikjell. It would only be a burden to Nels and Guro and the family in America if something has gone amiss."

"The same could happen to Siri, Mother."

Bergit felt that Elisabet took a morbid delight in dismal speculations concerning the sea and ships and railways threading across the new land. It was almost as though she had caught an infection from Kari herself. A faint woodpecker of warning tapped repeatedly at Bergit's tree of accumulated knowledge, and she sought to remember what Arne had once said about his wife many years ago, but she could not remember. To change the subject, she said pleasantly, "It will be easier for the child to say farewell now that she has survived a parting from Lars."

"That's silly," scoffed Elisabet. "Lars was just someone to tease—someone with youth."

"In that you are wrong," said Bergit. "She will love better some day for having learned to love Lars." Elisabet dropped the matter as one too foolish to pursue.

On a day in April Nels brought down the baggage for their journey. Guro complained good-naturedly about crossing so large a sea with so small a supply of clothing. "Suppose I lost the few things you have allowed me to take?"

"Then we'll put you to bed for the crossing." Nels laughed, much to Siri's delight and Bergit's amusement. "Never saw anyone so glad to see us leave our own home as Mons was," he remarked to Tosten, who sat by the window, idly turning the pages of a newspaper.

"Is that so?"

"He has lived alone so long," said Guro, preparing to set the table in the living room for their evening meal.

"Wonder if he will ever let us in when we come back?" asked Nels. "That's what is so foolhardy about charity—it can turn the giver into the beggar, you know."

"Mons will never be like that," defended Guro. "Anyway, he has been cutting logs to rebuild his own cottage."

In the remaining week Siri had begged to move in with Bergit; and this having been done, the two sometimes talked long into the night. When the child had fallen asleep, the grandmother often put a gentle hand upon the girl's face, tracing the contours of the nose and chin and cheeks with remembering fingers and an observing mind, resting her fingers on the warm mouth and on the brow; and when she lay back upon her pillow, the mystery of her own swiftly-spilled years overwhelmed her with wonder, and greater grew her wonder about the child beside her and what the years might hold for heart and mind and body.

Sometimes it was the child who lay awake after the grandmother had fallen into a light slumber. If the old one lay upon her back she sometimes snored with little exhalations of derision, which set the child to smiling. Siri had no will to sleep and surrendered only after a struggle. A thousand farewells had been said and a thousand more remained to be said! The carved cupboard gleamed softly in the spring moonlight, remembering the touch of a dimpled hand that had caressed the soft skin of its ancient wood. The bridal chest under the window had held her safely when her feet could not reach the floor. The three-legged stool beside it had wandered all over the house with her, and held Knuppe and her as they listened to many a tale of trolls or goblins. Outside in the quiet night she heard the stream racing in the moonlight toward the quiet sea. It seemed to run with a headlong urgency, like a stranger racing across the farm while the family slept. "I will not go!" she said and sat up in bed, unaware for the moment of the restive old woman beside her.

"What is it, child? Can't you sleep?"

"I don't want to leave, Grandma. I don't want to leave!"

"Perhaps this is so," the grandmother replied, drawing her into her arms. "But some day you will be glad, child, and for this reason alone I let you go. That's one thing you can do for Arne who was your father—to go and visit his brother. You will not be sorry. This I know."

"The child lay back upon the pillow, finally, but continued a recitation of loneliness. "I will miss you so much and Mother and Gunhild, and Lars I shall never see again—and I shall miss the Engs and the children and the church. I have grown to love the old church, Grandma, and the sexton I love too."

"Of course," said Bergit.

"Remember the time Mother went to Bergen and you gave me some treasures? Did you know, then, Grandma, that I might leave Norway? Is that why you gave me the pin and the mementoes?" Siri studied the old face, whose wrinkles had been almost erased by the moonlight. Her hair, more dark than gray, gave her a youthful look in the mellow light, but the child perceived suddenly the frail contours of the face and the heavy shadows which lay under the closed eyes and in the hollows under her cheekbones. A cry of pain, unvoiced, soundless, rose from the child's heart, for she perceived then, and was never to forget, the mortality which lay waiting for all things good and beautiful. Long after Bergit slept again she lay thinking—about Father and the splintered remains of the boat which had carried him to his death, about Balder, who no longer chased after her as she ran from copse to copse but lay with his head between his frizzled paws and yearned after her with longing eyes. The stream seemed to increase its running tempo, racing headlong into the sea, carrying her with it, into the fjord, into the ocean—into a swirl of troubled dreams

On the last Sunday they were together, they all rose early for church. Gunnar, who was to call for them, had assured Bergit that he could manage her wheelchair too, but Bergit insisted it was enough if she could lean upon both him and the cane. Elisabet at the last moment declared that she did not feel well enough to go and would tend to their dinner, for the Koppens, the Engs, and Kari would follow them from church. For Siri the crossing and the service had no reality. The small-windowed dim church, the high-backed pews, the minister's face above the round clerical collar all appeared as in a dream, for she who had been no farther than to Bergen once or twice was now to cross a great sea and half a continent, as the sexton had put it once. And as they left the old stone church and the greetings and farewells pressed upon Nels, Guro, and her from all sides, she felt so overwhelmed that she separated herself from them for the moment. The churchyard with its stone monuments and crosses lay newly greened in the April sunshine. She looked long and steadily at the Fjeldstrand plot and the small obelisk over her grandfather's grave, with the prescient awareness that should she ever return, this was where Grandmother would lie. Although she was not consciously alert to this changed state of mind, she looked upon the parishioners, the village, and the sweep of stone-rimmed fjord as a traveler looks who has more to bear in mind than the mind can bear.

The Sunday dinner and the crowded afternoon swept by in a

mass of confused impressions: of Gunhild blushing when the oldest
Eng boy, just returned from sea, invited her to walk in the orchard
with him; of Kari snuffling into her handkerchief; of Tosten growing
friendlier after each surreptitious visit to the storehouse; of Grandmother sitting straightbacked in her wheelchair—her great, unseeing
eyes turning from one to the other; of her mother tense and flushed;
of the pastor's wife showing Guro a new embroidery stitch—and this
on Sunday!

"So you are going to America," said the pastor, fingering his gold
watch chain. "Well, I have seen many embarkings at many a port—
the heartbreak of families separated until the Last Judgment. It's
a sorry business from start to finish and often a suffering endured
unnecessarily. But worst of all," he continued, his voice rising, "is
the chicanery of human beings bent on exploiting others—the steamship runners with golden promises, the Mormon missionaries promising sainthood with toil, though the latter is not stressed, you may
be sure." He shook his head. "It is a strange land you go to, Nels,
that would send such folk to our country."

Before he could reply, Bergit said, "It's hard to judge, for we're
so small and the world so large. Perhaps—"

"It is well known how *you* feel about emigration," interrupted
Nels.

"I am sure I have always kept such feelings to myself," the pastor
retorted.

"In any case *we* shall return to Norway," replied Nels. His attention was caught by Tosten's generous offer to finance Kari's passage
across the sea. Guro, however, saved him from any serious financial
involvement by saying that Kari must certainly wait to hear from
her son—for he could well be on his way back, both pockets stuffed
with American money.

"You must wait, Kari. You owe the poor boy that much considera-
tion," said Guro. Overwhelmed by the logic thrust at her from all
sides, Kari drew the handkerchief out of her bosom and gathered
new tears to its damp folds.

The evening came apace, and the pastor asked Elisabet if he might
have the family Bible. When the women had cleared a place at
the end of the table, they placed a lamp for him above the brass-

bound volume which had been Olaf's and his father's before him.
He read the One Hundred and Fourth Psalm and then bent his head
in prayer, petitioning for the safety of the travelers and comfort for
the hearts of those left behind. Siri had crept to her grandmother's
chair at the moment of his starting, and she felt the old woman's
thin hand grow tense upon her own. Soon came the farewells, and
at the very moment of his departure the pastor remembered that
he carried with him a gift for Siri from the sexton. So she unwrapped
a small black hymnbook with a gold-etched cross—a book which was
to carry her back, as nothing else could, to the fjord-girt land of her
childhood and the church which bore the smell of sea-dampened
wood.

And the last full day that remained to them came with bright
sunshine and a fair spring wind. "Fetch shawls for my head and
shoulders, Siri," said Bergit, "and wheel me down toward the sea."
Gunnar was to arrive the next morning to sail them to Bergen. To
all of them each hour was poignantly fleeting.

Elisabet watched the child and her mother as they moved down
the pathway. "Siri! Siri!" she cried, hiding her face in her apron.
"Guro, how could I have consented to such an enormity!"

Her old aunt set the coffee mill upon the table and went over to
the window, her arm about her niece's waist. "We'll have her back
next spring if that's the way you want it."

"What am I being punished for—what have I ever done that I am
so pursued!" cried Elisabet. So bleak and stricken was the small face
that Guro for a moment could almost believe the young woman to
be hag-ridden by the three Norns who sat toothless and cackling
under the branches of Yggdrasil.

In the meantime, down at the water's edge, Bergit was saying,
"Tell me, child, what you see."

"I see snow upon the peaks across the water and the gulls swinging upon the wind, and the trees in the orchard shaking out their
buds—but who will see for you now, Grandmother, when I am gone?"

"Have no fear about that. What we have seen together I will see
again and again."

For what she must say the child could find no words. Finally she
blurted out the fear that skulked with heavy feet throughout her

dreams. "Grandmother, do you feel strong enough to wait for my return?"

"It's not a matter of *feeling*, my child. Let it rest in the Lord's hands. God is love, and the compassionate Redeemer who took upon himself the burden of our sins was himself the Creator of the universe."

"I *know* that, Grandma."

"Many a man might wish to say the same, child. *Knowing* that should keep you from being afraid if I am gone."

"If you could only write to me!" pursued the child.

"I can."

"But how?"

"My idle fingers still can trace words upon a paper. Only I cannot promise that my pencil will sail an even course. But you must promise to write, child, so that I can see the land upon which your feet walk; and when you tell me a bird sings outside your window, you must tell me how the bird looks and the tree upon which he rests; and it would be even better if you could tell me why his song sounds sweet to you—for then I shall know how it goes with my little Siri. Your father Arne often said that a man sees with his eyes but perceives with his soul."

And then came their last morning upon the little strand below the mountain steeps, and still the weather held more fair than foul. The clouds were massing upon the higher peaks like the god giants of old, and raw chill had returned to the air. Breakfast over, Nels paced up and down, scowling out the windows to hasten Gunnar's coming. Tosten had announced his intention of accompanying them to the port, but at Elisabet's shake of the head, Nels said no, for someone should remain with the women. Without a handshake or a goodbye Tosten had left them; they did not know this until Siri spied their small boat well on its way to the village. At the same moment she saw Gunnar's boat rounding a little spit of rocky land and heading for their landing.

Constraint and confusion rode upon them all. While Gunnar and Nels toiled at the landing, Anna—unsought but hugely welcome—took charge of the women and announced her intention to stay with them until her husband's return with the boat. Her strong hand was upon the wheelchair, her voice upon Gunhild, her eyes upon Elisabet.

Now they were ready for everything but farewell. She clucked them down to the landing and gathered them to the boat, holding fast to the wheelchair which swayed with the movement of the pier. When Elisabet began to weep as she embraced the child, Anna drew at Siri's sleeve and said, "Your grandmother waits."

"Take my hands for a moment," Bergit said, "and then you must kiss me upon the cheek and be off. The rains will soon be here." The cold thin hands pressed sharply into the warm flesh of the child's fingers. The icy cheek she kissed was chill and salty. "We meet again," said Bergit.

Gunhild's eyes were aflame with weeping, and Siri flung her arms about the girl's waist. Then Guro had her by the hand and Nels swung them both into the boat. And as the boat moved out to sea, the farewells rang lustily from shore and planking. Fear and longing threatened to choke the child. She watched the wheelchair growing smaller; answered Gunhild's wave of arm with a fluttering of her hand; saw her mother move slowly shoreward. So fast they flew in the morning wind that soon the wheelchair was only something yellow moving slowly up to the house. She saw the gray shine of the stone escarpment upon which she and her father had sat and the snowy peaks above Ørnheim. When she began to look downward at the sea slipping behind them, she felt Nels' brawny hand on her shoulder.

"It's time to look forward, child."

Chapter 11

The Listening Land

Closing her eyes to shut out the tiresome monotony of the prairies, Siri leaned against the dusty plush upholstery of the day coach and thought again of her early childhood beside the fjord at Fjeldstrand.

As she often did in lonely moments, she tried to recall the sound of the little falls below Ørnheim. Soon she traveled in memory with the sharply falling stream, down ledges slippery with shining water, and even down to the final leap of the stream into the sea.

Even so fast, she thought, had the years slipped away since the day Nels, Guro, and she had stood in the vestibule of another train, pulling into the station at Minneapolis. How shy she had been that evening until the carriage drew up to the big white house and Uncle Roald had carried her up to the porch! At the moment of his setting her down in the carpeted hallway, she had nestled her bonneted head against his neck and felt the sweetness of recognition; here was a man so much like her own father that she had come home when she had left home.

But the rhythmic clatter of the train disturbed her thoughts and made memory an elusive game at best; but when she glanced out at the endless sweep of plains she was reminded of what Uncle Nels had said during his visit to America. "The whole land lies naked to the sky." But Guro had quipped, "No more bare than your beloved North Sea, Nels." She recalled her uncle's quick defense of the sea and how he had remarked that God had created the waters before the land, even as he created male before female—and that making the earth and its inhabitants had been such pure tediousness, he had rested afterward. As Siri brushed some dust off her skirt, she smiled to herself, thinking how infinitely dear to her the pair had been—bringing her to America in their old age and then returning to Norway to die, each in his own time and his own way.

Something had been lost from those early years. Once when she was home for vacation from college she had mentioned it to

Aunt Joanna, who had answered matter-of-factly, "It's your childhood lost, Siri. Nothing more—just childhood." In a serious moment she had asked the same question of her Uncle Roald.

His answer had come more slowly, of course, for in the words of Aunt Joanna, "the Gabrielsons are all dreamers." She recalled how he had drawn his tanned hand across the silky sheen of a strip of oak he was planing and how he had looked out the window of his carpenter's shop at the back of the barn. "I suspect it was old Bergit who held the threads together for you." Though she knew what he meant, she had not liked to think that life was essentially meaningless without another's presence. Something resolute within herself scorned such an admission, even as her grandmother would have scorned it.

Her thoughts returned to the present and the short letter from Leif which lay in her handbag. Although Leif had never been verbal, much less eloquent, his sharp disappointment over her decision to teach at Scotts Lake rather than to marry him at Christmas was edged with bitterness, and some of the phrasing had such a quaintness she suspected he had written the letter with his mother's assistance. If so, she thought, he *had* come back from his new job for the weekend and had not bothered to telephone or call. She could almost hear Mrs. Borland saying, "Don't go begging to her, son. It will do Siri good to miss you. Then maybe she will come to her senses."

Even Aunt Joanna had not agreed with her. "Why not marry Leif? I am sure you have kissed him often enough," she had said primly—although Siri was well aware of her aunt's pleasure at her own humor. "Go out and spend a month with that poor mother of yours. Just come back in time to let Dagmar sew you a wedding dress." Siri recalled how she had looked with great seriousness at her aunt when she continued, "You don't *have* to teach, child! Your Uncle Roald and I are only too happy to have you home with us."

She had never been able to tell her aunt how she felt about teaching, how it seemed to be the fulfillment of a pact she had made with herself in memory of her father. Something within her told her she would teach as easily and naturally as Aunt Joanna kept house and baked her Danish pastries.

Even though she did not like the land which stretched with such singular monotony out there, she felt that she might endure it for a year, and in that year she might grow closer to her mother again and learn to endure her stepfather. She drummed her fingers restlessly on the dusty windowsill, half aware of the treeless plains and a drying lake ringed by a sweep of white alkali. On a prairie road running parallel with the tracks, a buggy moved slowly, a man and a sunbonneted woman in the front seat, three towheaded children bobbing up and down in the back. Was this, a bleak life like theirs, what she was destined for? Was this what her grandmother Bergit had let her leave Norway for?

The train whistled sharply, pitching and jerking as it screeched and groaned for another stop. Two or three grain elevators, she thought dispiritedly, a dusty main street and a few wooden buildings lost in a world of prairie grass and stubble fields; a few cottonwoods and elms shading plank sidewalks; a scattering of gray and white houses, with sheets and underwear waving from clotheslines.

How little she knew of the land where her mother now lived! How little she knew of her mother really—for Elisabet had never been communicative, not even in those years when a little girl longed for letters from Norway. Her mother's marriage to Tosten seemed to have kept the clear waters of affection damned behind a cold wall of constraint. Yet in the letter lying in her handbag her mother seemed to have written with a sudden honesty more like her grandmother Bergit's forthrightness than her mother's habitual restraint. She recalled the words and their quaint, old-world dignity: "I have been told by the German Lutheran pastor, who himself speaks a few words of Norwegian, that a teacher of English is needed in the high school in Scotts Lake. Can you, Siri, for one year at least, find it in your heart to come out here? I ask for only a year, my child, knowing that in the time of youth one year is like many, but in the time of fading, it is only a day." It was a plea she could not in good conscience ignore, yet it would cause her to lose Leif, if it had not already done so.

Now the early September evening was turning the hills into shadings of soft green and mauve. A strip of cultivated land lay like a golden swath among the rounded hills, and in the declivity between the gold and the deepening green stood a small huddle of unpainted farm buildings guarded by a turning windmill. A meadowlark rose suddenly from beside the right-of-way, and above the chugging of the train she heard the tumbled notes of his song.

Suddenly, the land seemed as familiar to her as if she had walked through it in other times; she recognized it as a trick of her mind, which often gathered half-forgotten dreams and offered them to her in the semblance of experience. She began to gather her belongings methodically, the suitcase from the rack above, her valise, and her new leather handbag. She knew that in her nervousness she was collecting her baggage far in advance of her arrival in Scotts Lake, but still she drew her hat down from the luggage rack and dusted it off carefully and blew gently on the burgeoning roses that spilled over its brim. She slipped her arms into her narrow fitted jacket and set her hat on her head, tilting it slightly over her right eye and patting the loose sweep of her pompadour into place. When that was done there was nothing left to do but sit beside the window and watch the shadowy descent of evening upon the softened hills and wonder at the western bank of clouds with their tantalizing shapes like distant mountain ranges.

So out of a kind of shyness and a young dignity she disdained visiting with the other passengers in the coach and pressed her face against the pane as if some loneliness within drew her to the loneliness without. A small pond full of reeds and cattails caught a streak of red and gold from the sky and stared back at her like a cat's eye. "Almost there, young lady—let's see, Miss Gabrielson, isn't it? Is there anyone to meet you?" asked the conductor.

"No. But there is a hotel, isn't there?" When he nodded, she continued, "Is there a lake in town?"

"I can tell *you're* from Minnesota," he teased. "As a matter of fact, there is a lake out in the hills, but not very close to town. Here, I'll take your suitcase. You schoolmarms sign up for the loneliest places and then you marry a rancher and spend the rest of your lives wondering what foolishness got into you." She smiled at his badinage and nodded farewell to the old couple who had sat across from her and who were now extracting sandwiches and hardboiled eggs from an old shoebox.

He had swung the footstool into place and was helping her from the train

As they moved into the clanking vestibule, she felt an exhilarating slap of cold night air. As the train began to brake, the conductor steadied her with his hand. She heard the sharp whistling of the train, smelled the smoke which blew back toward them. She saw a sprinkling of lights, dark rectangles which were grain elevators, a lighted street deeply rutted from rain, and then the wooden platform slipping away below them. "Come to think of it," the conductor said smiling, "there's a young man who nearly always meets the train. I'll introduce you to him if he's here, and he'll show you to the hotel." She was about to protest, but he had swung the footstool into place and was helping her from the train. As a family kissed their farewells, she stepped back beside her luggage and watched her shiny new trunk leave the baggage car. "Miss Gabrielson," said the conductor, "here is the young man I was telling you about. Miss Gabrielson, Mr. Rittenhouse." The young man who had appeared, seemingly from nowhere, bowed slightly and extended his hand. Her first impression was one of incongruity—a well-pressed suit and a white shirt worn open at the collar, a mustache clipped with meticulous care, and eyes that regarded her with pleasure and interest, but nevertheless did not conceal a look of almost careless detachment. The brakeman waved his lantern, the conductor gave them a smart little salute as he swung himself upon the moving step, and the long train began to glide by them. They stood together upon the dimly lighted platform until the train had become a mournful whistle and a vanishing red light.

"Some part of oneself," he said in a voice that seemed as rich and deep as dark velvet under her hand, "always goes on with a train." She began to look around at her feet for the luggage.

"Eddie has it," he said. "He'll wheel it up to the hotel." They moved down the platform, their footsteps echoing after them. He took her arm for a moment to guide her up a street, and then he began to point out the lumberyard, the bank, the general store, and the post office. "Over there at the end of the street is the German Lutheran church—wrong kind, though, isn't it, Miss Gabrielson? I'm afraid it will have to do unless you want to worship with the Methodists or the Congregationalists."

"I'll look them all over, I suppose."

"My legal abode," he said, indicating a small doorway and a window on which she read "S. J. Rittenhouse, Attorney at Law." Except for a man who had just emerged from a place marked "Billiards" and was now unhitching his horse, the street seemed deserted.

"Is it always this quiet?" she said.

"Always. Except on Saturday nights." A sea of stars above them almost overpowered the low candlepower of the quaint street lights. "That massive building across the street is the Chatham Hotel."

"I'd never have found it," she said, allowing him to help her across the muddy street. When they were back upon the sidewalk, she stopped for a moment, listening.

"Oh, that's Eddie with your luggage and the post office mail."

"Not that sound," she said. "I noticed it before. The wind has such a high-pitched hum, but I don't suppose you hear it, you're so accustomed to it," she finished foolishly.

"In Dakota this is not a wind, Miss Gabrielson. This is a quiet autumn evening. Well, let's go in and meet the redoubtable proprietress of the Chatham, one Ellie McCarthy. I always introduce visiting young ladies to her." They moved up the short wooden steps into a narrow hall with dark wainscotting. "To the left, Miss Gabrielson."

The small lobby was equally as dark, except for a slumbering mass of flesh in a brown leather chair, a cat upon the lobby desk, and a spare, straight-boned, high-corseted woman with a bright topknot of flaming red hair. "Well, Scott," she said, adjusting pinchers on her thin nose, "whom do you bring tonight?"

"Miss McCarthy. Miss Gabrielson."

"Ah, the new schoolteacher." She rose briskly from the high stool on which she had been sitting. "Run along now, Scott. I'll take over."

"Thanks again, Mr. Rittenhouse," said Siri. "I did forget one thing, though. I forgot to have you point out the livery stable."

"Going somewhere?" he asked.

"Tomorrow."

Miss McCarthy interposed herself between them. "Scott, I'm quite able to point out the location of establishments in this town."

Scott placed an arm around the thin waist of the proprietress, drawing her backward a step. Siri could see that the woman was not entirely displeased, despite the pickled expression she wore. "I'll pick you up at eleven, Miss Gabrielson. I own one of the few automobiles in town." He nodded at the two women and then disappeared down the hallway.

"High and mighty, that young man. Well, I'd better take you into the kitchen for a bite to eat, and then I'll show you to your room." Siri found herself following obediently, through a darkened dining room with its counter and into a kitchen where a large kerosene lamp shone upon an immaculate sink. "Mrs. Swanson and Tammy have gone home. But I thought you looked a little tired. A little shadowy under the eyes." She lifted a teakettle from the large coal range and stepped briskly to a corner of the kitchen, where she lighted a kerosene burner on a small auxiliary stove. "They usually come to me first, the new schoolteachers, but they're always boarded out to folks around town. Mr. Willis—that's our superintendent—feels that a hotel is not the place for girls like you. There's no use arguing with him; he thinks that a traveling salesman spells corruption." She gave Siri another sizing up. "I fancy I could keep an eye on a girl like you—" Siri smiled to herself as she watched Miss McCarthy slip a metal toaster over a flame—"but there's one thing you learn in a small town like this, and that is that it's all give and take, coming and going."

She went over to a cupboard and took down a canister of tea. "Sit down. You make me nervous standing. Anyway, Mr. Willis has you staying with old Professor Lusk and his wife. Just don't let them starve you or freeze you, that's all I've got to say." She poured bubbling hot water into a Japanese teapot. When she had replaced the kettle, she whisked two slices of toast off the metal frames and said, "Help yourself to butter and jam. They're in the covered dishes at the center of the table." Siri began to thank her, but Miss McCarthy interrupted with, "I suspect you're a coffee drinker with a name like that, but I'm not going to give you coffee this time of night and hear you complaining the next morning about not being able to sleep."

"Do I *have* to stay where Mr. Willis tells me?"

Miss McCarthy poured two cups of tea, her sharp eyes growing bright behind the shiny lenses. "A little rebellion around here would be interesting." She stirred sugar into her cup. "But, no. You're not the kind of girl to try it." The sleeping coal range at their backs stirred in slumber and hummed a light tune of sleepy contentment. The cat slithered through the swinging door from the dining room and rubbed its fur against Siri's shoe. "Say, you're the one who has a family living somewhere out in the hills, aren't you?" Miss McCarthy's eyes grew narrow and speculating. "It seems to me—"

"My mother and my stepfather and their child."

"Ah, I think I've seen them, but I guess they do most of their shopping in Golag. Well I'm glad for your mother that you've come. Had enough?" She rose briskly. "Put your dishes in the sink. Mrs. Swanson will be here before daylight. You two'll have to meet." She caught up a dishrag and wiped the crumbs off the table. "I heard Eddie with your things a moment ago, so now it's to bed for you, young lady. Breakfast from six-thirty to nine. If I don't see you in the morning, you can't miss the schoolhouse—right at the end of the street, back toward the railroad tracks." She pushed Siri's thanks away with a flutter of her hand. "Don't *I* know what it's like to come to a lonely place like this!" she said suddenly, her voice grown husky. "When Pa brought Ma out here and built this hotel, I cried myself to sleep many a night. Get out of the way, you dratted cat!" she said suddenly, giving him a playful push with her long slender shoe. "Beats all how a tomcat will take a fancy to a pretty young thing like you. He and Scott! Two of a kind," she finished tersely.

"Well, how did you and Mr. Willis get along?" Scott asked, as the touring car nosed its way along a winding prairie road.

"I've been assigned all the English classes and two history classes and to sponsor the literary club."

"I don't mean that. Where are you going to room?"

"With the Lusks, of course."

"Of course." She did not particularly like the way he said it. She sat quietly beside him, holding her sailor hat with one hand, the other clutching the door frame. "It's actually a matter of arithmetic," he explained. "So many people wanting roomers. So many roomers. The Lusks are not a bad sort. He came out here years ago for his

daughter's health. Used to teach in a small normal school in the
East."

Siri was only half listening, having learned all these details from
Mr. Willis and the Lusks themselves. The winding prairie road
reminded her poignantly of a summer trip with Uncle Roald and
the family—and didn't all roads remind her of Leif? Again she
thought of space as a malevolent force, for so it had seemed in the
years she missed her grandmother and mother—and so it was now,
absence and space, space and absence, giant enormities against
which mind and memory battled vainly. If Leif were to write—and
Leif had never been one who liked to write even his college assign-
ments—could writing wipe out the space between them or speak the
powerful language of glance and touch and voice?

The road dipped into a muddy hollow and rose precipitously to
another crest of prairie where buffalo brush grew among a crown
of rocks. "The lake should be over here to the left. I'm a little lost
because we hardly ever take this road. There's a much better one
farther west that leads to Golag." She was only dimly aware of Scott's
voice, for she had begun to see the awfulness and futility of her
mother's life. If the years in Norway after I left could draw her skin
taut and change a softly molded face, what have the past two years
done to her, thought Siri. God only knows what kind of place
she lives in—hills rising upon hills, a single hawk circling in the
sky, and not a neighbor's chimney anywhere. "It's apparent you
don't care," said Scott.

"I do," said Siri quickly.

"Do what?" He saw her abashed look. "I'm sorry."

"Oh, never mind," he said.

"I was just thinking about Mother. What makes a man bring a
woman to a place like this?"

"It proves something, I suppose. Virility. Strength." The car
chugged up another hill, long grasses thumping against the spokes,
redolent sage and sunburnt grasses and weeds riding their fragrances
upon a singing wind. At the very crest he stopped. "Scotts Lake,"
he said. She looked down the steep hillside to a small lake disappearing around a hill. She saw a small sandy beach at one end, and
beyond, under the shelter of an overhanging hill, a lonely copse

of trees and bushes. The lake, she thought, lay among its enfolding hills like a captive of the glacial age. "At the other end, beyond the hills over there, Mother and Dad had a homestead once."

"And your mother's name was Scott?" she asked.

"It's what I told you back there," he teased. "When your thoughts were mooning across the prairies."

"How far is it to—to where we're going?"

"This road used to circle the north end of the lake, and from there it's only a few hills away." He was aware as he followed the faint tracks running through the now tall grass that she looked back and back again at the disappearing lake. She in turn was fully aware of his measured glances and even of his arm occasionally resting across the back of the seat, but he did not touch so much as a wrinkle of her clothing. She felt an easy pleasure in his company. When the car turned sharply to take another incline, she saw him remove his hand from the top of the seat and move the shift lever beside her billowing skirt. She sensed a sudden tension between them, like the recoil she felt when once she had thrust her finger into a light socket in the dark.

"I had no idea you'd have to drive so far, Mr. Rittenhouse."

"It's only about five or six miles at the most, but it's a wayward road made by a hungry horse cropping grass along the way. As a matter of fact, I'm going on to Golag. Have a client in the neighborhood." He grew quiet, and then he said abruptly, "And you, young lady, were going to hire a rig and come out here alone. "Don't do that around here, at least not for a year or two," he said seriously.

"You know," she laughed, "I hope I haven't jeopardized my contract going off like this with you!"

He slowed the car to avoid a boulder jutting out of the long grasses. "I'll give you some advice about that sort of thing. Just tell Ellie McCarthy where you're going and then tell the postmaster, and while you're about it, stop at Mercer's General Store and tell them. Before they get through telling one another where Miss Gabrielson has gone, they're sick of the whole matter."

"I get the idea," laughed Siri. "But Miss McCarthy doesn't look like a gossip."

"She isn't. Her tongue pulls a lot of weight when she uses it. Ellie took a liking to you. Or the tomcat took a liking to you. I can't remember which way it was." He braked the car at the top of a hill noisy with wind. "That's it," he said, pointing to a little valley lying lost between more hills.

She looked down at the ubiquitous windmill beside a cluster of nondescript buildings. "It certainly isn't much," she said. "Are you sure this is the place? It looks deserted."

"You haven't learned to read the signs, that's all. That strip of earth is darker than the rest. It's newly plowed. That brown smudge moving beside the barn is a dog. He'll start to bark soon. There is a small wisp of smoke rising from the building closest to the road."

"It's frightening," she said. Suddenly her tongue seemed to become unloosened, like a child pleading for time before he is sent upstairs in the dark. "You'd never know it, but once Mother lived beside the sea in Norway on a lovely little farm, and never did she want for anything. My father was a graduate of the University of Kristiania." She hid her face in her hands and said, "I'm sorry. I'm sorry." She put her hands down from her face and turned away from him. "It's only that—"

"Perhaps I know a little more than you think," he said. "This man—this stepfather of yours—has often come to town. Well, I hear the dog," he finished limply. "We'd best start down. The barn looks empty. The child and she may be alone."

The car began its descent down a steep road. The dog had now begun to bark, racing back and forth in front of the little unpainted house, sometimes altering his course to advance upward on the road. "I've seen so little of my mother—well, hardly at all since I was eight and a half. It was then I came to America." Although he appeared to listen, he made no comment. They had come to the bottom of the hill and were on a little downward stretch where uncut wheat lay on either side. As the dog advanced and retreated, loping gracefully across the grass, she thought of Balder, the Norwegian elkhound she had loved in childhood. "Hello there, boy!" she called, but the dog had run on to the doorway, his tail wagging furiously. They were down in front of the house now, and Scott set the brake, leaving the motor running.

Suddenly he was aware of the girl's sudden cry of "Mother!

Mother!" Before he could come around to help her, she had slipped out of the door and run up the pathway to the house. The little woman who stepped out of the doorway, shading her eyes, was soon engulfed in her daughter's embrace. He turned to the dog and said, "Come here, fellow! Come here!" But the dog was almost as excited as the women. They came up the path toward him, one so tall, the other so diminutive.

"Do you know my mother?" She made the introductions, and Scott shook hands with her, attempting to say *Goddag*.

Her small face brightened at his greeting. "You must tell her I know only a few words of Norwegian," he said hastily.

He watched the younger woman's face as she spoke rapidly to the elder one, the young one's quick change of expression, her creamy skin and the autumnal color of her hair and eyes, a delicate brown, not dark. "Mother would like to offer you a cup of coffee."

"*Nei tak*," he said. "Tell her I shall stop another time. I'll fetch your valise, Miss Gabrielson." When he returned, he said, "I'll pick you up again on Friday."

"Perhaps they'll take me back." He heard her question her mother, and then she stood uncertainly, looking first at her mother and then at him. "I'm afraid it's an imposition," she said.

"Not at all. Friday then, about four."

They watched him go, the little woman and the tall shapely girl, the dog beside her nuzzling her hand. They watched until the car had circled the slough north of the house and had begun its ascent up a hill, and then they waved and turned back to the little house.

In the little cottage which had two rooms and a lean-to at the back, Elisabet put out a small wash basin and an embroidered towel for her daughter. "The coffee will be ready shortly." Later Siri tried to protest her mother's covering the worn red-figured oilcloth with a cutwork cloth, until she had seen her mother's hurt and puzzled look. "Siri," she said, rolling the *r* in her daughter's name, "I wish you had let me know the hour of your coming."

"I really did not know myself until I heard from the school board, and then Uncle Roald and I talked it over and decided it would be best not to cause you any inconvenience in trying to meet me. It's a long way to town."

"Yet we would have met you."

"Well, I am here, Mother," she said cheerfully, trying to conceal the shock of finding them living with such makeshift possessions; yet the toil of her mother's hands was evident everywhere, on the worn scrubbed floor, on the ruffled calico curtains at the window, and on the bright woven coverlet on a cot in the corner of the kitchen. "You made that throw when I was small, didn't you, mother?"

Elisabet's eyes brightened. "The year that I took up weaving again, some time after your father's death. She stood at the sink pumping a kettle of water to put into the reservoir of the stove.

"Will Tosten and Sophie be back soon?" she asked, as her mother sat down at the table.

"It is hard to say. Tosten has had a cruelly hard time finding a part for a machine that broke down. He took Sophie along to buy her shoes. They come and go," she said suddenly, her defenses down, "and I have learned to let them be." I am sure of that, thought Siri, remembering the bold and wilful eyes of her little stepsister when they had met in Minnesota for the first time. Her mother had been no match for either of them—and now—

"Let's see, how old is Sophie?" mused Siri.

"Twelve. Last April." After they had drunk their coffee, Elisabet allowed Siri to wipe the china cups and plates, although she protested at first. "I have used my good dishes only twice since I came here," she said. "Once when the German Lutheran minister and his wife came out—the other time I cannot remember." She was untying the small white apron she had drawn over her lavender print dress. "It's time to milk the cow and feed the hens."

"I'll go out with you. I have never milked a cow, Mother, at least not since Lars let me play at milking. Do you hear from Lars?"

"The last time I heard he had married a girl from Trondhjem and that they had a child or two." Her mother's lips trembled with the shadow of a smile. "Such a love you had for Lars!" she reminisced. Siri followed her mother out into the evening sunlight. Such a love I had for them all! she thought. For Father and Mother and Grandmother and Guro and Nels—for the orchard and the little chatting stream, for the sea moaning softly against the rocks.

She did not follow her mother into the barn but sat on the planks covering the well. A clump of goldenrods nodded in the evening breeze. The semicircle of hills in the west had grown shadowy on their northeastern approaches. Along one gully she saw a feathering of stunted trees and small bushes. As her eyes moved back to the farm, she saw the remains of a little garden beside the barn, and beyond the garden another field of golden grain. If he has spent the money from the sale of Fjeldstrand, what are they living on, she wondered. When her mother appeared in the barn doorway she rose to help her with the bucket of milk. "When I am through straining the milk, perhaps you would like to sit outdoors longer. I myself do not care much for it. It makes me feel too small. But fetch some chairs from the kitchen. It may be that they will be home soon and then again perhaps they will come after dark." Her mother's voice seemed to have lost the soft tender lilt she remembered from childhood; and now she spoke in a monotonous tone, as people do who talk to themselves. When her work was done, Elisabet came softly out of the house and took a chair beside her daughter. The two sat together beside the little house in its nest of weeds until the fire of the prairie sunset had burned itself out and left a small glow like warm ashes above the dark hills. Even the lonely cricket beside the tar-paper shack grew strangely quiet; and the stars came out to watch the land, and the land itself grew quiet and listening.

"We'll light the lamp within," said her mother finally. "You must be growing hungry child." Siri rose and carried the chairs into the dark shanty and the darker room. She heard her mother's soft rocking footsteps ahead of her and then the sharp scratch of a match. When she had replaced the chimney upon the lamp, Elisabet looked across the room at Siri. "You have such a strange look on your face."

"O Mother," cried Siri, "out there in the starlight all those years came back to me—you and Father and Grandmother." She moved swiftly across the little sagging floor to embrace her mother. But Elisabet eluded her grasp and said faintly, bending down to the woodbox to grasp a handful of kindling. "It's well enough for you to think of the beginning, but for me it is the ending that must be thought about."

CHAPTER 12

Sophie

Because her early memories had always possessed so much vitality for Siri, she found herself wondering, during the short days of her visit among the hills, what kind of life her stepsister had had. Although she tried to communicate with Sophie, she had little success. At first she attributed her failure to Sophie's jealousy over her own place in Elisabet's bed, since Tosten had chosen during her visit to sleep on an improvised cot in the kitchen. But the child seemed actually to be indifferent toward her mother, the kind of indifference one exercises toward a person thrown by some exigency on a parallel course. Sophie never volunteered her help; when it was required by her father's unexpected comment or her mother's softspoken pleas, she helped with a graceless lack of interest that amounted to hostility.

For the most part she left Siri and her mother alone, as Tosten left them alone except for the first full day of her visit. The child had a swing hanging from a rafter in the barn—where she swung, so far as Siri was able to ascertain, quietly, steadily, without song or the small lonely chatter of an only child. Sometimes she went out to her father in the field, that is, until the sudden arrival of the threshing machine from a farm near Golag. Never had Siri been so glad to see anything mechanical as she was to see that machine! She never learned directly what the difficulty had been, but she deduced from several flareups between Elisabet and Tosten that the machine and some men had been there once already, on a day when Tosten was gone, and that the farmer who owned it would not, understandably, begin harvest until Tosten was there himself. As a result, the grain had suffered from a night or two of rain, and the rust spores which had been in evidence for a week or so had increased alarmingly.

It was on this day of threshing that Siri heard a string of expertly delivered Norwegian curses and saw Sophie come running from her father, her prominent eyes swollen with weeping, her florid face rigid with anger and sullen with stubbornness. "What is it now?" asked Elisabet, working steadily at the small range, for they would be giving the men their noon meal.

"I hate him! I hate Father!" Sophie flung herself on her father's cot.

Siri, peeling potatoes at the table, gave the child a glance and resumed her attention upon the task at hand.

"I hate him!"

Elisabet opened the oven door and pulled out a pan of rolls. "Why is that, Sophie?"

"He told me to stay away from the men. I was only watching. There's no harm in watching." She doubled the pillow on which she lay and thrust a balled fist into its goosedown plumpness. "I'm going out again. And I'll watch if I please!"

"When your sister gets through peeling the potatoes, you put a leaf in the table, and then you can put on the plates." Siri saw the girl's chin-thrusting stare.

Finally Sophie threw the pillow back on a corner of the cot and said, "How long is it going to take you to peel potatoes?"

"I'll be finished shortly."

"You look funny." Sophie rose and stood beside the table.

"Why?" asked Siri, finding herself somewhat angry and straining to keep her voice calm.

"Like an old schoolteacher. All schoolteachers look funny. Pa says so."

"Sophie!" Elisabet drew a towel down from a rack above the pump and wiped her perspiring face. "Don't get mean now."

"I'm not mean."

"Well, set the table. Go get the leaf."

"Where is it?"

"Where it is all the time. Behind the door."

Siri picked up the pan of peelings and set them aside for the hogs; then she handed a kettle to her mother. "Here are the potatoes, Mother. I'm going out for a minute," she sighed, "and then I'll be in to help you."

She heard the loud thump of a leaf being banged into the table. "Don't go out to the men, Siri! You're not supposed to go out to the men, either!" Siri settled herself on the small stoop outside the lean-to, her chin resting on her folded hands. How she longed to be back in Aunt Joanna's well-ordered home, with Uncle Roald striding in for dinner, the clatter of a buggy or two rolling down the brick pavement! Would she ever understand people, the reasons for their vagaries, the extent of their hopes, and the excuses for their defeats? Her mother's passivity both irked and hurt her; it reminded her, as she looked back, of the months following her father's death. She had had no real understanding then of her mother's withdrawal; it had come slowly through her own disappointments and experiences.

Back in the house she heard her stepsister's sharp retorts, her mother's monosyllabic replies. In the field back of the barn she caught a glimpse of spewn chaff rising in an arc from the long snout of the threshing machine. The Rittenhouse homestead, she mused, must have lain back of the hills to her right, in another lost valley. with a strong feeling of disloyalty to her mother toiling in the kitchen, she wished herself back to Scotts Lake—even that was better than this! She rose to her feet, thinking that never would she allow *herself* to be cowed by man or woman or circumstance as her mother had been; and her mother's lack of gumption seemed strange when she remembered how spirited her grandmother had been. *She* would have made short work of Sophie's outbursts! Habitual stubbornness, she thought, was a more serious matter than an occasional vindictive flareup. She recalled suddenly the day when she fled to the stream with Balder and had worked out her own despair and peevishness by herself—seeking within her its cause and fighting for a sense of rightness so necessary to her sense of well-being.

Elisabet gave Siri an apprehensive look when she returned to the kitchen. "What can I do now, Mother?" she asked. Sophie had disappeared.

"You shouldn't be doing anything at all," said Elisabet. "It's a sorry visit, having to help cook for the threshers. At any rate, it will all be over in a day, for there is still so little cultivated here."

"I am surprised they would bring a rig over at all," replied Siri, remembering the talk she had heard when the threshers were at the Pearson farm, Aunt Joanna's home place.

"Tosten will make it right with them," she replied.

It was a small crew that sat down at the table; and Siri would never have joined them, except that Tosten was in an expansive mood, holding a chair for her and insisting that such a pretty young thing like her—educated and all in a big city like Minneapolis—would honor them greatly with her presence. The result was exactly what Siri expected: she tongue-tied them all until Tosten began to argue about the folly of raising grain out in the hills. "Cattle," he said, holding his elbow firmly on the table and gesticulating with a fork from which a slice of beef dangled like the pensile hand of a metronome, "that's what I am going to bring in some day."

"Well, it'll take a dangside better crop than the one *you* have here to buy a herd," said Ole Braatvold, the owner of the threshing rig.

Elisabet refilled the meat platter and brought it back to the table. "Don't hold back," she said. "You must help yourselves." Siri noticed that Sophie had returned, leaning against the doorjamb, her hair freshly combed, one of the ribbons she had brought her from Minneapolis tied rakishly to the top of a long braid.

"Another thing about cattle, you'll have to build a better barn than the trap you've got," continued Ole, pursuing his argument.

Tosten pointed to his empty coffee cup and waited as Elisabet filled it for him and started around the table replenishing the supply for the rest of the men. "The *Rooshian* who first had this homestead, what did he know about building? Damn it, it takes time to get a farm going."

"*Ja,* especially when a man gets a thirst for old Egelmeier's home-made beer!" Ole laughed. The rest of the men joined in laughter until it became obvious that their host found it unfunny.

"That youngest Egelmeier boy," said Ole, undaunted by the silence, "he sure ain't goin' to amount to much. Funny thing, the old man and rest of the boys they ain't no slouches."

A burst of approval followed Elisabet's appearance with a heavily iced chocolate cake and two fruit pies. Siri had risen when Elisabet brought the dessert, attempting to get her mother to sit in her place.

"Pa," said a voice coming plaintively from the doorway, "if Ma doesn't want to sit there, can I? I'm starved." Tosten, apparently, had forgotten the morning's altercation, for he readily acquiesced.

The rest of the week slipped by quickly—too quickly for Siri because she felt that her mother and she had made little progress in intimacy. The animosity that Tosten had felt for her during the days of her childhood in Norway had seemingly disappeared. Occasionally he took a thrust at her "good fortune in being reared in a prosperous household" and warned her sententiously that such luck should be appreciated. "I have had many an undeserved blow in life," he said one rainy night when they sat around the kitchen table. "I don't suppose they've bothered telling you any good things about me, but I came from a good family in Bergen. The saddest day of my life was when my mother died and my uncle took over."

"He *was* pretty good to us," ventured Elisabet, looking up from the waist she was sewing for Sophie.

"That's a matter of opinion," he said. "Well, I could have taken some matters to law, but a fellow hates to give a lot of curious people a chance to talk."

"Papa," interrupted Sophie, who was lying on the cot playing with one of the kittens she had brought in from the barn, "was it Siri's pa who drowned in the fjord?"

"*You* know that!" snapped her mother.

"Why should I know that," retorted the child, "when I never listened to you and Tante Guro and all your silly chatter!"

Tosten struck a match. "That's a smart girl over there, Siri. Keeps that little mother of hers moving like a fish in a herring run."

On the day before Scott was to pick her up, Siri suggested that the three women pack a lunch and walk to the lake. "I never smelled such air as this!" she exclaimed. "Is it always like this, Mother?" She stood in the doorway looking out at the stubble field. When she turned, she noticed that her mother's eyes looked brighter at the prospect of an outing until she started to peck around at small excuses.

"Pa won't be home until dark," Sophie argued, for once on the distaff side, "so let's go, Mother." The two girls finally prevailed with their arguments, and soon they had packed a woven egg basket with food (Siri recognized it as one Bergit had). Even after they had gone some rods up the hill, Elisabet continued to look back, worrying about the small fire in the range and the cow in the pasture and the washing left on the line.

"Don't you ever go anywhere, Mother?" asked Siri.

"She never goes anywhere," volunteered Sophie. "Well, hardly ever."

Siri found herself speculating about unfamiliar plants at their feet, outcroppings of rocks on a hillside, a bird startled suddenly from its nest. But neither her mother nor Sophie had many answers and she began to wonder about their lack of curiosity, particularly her mother's, for Elisabet had lived so close to the soil and its growth when Siri was a child. She has to think about *something*, she said to herself again and again. Yet she did not allow such unanswerable perturbations to spoil the day.

Sophie had run ahead and her mother asked, "What has become of that tall blond boy you liked so well—Leif Borland? And he was Norwegian, too," she said offering the ultimate recommendation.

"He's fine, Mother," she answered, looking back at the hill they had just climbed, her face averted.

"You're betrothed, then?" asked her mother timidly.

"There are problems," extemporized Siri. "You know, getting started in his career and—"

"And *you* out here," said Elisabet shaking her head. "You must keep up your letters."

"There's the lake!" Sophie stood teetering on the tallest pile of rocks.

"Look out for snakes!" warned Elisabet.

"You have poisonous ones here?"

"Don't you know anything? Rattlers," said Sophie. When they reached the small clump of trees and bushes Scott and she had seen from the car, her mother suggested that Sophie have her swim immediately so that they might eat and get back, for she did not like to be gone long, she explained. Siri settled herself upon the grass. A few trees out here, she thought, look like a forest; and she lay down to enjoy their wind-swept shadows, the small tinkling sounds of their restless leaves, and the varied voices of the prairie winds. The wind was full-toned in the branches above, she noticed, but came whispering through the grasses at her feet.

"You're like your father," said Elisabet suddenly. "In the turn of your head and in the eyes."

"I'm glad, Mother," said Siri earnestly. Elisabet did not reply, but walked to a small clump of chokecherries near the edge of the copse. Siri saw her fingering the leaves, then pulling at a small dry twig which she threw to the ground. Before she returned to Siri, she called to the child, who was splashing about in the water.

"You should have gone in too," said her mother as she began to unpack the basket.

"Some time, maybe. Today I didn't want to." A smile hovered about her expressive and sensitive mouth. "I was thinking about the time Grandma Pearson and Aunt Guro went swimming in the lake on the farm—" but Elisabet was not listening. Siri rose and helped unpack the remainder of the food. She saw her mother stretch a blue and white homespun cloth as familiar to herself as her own hand. Elisabet called to Sophie several times, but the child sent up ripples of amused laughter, reiterating that she didn't have to come in. Laugh. Laugh.

Siri walked down to the small sandy shore. "Sophie, you are coming out. Right now!" The child returned level glance for level glance; then she dropped her eyes and came wading out of the water, her long black sateen bloomers dripping. The undershirt clung to her body and Siri saw the small rounded mounds that promised large full breasts. If a man like Leif, she thought suddenly, found a girl like that of my age—. She was hardly aware of Elisabet's call to her, for something about the swaggering voluptuousness of the girl's young body made her feel apprehensive for both the child and Elisabet. Sophie did not want to dress before she ate, but snatched up some food and went down to the water's edge, where she lay on her side looking out at the water. When they were through, Siri saw the hopeless little droop of Elisabet's shoulders as they gathered the remnants of lunch.

"I am afraid this wasn't much fun for you, daughter."

"Oh, but it was," said Siri politely. She took the basket from her mother's hand, and together they followed the course of the lake, looking for remnants of wild currants and gooseberries the birds might have spared them.

"It's a little late," said Elisabet, "but they'll make good jelly if Tosten remembers to buy some sugar."

"You should go buying with him. I think you're alone far too much."

"I went several times when he bought in Scotts Lake, but he has taken to buying in Golag lately, and anyway there is always the worry about the cow needing milking," she finished lamely.

"Where is Sophie?" asked Siri, glancing down the shoreline and up the slope of hill.

"O, Sophie. She will come when she is ready. She knows all the hills and the gulches for miles around."

On the morning of her leaving, Elisabet asked with a frown, "This man who's coming after you, Siri, do you—well, how can you know him in so short a time?"

Siri set the platter she had dried into the cupboard above her. "Someone had to bring me, Mother. Some *man*," she emphasized.

"That's true," agreed Elisabet. A buzzing hornet of peevishness stung Siri's mind and she thought to herself, you let me leave Norway, Mother, when I was too small to venture a word in my own defense. Now that I am a woman you begin to worry about me. Instead she said, "There were so many questions I wanted to ask you about Norway, but there will be other times to visit."

"We have been together. That's good," replied Elisabet, wiping the sink carefully with a cloth cut out of discarded underwear. Siri had repacked her small valise when she had risen, had made the beds in the front room, and now she had a desire to get out of the house and orient herself to the morning world. It was a habit from earliest childhood, in which every day brought with its sunrise a newly made world. It was a habit and a frame of mind that she never essentially lost, but one which could be sustained only with well-fortified defenses from the frontal and rear attacks of others, who apparently found yesterday's world rising with today's. A small frost had come during the night, and the September air had a cold freshness and a clarity that lent surprising detail to the farthest hills. On the south side of the house, against the heavy bank of insulating sod, she saw the drooping faces of zinnias, like a little line of watching spectators felled by a night's plague. She heard Tosten out in the barn hitching up a team to the wagon. He had been taciturn at breakfast, escaping the house without a word for anyone; yet she knew that he was aware of her leaving, because she had thanked him for the visit, an amenity that won only an absent-minded nod from him. Sophie had, strangely, not begged to go to Golag with him, disappearing as soon as they rose from the table.

Siri walked around to the north of the house, where her mother had set out a half dozen spindly cottonwoods no taller than Elisabet herself, hopeful some day of a windbreak against the roaring north-westers from Canada. One of the kittens mewed his little wails of neglect at her feet, and she picked him up absentmindedly. The soft furry life nestled against her breasts reminded her of Troll, the little Boston terrier Uncle Roald had given her on the day of her aunt and uncle's return to Norway, a small waddling bundle of worry and fun "ruddered by a screw tail," as her cousin John had put it, a little dog who had never been fully convinced that it was not Siri who had been given to Troll.

When she came back to the house she saw that Elisabet had turned out a little wash and that Tosten was loading some sacks into the wagon—potatoes, presumably, because she had heard her mother protesting that the family needed more potatoes "than that" for their own cellar. He had changed little in the years that had shrunk her mother; his shock of sunburned hair showed only a small peppering of gray along the sideburns, but his features had a bloated look, and the abdominal paunch had at last threatened to surpass the massiveness of his shoulders. As he took up the reins and started the wagon rumbling across the lot, he passed Elisabet leaving the hencoop with a pan of eggs. He did not look down at her and she did not look up at him. Siri was suddenly struck by the unreality of the scene, played out with the unrehearsed competency and in-difference of a pair of chautauqua troopers.

By lunch time Sophie had not appeared, but Siri had seen her once, wandering along the closest hilltop, dragging what looked like a stick. By two o'clock, however, she had appeared, and when Siri looked up from the gooseberries she was picking over for Elisa-bet, she saw with surprise that the child had put on the dress she wore the day of the threshers, and one of the ribbons she had not worn before was tied to her hair. "She wants to ride back with you part of the way," said her mother matter-of-factly. Siri had a protest on the tip of her tongue. Why, she herself felt a timidity about the moment of Mr. Rittenhouse's arrival, and to ask him to take a passenger! "You must realize, Siri, that the child has had few of the pleasures you are accustomed to," she said. "She has ridden in an automobile only once, and that was when we stopped off in Minnesota to see you," she finished, seeming to chide her older daughter gently. "She'll get off by the lake or a little beyond and walk back—such a walk means nothing to her. She walks back and forth from the school in Golag."

"But not on stormy days!" hazarded Siri. "Surely not then!"

"I'm afraid she doesn't like school well enough for that." Elisabet stirred up the fire in the stove and asked, "Will he drink a cup of coffee when he comes?" Her mother's face was a strange mixture of long-practiced courtesy and some timidity.

"I can ask him."

Sophie, of course, was the first to discern the car chugging along the crest of the hill, even before Shep's alerting bark. From the narrow front window above the treadle sewing machine—Tosten *had* bought something worthwhile for her mother—she saw the girl perched on a rock, her arms flung backward, her legs sprawled out in front. "I don't think I have forgotten anything, Mother," Siri said, glancing out the window to check the progress of the vehicle, from which a small swirl of dust rose like pursuing smoke. "Why, there's someone with him!" They both watched the approach of the car in the rapt manner of farm folk observing the disquieting but usually pleasant upheaval of monotony. "It's Miss McCarthy, Mother," exclaimed Siri, feeling a surge of pleasure at the discovery. Elisabet looked at her daughter blankly, as though Siri expected her to know the residents of Scotts Lake.

Out beside the house Elisabet's invitation was duly offered, but the two arrivals declined. "*Nei tak, jeg maa gaa hjem og stelle med huset,*" said Miss McCarthy in a surprising jumble of stiffly spoken but quite accurate Norwegian. Siri laughed and explained to her mother that the house Miss McCarthy spoke of returning to take care of was Scotts Lake's hotel. It was clear that Miss McCarthy's unexpected use of Elisabet's tongue had pleased her mother. Miss McCarthy, in the meantime, had climbed out of the car to exclaim over a little kitten making its difficult way across the high grass, like a swimmer paddling through a fringe of bothersome weeds. "Isn't it cute?" she said, catching it up in her arms. "Scott, I'm going to take it home with me. Little girl," she said, turning to Sophie, who was watching the scene with critical detachment, "will you sell this darling kitten to me?"

"Ellie, you've got *one* cat!" said Scott, giving Siri an amused look.

"Of course I've got one cat!" exploded Miss McCarthy. "One good-for-nothing fat old cat that's too tired to get off the lobby desk!" She turned to Siri. "You see, I need a mouser for the basement. Would your sister sell him to me, do you suppose?" She tossed the cat into Scott's arms.

"I'll sell him," said Sophie. "I've got three more out in the barn."

"One will do," said the woman. She reached across the seat and rescued the kitten from Scott's flailing arms. "Lend me fifty cents, Scott." He dug into his pocket and came out with the required cash.

When the transaction was completed, Siri said with a timidity that embarrassed her, "Sophie would like to ride with us as far as the lake. She hasn't ridden in many cars."

"Well, climb in," said Miss McCarthy hospitably, following the child's quick scramble into the back seat with her own dignified ascent. "You haven't missed a thing, either," she went on, knotting a scarf around her motoring hat.

Siri kissed her mother on the cheek and turned to find Scott beside her, his hand extended to help her into the front seat. Before he went around to his side of the car, he shook her mother's hand and said *Farvel;* it was a gesture that seemed to please Elisabet, and it occurred to Siri that Scott must have been familiar with the way of newcomers, whose manners might seem more formal or quaint than the casual amenities of the plains. Siri waved to her mother several times as the car wound up the prairie road. The double doors of the barn stood ajar, and the light struck the opening in such a way that the doorway looked like a giant maw threatening to swallow the small house beside the barely discernible fringe of cottonwoods. When Sophie did not ask to be let out as they circled the end of the lake, Siri turned and attempted to catch her eye. If she was aware of her sister's glance, Sophie did not let on—but sat there, unblinking, rubbing the fifty-cent piece between the palms of her hands. Miss McCarthy seemed oblivious to all of them at the moment, her glance grazing the surface of the hills, her mind bemused by reflections of one kind or another, while her gloved hand held firmly to the kitten lying on its stomach in her lap.

Siri turned to Scott and found his eyes upon her. "We must let her out, Mr. Rittenhouse."

"Oh, for heaven's sake!" cried Miss McCarthy suddenly. "Call him *Scott!* Siri, meet Scott. Scott, meet Siri!" she said caustically. When the car came to a stop, the child put the fifty cents in her left hand and pushed at the door handle.

"Shall I help you out?" asked Scott. Sophie shook her head and climbed slowly from the runningboard. She stood beside the small road, the grasses reaching up into her skirts as they called their good-byes.

"Goodbye, Sophie! Be good to Mother!" The child did not reply, but stared at Siri with a kind of cunning malevolence.

"If you don't mind my saying it," said Miss McCarthy resettling herself in the back seat, "that stepsister of yours is a peculiar child."

"I know it. Something tells me we shall always be strangers," said Siri with a sigh.

CHAPTER 13

Scotts Lake

Mrs. Lusk, decided Siri, had achieved the rather grim look about her mouth from pursuing fleeing dollars, but their flight to the butcher shop and the grocery end of Mercer's General Store was certainly a slow one. "You see, dearie," she confided to her roomer and boarder one day when Mr. Lusk had taken a walk, "I am actually feeding poor Esmer. It's a long and involved story, but my father left me a little money from which I draw a small dividend." She was gathering bits of complexion and laundry soap into a small metal receptacle with a handle so that they might be salvaged for dishwashing. "Now Esmer himself has a small pension and a little savings, but I have figured that actually my father, bless his soul, and the investment he left me sets this table—she indicated the dark oak structure in the room beyond—two-to-one to Esmer's contributions." She swished the container in the dish pan several times. "Now, I am not complaining, Siri, but when Esmer tells me, as he did at the supper table, that the woman's vote would *ruin* this country, I'd like to get up and stick our bank book under his nose. It's one thing arguing and another thing doing."

"Oh, he means well, Mrs. Lusk," said Siri attempting to wipe a streak off a water glass Mrs. Lusk's myopia had caused her to miss, or perhaps it was the discouraged state of her dishwater which smelled faintly of Cuticura, Jap Rose, and Fels Naptha. She didn't feel exactly like taking sides either, but she grew a little weary of semantics and fried potatoes served together. She had the feeling that Mr. Lusk had small regard for "female instructors," as he put it; and once in a while when she came home burdened with a leaning tower of books and a stack of folded themes for correction, he coughed her into the room from the comfort of his leather chair by the front window with small "ahems" and "Miss Gabrielsons." "Well—ahem—Miss Gabrielson—ahem, what great learning has taken place in that red brick building euphemistically labeled a place of instruction?"

"Oh, English and history, Mr. Lusk."

"Let's get down to particulars, Miss Gabrielson. Now it cannot be assumed that when you say English you mean the same thing as I do when I say English." He waited for evidence of her insatiable curiosity. When she merely shifted the books and papers to a more comfortable position, he pursued his little drama of self-aggrandizement. "I assume your birthplace was Norway?" He waited for her nod (Oh, nod quickly, she thought! My aching arms! Some day I'm going to toss the whole load right into his lap!) "Of course, I am sure it is obvious to you that the language you speak—your phrasings, your choice of words, to put it simply—is chosen with a different purpose from the one I might have. Your thoughts are conditioned by your experiences, and you and I do not share like experiences. Ahem."

"If you'll excuse me, Mr. Lusk, I'll take these books upstairs, and we can chat later."

He raised his hand in a gesture of patient restraint. "Miss Gabrielson, now let us not move precipitately. One does not raise a question and then toss it lightly away as one would strike a match and waft the extinguished little sliver of pine into a wastebasket. The point we have raised here is this, put succinctly: What *is* English in the year of our Lord 19 and 11, in Scotts Lake, North Dakota, in the red brick building at the end of Main Street? And may I further say on—ahem—the twenty-second of the tenth month, to be exact?" He eyed her restless movements with disfavor. "Now, Miss Gabrielson, what is English today?"

"*Which* English, Mr. Lusk? Eighth-grade English? Freshman English? Sophomore English? Junior English?" She clutched the slipping papers firmly in a desperate embrace and sped up the stairway with its worn carpeting.

Her thoughts returned to Mrs. Lusk fretting about baking a one-egg cake for the ladies sewing circle. "I don't mind giving of my time or helping fill a barrel of clothing for those benighted heathen, but this new-fangled idea that one must serve something solid to eat when we get together is about the silliest thing I've ever heard. A cup of tea used to be ample. I don't want to hurt your feelings, Siri, but I am sure that the whole idea started with those Lutherans

over on the west side of town. They are the *eatingest Christians!*"
She reached across the cupboard and looked into the brown sugar
crock. "Lordy me, child," she sniffed, setting the crock down with
a clatter. "Here I'm about to burn the cake, and eggs ten cents a
dozen!"

After a month or two Siri became accustomed to the growlings in
her stomach. Once in late September she had told Mrs. Lusk that
she was "eating out" and had gone to the McCarthy diningroom
and ordered a pot roast dinner and pie à la mode. Ellie told her
afterward that she had held out longer than the girl who roomed
at the Lusks the year before. "You better take your meals at the
hotel," said the proprietress briskly, "and I'll give you a rate on
them. Get the price on just the room alone over there. That ought
to appease the powers that be." Siri told her that she would think
it over, but during her first year in a new place she was reluctant
to show any rebellion—anyway, Mr. Willis asked her at least once
a week how she "enjoyed" living with the Lusks. "Fine people,"
he always said as he terminated the conversation. "I knew you'd fit
in there—hand and glove. Esmer's a gentleman and a scholar, and
Violet—that's Mrs. Lusk to my wife and me—is a charitable woman.
A real charitable woman."

Since her visit to the hills early in September, Siri had not been
out again. On an afternoon in November when the prairies were a
shimmer of blue sky and golden earth, with a sudden return of
Indian summer, she came up the short wooden steps to the front
porch of the Lusk residence, humming an autumn song she had
heard the glee club practicing. She was startled to find her mother
sitting in a straight chair beside the front door, a welcoming smile
on her face, a brown paper parcel on her lap. "Mother!" she cried,
running up the steps to embrace her.

"Tosten came in today on some business, and this being your birthday week, I had to come in and see you. Wear it with health,
daughter." She put the soft parcel into Siri's hands.

"We'll go right upstairs to my room, and I'll open it there. You
could have waited inside, you know."

"Mrs. Lusk, she invited me."

"You said that in English, Mother! You've been practicing!"

"Oh, a little," her mother admitted, as Siri opened the door to her room.

"So pretty," said Elisabet, looking at the four-poster and the crocheted bedspread, the flowered carpet on the floor, and the wide bureau with its swinging mirror, the small study table.

"Yes, it is pretty. You sit here in the rocking chair by the window, where you can look out at Mrs. Lusk's little garden. Just about everything is frozen except for a few asters and crysanthemums. She keeps on covering them at night. I'll open this package." She took manicure scissors from the little case in the upper drawer and clipped the ribbon carefully. It was an old pink ribbon, carefully ironed, and she folded it before she put it on top of her dresser. She unwrapped the brown paper and found a white lawn petticoat, with three or four miniature tucks above a scalloped hem delicately embroidered in a satin stitch. "Mother," she said putting on an accusing face, "did you use the lawn I brought *you* to make something for me?"

"For both Sophie and you. There was so much."

She thanked her again and again, as was their custom, and then said, "How long can you stay? Over night?"

"No. Sophie stays with the Egelmeiers this night, and I must get home for the chores. I meet him at eight, where the buggy is hitched beside the store."

"Then we'll go out to dinner, you and I." She flew down the stairs to inform Mrs. Lusk of a situation that benefitted both of them, the Lusk budget and Siri's stomach. When she came back into the room she observed that her mother's face was more pinched than it had been in September, with a strange translucence in her finely textured skin. "You don't eat enough, Mother," reprimanded Siri as she finished wiping her hands at the commode in the corner. "I don't really, either," she confided, politely lowering her voice as though the Lusks were capable of understanding her Norwegian. Yet she regretted her impetuous disclosure immediately because Elisabet began to fret about Siri's problem. Siri soon reassured her that it was not quantity lacking so much as quality, and that she had been inordinately spoiled by all the good food she had enjoyed at Fjeldstrand as well as in Aunt Joanna's kitchen. When this brought a flood of backward glances, Siri discovered that her mother was chatting with animation, much as she had in the old days before Papa's death.

As Siri brushed her long hair and swept it into a loose bun and pompadour, her mother asked her timidly, "When did you last hear from Leif?"

Observing the intensity of her mother's interest in the subject, Siri lied, "O, Mother, not too long ago." How could she tell her mother of their quarrel? Even though she might not attribute it to her coming out here, she sensed that the disclosure of a break between them would be upsetting. She could readily imagine her mother going about the house, reflected Siri as she fastened a gold barpin at the neck of her shirtwaist, dreaming about their felicity!

They walked together down the sloping street where the Lusks lived, across a little footbridge that spanned a now dry creek bed, and turned down another shady street which led to the schoolhouse.

"This is where I teach," said Siri. "The room on the corner up there—the one that the boxelder touches—that's my room, Mother."

For the occasion Elisabet had put on the dress that Aunt Joanna had selected when they were shopping in Minneapolis, a soft two-piece silk of a figured teal shade that made her great eyes look bluer than ever. Her silky hair, still silvery blond, but grown drab with washings in the hard water of the plains, was parted at the middle and swept gently over her small ears. She wore a small feathered hat riding the crown of her head like an iridescent ship caught on the crest of a wave. "How proud your father Arne would be of you, child!" They turned up the small main street and Elisabet continued, "I know the school well; and when Tosten drove me by a time or two I had the greatest longing to see you there. I hope you have not regretted coming."

Siri spoke pleasantly to a pair of boys who came down the sidewalk, hands in pockets, swinging with that careless, rolling gait she associated with their newly discovered sense of manhood. "Hello, Miss Gabrielson—hello, Miss Gabrielson." They spoke almost in unison, stepping to the dried grass to let them pass, darting quick, covert glances. "My boys," she explained needlessly. The evening dropped so gently upon them, with a smell of smudged leaves, that it seemed to settle upon the darkening earth like a drifted veil. The little street lights with their blinking globes had a kind of comic look, like a row of tin soldiers with yellow caps. "It's too early for the train," said Siri. Nevertheless, she looked down the track hopefully, yearning as she always did when she crossed the steel ribbons for wings of the wind to drop her in Aunt Joanna's kitchen or beside Leif. Where was he eating tonight? Somewhere in a small cafe in a town in Kandiyohi County? Her cousin Tommy had written that the last he had heard of Leif, he was working for the highway department. She looked up from her musings to see Scott cranking his touring car. He threw them a hasty wave and bent to the task again.

"Is that the young man who came out to the farm?" asked Elisabet. "Do you see him often?"

"No," said Siri honestly, "I've hardly seen him for two or three weeks." As they waited for a buggy to roll by, she wondered about Scott, concluding that he must be on a case in the county seat. She felt the sudden winged rise of spirit that perhaps only the young can know, and with this euphoria a sense of detachment, as if she floated above all that was pedestrian and troublesome. "Mother," she said, detaining Elisabet with a hand upon her thin upper arm, "have you ever smelled air like this or seen such a glow in the western sky?" The mother made no comment, but watched her daughter's face as they stood beside the hotel steps. She was well content.

Ellie had not eaten and told Siri that she would join them at the table by the windows, so the three of them sat down to stuffed pork chops, mashed potatoes, buttered peas and carrots. "It's a little starchy," she said, passing Siri and her mother a plate of hot biscuits, "but that's the way these traveling salesmen like it." She chatted briskly with the mother and daughter, sometimes in a brave mixture of Norse words she had picked up in the locality, sometimes directly to Siri, so that the latter was obliged to translate for her mother. Ellie kept on thinking as she watched the older woman: that *poor* woman, she's a pretty little thing, all dressed up like this. I wonder if her daughter knows what's wrong with her. She's lost her sense of dignity, living the way they do. Ellie was insatiably curious in a harmless way, keeping her observations to herself, adding and subtracting human values with the same absorbed attention some people give a game of solitaire.

"I must call Mrs. Swanson in!" exclaimed Ellie, suddenly inspired.

Then followed a scene that Siri would always remember with heartwarming delight, for it seemed to epitomize the easy cama- raderie of the western plains: guest, proprietress, and cook chatting until Elisabet's food grew lukewarm, until Tammy was obliged to bring cup after cup of coffee, with only Siri remembering to drink hers while it was hot. She watched the clock on the wall point to seven-thirty, finally to eight. Siri nudged her mother and remarked about the time. Then both the women rose and shook hands, Mrs. Swanson promising to drive out some Sunday afternoon.

Outside the night had grown dark and so chilly that Siri worried about her mother's light cloak. "The brown-checkered homespun blanket is in the carriage," she assured her daughter. When they reached the buggy and the patient horse, there was no sign of Tosten. Elisabet reached into the back of the vehicle and brought out a bucket of oats for the mare. "You must go, Siri, for it grows late. I know there is much work to be done preparing lessons. It was always that way with your father."

After some convincing, Elisabet allowed her to climb up to the seat beside her. Siri's earlier elation had now disappeared, for she had grown sleepy from the unaccustomed quantity of food and the warm air in the little diningroom. Her mother, however, talked hap- pily about the afternoon and evening, of the kindness of Miss Mc- Carthy and the Swedish woman. "She is a widow, you know, and lives with a brother only recently come from Sweden," offering this information with the enthusiasm the middle-aged and the old often evince for scattered facts relating to people they meet. The mare stamped restlessly. Siri began to yawn. The nine o'clock curfew rang from the Congregational tower.

For a few minutes mother and daughter argued pleasantly, Siri protesting that she would *not* leave her mother, and her mother fi- nally conceding that it might be better, after all, for Siri to remain with her, since it was getting too late for any woman to be out on the streets.

"Where *is* he, Mother?" Siri asked with some exasperation. "Is he in the pool hall?" Elisabet reverted to one of the evasive moods the child remembered from her last months in Norway. It could be possible that he was there and then again he might be visiting a friend or two. Scotts Lake was clearly putting itself to bed, for lights began to wink out one by one. "Mother," she said sharply, "how often does this kind of thing happen to you?"

"Not too often," said Elisabet with quiet stubbornness, evading a direct glance. "For I most always stay at home, you know."

"Who milks the cow and feeds the hens?"

"That," said her mother, "is what worries me most of all."

They sat there for what seemed an endless drag of hours. "They put the lights out at midnight," said Siri.

At that moment her mother sat up in the buggy. "You must stop your worrying now, for he is here." She patted her daughter's thigh and said gently. "Move over now and give him room."

Tosten came down the sidewalk whistling a tune that Siri recognized as "Paul and his chickens." He stopped to unhitch the mare—a process that seemed to take an unconscionably long time to Siri—and then he swung himself heavily into the seat beside the women, suddenly discovering not only the presence of Elisabet—whose company on this junket he had quite forgotten—but Siri, as well. "You must take her home, Tosten," said Elisabet. He agreed pleasantly that such a side excursion was quite possible but when he had turned the horse, the horse did not want to go in the direction of the Lusk residence. The mare had from long experience learned to trust only her own directional sense, and no amount of Tosten's pulling on the reins would alter the stubborn mare's direction. "Oh, get back in the other seat!" said Elisabet with a satisfying flare of temper. Tosten did not argue, and soon he was snoring on the leather seat above the bucket of oats. The mare had complete confidence in Elisabet's gentle commands. But long after they had left her at the Lusks Siri lay awake under one of her landlady's piece-quilts. In her mind's eye she could trace the long journey across the swelling hills and hear the sharp bark of a coyote. Not until a blunted circle of moon began to move across the starry sky did she feel composed enough to settle her pillow under her head and think of sleep.

CHAPTER 14

The Hilltop

On the day following her mother's unexpected visit Siri received a letter from her cousin John informing her that he expected to stop off on his way to Montana, where he planned to look into a medical practice for sale. As was often her custom, she had picked up her mail before classes started in the morning, and John's welcome letter and her lack of sleep combined to give her a sense of vagueness, a fact which would have given Mr. Lusk, had he been observing her, cause for another syllogism. She had also allowed herself to be tricked into one of those specious arguments which frequently flare up in secondary classrooms, this one concerning the validity of the Monroe Doctrine in an age so different from the 19th century. "Bugs" Sokolsky had argued with a lack of respect that bordered on insubordination, but Siri's firm but pleasant air quickly restored classroom quiet. As she straightened her desk after four o'clock it occurred to her that Bugs's attitude had a personal element and was not entirely simple belligerence, for he had won the reputation in his two years of high school of being a sensible and cooperative boy. She hazarded a guess that he had, somehow, connected her with Tosten, the latter having been and being one of the frequenters of the Sokolsky pool hall. She went into the cloakroom for her jacket and shrugged off unpleasant speculations with the thought that her taking a position in Scotts Lake had been a calculated risk, for her Uncle Roald and she had spoken of possible tangled relationships, but he had echoed a conviction which her own father had written in the small journal he had kept—that any progress of worth in this world depended upon the confident assumption that good has more enduring power than evil.

When she walked out the door with Miss Hennesey, the little sixth-grade teacher from downstairs, she saw a massive bank of gray clouds in the northwest and observed that the air had an unsettled quality. "Winter is coming," said Flora. "Gramps fussed about his rheumatism all last night." She looked up at Siri. "I suppose you have an invitation to old man Rittenhouse's annual birthday party, you and Scott being friends."

"Do you, Flora?"

"Listen, you haven't been around here very long or you'd know that Gramps and he don't hit it off very well. One of those old feuds—property lines and an argument about a well. 'Bye, Siri. See you Monday," she called, sprinting up a well-clipped pathway to a small bungalow, where an old man sat rocking on the front porch, a pipe clamped between his teeth and a grizzled Airedale at his feet.

A small sprightly wind with a cold breath scooped up a drift of autumn leaves and swirled them about her skirts, scattered the tumbling leaves upon the road and ran across to the McKail yard for more devilment. Despite her wish for Scotts Lake to put on its best company manners for John, Siri felt the excitement that a weather change often incites in the young. The plains with their massive weather patterns left her with an increased awareness of the smallness of man upon such sweeping areas of land and under the mysteries of sky. It continued to surprise her that many folk were oblivious to weather, except as it touched their personal comfort. Wasn't it in Chaucer's *Troilus and Criseyde* that Troilus was caught up in the eighth sphere and looked down to see "This litel spot of erthe, that with the se embraced is"? If she could only lead her literature students to wonder at the greatness and smallness of man, a creature with his feet chained to the ground but an unfathomable universe above his head!

"Siri!"

"You startled me, Scott."

"Want a spin?"

"Well—"

Scott held the door open for her, apologizing for not assisting her. "Got a sputter in this monster, and I thought I'd take a run south of here. Try her on a hill. Fortunately I just happened to see you." She settled her books between them while he commented about how long it had been since he had *really* seen her. "Father celebrates his eightieth birthday on Sunday afternoon, and we'd be greatly honored by your presence, as the etiquette books say." She explained that her cousin John was coming in on the Saturday flyer from Minneapolis. "Bring him along—that is if he'd care to sample the hectic social life of Scotts Lake." She thanked him somewhat primly, but Scott's ebullience overrode the shyness that suddenly plagued her. "Anything that I ought to know about this cousin John?"

"He just finished his internship and is investigating a practice for sale. Lewiston, no Livingston," she said.

"Good for him!" He increased his speed and said with amusement, "Let your hair fly. I hate hats on women." She could see that he was in exuberant spirits. "Wasn't that your mother that I saw you with last night?" he shouted as the speeding car and the wind set up a roaring duet. Siri began to laugh. Scott's carefree mood, the spinning earth, the approaching Jotunheim of clouds, and the put-put up the steep hillside gave her a childish sense of abandon, like a funny rag-doll in a runaway carriage.

When they had reached the top, Scott said, "She's hitting better than I thought she would." Siri ran her fingers through her hair and attempted to pat escaping strands into place. "Brown and topaz," said Scott.

She knew that he was talking about her hair, and she turned her face to look down the rocky slopes to the prairie below. "I love mountains," she said, ignoring the personal challenge in his glances. "Just being up here makes me lonesome for Norway." When he did not say anything, she went on with, "A few seconds before you came along I was thinking about a long poem by Chaucer in which there is considerable argument about predestination, and—" She looked at Scott. He still wasn't saying anything. Feeling somewhat pedantic and more than a little foolish for having brought up the subject, she finished rapidly, "Well, his conclusion is that we actually do not have any freedom of choice—well, for instance, here I am when by all reason I should be living in Norway—"

Scott caught her roughly in his arms, pressing her so tightly that the row of buttons on her dress sent sharp prongs of pain into her breastbone, and when he began to release her, he lifted her face upward and held her with a long kiss. She felt a melting sensation, a weakening that flowed down and through her body until she seemed to become weightless and unresisting.

When they pulled apart, Siri sat motionless beside him. The tall,

"ou and I have just
ade a discovery
ore important
a man and
woman than
ything else
this world,"
said

dry grasses beside the car rustled sharply in the rising wind. She pushed back the jacket she wore and felt for the black-ribboned watch fastened to her waist with an oak-cluster pin. "It's five o'clock," she said, suddenly amused and chagrined by the absurdity of her observation.

"You and I have just made a discovery more important to a man and a woman than anything else in this world," he said, "and you pull out your watch and say, 'It's five o'clock!' Siri! Siri!" he said.

"What *do* you say?" she asked.

"*I'm* going to say, 'I love you.' "

She saw his arms moving toward her, but she restrained him with a small push against his wrist. "Is there anyone else?" he asked.

"I don't know. Perhaps." She watched him put the car in gear and turn the front wheels toward the narrow, descending trail. As they reached more level ground, she felt the first needled pricks of cold rain upon her face.

"I'll try to get you back before the storm sets in." They drove down the winding road toward town, the air growing increasingly sharp and wintry. "Thank you for being genuine," he said, giving her an odd smile.

"What do you mean?" she asked in a small, puzzled voice.

"I don't know, really—except that you didn't say all the foolish things women are supposed to say when a man does something they know he is likely to do." The streets had a deserted look, with only a few homebound people ducking their heads against the cold rainy wind. He stopped under the scraping elm trees in front of the Lusk residence. "I'll take you to the door and say a few words to your keepers." He helped her up the slippery stairs to the front porch. "It's what I told you before, tell them where you're going and where you've been."

"But not what you've done!" she said, giving him a mischievous look as he opened the door for her.

Dinner over, Mrs. Lusk suggested that Siri bring her school work down to the diningroom table. "There's a good fire in the base burner here, and it seems foolish to build another fire in the hall-way upstairs, since you'll soon be going to bed." She took the crumb tray and its matching scraper and brushed the white linen tablecloth. "I was just telling Esmer before you came in with Scott that it beats all how changeable this country is. One minute Indian summer as pretty as you please and the next, a howling wind right out of the Arctic."

"Thanks, Mrs. Lusk, but I'm not cold, really. I'll work for a few minutes upstairs and then crawl into bed." Apparently cold weather, concluded Siri, had a paralyzing effect on Mr. Lusk's mental faculties, for he hadn't given his wife a word of argument when she remarked that the Taft administration, so far as she was concerned, was doing all right. He sat by the glowing burner warming his felt-slippered feet, the *Fargo Forum* in his hands.

"Don't forget, dear, where the extra quilts are!" Mrs. Lusk called, after Siri had bade them goodnight. "Shake the mothballs out of them. Better pick them up or we might step on them. Anyway I can use them again."

Siri smiled at Mrs. Lusk's squinting pronouns and said goodnight again. Seated at her desk, she began to score a half dozen or more papers and decided she would let them go until morning since a stormy Saturday would suit the purpose more than the present moment. She began to undress methodically, stepping out of her black and white shepherd's plaid and shaking it gently before putting it away in the clothes closet. As she wound her watch, she smiled at the recollection of Scott's rebuke.

A cold jet of air shot under the closed window. The first big storm of winter had caught the Lusks without their storm sash on. A breakfast argument came to mind, Mrs. Lusk declaring that she would hold out all winter before she would pay Herman Potz the two dollars he wanted for puttying the windows and setting in the storm sash. "Your vertigo isn't that bad, Esmer, but what I can brace the ladder while you take it nice and easy up there. Trouble is," she had argued, "you get so all-fired mad about having to do a few jobs around the place, you raise your blood pressure before you leave your chair. No wonder you get those dizzy spells." Siri chuckled to herself.

When she had put away her clothes and slipped into a nightdress, she stood by the window looking out into the storm. Try as hard as she might, it was almost impossible to imagine what it would be like on the little farm tonight. Even during the rainstorm when they had sat by the fire, she had felt the permeating chill from outdoors and the bleak loneliness of their situation. If something should happen to Tosten on one of his numerous pleasure jaunts, she'd be almost glad! It would be one way of putting an end to the folly of allowing her mother to waste away for such untenable reasons.

She turned away from the window and found a cloth which she used for shining shoes, folding it carefully along the sill where the snow had begun to drive in. Then she opened the door to the hallway so that she might have enough air. It would serve them right, she thought, if she opened the window to let the snow drift in on the carpet—anyway, regardless of what everyone said about night air, she liked it!

Disdaining the mothballs and extra quilts, she found her winter coat with its fox collar and stretched it across the foot of the bed. Then she blew out the kerosene lamp and slid into the cold sheets. From trundle-bed times she had always enjoyed the first icy contact with a cold bed, the slow warming of the human nest, and then when body warmth had conquered the chill, little exploring thrusts into the icy wastes of cold sheeting. Listening to the battering assaults of wind, she lay on her back, her long hair soft under her shoulders and fragrant from a recent washing in Jap Rose soap and a vinegar rinse. Despite the fact that a portion of her mind tried to label her a hussy for enjoying the memory of Scott's kiss, she felt a strange contentment with herself and tried to remember Leif's goodnight kisses and compare them with Scott's unexpected theft. Perhaps I take "clasping" too seriously, she thought. Perhaps I have read too many novels and magazines that skirt the subject too gracefully and unrealistically. Perhaps the standards expressed optimistically in magazines and from the pulpit are not so much the reflections of current social practices as they are social *wishing* by men and women often beyond the age of temptation.

She recalled the contradictory aspect of her upbringing—Bergit's occasional and surprising lack of shock over against Elisabet's sense of small rectitudes. Let me be like my grandmother, she thought—above all, honest with myself so that I can be honest with others.

What is my mother *really* like, she wondered. How much erosion of spirit has she suffered? Am I disloyal when I think she almost welcomes her sufferings now as achievements beyond the scope of some people: see how I have borne what others will not bear? How evil of me to think it, thought Siri—well, not really, she concluded defensively, for these thoughts have grown with my years.

As she lay there thinking about the afternoon, she concluded that she had made it impossible to accept the birthday invitation—actually *he* had—*they* had, she reasoned more logically. Probably John wouldn't want to go, anyway, and Scott's inclusion of her cousin was simply a matter of courtesy. She commenced to grow sleepy, her mind picking up fragments of memory: Grandmother's phrase "as fickle as hares in a hayloft"; Leif's good-natured boyish face and his fresh blond looks; Elisabet bringing in eggs from the forlorn little chicken coop; Tosten on the night of her grandmother's accident. Her reflexes snatched her suddenly from a well of sleep and she remembered that she had not said her prayers. None of the Lutheran prayers she had memorized seemed to fit her frame of mind, and she put her arm under the cool pillow, turned on her side, and soon fell asleep.

Saturday evening the flyer was an hour late. Although the first seasonal storm blew itself quickly away, small flurries of wind-driven snow eddied across banked drifts, and the telegraph lines above the depot whined and sang in the wind. A few minutes previously Scott had swung into the little waiting room berating her for having walked down alone. "You knew I'd come down for you on a night like this!" he scolded. "And why in the name of common sense don't the Lusks have a telephone!"

"For the same reason they don't have anything else, I suppose." She felt slightly resentful over Scott's implication that she couldn't take care of herself; furthermore, she did not wish to share John with anyone.

As though he read her thoughts, Scott said, "I don't intend getting in on the act tonight, but it's devilishly dark and windy out there, and your John wouldn't like knowing you came down alone."

"I like stormy weather," said Siri, with more honesty than pugnacity, though Scott could not be expected to know that.

He gave her an amused look. "Well, let's wade up to the hotel then and have a cup of coffee with Ellie. There's no sense in hanging around here." They crunched down the platform and turned up Main Street. "Rather deserted for a Saturday evening, isn't it?" She stumbled as one foot unexpectedly sank into a soft portion of the drifted snow. He caught her, steadying her with his arm as they walked on.

She gave him a foolish little laugh and said, "Silly, wasn't it?" In the dim light of the street lamp he saw her pert young face under its three-cornered hat, a trace of snow on her eyelashes, her creamy flawless skin rosy from the cold, her provocatively sweet mouth upon which lay the memory of a kiss, and the brown eyes with their disturbing habit of inviting and withdrawing.

"Siri, who is he?" he asked suddenly.

He grew angry with her coy, "Who, Scott?" and said, "Why can't you be honest?"

She pulled away from him and hugged the muff against her waistline, picking her way carefully across the little drifts that lay upon the sidewalk. "He was a boy I went to school with."

"Was?"

"Well, *is*. We had a misunderstanding over my coming out here. Oh, you know," she said with an attempt at levity, "one of those Victorian scenes: marry me now or leave me forever!"

"I like the *forever*."

She stamped the snow off her overshoes and said, "Ellie's coffee is going to taste awfully good." He followed her into the narrow hallway, helping her off with her coat, aware of the lifted sweep of her breasts under the soft draping of the green wool she wore.

When they walked into the lobby an animated chatter suddenly broke off as the Saturday night crowd took a measure of the newcomers. "Say, Scott, you're just the fella we want to see. We got into an argument about a railroad right-of-way." Scott frowned for a moment and said softly, "Find Ellie. I'll be in shortly."

She found Miss McCarthy on a ladder replacing a lampshield. "You'd think with all those men in there a woman wouldn't have to do a thing like this. Freeloaders, every last one of them. Don't want to spend a Saturday night staring at the wife and kids so they come down here and burn my coal and use my kerosene and argue about politics and wheat and the weather. Scott with you? This the night your cousin's coming?" Siri held the rickety ladder while Ellie brought down the old lampshield. Ellie washed her hands in a basin in the sink and commented, "Weather like this is awfully hard on business."

Siri walked about the kitchen restlessly. "Nervous as a cat, aren't you? Speaking of cats, is that cat we brought in from the hills a mouser! The darn thing's a female, though, and I don't like the ideas she's putting in old TC's head. Going to have more cats than customers."

"TC?" asked Siri, sinking down into a chair beside the table.

"Short for tomcat." Ellie looked up as the door swung open. "Speaking of tomcats, Scott, and there you are!" She stirred up the fire in the range and set the coffee pot forward. "Well, what's the matter with you two?"

Siri didn't say anything, but sat with an elbow on the table, her eyes following the faded pattern on the linoleum floor. Scott had his watch out, comparing his time with that of the clock on the wall. "I'm sorry," apologized Siri. "I didn't see what you were doing, Ellie." She took the coffee cups from Ellie's hands and placed them carefully around the table and went back for the pie Ellie held out to her.

"Your cousin planning to register here?"

"Where else can one 'register'?" Scott laughed. "Ellie, you kill me."

"As a matter of fact, Mrs. Lusk offered me—I mean offered him for me—well, she has a room for him."

"Gratis?" said Ellie, bringing the coffee over.

"You're coming to the party tomorrow afternoon, aren't you, Ellie?"

"Belle of the ball, Scott." She poured some cream into her coffee. "You two mad at each other or something? You're going to the party, aren't you Siri?"

"It depends upon John."

Scott consulted his watch again and said, "We probably ought to start down there. Thanks, Ellie."

Ellie rose with them and said, "My pleasure. Don't mention it. I can't tell you how you've brightened this gloomy winter evening."

Down at the station Scott was as good as his word. A crowd of the more venturesome loafers had walked down to the depot with them, waiting patiently in the yellow gloom for the first long whistle of the flyer. When they saw the train coming toward the depot, the men crowded closer to the rails, huddled together, their backs against the wind. When it came hissing and steaming past them, throwing yellow squares of light on their faces, Siri cried, "I saw him! There he is!" and began running down the platform.. Scott caught up with her as a tall young man swung down from a sleeping car and pulled her off her feet. Siri turned around and made the proper introductions, Scott shaking the stranger's hand and murmuring something to the effect that he hoped Dr. Gabrielson would accept his invitation and that Siri would explain further. He smiled, doffed his hat, and disappeared into the night.

Mrs. Lusk awaited Siri and her guest with a pot of hot chocolate and a plate of small decorated cakes she had brought home from a missionary meeting at the church; in fact, she had stood staring at the five or six cakes left in a tin until the creator of these dainty splendors asked, "Violet, what's the matter? Is there something crawling on them?"

"You're not going to throw them away, are you?"

"I hadn't thought of it."

"Would you *sell* them to me?" Mrs. Lusk felt immediate qualms about the financial risk she had committed herself to.

"Take them, dear, but be sure to return the tin," said her sister-in-faith with largesse and caution neatly balanced.

Fire was burning briskly in the parlor stove when Siri and John came chatting and laughing to the front porch, where they removed their overshoes to deposit them on a paper in the front hall. Mrs. Lusk fell in love with John immediately. "Such a tall, handsome young doctor," she told the owner of the cake tin when she returned it after church the next day, "and it was such a nice thought on your part offering the cakes to me." She accepted a cup of tea from her neighbor. "I'm sorry you couldn't have been with us last night, because you have heartburn, too—but I asked him right off what to do about it and the sinking spells I get in the morning while I'm cooking breakfast. Well, it's too bad we can't have a young man like that here instead of Dr. Torrence, because I don't think I'd mind undressing a little in front of him. We've discussed that before, you know." She got up and retrieved her shawl, saying, "Well, ta, ta, my dear. As soon as they're home from their church, Dr. Gabrielson is taking us to dinner up at the Chatham. If I can do anything for you sometime—" and Mrs. Lusk was off, a shawl over her head, to keep their dinner engagement.

After lunch when they had left the Lusks in the lobby with Ellie, John and Siri set out on a long walk, feeling that they would have more privacy that way, and, anyway, Siri wished to show him the town. After John had admired the schoolhouse and Mr. Willis' house—at Siri's insistence, at a respectful distance—and Mr. Rittenhouse's Victorian showplace—at an even more respectful distance, they began wandering away from the town itself, along the hard-packed snow that did not in most places obliterate the faint trail of the prairie road that led across tens upon tens of hills down to the valley and what she termed "Tosten's Folly."

"I wish you could take time to see mother," she said. "Someone ought to look at her. She's getting thinner all the time and is very pale." Siri had tucked her arm in John's and he looked down at her from time to time, recalling with affection what a small quaint and shy brown-eyed girl she had been when she had come to live with them. "I suppose we could have hired a cutter from the livery stable and gone out to see her this afternoon." Whereupon John scolded her in a most brotherly fashion and made her promise that she would never set out across such a wilderness alone, and, anyway, she ought to realize that after a storm such as they just had, every landmark would be obliterated, if there *were* landmarks in a country marked only my monotony. Siri asked him about the practice he had in mind, and John confided that he had never given Montana a thought until he met a beautiful girl from Livingston while he was an intern in Chicago. This information naturally called for many detailed questions from Siri and set her to wondering about people— John, for instance—who could meet someone and know immediately that they were meant for each other.

"Brun's getting married too," he said. "Two guesses." Siri tried in vain to recall a girl—any girl—Brun was ever interested in, for Brun had been a plodding, intent, unimaginative boy in love only with whirring blades on reapers and with balky gasoline motors. Finally John asked, "Give up?" He prolonged his moment of disclosure as long as he could, then yelled, "Teresa Hickenlooper!" This sent Siri into gales of laughter, for Teresa had been their highschool valedictorian, a thin, emaciated looking girl with hornrimmed glasses, who moved through her school books with the steady, gnawing precision of a termite working up a strip of siding.

"When?"

"Perhaps I'm not supposed to tell, but when you come home for Christmas."

"I can't leave Mother," said Siri, her glance very sober.

"Mother and Dad have it all figured out. You get two weeks, don't you? Allow for the time it takes coming and going, and divide the time equally—or, better still, give us a day or so more."

"John, John!" Siri hugged him tightly. "You don't know how I have missed you all! Once, I didn't think I could ever live after I left Grandmother in Norway, and I've had to go through it all again here."

"You'll see Leif, too, probably."

"Oh."

"I like Leif pretty well, I guess—one of those easygoing fellows, in my judgment, who never spend much time worrying about other people's feelings unless they relate in some way to themselves." He looked intently at Siri to see whether he had hurt her feelings. "He's not selfish. I don't mean that. He's just not too perceptive, that's all." They climbed to a small rise and stood looking about them, forward to the hills and back to the small town, where smoke rose straight into the air from at least a hundred chimneys. "Tell me about this Scott Winterhouse."

"Rittenhouse," corrected Siri. After a few paces she said, "There's really nothing to tell, John."

"Want to go tonight?"

"I don't know." Suddenly she turned to him and said, "He kissed me."

"I'd have done the same thing in his place." He smiled at her affectionately. "You mustn't be afraid to fall in love." He reached into his jacket and extracted a pipe and some Duke's Mixture. She waited at his side, remembering her first day of school in America and how John, then a senior, had taken her to Miss Blomquist's fourth-grade room and helped settle her down in one of the newly varnished desks beside the blackboard. When he had the pipe drawing properly, he said, "You laughed about Brun and Teresa Hickenlooper, but actually it's not such an odd marriage, after all. Brun's out there on Grandma Pearson's farm—by the way, she sends her love—and Teresa is going to fit in very well. She'll go to bed with him and produce some fine hardworking youngsters, she'll pitch into the farm work and make Brun a real—"

"You sound almost indecent." Siri laughed.

"They're the kind of people who have made this country," said the young man seriously. If we ever get afraid of pitching in and working things out day by day with an eye on the long haul, we won't be the kind of country we're trying to be today."

"Teddy Roosevelt would have liked you," teased Siri. Yet John was talking like home, she thought proudly. Like the people in the little area John came from, people who bought a quarter's worth of roundsteak from Himmelhoch's market and sat down to a sumptuous meal from garden, orchard, and henhouse.

Before they returned to the Lusk house, John had convinced her that he actually would like to drop in on Scott and his father, since the train West would not be in until after eight o'clock and he could see nothing to prevent their going. "Anyway, Siri, I want to see everything that's important to you here so that when I go back to Mother and Dad I can answer their bombardment of questions."

After John had thanked the Lusks for their hospitality, the cousins walked slowly down to the little depot, where John was introduced to the station master and left his valise. The clear winter sky was deepening into a cold, blue-black dome as they walked toward the better residential section of Scotts Lake. "Wonderful air in this country," said John as they turned up the Rittenhouse walk between neatly shoveled banks of snow.

"I keep on saying that, too."

Twin lights set on either side of the red-stone porch railings lighted their steps to the door. As John twisted the bell-buzzer, they heard the sound of chimes mingling with talk and laughter. Scott himself opened the door, and John was quick to perceive the quick wash of pleasure when their host caught sight of Siri. He ushered them in with warm greetings and called to an elderly woman who appeared in the doorway of one of the rooms, "Aunt Vinnie, come here. I should like to have you meet Siri Gabrielson and her cousin, Dr. Gabrielson." After he had made the introductions properly, the straight elderly woman with a handsome sweep of silver hair said, "I've heard about you Siri—what a strange and lovely name! You're from Minneapolis, aren't you, Dr. Gabrielson?"

As Scott moved with them to one of the parlors, he went on to explain that Aunt Vinnie was his father's younger sister. "You must come right in and meet Dad." Introductions were made on every side, and Siri soon realized that a good half of the people were from out of town. Scott waited, his hand on Siri's arm, while his father finished a humorous story about a pioneer altercation between a Norwegian and a Swede. "Better be careful, Dad," warned Scott. "I'm going to introduce you to a couple of Minnesota Norskies right now."

Old Jacob Rittenhouse rose from his chair with an air of massive dignity and shook their hands. Except for the twinkle in his heavily-creased and somewhat puffy eyes, his bristling mustache would have made him appear quite formidable. Heart trouble, said John to himself, when it came his turn to shake hands. Aunt Vinnie brought them a tray on which sparkled glasses of birthday wine. Siri looked uncertainly at John, remembering her contract which forbade "spiritous liquor," but Scott amused all those listening by assuring her that if employment in Scotts Lake were at stake, here stood the best legal counsel in the county.

Finally supper was announced, and as they moved into the big paneled diningroom, she saw Ellie leading Mr. Rittenhouse to the buffet table. A dapper little fellow who said he was the clerk of court in the county courthouse assisted Siri down the buffet line. She noticed that John was being helped by charming brunette twins who had taken their places on either side of him and were flirting michievously as they helped him fill his already overloaded plate with relishes of all kinds. As she was picking up her napkin, Scott

came by with a "Save a place for me in the library." She looked
about uncertainly until the dapper little gentleman in the string
tie steered her safely through several rooms to a room with a tall
fireplace and the dry scholarly smell of books mingling with the
sharp odor of burning logs. Her self-appointed escort bowed her
nattily to a cloth-covered table under a window with leaded rose and
green panes. "I think we should wait for our lord and master," he
said, "don't you?"

She nodded. Then they were joined by a fleshy woman with a doll-
like face, whom string tie introduced as his wife. Scott followed almost immediately. "You have met the Lakes, I see," he remarked
as he sat down at the small table with them. Then followed the
usual conversation about geographical origins, since almost everyone
at the party came from somewhere else, according to the clerk of
court. "I knew the minute I heard your voice that you were foreign-
born!" Mr. Lake commented to Siri. "There's always something that
gives it away, a lilt or a shade of difference in pronunciation, but
always something." He cocked his head slightly and said, "Say something!" Francine looked at her husband with tolerant amusement
and Scott began to laugh, until all joined in, but Siri felt that Mr.
Lake really didn't know what he was laughing at. When coffee and
dessert were over, Scott glanced at the clock on the mantel and suggested that Siri might like to see the rest of the house. Francine,
curiously graceful and supple despite her size, rose with them and
said she never got tired of seeing the house.

When the little tour was over (others had joined them, including
John and the green-eyed twins) Siri and John became aware of the
late hour and sought out their elderly host and hostess. Soon the
expedition to the depot gathered forces, and when they stepped
out into the frosty starlight they were accompanied by many of the
younger guests. "You're coming back again," said Scott, who
crunched along with Siri in the wake of John and the twins. At first
she said no because there was school in the morning, but then she
thought how lonesome she would be when the flyer streaked across
the plains with John, and said yes. "It's such a long time until
Christmas," she said, sounding terribly out of context, but Scott
seemed to understand, for he replied, "And you'll be going home."

Despite the feeling that she would be lonesome during the interim until Christmas, the days passed with surprising swiftness. She liked the boys and girls of the prairies, youngsters who came from homes like the little one where her mother sat sewing or knitting, but homes not nearly so far away and isolated, probably—youngsters who came from Scotts Lake and lived in houses typically furnished with golden oak or Circassian walnut and a parlor organ for amusement. They all knew that wheat was currently selling for about ninety cents a bushel and that the future looked promising enough; still they wondered about such phrases as "spheres of influence" and "militarism" and argued with adolescent zeal about editorials in the *Fargo Forum* or the *Minneapolis Journal.*

During the first week in December she rode out with Mrs. Swanson and her brother Harald, who had recently arrived from Sweden. The weather having remained sharp and clear, Harald was able to drive a sleigh raucous with bells; and Siri, who sat between his sister and him, was often weak with laughter over Harald's pride in his jingle bells. "Yust listen to dat yingle, yingle!" he exclaimed repeatedly, telling her several times that some of the bells had come from the old country and some from a "damn Norskie" over in a neighboring county who owed him for some work he had done on an axle. When Mrs. Swanson reproved him for swearing and told him that Miss Gabrielson was a Norwegian, he "ex-shused" himself again and again, until the sled bounced over a hummock and set the bells to clanging and restored his happy frame of mind. Siri was glad to learn that he owned the Scotts Lake livery stable, for she might have occasion to hire a rig when spring came.

She had sent a letter to Golag, telling her mother of their plans, and rode the remaining miles wondering whether her message had come in time. But as the sleigh sang down the last hill, she saw smoke rising out of the chimney and Sophie plodding toward them through the snow, apparently waiting for a short ride. They all hit it off well, with Mrs. Swanson able to draw Elisabet out in a way her own daughter could not. Tosten, in a good humor and apparently sober, discoursed on the future of the country, while Mrs. Swanson studied the photographs Elisabet handed her. Siri had brought them a stereoscope with pictures of several national parks and the Golden

Gate, and although the company was obliged to view the breath-taking splendors of the American West with Sophie's warm breath upon their necks, everyone was properly impressed with Siri's gift. Sophie herself gave her stepsister several smiles before the afternoon was over.. After an early meal after which Tosten was showing the guests about the farm, Siri wiped dishes for her mother and was able to discuss Christmas plans with her.

It was soon apparent that Elisabet had anticipated having Siri at the farm throughout the holidays, saying softly with sad eyes, "Our last Christmas was fourteen years ago, Siri. Fourteen years!" Elisabet began to scrub vigorously the kettle in which she had simmered meatballs and said in a small voice, "Yet I suppose that Roald and Joanna have been mother and father to you for more years than I have been with you. It is a decision you must make for yourself. But make it soon, for if you can be here on Christmas Eve, I shall make many of the dishes we had that evening when old Nels read from the family Bible."

"I'll come here first, so we can have Christmas Eve together."

"And we shall fetch you ourselves!" promised her mother, looking very much relieved. "You name the day and the hour." Before they gathered their wraps together, Siri had an opportunity to press a folded bill into Elisabet's hands, though her mother protested and seemed considerably disturbed over Siri's generosity.

"It's for all those special things you have promised to bake, Mother. And *you* do the buying yourself. Don't let Sophie or Tosten do it."

All the way back to Scotts Lake, with Harald's bells yingle-yangling against the long flow of her backward thoughts, she thought back to the Christmas her mother had cherished through all these years, remembering Lars and the Christmas goat, her old aunt and uncle, but most of all Bergit, who slept beside the old stone church.

CHAPTER 15

The Wedding

"And your stepfather didn't come at all?" asked Joanna sympathetically as Siri and she sat in the Gabrielson kitchen drinking mid-morning coffee.

"As mother promised, he picked me up on Friday afternoon—Sophie was along too—and helped me bring in the Christmas packages and took a drink of water at the kitchen pump. Then he was gone—poof! Like that!"

"What did you do then?"

She brushed some cinnamon sugar off her fingers. "Mother, of course, wanted to wait supper. Oh, Aunt Joanna, she had cooked all the good things she remembered from our last Christmas together. Well, we waited an awfully long time. I remember going out in the starlight thinking I might hear his sleigh, but there wasn't a sound outside at all—just complete silence, and once the howl of a coyote way up in the hills past Scotts Lake. It was the most beautiful Christmas evening I think I *ever* saw." Aunt Joanna shivered slightly as though to say, Well, have it your own way, Siri. "There was nothing out there, really, nothing except heaven and earth—stars and land and silence." She sighed. "Finally Mother called me in."

"I should think so!" said Joanna emphatically. "Then what did poor Elisabet do?"

"She didn't say anything at all about Tosten's absence—she can be very evasive at times, you know."

"It's a little difficult to say anything under circumstances like that, but she shouldn't have to dissemble in front of you."

"She has become frightfully self-contained though," argued Siri, "and I don't think that's good for her. She wasn't that way always, because I can remember back in Norway she'd spit at Grandma sometimes, and Grandma just passed it off and said something humorous and let it go at that."

"When did you have Christmas Eve supper then?" asked Joanna,

getting Siri back to essentials, yet enjoying her little asides and remembering how quiet she had been when she first came from Norway,

"Almost right away. She quietly dished up supper and called
Sophie and me to the table. After grace we sat in the kitchen with
its cracked walls and lopsided, grumbling stove—and a table pretty
enough for the best hotel in this city. I sat there eating *lutefisk* and
her delicious meatballs in cream sauce, thinking persistently that
she ought to be glad he didn't come home."

"Siri, how awful!" said Joanna. "You're talking about a marriage,
you know."

"I *thought* it, Aunt Joanna," she said, "and I'll bet you and Uncle
Roald would have thought the same thing." From the expression
on her aunt's face Siri concluded it might be safer to rely on facts
than on interpretations, so she continued with as few digressions
as possible to relate how they had continued eating and how her
mother served them pudding with an almond tucked into a dish,
and Sophie got the almond. "Sophie was such a good girl all evening
I can't help thinking that the entire Christmas Eve impressed her
terribly—and if it impressed her that much, how *had* they celebrated
Christmas after Grandma and Aunt Guro died?"

"And when did he come back?"

"Christmas afternoon. He didn't look too terrible, but he was
awfully surly and didn't want to look at the presents or have a cup
of coffee. He didn't want to do anything but sleep—and that wasn't
too easy an arrangement considering they actually live in two rooms."

"I could see that Mother wanted me to stay longer, but there was
a kind of strain in the air, crowded as we all were and the weather
blustery for two days, so I suggested that Tosten take me back if
it was convenient, and I made Mother come along because I thought
she needed a change." She looked at her aunt hesitantly. "You will
probably tell me that I did the wrong thing, but when I caught
Tosten out beside the barn one afternoon, I told him he had treated
Mother rather shabbily at Christmas, and that she looked tired and
unhappy."

"What did he say?"

"Oh, you know how he is. He said that women don't generally

take to the prairie country, not way out there alone as she was, but when spring came she'd pick up a lot. He even said he'd bring her in to attend church with me some morning."

"Goodness!" exclaimed Joanna, rising to put their coffee dishes in the new sink Roald had installed for her, "I'm glad you are here this part of Christmas anyway. I'm not sure we made the right decision, letting you go so far away."

Roald and Joanna had discussed at some length how to entertain Siri for Christmas, since she had missed the heart of the holiday by being away on Christmas Eve and Christmas Day. Finally they concluded that she might enjoy a family gathering. Roald had been firm about Joanna's not cooking a sit-down dinner. "Let's serve a buffet about nine-thirty or ten. The tree is up and still looks pretty. The main thing is being all together."

"Except for John!" his wife exclaimed, missing her first-born acutely, now that he had bought a practice in Livingston. She began to count the guests on her fingers, but soon found the process to be an anatomical impossibility and finally took out a paper and pencil. "We are four; then there's Ma, Brun, and of course Teresa. Shall we ask the Hickenloopers?" After Roald's affirmative nod, she continued, "And then there's Dagmar and Elissa and her Gordon and Dagmar's two girls and her grandchildren and—" Roald suggested that she stop counting and merely wait to see who came. She didn't need to name them off for him, because, goodness knows, he had fed them often enough. "Shall we ask Pastor Sandvik and his wife? Siri always liked them so well," she affirmed; and when Roald said he thought it would be fine, Joanna felt that her guest list was complete.

On the night of the little party Joanna was in that happy nervous state of the good Scandinavian hostess, ready for a complete collapse. Tommy and Siri were acting terribly, however, engaging in a pillow fight somewhere upstairs and probably upsetting the perfection of carefully draped bedspreads and primly spaced chairs. She thought of calling up to them until she realized that she had waited four months for the sound of such happy bedlam. If I could just take time to slip into my bedroom, she thought, and loosen the strings on my new corset, pillow fights and Roald tracking in snow wouldn't seem so drastic.

"Hey, Mom! Look who's here!" Joanna turned around from the sink, where she had been curling celery, and found herself embraced in Brun's great arms. "Mom, here's Teresa." Teresa's glasses had misted over in the change of temperatures so that she extended a waving, indeterminate hand toward her prospective mother-in-law, like a child playing Pin the Donkey. She was followed by Mrs. Pearson, lugging a basket of edibles, who embraced her daughter with pleasant efficiency and said, "We brought you a few extra things for the table."

"Why did you come in the *back* door, Ma?" asked her daughter. "This is a party. You're supposed to come in the front."

Meanwhile Roald was ushering in Dagmar and Elissa and their families. Dagmar, Joanna's sister who owned a dressmaking shop, overawed them all with the tightest of hobble skirts and the flattest of figures. Siri took a stiff and dutiful kiss from her hobble-skirted aunt and a good thorough bussing from Elissa. Of Dagmar's two girls, only Jenny had been "able" to come, but the family accepted the news with practiced equanimity, for they had grown accustomed to Pat's absences, since Patricia had married what was frequently termed a "scion" and moved in circles that did not touch theirs.

Jenny's two little blonde girls, wearing identical Dutch bobs, were taken over by Siri to inspect "Gwama's" tree. In a few moments the doorbell buzzed again, and Roald brought in the pastor and his wife, an amiable plump couple liked by everyone in the congregation and certainly loved by the Gabrielsons. Soon they had taken Siri aside to inquire about her four months "out West" as they termed it. "And no *Norwegian* Lutheran church there, Siri?" asked Mrs. Sandvik. "Your poor mother, what does she do?"

"My goodness," interrupted Joanna, "I just happened to think— where are your parents, Teresa?"

"Mother and Dad decided not to come but sent a tin of pepper nuts instead," said Teresa somewhat irrelevantly. Roald passed glasses of brandy, after which he settled down beside Siri and listened to her small descriptions of life with the Lusks and Ellie's cats. Roald watched her shrewdly and noticed that she avoided all mention of the Rittenhouses and Scott, names familiar to him since John's short visit with Siri. Since she was his one direct and vital link with his brother Arne and all the memories of their proud impoverished youth, he cherished her for this, but most of all for what she was herself. From the very beginning she had seemed as one of their own, and he felt that he understood her sensitive nature even better than Joanna did. He recalled the first Sunday she had been with them and how she had put on the costume of their province to please him, coming down the stairway holding on to Guro's hand, a rosy apple of a child with shining yellow-brown hair hanging to her shoulders. He had swept her into his arms to examine the embroidered blouse, the snug little kirtle, and exclaim over the little pin or *sølje* which she wore at her neck. "She's funny!" said Patricia.

"Quaint, not funny, dear," corrected her mother Dagmar. Though the child did not understand all their words, she had been quick to pick up the tone of mild ridicule in the mother and daughter, and never, thought Roald, had her defenses been down around Dagmar. He recalled that even *he* had an occasional tussle with his sister-in-law—for example, at the time he and Joanna had announced that they were sending for Siri. "If you must have a child," said Dagmar, "why don't you adopt one here?" He had explained that it wasn't a wish to have *any* child that had prompted him to do this—it was his desire to have his own brother's child. "Well, she's likely to be a queer one, foreign and all that," persisted Dagmar, who seemed to forget that her Norwegian father and her Danish mother had reared her in a bilingual home. Perhaps the best word for Dagmar, he thought, was that she was "ambitious," and after Mike's sudden death, she had taken to dressmaking, working hard to establish her own shop and succeeding well too.

Now he watched Dagmar crossing the room to them, to exchange a few amenities with Siri. She had developed through the years an airy briskness with a slight touch of malice. "Well, Siri," she remarked as Mrs. Sandvik vacated her chair to help Joanna with the coffee, "is it going to be a Dakota farmer for you out West or are you back to catch up with Leif?"

"Must it be either?" parried Siri.

"Then you have found someone else?" asked Dagmar, shifting gracefully to arrange her tight skirt comfortably.

Siri didn't like the sound of Dagmar's tone and replied in a voice that was a mild imitation of Dagmar's, "I haven't really been looking, but if you're interested, Dagmar, there are a lot of men out West. Maybe I can look around for you."

"No thanks," said Dagmar. "I can meet all the interesting men I want to in the *city*." She turned to Roald, asking his advice about a remodeling problem, since she had plans to enlarge the shop. While Siri held one of the little girls on her lap and answered the child's questions with an abstracted mind, she found herself thinking of Leif, when he and she had sat on the same flowered sofa only four months ago. Out in Scotts Lake the sharp, visual memory of Leif had often threatened to recede, except in surprising little images that came like a flash from a magic lantern; but here, in the matter of a single second, she was overwhelmed by a vision of him. How strange, she thought, to be home and not have Leif coming in with Tommy, amusing them with their good-natured antics, rolling back the rugs to dance—and the dances invariably becoming mimicries of college friends: of the girl who always danced with her head bobbing like a horse trying to shake off its collar, or the old professor who clicked his false teeth to the beat of music.

Joanna stood in the doorway inviting them in for coffee at the moment when its aroma had become too persuasive for them to wait any longer. Siri walked in with Jenny and Teresa, whom she had observed chatting beside the Christmas tree about linens and dishes, though clearly Jenny appeared more excited than the bride-to-be. In fact, the colossal matter-of-factness of both Brun and Teresa had troubled her vaguely all evening. It reminded her of one of Ellie's remarks when Scotts Lake was apprised of the birth of a baby to a heretofore childless couple, "Land sakes! And all this time I thought they were just friends!"

When all had eaten far more than they should, Mrs. Sandvik sat down at the organ and began to play their favorite Christmas carols and hymns. Siri joined in with her alto until they began a little song of her childhood beginning with the line, "Oh, how beautiful the sky," a song which brought poignantly to mind the last evening

her Aunt Guro and Uncle Nels were in America, so she slipped away
to stand in the bay window, remembering, how her little aunt had
spoken of America as a great and beautiful land and she had cried,
"But it isn't beautiful. The sun shines so brightly I want to cover
my eyes; there is no sea, and nothing is the same."

"Yet I venture to say that the stars will be the same. Perhaps
even now your mother has risen to go out to the sheds and is looking
at the same stars. Faith is what you must have, Siri. The mind can
play tricks on us, so it is necessary to call upon something more
within. It must be an act of will, child." She could not remember
all her words, but she remembered her concluding with, "Learn to
be brave in youth; it is the early practice of character that sustains
you in old age. It takes God's own miracle to turn a selfish witch
into a saint."

"What's the matter, Seer?" Tommy put his hand on her shoulder,
calling her by a favorite nickname.

"Just thinking."

"Leif may be at Brun's wedding tomorrow," he said softly.

"Oh?" She heard Mrs. Sandvik getting up from the organ and
some of the other guests insisting that they must leave. Her favorite
of the two aunts, Elissa, stopped to invite her for a day, and Pastor
Sandvik assured her he would write the Norwegian Lutheran pastor
in the county seat and see whether *he* could call on her mother. All
in all, she concluded, as she helped Joanna dry the last of the china,
it had been a heartwarming evening. It was *home*.

＊　　＊　　＊

On the morning of the wedding Siri wrapped her gift for the
newlyweds, a Daisy and Button pressed-glass plate. "Of course, I
should have gotten it there sooner," she commented to Joanna, who
was cutting small tea cakes to take over to the German Lutheran
Church for the wedding reception, declaring that Teresa's mother
needed a little assistance at a time like this. "But I couldn't have
found anything as pretty as this in Scotts Lake."

"I suppose that's so," conceded Joanna. "But it seems to me that
John said the Rittenhouses had a beautiful home. Where in the world
did *they* get their furnishings?"

Siri, well aware of her aunt's devious investigations, answered pleasantly, "Back in the boom days of the community some of the families sent as far away as to Chicago for things."

"Is it a large family?" asked Aunt Joanna. "Any girls your age, for instance?"

Siri found herself amused by her aunt's calm assumption that she was putting something over on her but said, "I've never met any Rittenhouse girls." She observed Joanna's small frown of disappointment and added, "There's an only son. He's the one who drove me out to see Mother the first time I went out to the farm."

"I hope he's nice," said Aunt Joanna. "A girl has to be careful in these times." Since Tommy was upstairs or even closer, she said softly, "With skirts way up to the top of their shoes and heaven knows what's missing underneath."

"Do you want me to take the cakes over to the church?"

"Better have Tommy help you."

On the way over, Siri, said, "I don't think I've ever been in Teresa's church."

"It looks terribly austere," commented Tommy, "but the minister's a fine chap. Modern times," he said philosophically. "Here we are with a German in the family, and who knows what you and I will come up with." He held the door open for her and they walked down a narrow flight of basement stairs. Before they had emerged through the inner door, Mrs. Hickenlooper spied them and came rushing toward them with the curious little running steps Siri remembered from her childhood.

"Siri! Siri!" she cried. "Ach. So goodt to see you." She went on to explain as Tommy set the cakes in the kitchen that Teresa would have had her for a bridesmaid but they couldn't be sure Siri would be able to come. They chatted for a few minutes, and then she and Tommy walked back to the house.

Later she dressed with fastidious care, as only a young woman can who knows that a former sweetheart's eyes might be upon her. They drove over in Uncle Roald's car, and when it refused to start with the first crankings, they had all they could do to restrain Brun from getting out of the front seat to show his dad how easily such a matter could be done if one had a feeling for the gasoline motor.

Buggies and a few automobiles crowded the little street on which the German Lutheran church sat between two rows of sighing fir trees. Inside, the groom's family was ushered in with all the proper ceremony necessary to assure a fleeting hour of extraordinary importance. As she followed Aunt Joanna up the aisle, Siri did not look to right nor left, but she felt such a weakness in the limbs under the bouncing fringes of her new green dress that for a moment she thought of collapse. As a towheaded boy with freckles across his snub nose began to pump the bellows of the organ, a heavily built blond with an aggressive air began to play the wedding march. All craned their necks to catch a glimpse of a not very beautiful bride squinting behind steel-rimmed glasses; but Teresa came upon her father's arm with her small narrow head held so high that all the middle-aged women caught the aura of love that gave winged lightness to her steps and drew out their handkerchiefs to weep for the tarnished vows of their own marriages. Joanna sat proud and dry-eyed, but Siri felt in her new gold mesh bag for a handkerchief and lamented the lack of poise which might redden her eyes. When the short semi-formal wedding was over and the minister had delivered his words of admonition, Siri realized that the moment of meeting Leif, should he be there, was imminent. After she had kissed Teresa and hugged the startled Brun, she felt suddenly old and unwanted, with the thought that both John and Brun had found life partners and she—only a little younger than both—had been washed aside by the romance of life to grow shrill-voiced like Ellie and waste her affection on a cat or two.

"Siri!" The familiar voice coursed through her like rich wine and she broke off a phrase to turn and find Leif's strong hand upon her arm. She looked up into a pair of blue eyes in which laughter had been caught and held. As she gave him her gloved hand, she felt as though they stood there completely unrelated to the people milling about them and could not remember afterward what their first words had been—only that she had had a kaleidoscopic picture of all their merry school days. She recalled his asking her how she liked it out West and her reply that she liked it fine. Then he turned to a short young girl who wore a hat with feathers falling over a large brim and said, "Andrea, I should like to have you meet Miss Gabrielson. Andrea Slate."

Andrea smiled hugely and said, "We have met. But I don't suppose Miss Gabrielson remembers a skating party in St. Paul." And Siri remembered a girl, somewhat younger, who had lived not far from Leif's parents. She had had a terrible time with her skates, coming to Leif again and again for help. The two women took each other's measure, the tall one not too successfully because she found it difficult to dissemble, the shorter one self-assured and slightly amused. At that moment Joanna came in a flurry of words to remind Siri that she was to pour at the north end of the table. Her aunt caught sight of Leif and the young girl beside him and murmured that it was nice to see him, not waiting for an introduction to his companion, but hurrying Siri down toward the basement.

Joanna had to be in the reception line in a moment and felt pleasantly distraught by her various duties (Roald said that was the only reason women like her insisted on large weddings), but not too distraught to wish that with all the things she had been able to teach Siri in her fourteen years of tutelage, she had been able to teach her to "pretend" at the right times. Heaven knows, she thought to herself, the girl carried on easily enough about other things— mooning over beautiful thunderstorms and pretending to like those awful prairies full of howling coyotes.

Although Leif had attempted to draw Andrea to the other end of the table, Andea wanted her coffee from Siri, not in so many words, of course, but she moved steadily in the direction she desired, until at last Leif and she stood waiting their turn. By this time, however, Siri had regained her composure and achieved a climb to the cold emotional plane to which her strong mind often drew her. It was a slightly different Siri who handed Andrea her cup and smiled coolly at Leif, who she knew was not particularly comfortable. She saw Tommy and Brun some minutes later laughing and talking with Leif, while Andrea stood waiting beside one of those gloomy church-basement windows showing dried grasses and rimose patches of snow streaked with dirt.

At last the bridal pair was gone, and the Hickenloopers and the Gabrielsons united for life by mutual concerns and pleasures. Joanna

wrapped a piece of wedding cake in a white linen napkin for Siri's
pillow that night. "Ach, nice wedding!" exclaimed Mrs. Hickenlooper, placing an arm about Siri's waist. "And for you we do it
next. Is that not so?" Siri shook her head, but Mrs. Hickenlooper
wagged a finger at her.

On the short ride home the family discussed the affair. "Nice little
wedding. Warmhearted and not fancy," pronounced Roald.

"That's the way Ava Hickenlooper wanted it," said Joanna. "She
told me she wanted it nice for Teresa, who always demanded so
little of them, but she didn't want anything pretentious so that people
could laugh at their attempts to be society. She's a sensible little
woman, and I'm glad to have Ava in the family!" said Joanna loyally.

Aunt Joanna slipped upstairs to have a proper chat with Siri before she fell asleep and leave the wedding cake beside her pillow.
"Leif isn't a bad sort," Joanna said, after she had adroitly turned
the conversation in the right direction, "but you will have to learn
how to handle him—and, anyway, I happen to know that Andrea
deliberately got that wedding invitation because Mr. Slate works
for the same plumbing concern Teresa's father works for. Siri," she
said, giving her niece an affectionate pat on a shoulder, "I think
you're a little too naive sometimes for your own good. I'm afraid
that's what comes of being an only child for so long in a household
of elderly people."

Siri agreed that it was quite possible, but after Joanna left, she
thought with amusement that many a vocal individual could easily
underestimate the thought processes of those who did not resolve
all issues with easy loquacity.

CHAPTER 16

The Inheritance

When the evening flyer slid into Scotts Lake only five minutes late, Siri had every expectation that Scott would be there; but when she alighted, the depot had a scattering of strangers, a young boy who appeared slightly familiar despite the dim lights and the fast-falling snowflakes which tended to hide him from view, Eddie with his handcar, and the station master who greeted her by name. "Want Eddie to take your luggage up to the hotel for the time being or leave it here?" he asked kindly.

At that moment the young lad whom she had seemed to recognize came into the bright light from the telegraph office. "I'll take them for you, Miss Gabrielson."

"Why, Bugs," she said with surprise, "are you in the habit of meeting trains?"

"No ma'am," he said. "I'll get your suitcase."

"I'm glad you were there," she commented as they made their way down one of the quiet residential streets. "It's so terribly dark on a night like this."

"Miss Gabrielson," he said suddenly, "your old man got in an awful brawl in Pa's place the day after Christmas."

Siri stopped short. "Oh, no!" she said. "Bugs, I'm not trying to be disloyal to my own family, but Mr. Vegg is not my own father. He's my stepfather, you know."

"Gee, I'm glad. Hey, let me carry that valise too, you look done in. Siri did not protest, and when she said nothing further, he looked abashed and somewhat ashamed of his role as purveyor of bad news. "Pa don't know how this brawl started, but your—Mr. Vegg, I mean, owes some fellows quite a lot of money. Of course, it ain't really legal, settin' up bets and all that."

"Was anyone hurt?"

"Mr. Vegg got a real shiner, and someone called Mr. Hocking and Mr. Hocking told him not to come into town again, not for a long, long while."

"Poor Mother!"

"I know," said Bugs sympathetically. "She's a real nice person— say is that girl of theirs *your* sister, Miss Gabrielson?" After a moment—"I sure didn't think so."

"Why? Sophie was in town with him?"

"No. I've seen her around, that's all."

When they reached the Lusk porch Bugs said, "I better be gettin' on home, Miss Gabrielson. But I had a kinda hunch you'd be in tonight, school tomorrow and all."

She thanked him several times, and as he was about to leave, he said suddenly, "Say, I almost forgot. Old man Rittenhouse had a heart attack."

"Is it very serious?"

"I dunno. Just thought you'd like to know."

Mr. Lusk had by now opened the front door with considerable caution, and when he discovered that it was Siri, he stepped out to the porch and helped her with the luggage. "Waited to the last moment to come back, didn't you?" he said with an attempt at humor. "Be all fresh for your morning classes." Mrs. Lusk's chocolate was three parts hard water, one part skimmed milk, and an afterthought of chocolate, but Siri accepted the hot drink gratefully. She asked them whether they knew how Mr. Rittenhouse was getting along, but the Lusks proved to be unaware of his attack, for they had been out in the country to call on friends. For a moment Siri considered walking up to the hotel to see Ellie, but thought better of it for several reasons, including the fact that it behooved her to be circumspect about any perambulations after nightfall—that is, if Tosten's post-Christmas escapade had become general knowledge.

After she had left her books and papers in readiness for the morning, she undressed, and lay down with little intention of sleeping. Both of the evening's news items had upset her greatly—not that she had been unaware of trouble and disaster at any time in her life, but events seemed to touch her at this time in a personal and singular way, now that she was without the support of her family. She recalled how difficulties were aired and discussed in the little Gabrielson sittingroom between the parlor and the diningroom; and if the family did not arrive at any solution, they did achieve more solidarity. Poor Scott, she thought, with old Mr. Rittenhouse ill! She could not imagine the house without his dominating personality. What had Scott's childhood been like, she wondered. Aunt Joanna on the last night of their little visit together had said, "Siri, why would a mature person like this young Mr. Rittenhouse you mentioned (*I* mentioned, she thought!) be content with a small practice in a small town?" Aunt Joanna had been very clever about making her opinions known, speaking often in generalities.

Eventually the conversation had turned to Leif, as Siri had known it would, and Joanna had said with some perspicacity, "I don't think Mrs. Borland was ever really comfortable around you. Sometimes when you had been there for Sunday dinner, you used to say, 'I don't think Leif's mother really approves of girls going to college.'"

As they had visited, their talk naturally turned to the encounter at the wedding, with Aunt Joanna saying, "She was a forward little thing, and did you notice that in this age of free necks, her neck was a little too free—at least for a daytime affair in a church?"

Siri had always appreciated her aunt's loyalty in times of trouble. In this respect Joanna was different from Dagmar, whose loyalty to her daughters was a matter of mood, she remembered. "If you want Leif, I suspect all you have to do is wriggle your little finger, especially after what has happened," she said significantly.

Whatever she knows, thought Siri, she is bursting to tell it—with a little persuasion, of course. "Oh?" questioned Siri blandly.

"I don't suppose I ought to tell you. Some of it may be only gossip, and I don't imagine that repeating it would be the *Christian thing* to do."

"I suppose not," agreed Siri.

"On the other hand—" Siri took up the square of wool which lay beside her on the drum table and began to work on a piece of crocheting which might, by some miracle, grow into an afghan some day. "On the other hand, I think you should know the truth just in case Leif and you patch it up some day—not that as a *wife* you should hold it against him, but still you'd have the right to know."

"Are you sure you want to tell me then?" asked Siri.

"That's what I'm trying to say—that it might be my *duty* to tell you! You remember the girl he brought to the wedding? Well," said

Joanna, taking a deep breath, "Leif's mother is a friend of the Mrs. Olafson who raises Plymouth Rocks and sells me eggs when I do a lot of extra baking." Siri thought with amusement that they were getting down to essentials, now that the source of information had been indicated. "Well, Mrs. Olafson said that Mrs. Borland agreed that Leif and Andrea *have* gotten into it pretty deep. In fact," continued Aunt Joanna, lowering her voice and glancing toward the diningroom and kitchen to make sure they were still alone in the house, "they've been using the Olafson cottage as a place of rendesvouz."

"If Mrs. Olafson is allowing them to use her cottage, *she* shouldn't be carrying tales abroad!" said Siri hotly.

"Friends have always used their cottage. If you'll think back, you've warmed yourself at their fireplace after many a skating party."

"You mean they go there alone," said Siri. "It might not be the circumspect thing to do, but they're both grown up."

Joanna sighed. "You make it hard for me, Siri. What I've been trying to tell you is that they have been using it for *immoral* purposes." Siri gave her aunt a quizzical look. "Well, to put it bluntly. They've slept there."

"Any proof?" asked Siri.

"If you're going to be so skeptical—well, I'm sorry I told you," said Aunt Joanna, tossing her embroidery on the sofa cushion beside her. "You surely don't *approve* of anything as wrong as that, I hope!" Her aunt's stare was so steady and demanding that Siri felt for a moment very small and vulnerable. "I'm sure that going out to Dakota hasn't been the right move for you. I opposed it last summer and I still oppose it."

"What has that to do with Leif and Andrea?"

Aunt Joanna searched desperately for words of logic to cover her non sequitur pronouncement. "Well," she said firmly, "if you had stayed in Minnesota, Leif wouldn't be taking Andrea out to the Olafson cottage."

Although Siri was on the point of quipping, "No, he'd be trying to take *me*," she saw how seriously Aunt Joanna was taking the whole matter and said, "I'm glad you told me—I'm sorry for them both if they're in trouble."

"Of course you are," said Joanna, appearing relieved. "But being sorry for them doesn't make what they're doing *right*." She walked over to the bay window and pinched a yellowed leaf off a house plant. "And since what's done is done, it wouldn't be right holding all this against Leif if you two should make up again." Returning to the sofa, she picked up her embroidery and folded it neatly into her sewing basket. "You're old enough to realize, Siri, that most men are going to have experience in *such matters* before they settle down with one woman." Aunt Joanna came over to the chair where Siri sat with her knees drawn up behind intertwined fingers. "You know, your Uncle Roald and I love you like we love our boys," she said impulsively. "Well, I suspect it's time to fix supper."

Siri watched her aunt's straight figure move toward the dining-room. "I know you do," she said—and, then, "I'll be right in to help you." But even after she heard Aunt Joanna rattling pots and pans, she still sat staring out the front window to the snowy yard below. There were so many subjects she would like to chat about—but with whom? Aunt Joanna, she reflected, was not alone in handing out moral pronouncements as if they were immutable laws. Every home in the land, perhaps, had its august lawmakers; and what was law in one domestic kingdom did not necessarily constitute law in another. And though Aunt Joanna's tale was both depressing and disillusioning, Siri felt that the whole matter of moral judgment was most puzzling. And what was one to do about the "legal" voice that constituted one's conscience? And had she been able to talk with Aunt Joanna without restraint on either side, could her aunt have pointed out why *Andrea's experience* was less excusable than Leif's?

And while she was thinking about all this, why not ask herself what *she* would do if Scott and she were tempted beyond discretion? Of course, she thought, that was what Aunt Joanna was getting at when she brought up my going to Dakota—it was another way of saying, Dakota puts you out of our reach. Siri untangled her legs and rose from the easy-chair, stretching to ease the tension induced by their conversation. As she neared the kitchen, she thought: maybe even Ellie McCarthy has a past.

❁   ❁   ❁

When Siri finished her first day of teaching after the holidays, she walked to the post office to gather her mail and then went on to the hotel to see Ellie. They greeted each other warmly, though Ellie took some care to disguise her pleasure by pushing TC off the lobby desk. "He hasn't moved an inch since you left for Minnesota." She studied Siri shrewdly. "Well, have a good time? Bring me any *lefse?*" Siri pulled aside her muff and handed Ellie a candy tin full of Aunt Joanna's Christmas treats.

"From Aunt Joanna," she said happily. "How is Mr. Rittenhouse?"

"Holding his own. That's all. Scott was in a few minutes ago and said to tell you hello. They're talking about taking Charlie to Mayo's when he feels well enough to be moved." She sighed profoundly. "The news surely put a coating of gloom on this town."

When Siri left the hotel and started homeward she saw that the sun was setting behind a threatening bank of clouds. "More weather," she said to herself, not so much angry with the prospect of a storm as disturbed by the pervading atmosphere of sadness that seemed to lie upon everything. A small town, she thought to herself, is like a family, and when something fells its most important member there is a heaviness upon all.

When Mrs. Lusk was dishing up supper, she went into her room and skimmed over the mail. She had read her mother's short letter when she was in the hotel, but had postponed reading an enclosure, a letter from Kari Moen. It proved to be a collection of lachrymose paragraphs, most of them lamenting the changes along the fjord and the changes in Kari herself, apparently all for the worse. With her effusions of sorrow out of the way, Kari at last got down to the main issue: she was booking passage on a steamer in the spring and coming to America. Mikjell, she wrote, was now a man of some means and her faith in her son was vindicated. Naturally she would stop off to see the Gabrielsons in Minneapolis and hoped to see them all there—Elisabet, Sophie, Siri, and Tosten! Siri smiled at the widow's disregard of distances in America—but hadn't they all been like that when they first came, completely ignorant about the length and the breadth and the sweeping immensity of America? "Siri! Siri!" called Mrs. Lusk cheerfully. "You must come right away. The macaroni with cheese is growing cold!"

The storm she had seen on the horizon raged into Scotts Lake that night, trying its teeth on all the storm sashes and doors, and then went blustering southeast-ward. By Friday the snow lay in hard-packed drifts and a cold winter sun shone through the school-house windows; the boxelder outside her room looked more gaunt and wind-whipped than ever, but upon its branches a little sparrow hopped up and down with summertime grace.

On Friday afternoon she left her books at the Lusks and went down Main Street, angling off toward the livery stable. The weather looked settled enough for her to go out to the farm by herself, and her mother *had* sounded very lonely. She peered into the barnlike structure and discovered Harald wrestling with some harness. "Hello, there," she said pleasantly. "You have a customer, Harald. I'd like to rent a cutter and go out to Mother's tomorrow morning."

He looked away for a moment and then he said sternly, "I ain't got a sleigh to rent, Miss Gabrielson."

"Is the snow too deep for a saddle horse?"

"I ain't got a saddle horse."

"You're just kidding, Harald."

"I yust ain't got a ting." He followed her out into the snow by the doorway. His handle-bar mustache began to tremble, and he blinked his round blue eyes several times.

"Yes?" she said expectedly.

"Yust run along, because I ain't even got a vord to say." She stood uncertainly for a minute and then she started back toward Main Street. Now, what was the matter with Harald, she thought—or, maybe, what was the matter with Siri Gabrielson?

As she was puzzling over Harald's strange behavior, she ran into Scott coming out of Mercer's. She could not get over the little tremor of pleasure this meeting gave her. "How is your father?" she asked.

"Getting along as well as can be expected and apparently a little on the mend today."

"What brought it on, or don't you know, Scott?"

"Christmas," said Scott. "One or two pheasants. A crown roast of pork. To say nothing of plum pudding and mince pie." He smiled in the familiar easy way Siri enjoyed. "Dad always said that if he couldn't eat what he wanted and smoke what he wanted, we might as well write his epitaph." Before they parted, he said, "The way things are, I can't say when I'll see you, but seeing you is wonderful. One of these days I must hear about your Minnesota visit."

On Sunday about one o'clock Charlie Rittenhouse sat up in bed with two plump goosedown pillows supporting his back. "I'll lick this thing yet, Vinnie, but I need a little help. Bring me a glass of wine and then some of whatever is cooking downstairs."

"Do you think you should?"

"Of course I think I should or I wouldn't have asked you. Where's Scott?"

"Mailing the letter you wanted mailed."

When she came back with a tray he studied it critically. "Is that all the damn roast beef you can spare?"

"It's more than you should have," said Vinnie as she flicked open a linen napkin.

"Coffee?"

"I don't know about that," she said uncertainly.

"All right, you old hen," he said affectionately. "Sit down, then, and keep me company." He looked better, she thought; and a Charlie who didn't take interest in food was no Charlie at all.

"The weather is beautiful today," she said. "It's something I couldn't get used to about Dakota when I first came to stay with you—that deceptive winter sun shining so brightly on the coldest day. It's twenty below out there," she said.

"Coffee now, Vinnie? No, don't be so quick about taking away this tray. She watched him start eating again, cutting the thin slices of meat carefully. The veins stood out on his hands, and there was an angry red spot on his lower left cheek. "Maybe I better call Dr. Torrence first—" she began uncertainly.

"Maybe you better not," he said. "Vinnie, if an old codger like me can't make up his mind about whether he should have a cup of coffee or not, what is there left of him? Tell me that."

"All right, Charlie. I'll bring you a cup."

When she had left, he looked out at the dazzling sweep of plains and the small white hills against the blue horizon. There isn't a rod of land for twenty-five miles around here whose pedigree I don't know, he said to himself. As soon as he was up and around, he wanted to see what could be done about bringing in electricity. Of course, there'd be some argument and a lot of struggle, but there was a lot of fight left in him. He reached for a cigar in a box beside the bed.

When Vinnie brought in the steaming coffee, she found him slouched over the silver tray, from which a thin trickle of gravy ran upon the bed. Before she rushed down the stairway to call Dr. Torrence, she threw the burning cigar into the coffee cup and stamped vigorously on the rug. "The old fool could have cremated us all," she said tenderly.

Nothing was ever simple, thought Scott—not even death. His mother had been a Presbyterian in a town where there was no Presbyterian church; his father had been a Lutheran once, but had never taken kindly to the local church since the time it became embroiled in so many petty arguments that a man who could make large problems seem small could not imagine enjoying a situation where small problems grew so large. So the Methodists buried him.

The funeral was on Thursday afternoon, and school had been dismissed because the land on which the school stood had once been Charlie's and the little park beside the city hall had been donated and landscaped by Charlie. Even one of Charlie's bitterest critics, the town ne'er-do-well who used Charlie's park more than anyone else, said begrudgingly, "I have always said, and I say it again, no man should ever be allowed to grow as big as Charlie Rittenhouse has in this town, but if we gotta put up with that kind of inequality, guess Charlie was the best of his kind." He liked the sound of his words so well that when he went home to supper he said them again to Hope, his wife, who was late in dishing up the meal for her philosopher husband and the six children because the funeral in town had given her more washings, everyone needing to dress up for the occasion.

Siri sat with the Lusks in the little Methodist church near the park. She saw the handsome brunette twins again, who, she discovered, were Scott's nieces from Illinois. She saw many of the people she had met at Mr. Rittenhouse's birthday party, and Ellie with the family. She saw many faces of her own countrymen, recognizing the Andersons and the Larsons and the Oscarsons by a kind of telepathy.

She saw the Schwartzes and the Zumpfs and the Eilers, whom she also recognized by something indefinably there in manner and carriage. She saw Tosten, too, with someone Ellie later told her was an Egelmeier from up near Golag. She had wanted to catch her stepfather before he left to ask about her mother, but he had disappeared in the crowd. Out in the cemetery, where the sun shone from behind a curving swath of pink and red clouds denoting tomorrow's wind, she saw Scott's face upon her for a second and wished in the way of a woman with a tender and romantic mind that she had been kinder to him that day on the hill.

When she left the Lusks she told them not to expect her for supper, that she would go up to the schoolhouse and write tomorrow's work on the blackboard and perhaps eat a sandwich in the hotel if she was hungry. She worked in her room for almost an hour, and then, instead of walking up to the hotel as she had planned, she set out on a small country road and walked until the sun had set. When she came back to Main Street she saw that it was unusually busy, for in the way of farm folk, many had lingered to trade and talk. She entered the hotel through the kitchen entrance and found Mrs. Swanson almost unable to keep up with the orders coming in from the busy dining room. She took off her coat, rolled up her sleeves, and set to helping her dish up plates. When Ellie came in, she did not look at all surprised, but said, "Good girl!" and gave her a pat on her shoulder. The three of them toiled in the kitchen until almost nine, and then they sat down and ate together. "I should have had my head examined," said Ellie. "I never thought of extra help." Before she left, Mrs. Swanson told Siri that she and Harald would be glad to drive her out to the farm on Sunday if she cared to go. She was about to mention Harald's strange behavior, but decided Mrs. Swanson had survived enough problems for one day without adding another for her tired feet to carry home.

On Friday and Saturday the dry snow blew around in powdery swirls and the wind cracked brittle branches and sang a January melody in the telephone lines; but no new snow fell, and on Sunday after church they drove out to the farm. After dinner was over Harald and Mrs. Swanson took Sophie out for a short ride, leaving Siri alone with her mother. Although Siri felt that Mrs. Swanson had done it to enable them to have a little time together, she was grateful for a little private chat with her mother.

Elisabet had seemed perturbed ever since they came, and when they were alone, she told Siri that she had not been able to sleep because of a terrible thing that had long lain upon her conscience. Siri deduced that the matter was of no small consequence, but that her mother would have to tell it in her own way, so she continued setting the table and speculating with compassionate amusement about this awful thing Elisabet had done. "You will never understand, Siri, until I am gone and you are a wife yourself."

"Perhaps that *is* so," answered Siri, "but first I shall have to know what I shall never understand."

"Well, your Uncle Nels," she began, "you know we saw him before we left, there in the old seaman's home in Bergen. I suppose you have thought, daughter, that the sale of Fjeldstrand gave us *all* our money for our journeyings and the farm here, but when Tosten's gambling debts had been paid, there was not too much to be gained out of Fjeldstrand." Siri felt a shadow fall upon her and thought, oh, no—but let her mother continue.

"You yourself know that Tosten was never one to tell me anything, and even Grandma had a way of treating me, her own daughter, like a child. But of course *you* wouldn't remember that, for you were too young. There must be some weakness in me—" she said sadly. "Well, it was like this, you see. Tosten left me to visit with old Nels, for he had no wish to see him." At this point she began to wipe her eyes. "Nels was delighted to see the child and me, you may be sure, and even more delighted to know that within some weeks' time we should be seeing you in America." She looked at Siri with the saddest of eyes. "You know what store he and Guro set by you. Well, the upshot of it was that he gave me a packet of money for you, something he and Guro had set aside for your inheritance—" At this point she began to weep, but shook off Siri's hand upon her arm.

"It might be better," she said, "before you put your arm about me, to see whether, when I am through, you'd rather strike your old mother."

"Oh, Mother!"

"But it happened that I fell very sick upon a rough sea, and Tosten, who is very clever about such things, found the money which was meant for you." She gave Siri such a hopeless look that the girl wondered how her mother could have kept her wits, worrying as she had. "I discovered the loss of some of the money when I unpacked in New York. But Tosten painted such a picture of empires of wheat and cattle out in the West and assured me so convincingly that in a year's time he could double what Nels had left you, that at last he won me over. You must also understand, daughter, the fear and the loneliness I felt in this strange and busy land, and that anything looked better than being left at the mercy of strangers should Tosten grow wilful and angry."

"Is it all gone? All of it?" asked Siri.

"No," she said with alacrity, "I have hidden a hundred American dollars which you must take this day. And soon Tosten must get the rest together for you." At this juncture Siri was not really listening, but attempting to discover whether there would have been time for Uncle Nels to have a letter of thanks from her before he died had not the money miscarried. She sank into a chair and put her head in her hands and began to weep. Elisabet came up to her softly, patting her gently on the head. "I deserve it all," she said, "for I have been weak."

Siri told her finally that she must keep the hundred dollars, that the money really did not matter, for America seemed always to have been good to the Gabrielsons. The thing that really mattered was whether there had been time for a letter to reach Uncle Nels, "How terrible it is to think that he might have considered me ungrateful!" She looked up at her mother and said, "Can you not remember how good he and Tante Guro were to me? Ah, how they smiled and made merry for me on that long, long journey across the land and the sea!"

"Don't you think I, too, have such kindnesses to remember!" exclaimed her mother. "I who have more than twice the years upon me?" She brightened a little and said, "Let me fetch an almanac, for it is quite possible that he could not have heard from you. She rummaged around in an old chest and came back with the almanac and a stubby pencil in her hand. "Now we shall see," she said, using the comforting tone one uses for a small child with a big sorrow. "We left Bergen on this day, and we came to America on this day, I think. About a week later we would have been in Minnesota—now, let's see." She bit on the pencil stub and frowned. "He could not have heard for over four weeks at least, and he died on the first of June."

Siri took the almanac out of her hands and studied the markings on it. "He had *some* days of waiting, mother, and this is what I am bitter about." Her mother's eyes had such a woebegone look that Siri said gently, "Better see to the coffee, Mother. The hundred you must keep and hide so well that—"

"Perhaps it is better that you keep it for us—for me," she amended quickly.

"No," said Siri. "This you must do for me: put it away yourself so that if any emergency arises, you have it. Do you always eat well out here? It has worried me."

"We have had enough. I am thrifty, and Tosten always has a little jingling in his pockets." And with a small return of wry humor, "And always hope for more!"

They saw that the sleigh was back, but Sophie was not with them. "Elisabet, I could do nothing with the child. Before I knew it, she had leaped out of the sleigh and was running out across a field where a boy was shooting rabbits," fretted Mrs. Swanson.

"Don't worry about that," said Elisabet. "That was the youngest Egelmeier boy, and he is sure to have a horse somewhere. Together they will ride back to his house, and she will find her father there." She invited them to the coffee table. "They tell me Mrs. Egelmeier cooks a fine rabbit dish—*Hasen*-something, I think."

They left a little before sunset, with the light blue look of spring in the sky and a small drift of clouds catching the blue and rose of the setting sun. Siri never ceased admiring the whiteness of the prairie snow, which seemed to lie for weeks at a time untouched by streaks of soil, unless a strong wind after a thaw and the return of freezing weather blew veins of dust into it. She had little to say and there was a look of sadness about her mouth. The brother and sister exchanged knowing glances, and finally Harald put a cautious arm around the girl's shoulder and said, "You must not be sad, girl.

If I were a young man and as handsome as I was vunce"—here he looked to his sister for confirmation—"I would marry you and make you happy."

Mrs. Swanson began to laugh heartily, and Siri joined with her. Harald felt so exhilarated by the success of his safe proposal that he gave the horse a light tap and set the bells to jangling.

The end of the first semester was soon upon them, and Siri was extraordinarily busy with reviewing, testing, and grading. Occasionally she thought about her mother on the farm and realized that she had not asked her how much Uncle Nels *had* left her! She must remember some time when they were alone to broach the subject delicately, for she treasured everything the old couple had ever done for her and wanted to tuck away in her mind a further measure of their love for her.

She had a letter from Aunt Joanna saying that they had missed her greatly and had been talking about some arrangement whereby Siri could return to Minnesota next year—if need be, perhaps Roald might find some work for Tosten in the lumber yard he had purchased recently. "This will surprise you greatly," Aunt Joanna went on, "but on Sunday last Leif appeared with Tommy and said he was planning to write to you. I cannot say that I felt any warmness toward him, not after the way he flaunted that girl at the wedding." She went on to say that Teresa and Brun appeared happy (How can you tell, wondered Siri). "Oh, yes, I had a small note of thanks from your friend Ellen McCarthy, and she said Mr. Rittenhouse had died. I can't remember that you wrote us about that," scolded Aunt Joanna. "You must remember we are always interested in *all* the news from Scotts Lake." Although Siri did not haunt the post office, she went regularly enough to pick up her mail and wondered how she would feel were she to discover a letter with Leif's familiar handwriting.

During the second week in February the weather turned warm and springlike; the sloughs were full, and some of the draws ran with little creeks. On Saturday morning when she was drying her hair out in the back yard (Mrs. Lusk predicted pneumonia), Scott left his car running at the curb and rang the bell to see whether Siri would like to ride with him on an errand to the county seat. Mrs.

Lusk made several valiant attempts to keep him from seeing the girl with her hair down; but she was no match for a Rittenhouse, apparently, for Scott had gone around the side of the house to the back before Mrs. Lusk could apprise Siri of the danger. "Good!" said Scott, when he had properly surprised Siri with a brush in her hand and her hair shining brightly from its vinegar rinse. "I never did like hats." She understood that he was referring to an occasion in the past, smiled, and excused herself to prepare for the ride. Upstairs she drew her wavy hair into a figure eight at the back, slipped into a suit she had worn in the fall, and threw a duster over her shoulder. In no time at all she was ready, with Mrs. Lusk standing behind the lace curtains and watching them leave. "Sometimes, Esmer, I think that longlegged girl of ours bears watching," she said.

"You can never tell about foreigners," said Mr. Lusk. Their *mores* may be quite different from ours. Anyway, higher education is wasted on women, and whatever she has done, I am sure it proves it."

The roads were still quite muddy in lower areas, and Scott was obliged to maneuver carefully. "Things have settled down a little for us," he remarked when they were on a long sweep of hill. "The twins are back in school, and my sister Maude left yesterday. I'd like to have had you meet, but you can imagine that there was a lot to be done." He glanced at her. "How are things out on the farm?" She assured him that everything was all right, and waited for him to go on talking.

He glanced at the brown hills interspersed with traces of snow in the hollows and shaded places. "Dad came out here in the days of sod huts and buffalo chips for fuel. He practiced some ruthless economies in those early years and so did the Scotts, who had the homestead next to him. Both families did well, but it never was as easy as it looks afterwards. Later when lean years had others clamoring to sell, he dug into his savings and bought them out." He paused and looked at her. "In a way, that may be taking advantage of others' hard luck, but I don't think so."

"I can't see why, if he gave them what they wanted for the land."

"As I understand the cracker barrel critics, however, people don't want *enough* when they're desperate and actually ask less than it's worth."

"But what's *worth?*" asked Siri, taking a leaf from Mr. Lusk's favorite book.

"Spoken like a true Rittenhouse." He laughed.

"Something has been bothering me," said Siri, as they reached a newly graded road. "You know there is no apostrophe in Scotts Lake. Why?" She grinned impishly. "That kind of oversight can throw an English lesson on possessives completely off its course."

"Just practicality, I suppose. Chances are, people would leave out the apostrophe, anyway. This legalizes the omission with the United States Post Office." He passed a horse and buggy and waved at the occupants. "I hear from Mr. Willis that you are doing right well as a teacher—a little unconventional, perhaps, but—"

"Unconventional, am I? What do you mean?"

"Got your dander up, didn't I? Oh, I don't know what I mean—guess the youngsters have fun learning, that's all, and in some pedagogical areas that's a crime. Lawyers, too, you know are sometimes accused of putting on a show. Just keep it up, Siri, whatever awful thing you're doing. The boss seems to like it, and so does the town." He could see that she was a little troubled by the whole thing, and he was sorry he had started it, so he concluded with, "I've had a few old beldames at Scotts High myself, and sometimes I think these desicated old minds get high standards mixed up with their own ego satisfactions—in fact, if you substituted rag dolls for lively youngsters some morning, they wouldn't notice the substitution, but go right on teaching."

"I have been lucky," she said, "because I have had so many dedicated teachers, and each one of them had a personality that reached out and beckoned us to follow into new and curious lands of learning. To teach like that is so very simple and so very difficult."

She felt Scott's arm move tenderly across her shoulder and gave his closeness no particular analysis except to realize that they had achieved a rapport on this little expedition that had never been achieved by them before. When they reached the county seat, he left her to her own devices, and she made a leisurely tour of the two little business streets and their stores, meeting him for lunch in a little cafe that boasted home cooking.

On the way home the spell cast upon them in the morning had not been broken. "Siri," he said finally, "I keep on talking about Dad and the early days; and when I was in the register of deed's office it occurred to me that I had never asked you about your childhood and why you came to America."

"What an odd time to think of that!" She laughed. Yet she began to tell him, seriously enough, about the family at Fjeldstrand and the chatting stream and the old *saeter* path.

When she had finished, he said, "You can have your misty sea and steep precipice. Siri, my girl, I'll settle for your Bergit!"

She felt an inordinate life of spirit at the way Scott had trod through her light tale of reminiscence, to stand, as it were, beside a rocking chair, where sat an old woman with restless hands and a probing mind.

CHAPTER 17

The Swing

March had been so blustery and unpredictable that Siri found herself unable to get out to the farm; so she wrote Elisabet at weekly intervals, relaying news from Minnesota. In turn, Elisabet sent on a letter she had received from Gunhild, and Siri was much flattered by Gunhild's naming her youngest child after her, but a little amused by the strange musical effect of "Siri Eng" for the combination seemed to float like a bird call.

Late in the month Siri found a letter in her box that could have originated only with Leif. It was not a letter to be read as one walked down a windy street hanging on to skirts and coat, nor was it a letter to be read under Ellie's surveillance—and she *had* promised Ellie she would come by. Even unopened and lying between her fingers, the letter exercised a curious emotional effect upon her, like a bit of mercury held between one's fingers. The wind, the letter, and the prospect of a coffee chat made Siri feel light-hearted and swift of foot. Though so many were heard to complain about the incessant winds of Dakota (Mrs. Lusk said they wore out her bed sheets), Siri liked them: hurrying down from Canada, they raced across the hills and plains; and where men believed themselves foolishly permanent, the winds shook trees and rattled doors and windows and roused men from their dreams at night. She often recalled her first evening in Scotts Lake when she had heard the traveling prairie wind humming in her ears and how she had suddenly stopped beside the hotel to listen. Since then she had never stopped listening, any more than her grandmother Bergit had ceased hearing the sea because the sea was as familiar as her own breathing. Elisabet had been reluctant ever to tell her about the years following her departure to America; but this she had wrung from her mother, that Grandmother had slept away peacefully on the stormiest of fall nights.

Now the wind literally blew her into the entry of the hotel, racing ahead of her to lift a calendar off the wall and startle Ellie into yelling from the lobby, "Good grief, girl! Close that door!"

"I did once."

"Give it a good slam." After Siri had taken off her coat, Ellie said, "Well, I got to thinking about something and that's why I wanted you to come down this evening." She passed a piece of Mrs. Swanson's proud angel food cake to Siri. "I've lived too long to expect anyone to commiserate with me, but I have sat here—child, girl, and spinster—until I can taste the wood of that stool behind the lobby desk. Ellie, I say to myself a hundred times a day, is this what you were born for: an old wooden hotel where the moths and you are fighting for the last square of blanket and the termites are forming battalions for an Armageddon over the last splinter of wood?" Siri grinned. "It may be funny to you, child, but hear me out anyway. I have heard the whistle of that danged flyer for about thirty years—tootin' across the wilderness, shrieking on lonely nights—and has it ever picked up Ellie McCarthy and taken her anywhere?"

"Hasn't it—ever?" asked Siri innocently.

"Oh, it took me East once to one of those blasted academies for ladies so popular in bygone days, but what *I* wanted to know, an academy never taught. Well, anyway, Siri, Mr. Willis said you have a week at Easter and Easter comes before the traveling men start pussyfooting in with sample cases and mouldy stories, so how about us taking off for a little vacation—maybe to Livingston and a peek at the Yellowstone River? That's where this medical paragon of yours lives now, isn't it? We'll stay in a fancy hotel and see how it looks on the other side of the desk. How about it?"

"I'll have to go home and count my savings, but it sounds wonderful, Ellie!" She began dancing around the room. "Mountains! Mountains! Mountains!" she sang.

"Honey, go ahead. That's how I feel," cried Ellie.

"Pardon me, but is this the place where the bacchanals are being held this year?" asked Scott.

"Sure is," said Ellie happily. "Pull up a mossy stone and join the rites."

Scott sat down at the table while Ellie poured a cup of coffee. Absentmindedly, he pushed aside Siri's mail and caught a glimpse of the words *Leif Borland* . . . . *Minnesota* and thought, so that's what a letter does to that brown-eyed girl over there. Ellie saw his sober look and sat down to explain what she and Siri had hatched up.

"I think that's fine, and exactly what you should do under the circumstances, Ellie," he said, a look of secrecy passing between them. The three of them chatted about timetables and accommodations until he observed Siri's eyes growing remote and sober, as Scott had discovered her eyes frequently did.

"I was just thinking about Mother. Maybe I shouldn't go so far away. Especially at Easter."

"I'll look in on her once," promised Scott. "I have business over near Golag." So it was practically settled.

"Mrs. Lusk's ham-bone dinner will grow cold," said Siri, glancing at the wall clock. "And I do mean bone." She picked up her mail and rose. "Ellie, this has been about the happiest day of my life."

"Don't say that," said Scott. "It excludes some I remember," and he winked at the older woman. "I'll walk you down past the depot. Don't have my car today." So after arranging for more conspiratorial meetings with Ellie, she walked down the wind-swept street with Scott. "Siri," he said, "I haven't forgotten what you told me about your childhood. You carry a disgraceful sense of responsibility on those young shoulders. Your mother once made a choice—I think a poor choice and you honestly think so too. You can't go around protecting her against every shock."

"But she *is* my mother and I love her."

"Just be careful that you don't go around thinking that two wrongs can make a right.

"What do you mean, Scott?" she asked, catching on to her coat, which threatened to blow over her head.

They stopped at the street where he had to turn off. "I don't know exactly. I guess my profession makes a man too aware of trouble. Lawyers are always extricating people from their own or others' foolishness." He tipped his hat and started down the street. Suddenly he called back to her against the wind, "And remember one Scott on hand is better than two Leifs in Minnesota!" She made a silly face at him and hurried toward home.

On the evening they were to leave, Scott and his Aunt Vinnie entertained the travelers for dinner. It was a gesture well meant, but it did not leave Ellie and Siri in as good spirits as they had been prior to their coming; for the house seemed to miss old Charlie Rittenhouse, his noisy laughter, his good cigars, and his robust stories about the good old days. Yet his aunt remarked before Scott drove them to the train that it was one of the best times she had had since her brother's death. "Something has to be done about this," she said, "for Scott and I cannot continue living alone in this big old place. We're hoping the twins will come out again this summer."

There was quite a gathering at the depot when the evening train pulled in. Siri realized that Ellie's trip was the talk of Scotts Lake, and there were many last-minute offers to run the hotel for her, much joking about Ellie's new hat, and many warnings about not stealing linens and soap. When almost everyone had kissed Ellie goodbye (and some taking advantage of the general bussing to kiss Siri, as well—especially Scott), the two stood at last in the chilly vestibule waving goodbye.

Eventually they went to bed in their lower berth, laughing uproariously over the difficulties encountered in finding room for their long limbs. This continued until someone tapped on the partition between them and a masculine voice hissed, "Quiet, please." Ellie said it was the first time she had ever slept that close to a man, and wasn't it exciting? Siri could not sleep at all because it was necessary to keep her eye open for the first glimpse of a mountain, so Ellie remarked, "Why waste our time sleeping? We can do that at home." They rose long before dawn and donned their clothes in what amounted to a private dressing room and went through several sleeping cars with their assortment of snores and groans to sit out on the observation platform bundled in scarves and coats. Their morning zeal also enabled them to be the first to answer the dining-car call. All in all, they were foolish, hilarious, and completely happy. Siri's first sight of a mountain and a stream coursing over a bed of bright stones set her to searching for her handkerchief like another Kari Moen, until Ellie threatened to range through the cars and find more pleasant company. "Ellie," said Siri, dabbing at her eyes, "I'm crying because I am so happy."

When the train pulled into the station, there were John and

Maryanne White, one of the prettiest blondes Siri had ever seen. Ellie delivered her ultimatum almost immediately. "You young people go on. I want it strictly understood that I am on my own, and no one needs to worry about me at all." She started down the platform, her scuttle hat held inordinately high, but when John and Siri caught up with her and marched her back to the waiting conveyance, Ellie looked extraordinarily pleased.

That evening she curled her hair with an iron held grimly above a coal-oil lamp she had inveigled from a bellhop. "Siri," she said, spitting on her finger to test the curling iron, "do you know *the park* is above us?"

"Or course."

"You did?"

"It's closed this time of year, Ellie." A few mornings afterward, however, a carriage awaited them shortly after dawn, and the delectable Maryanne and her parents picked them up in front of the hotel for the tortuous and somewhat frightening ride parkward. When Ellie discovered the frightening nature of the terrain, she closed her eyes and told Siri to look for both of them and tell her about it later. Gradually, however, Ellie's courage overcame her caution and she began to exclaim loudly over the tumbling stream, so that although it continued to tumble, no one was able to hear it.

"We won't be able to see much this trip," said Mr. White—just a few little geysers. Everything's closed during the winter season."

"I didn't know the geysers closed too," said Ellie.

"The hotels," whispered Siri.

Mr. White was able to show them a few phenomena; but Ellie had an uncomfortable feeling treading on *terra loosa*, as she called it, and although she thanked them again and again for showing her the sights, she told Maryanne privately that this was the first time she realized God had not finished his work and sealed up all the holes in the earth. Of course, Maryanne and the Whites realized that Ellie was a lot smarter than she pretended to be.

By the third day of their visit in Livingston, Ellie was searching the paper to see if someone—just someone—didn't want to trade a hotel in Livingston for one in Scotts Lake. Siri knew how she felt, because she never, never wanted to go back—not to the plains, not

to Minnesota, not even to Norway.. There was something about this
country that spoke to her so fervently she felt like going out and
talking back. Whenever she went walking or riding, she kept on
saying to the river, to the trees, and to the mountains: I love you,
I love you, I love you!

On their last evening, the Whites invited them to dinner in their
charming and comfortable home, and afterward they listened to John
and Maryanne discussing their wedding plans for the twenty-fifth
of July. "Of course I'm young, and it's going to take some time to
establish myself, but I have a few more patients every month. I think
I'll be able to give Maryanne the kind of life she wants." Watching
them, Siri concluded that what they really wanted was simply each
other. It amused her to compare John's open adoration of Maryanne
with Brun's matter-of-fact acceptance of Teresa, yet she felt that
her younger cousin was equally as devoted to his sweetheart as John
was to Maryanne.

After they had left the Whites, Ellie and Siri talked long into the
night. "It's odd," said Ellie once, "how you and I strike it off together,
for most girls your age wouldn't enjoy rattling around with an old
maid like me." She added, "I suspect you're used to being with older
people, aren't you?" Although Siri had talked about various aspects
of her childhood, their conversations had rarely been confidential.
Later Ellie asked, "There's a young man back East, isn't there?"

"How did you know?"

"There has to be. Anyway, Scott told me."

"He doesn't know anything about it."

"Sometimes Scott knows a lot more than you think. Old CJ was
like that too."

Siri found herself telling Ellie about hearing from Leif. "After
all this time!" she exclaimed, sitting up with a pillow propped behind her back and listening to the sounds of the town and smelling
the cold air that billowed through the curtains.. Ellie lay on her back
staring at the ceiling and thinking that she would never feel at
home anywhere but in a hotel. She turned her face and noticed
the girl's attractive profile and the long hair caught up in a ribbon
she used at night. "He said the oddest thing—I'm talking about Leif,"
she said dreamily. Something about waiting to write because he had

something to get out of his system. I think he means a girl named Andrea. I saw them together at my cousin's wedding."

"What's Leif like?" asked Ellie, but her mind was really upon the hotel. Why hadn't her dad gone farther west, she wondered.

"Oh, he's very tall and well built and looks awfully sure of himself. He walks with a hint of—well, not swagger. Like a sailor walks, perhaps."

"I've never seen a sailor walk," said Ellie. I wonder if I could ever sell the Chatham, she thought.

"He chuckles a lot when he feels good, and when he's angry, he grows very quiet."

"Isn't that nice!" said Ellie pleasantly.

"You weren't listening—not at all!" Siri straightened out her pillow and lay down on her side, pretending that she was going to fall asleep.

"I can tell you some things about CJ," said Ellie.

"You can?"

She saw her sit upright, grabbing her pillow for another chat, and Ellie smiled to herself. "I went on this trip because CJ left me a little money."

"Now why would he do that?" Siri felt immediately that she had said something tactless and covered quickly with, "I didn't really mean that."

"CJ was like that," Ellie said. "There was a time after his wife's death when we were perhaps a little sweet on each other. Oh, not the way you young people are. We just liked to insult each other and got a lot of pleasure out of each other's company. But I'm not the marrying kind, and he was the marrying kind only once—Scott's mother was beautiful through and through. I'm afraid that can be said about only a few women, Siri. Well, he always said, 'I'll remember you in my will, Ellie,' and I always said, 'CJ, you do that.'" She sighed. "You know, that's the last thing I said to him when I was up at the house the Saturday evening before he died. When I left I said, 'Remember me in your will, sweetheart,' and bless me if he didn't."

"I think that's nice."

"It's not common knowledge, so—"

"I understand," said Siri. She sat with her arms about her knees, staring out at the night. " 'How sweet the moonlight sleeps upon the bank,' " she said.

"What did you say?" asked Ellie.

"Just a quotation from Shakespeare. Isn't it lovely? 'How sweet the moonlight sleeps upon the bank!' "

"It doesn't make any sense to me," said Ellie. What kind of a bank? A ditch bank? The First National Bank?"

"The Yellowstone."

"But, dear," said Ellie. "you can't see the Yellowstone from here."

"Oh, yes, I can!" insisted Siri. "I've seen the Yellowstone at least twenty times since we came. I've seen moonlight thousands upon thousands of times. Why can't I see moonlight on the bank of the Yellowstone? It's very simple—you just put them together. My grandmother always remembered things like that after she was blind. She could see the glaciers and the storms moving across the water and the little stream curling through our orchard."

"Well, she just remembered them," said Ellie.

"Not just remembered them. She perceived them with all her senses and kept them in her heart. When you see things that way, Ellie, you never forget them."

"Now, what was that quotation?" asked Ellie. Siri repeated the words. "You're killing, kid, just killing. One of these days you're going on a honeymoon with some single-minded chap and you're going to sit up in bed and say, 'How sweet the moonlight sleeps upon a bank'!" Ellie chortled. "All I can say is that I'd like to be there!"

The next day they were speeding through the mountains again, moving gradually down to the high plains country. All good things must come to an end, thought Siri, but she was almost inconsolable over leaving pines and streams and towering peaks. "John is so lucky," she said. As travelers do, they began to talk less about what they were leaving behind and more about home. "I keep on wondering how Mother is," said Siri.

"If Scott said he'd go out, Scott went out."

"I'm sure of that, but I have the oddest feeling sometimes."

"What do you mean?"

"As if Mother needed me."

"Honey, your mother needs a different kind of life from the one she has. But I'm afraid there isn't much that can be done about that." She picked up a magazine. "I might have made a mistake buying that hat at Mercer's. I see more Merry Widows than anything else." She threw the magazine on the plush seat. "Darn it, I hope Mrs. Swanson remembered to open a can of salmon for TC while I was gone."

"Mrs. Swanson's brother did an awfully strange thing when I asked for a rig some time ago."

"How was that?"

"He kept on saying he 'yust' didn't have anything for me. He even said he didn't have a thing to say to me!" Siri could not conceal her hurt. "Shortly afterward he and Mrs. Swanson drove me out to the farm as nice as you please."

Ellie's eyes twinkled. "You're awfully naive about some things, child. I thought Scott told you never to go out to those hills alone. If Harald had let you take a rig—well, poor Harald, we'd have had his neck."

"Do you ever get to keep a secret in Scotts Lake!" sighed Siri.

"Honey, I have kept a thousand secrets! Everyone takes a look at me and my sour old face and says, 'It'll be safe with Ellie,' and I guess it usually is."

They started to prepare for bed as soon as the porter began to unlock the bed compartments. Then they settled down for the night, feeling an easy companionship and visiting in a pleasant, desultory fashion. Finally Siri heard Ellie's regular breathing and knew that she had fallen asleep. She pressed the little snap-lock and raised the curtain so that she could look out to the prairies. Here the train seemed to have a lonely whistle as though it blew to keep itself company, like a traveler whistling his spirits up in the dark. Elisabet had once remarked that on some nights when the wind was right, she could hear the flyer; and since then she had always listened for it. It was very well for Scott to talk about her disgraceful sense of responsibility, she thought, but how could he know the memories she carried from childhood! She remembered her mother putting her to bed when she was very, very small and leaving her with the door slightly ajar, so that she caught a sense of comfort from the small light that came through the door—and how she lay listening to the laughter of the descending creek and imagined it to be the hiss of a serpent gliding into the sea, and how the rumbling snowfields became to her the voices of heathen gods roaring upon the windy heights. Yet if she became frightened or called out, her mother was swiftly beside her, assuaging her fears with caressing touches and a soft, lilting voice.

"You didn't sleep much, child," said Ellie as they were gathering their things together for Scotts Lake.

"Oh, well enough," replied Siri. "But it was one of those odd, restless nights when the mind skitters across a thousand memories."

"A girl like you has a thousand memories!" scoffed Ellie. "Well, I'm glad to be back, after all. The termites are going to have to fight *me* for that last splinter of wood." They began to recognize small landmarks, and soon they felt the braking of the train and heard the whistle of the engine at half-mile crossing.

Ellie was the first one off, and when she saw a small gathering on the platform she waved gaily and said, "Your postcards are on the same train—we forgot to mail them, folks." She looked about her with an odd expression, for she did not meet the usual good-natured greetings nor hear a single person say, "Hi, Ellie old girl!"

Scott came forward with a slightly crooked grin and took them both by the arm. "Something rather awful has happened while you were gone. No, Siri," he said reassuringly as he led her toward the car, "your mother is all right. Don't worry about that. I have her up at the house with Aunt Vinnie."

The following morning Siri asked, "Why didn't you tell me, Mother, that you needed doctoring?" Her mother had been relating a small portion of the events which occurred when Ellie and she were returning from Livingston. Now Elisabet lay in the large bed like a small lost child, thought Siri, as she noticed how much she had failed since the last visit.

"Who can feel well out here?" her mother said. "All the wind and the loneliness and the land." She tried to rise from the pillow, but Siri restrained her. "You must leave this country before it is too late," she said with a sagacious look.

Remembering Dr. Torrence's advice to let her talk herself out but not become too excitable, Siri said in a placating voice, "Don't worry about me, Mother—school will soon be out."

"I am glad you are here," said Elisabet, with a little return of good spirits. "It was almost impossible to make Mr. Rittenhouse understand how I could not leave the farm until everything was taken care of." Occasionally Siri caught a glance or a turn of her head that reminded her of Bergit during those days before she left for America with her aunt and uncle. But she wished again, as she had often wished throughout the years, that Elisabet had some of Grandma's spirit. "Why did you drive way over to the county seat to see a doctor? Why didn't you come into Scotts Lake, Mother?"

"I do not know myself," said Elisabet, moving her fingers restlessly, "but Tosten kept on telling me there were better doctors in a larger town." At the mention of Tosten's name, Elisabet made a strange grimace of weeping, but appeared to hold herself in check. "How long must I stay here?" she asked suddenly, lowering her voice and looking toward the hallway. "I must get back to the farm, for there is much to do. You must see to it quickly that arrangements are made to take me back to the farm and Sophie."

"But Sophie is with the Egelmeiers. You remember that."

"Who milks the cow?" she asked, pulling at the edge of the sheet which lay folded over a lavender quilt of delicate design. "Who feeds the hens?" She looked out the window with a glance that told Siri how far her mind wandered. "It is a pity conscription took Lars, for one could always depend on him."

"It's all taken care of Mother," said her daughter, taking her mother's restless fingers in her hand. "Why don't you sleep now?"

"I waited so long for you. I must tell everything to you, Siri, for the truth of it all must be known." She gave her daughter a reproachful look. "Perhaps Tosten was kinder than you think, for he took me to a *Norwegian* doctor. But you yourself with your English learning cannot know how good it is to talk in one's own tongue."

"Of that I am sure," said Siri amicably.

"He was a most kind old man and did not hide my heart sickness from me." She looked out the window where the tops of the trees were tossing in the spring wind. "I could have told him where the sickness comes from. From the land and the hard water and the worry which always rides upon the wind—will the seeds sprout and will it rain? He gave me a little box of pills and told me to come in and see him again within a few weeks."

"I am glad you found one of our own countrymen, Mother."

"You must let *me* tell it, Siri. When he was through, Tosten began to rummage around in his pockets for money for the doctor. So I dipped into my reticule and came up with the fee. Then I went to the carriage and Tosten talked with the doctor for some time."

"Mother, I have the sexton's little hymnbook with me. Would you like to have me read a hymn to you?" she asked, remembering her mother's habit of reading the old hymns which had been sung in the white stone church.

"No, not now. I must continue with the telling of this, for the truth of it all must be known. Finally Tosten got into the carriage beside me and said, "How much has my frugal little Elisabet hidden away this time?" She withdrew the hand which Siri had been holding. "I would have given him what was left, but I had made a promise to you, Siri." She looked questioningly at her daughter. "I had made a promise, had I not?" Siri nodded. "Well, he sat there hanging his head, so to speak, and said that maybe it was for the best, after all, because the way things had been going he saw little hope for any of us. He said it was a land calculated to make the rich richer and the poor poorer, and such as we should have remained in the old country." She closed her eyes and rested her head upon the pillow. "Now I am sorry I did not give it all to him." She opened her blue eyes and stared fixedly at Siri. "Perhaps it would have been better had you not interfered about the money, but of course you cannot know that there has been such great contrariness for me to deal with. Well," she said, beginning to finger the hem of the sheet again, "I told him we must stop for supplies, for the flour and the sugar were almost gone, and I asked him to come in and help me. But he would not come, saying stubbornly that he wished nothing more to do with the money, and the clerk in the grocery could carry out the box for me."

"I should have come out for Easter!" exclaimed Siri. "You went through all this when I was having such a good time." She brightened and said, "John sent his regards. Some day when you feel better perhaps you can go out and see the country I saw—streams and mountains that will remind you of Norway."

"You must not keep me from the telling," chided Elisabet. "Anyway, I have seen all the land I wish to see. Well, I made the necessary purchases, and then I had them put in the back of the carriage and asked Tosten if there was anything he needed—tobacco, perhaps, but he shook his head and said he had no need but for me to get home. So he put his arm about me and I leaned my head on his shoulder—" At this juncture, Siri thought her mother would weep, but she took a deep breath and continued, "So we rode for a long, long time, for it was still some distance from the farm. But at last we were on the hill where I could see the farm and Shep coming to meet us. I was weary with it all and had some pain again so Tosten told me to lie down." She sighed deeply. "Well, I told him I must tend to the chores, for I knew his habit of driving up to Golag when he began to look sad or glum, but the chores he said *he* would tend to. He helped me take off my good blue dress and brought me a wrapper which I put on. Then I lay down, and he covered me with that throw I wove when you were a child and Bergit was still with us." Her recital had been such a long one that Siri tried to restrain her, but she seemed moved by some compelling need to go on.

"How long I slept I do not know, but it was almost dark, for Tosten had lighted a lamp for me in the kitchen. I heard Shep at the back entry, whining and pawing. It took me some time to get my wits about me, for of late I have been very weak and muddled when I rise. Finally I saw that the milk was in and the eggs had been gathered. I looked out into the near darkness, pushing Shep away, and saw that the carriage was gone or put away. I knew not which."

"Poor Mother!" said Siri, unable to restrain herself.

"There is a weakness within me somewhere," said Elisabet plaintively, "or else all this would not have happened. I myself was not hungry," she said, resuming again the monotonous tone of her recital, "but I set about cooking something—an omelet, I think it was, and warmed over some potato soup left in a crock. Oh yes, I also had a bowl of cooked fruit—and the fresh bread I had baked the day before. When it was all on the table, I called him, but there was no answer, only Shep pawing and whining at the back door. Even then I did not think too much about it, and told Shep he was a bad dog, a very bad dog this night. I noticed then that the moon was rising behind a bank of yellowed clouds and that the wind was beginning to blow. You cannot imagine how much the wind blows out there, Siri.

"Well, there was nothing to be done but look in the back entry for the lantern and see whether he had gone on to Golag and left something so amiss that Shep was not himself. So I lit the lantern, following Shep who went whining out to the barn." She turned her face away and said in a tight voice, "We should never have come to this country—it was never this bad for me in Norway."

"Mother, I have been told what happened," said Siri gently. "You need not retell it."

"It must be told as it was," she replied. "The barn door was open, and in the yellowed moonlight I could see partly in. Shep was almost demented . . . like Balder on the morning after the storm." She gripped Siri's arm. "Oh, there is such a weakness in me, child. You cannot tell me that I am not being punished for something."

"You mustn't say that, Mother!" Siri tried to comfort her, but her mother thrust her arm away. "I took the lantern and held it so—" Here she indicated by her eyes and a hand the level at which she had held it. "At first I could see nothing, for the light blinded me, and then I saw a foot swinging and then another foot and then his face and the long single rope of Sophie's swing hanging from the rafter." Then she began to weep unrestrainedly and did not push her child away when she sat upon the bed with her, but said again and again, "Siri, Siri, there is no one but you now—for Sophie I have never had."

After dinner when Siri joined Scott in the little library, he said, "How is she now?"

"Much, much better."

"We might as well get some things over with," he said, "while Aunt Vinnie and Ellie are out in the kitchen."

"I have been thinking about everything," said Siri, "and I feel I should write Aunt Joanna tonight and get the letter off on the morning train. As soon as she's able to travel, I'm sure they'll want her

with them. And then there's the matter of Sophie. They may want
her too. They're like that, you know."

"She'll never leave the Egelmeiers," said Scott.

"But they can't be expected to keep Sophie! Next year, perhaps,
I can make arrangements to keep her with me—as if anyone ever
kept her anywhere," she added ruefully.

"And then there's the matter of the funeral, Siri. Your pastor thinks
it should be held on Tuesday morning, just a quiet graveside ceremony up at the little cemetery at Golag." Scott opened his desk and
set out writing materials for her. "If you feel like it, why don't you
write them now? When I take Ellie home, we can mail the letter.
The air will do you good. Anyway, there are some things we must
discuss, since you want me to handle the farm and the payment
of his debts." She accepted the chair he held out for her, and when
he asked if she wanted him to leave, she shook her head.

"I feel better with you here," she said. Scott took a book down
from a shelf and seated himself a little to the side and back of
her. She wrote a salutation and then held the pen in front of her
face thoughtfully. "Scott," she said suddenly, "do you believe in
fate?"

He set down his book and turned his head so that he was able
to see her at an angle. "Well, I don't wish to sound like that sainted
professor of yours, but I think 'fate' is such a vague and generally
overused term, I can't answer your question, honey." The last word
came out as a surprise to him and certainly to her, for he saw the
blush which rose suddenly on her cheek.

"I don't suppose I make sense," she said, "but this awful thing that
happened I think I almost perceived happening on a day that Tosten
came up the fjord in his boat, Mother along with him. I remember
standing beside my grandmother and not wanting to go down to
the pier to meet them. When I hid my face in my grandmother's
skirts, I sensed a blackness at that moment beyond the blackness
of absence of light."

Scott set down his book and began to walk up and down between
the cold fireplace and the doorway. "You're a strange girl," he said,
"almost prescient, at times—perhaps that's not the word I want,
either." He came up to the back of her chair, then turned, putting

his hands at his side and holding them clenched. "One of your ancestors, I think, must have had something to do with incantations and rites—I see it in your eyes at times." He threw up his hands in a small gesture of dismissal. "Oh, get on with your writing."

Siri smiled to herself, dipped the pen into a glass inkwell, and began to write swiftly. She knew that the tragedy out at the farm would affect Uncle Roald more than anyone else at home, for Elisabet was, after all, his own sister-in-law. Omitting as many details as possible, she wrote a short letter; still she did not deceive them about the manner of Tosten's dying, feeling that they deserved to know the events so that their decision would be based upon knowledge rather than emotion. When she was almost done, the women came into the room carrying trays of food. "It just occurred to me," said Aunt Vinnie, "that it would be a lot cozier in here." Scott rose to help them, and soon they had a table set under the little window where Siri had eaten at old Charlie's birthday party. "Your mother is still sleeping," said Lavinia. "She's the smallest thing. How did you happen to grow so much taller, Siri?"

"She was the exception, I suppose. Anyway, Dad was quite tall."

Ellie, always unpredictably predictable, said sharply, "Scott, you might be interested in one of Siri's favorite quotations."

"What is it?" he asked, as he finished buttering one of his sister's praiseworthy Parkerhouse rolls. He had not observed Ellie's teasing look. Thereupon ensued much playful threatening between Ellie and Siri, but after it was all over, Siri felt a deep sense of something like guilt, thinking about her mother upstairs and Tosten lying in a shed back of the general store in Golag. Ellie saw the girl's face grow pensive and could have wished her tongue out.

When Siri went out with Vinnie to prepare a tray for Elisabet, Ellie said, "That was stupid of me, teasing her like that. I'm afraid I've hurt her feelings, Scott."

Scott said, "I don't think so. She always enjoys your horseplay, but the poor girl has a lot on her mind." Affectionately, he put a hand on her shoulder. "It doesn't become you, Ellie, to get so self-conscious. You have your reputation to uphold in Scotts Lake."

"All right," said Ellie, turning around swiftly and looking at him directly, her hands on the lapels of his suit coat. "Why don't you marry that girl, Scott?"

"Now, look here, Ellie, that's my business."

"When did I ever keep my nose out of others' business?"

"All right, then. Don't think I haven't thought of it."

"Scott, she's awfully pretty with her hair down," said Ellie wickedly, "and that complexion is for real—and she holds up well, day or night." She gave him a mischievous look. "You know what I mean."

"Oh, leave me alone, will you?" exclaimed Scott, pushing her aside.

"Well, I've done it again," said Ellie picking up a loaded tray and pretending to be hurt, but she flounced out of the room with a twinkle in her eyes.

The letter was safely mailed and Ellie delivered to her waiting tomcat. "Let's take a ride," said Scott. "Vinnie will be at your mother's call."

"If she'll only call," said Siri. "She's so afraid she'll trouble someone. I'd like a short ride, anyway," she finished.

"I'll get right to the point," he said. "Your stepfather left your mother in somewhat of a predicament." Siri did not say anything but watched the land suddenly lighten as the moon appeared above a frosting of clouds in the east. She heard the evening train whistle in the valley below them. Scott was aware of it, too, for he turned suddenly and said, "I'm no longer a train meeter, Siri, the obsession has been cured. The very first night a young woman came swinging down the steps, the patient was cured, but he has been miserable ever since." She felt his hand tighten about her shoulder, but soon he went on, saying, "I never mix love and law, so—well, old Egelmeier owns the horses now, the wagons, the carriage. He showed me an overdue note. These were his security. A farmer up above Golag owns the cow, another the plow. It goes on and on, Siri. Nothing in the house is touched, though." When she did not say anything, he said, "This isn't going to be too much for you, is it?"

"What about the land?"

"He couldn't touch that. It's a homestead, you know. Old Egelmeier told me that Tosten was planning to leave as soon as school was out—going to try his luck elsewhere, he said."

"And poor Mother and Sophie?"

"He talked as if he was going to take them along." He looked down at her. "They're a wild lot up at Golag. Always have been. But I never heard one thing about Tosten's being untrue to your mother, if that's any satisfaction."

"Sometimes I wish he had been! From the very start!" she said bitterly. "Then she might have had her eyes opened and someone could have talked some sense into her!"

She heard the chug-chug of the flyer as it began to leave the depot in town and wished she were out of Scotts Lake, far, far away somewhere where the land was not so sweeping and malevolent in its watchfulness. Despite his kindness and his chivalry of some minutes ago, she detected a tension in Scott, too, and felt that whatever interest he had in her could not withstand the disgrace that now embraced this little family of hers. Everyone had been immensely kind—even Mr. Lusk had put his arm about her and assured her *she* was well thought of!—but she knew small towns and how they never quite forgot scandal and kept their scabrous little descriptions through the third and fourth generations. "I'll do everything I can to straighten out matters as quickly as possible," Scott said. He turned the car around at a crossroad and started back to town.

"Scott, your aunt Vinnie persuaded me to stay until after the funeral," Siri said, "but tomorrow is Monday and I must get back to the Lusks and get ready to resume teaching on Wednesday."

"You're not thinking of your mother when you say that," he said. "Some point of etiquette is bothering you, I'm sure. You know, Dad always used to say, 'Damn etiquette if it makes you do the wrong thing.' Stay until Tuesday evening, anyway. You know, don't you, that your mother won't be allowed to attend the funeral?"

"Yes, Dr. Torrence told me." Scott had driven the car into the old remodeled carriage house at the back of the yard. They walked slowly up the pebbled walk to the back door, where the light from an enclosed porch shone on her troubled face and the wavy sweep of golden brown hair. Ellie's words drummed in his ears and he wanted to take her in his arms and let all the troubled tomorrows take care of themselves. "Thanks for everything, Scott." She fumbled for the latch, but he reached across and let her in.

On Tuesday morning Scott and Siri were finishing their breakfasts when Vinnie said, "I'm going to get Annie in to stay with your mother. She's the best practical nurse in town, and your mother needs a lot of care with a cold coming on top of everything else." Vinnie rose and said, "You two take your time.. I'm going to put a shawl on and run over to see Annie."

"I was afraid this would happen when I saw her the morning after she had found Tosten."

Siri looked at him questioningly. "Why? What happened?"

"I thought your mother told you everything," he said, looking surprised. "It doesn't matter," he said.

"It does." Siri's eyes held his demandingly.

"She didn't tell you that she stayed out in the barn all night?" He shrugged helplessly and said, "Well, you'll hear it, anyway, I suppose." So Scott told about coming down the hill that morning and finding Elisabet running to flag him down. "She was terribly distraught or she would have known I'd stop. I couldn't understand much of what she was saying, except about Tosten being out in the barn. I thought at first he might have cut himself with a scythe or on a farm machine." Scott went on to tell how he had bundled her up and taken her to a Scandinavian family on a farm some miles east of Golag. "I had to get her to people who could understand what she was saying. Alone there with that dog and the small light from the lantern, she had apparently tried to find some way to get him down.. But she could not bear the thought of dropping his body, so went into the house and turned out the lamp and looked to the fire and then wrapping herself in a blanket of some kind, she lay down on the hay and waited until morning."

"Only Mother would have done that," said Siri.

"I am sure of that," said Scott. "But I had these people ask her why she had not hitched up the horse and gone for help. She told them that the horse had broken out of his stall and run somewhere and if she could have cornered him, how would she know one prairie road from another in the moonlight?" He looked fondly at the girl who sat with her coffee growing cold, the food almost untouched. "In that respect, she was smarter than her daughter, from what Harald has told me."

Later, Scott picked up Mrs. Swanson and Harald and took them along with Siri and him to the funeral in Golag. They took the much better-traveled road, a way which missed Scotts Lake and the little farmhouse, stopping at the Egelmeier farm to pick up Sophie. She did not want to ride with them, but chose to go with the Egelmeiers instead. Still, Siri sought out the child and stood beside her as the pastor read in English the fourteenth chapter of Romans. The words seemed to come whispering on the wind: "But why dost thou judge thy brother? or why dost thou set at nought thy brother? for we shall all stand before the judgment seat of Christ . . . . Let us not therefore judge one another anymore: but judge this rather, that no man put a stumbling block or any occasion to fall in his brother's way."

When it was all over, she said softly in Norwegian to Sophie, "Sophie, will you come back with me and stay?" But Sophie fled to the generous arms of Mrs. Egelmeier, so she beckoned to Scott to help her talk to the middle-aged couple. "Led her stay mit us until sgool is oudt," Mr. Egelmeier said. "Den ve zee." He looked at his plump, florid wife. "Mamma and me ve haf no girls." So Siri shook their hands and walked with Scott to the car, where Harald and Mrs. Swanson sat drying their eyes. As the car drove away from the neglected cemetery, she saw the black earth waiting for a man she was constrained not to judge. Some vestigial memory brought to mind a tale of a little boy in plum-colored breeches reciting

There lived a curious gray-haired man
On the outermost naked isle.

CHAPTER 18

The Ride to Golag

May came, and with it a short snowfall to remind northern prairie folk they were still thralls of winter, no matter how much the sun had shone upon them in April and the meadowlarks had sung. Siri recalled Bugs's telling her that the Indians called the meadowlark the bird of promise, and that in Dakota language he sang Hi-ya-he-he.

As kind as Scott and Vinnie had been to her mother, Siri could not understand her mother's uneasiness around Scott. After her near tussle with pneumonia, Elisabet's health had slowly improved, and in time Aunt Joanna came to take her home to the Gabrielsons. Siri had mentioned her mother's reluctance to warm up to Scott, and her aunt Joanna had tossed it off with, "Siri, must you always run about weighing everything on those little golden scales of yours?" Then she had said more sensibly, "Who could welcome a son-in-law she can't talk with?" But Siri had been quick in setting her right on that point: Scott and she were very good friends, that was all.

What a help bustling Aunt Joanna had been! Together with Mrs. Swanson and Harald, her aunt and she had gone out to the homestead one Sunday to make disposition of the things which remained in the little house. Again and again Joanna exclaimed over Elisabet's pathetic bravery in enduring such a forsaken place. "You should have told me!" she scolded, as Siri was pumping water for their coffee.

"But I did, Aunt Joanna. At Christmas," she said, her eyes filling with tears.

Mrs. Swanson was wrapping dishes in newspapers and said kindly, "Nothing could have made her leave that man, Mrs. Gabrielson. I suspect our Siri here knows best what gave her that endurance." Siri recalled now how difficult it had been to determine the disposition of the few things remaining from Fjeldstrand. Having learned so early to say farewell to so much, there wasn't really a lot that she herself wanted. She packed a box for Sophie and one for herself and another for the Swansons, whose protests were silenced by saying that Elisabet had ordered her to give them a few things because had it not been for their kindness, Elisabet would have been lonelier the past winter. She kept the woven coverlet for herself, since she alone remembered the child-enchanted hours of its weaving, Bergit's shawl, and Guro's quaint tapestry from Ørnheim. She wondered what had become of Nels's old dragonheaded fiddle whose music once set them to dancing. Had he taken it to the seamen's home or had it been cast upon old Per's heap of treasures? She hesitated over the old jewelry and decided that it should be sent to the city, for Elisabet might feel well enough again to make her own disposition of it. Finally she was obliged to take the little set of china, too, for Harald said they had run out of paper for packing. When all had been packed and stowed away, Joanna put a cloth around her head and swept out the house, though Mrs. Swanson said many a storm would blow upon the place and only put the dirt back in it. Then before Harald started the team up the hill, she saw the little weather-warped house as Elisabet must first have seen it, and the awful thought occurred to her: I once hesitated coming out here to teach—suppose I *hadn't* come!

"Poor Shep," she said, "I feel sorry for him. He loved Mother so."

"*Ja*, vere did he go?" asked Harald.

"To the Scandinavian family where Scott took Mother. At least he'll understand their language."

      ✸   ✸   ✸

As Siri pushed a letter to Leif into the mail slot, she thought how glad she was to be done with the little farm; and never again would she think about it too much, for Bergit had taught her the folly of useless thoughts—with what words and when, she could not recall, but Grandmother had done that task well. She opened her mailbox and found a letter from Joanna and decided she would go on to the hotel to read it there and have cake and coffee, for the Lusk economies were growing worse. In a way, it was her own fault for having praised the mountain country so much; for the Lusks were planning on a summer journey to Yellowstone themselves, to be paid for by herself, Siri feared, if strictest economies of the table could advance their expeditionary forces.

When she came into the diningroom, Tammy told her that Ellie was out marketing; so she sat at the little counter and ate her cake and drank her coffee, reading Aunt Joanna's letter at the same time. "You must come as soon as school is out," she wrote. "I don't mean to alarm you, but the doctor here concurs with yours in Scotts Lake: it's only a matter of time." She went on to send her regards to the Rittenhouses and Ellie, adding a postscript to the effect that Teresa and Brun were expecting a baby.

"Do you realize," said Ellie's voice behind her, "that everything you eat here has to be ordered by me, planned by me—Lordy, don't ever run a hotel!" Ellie sat down with a generous piece of apple pie, and soon began to grow more cheerful. "Where are we going next Easter? Have you planned that?"

"I'm not sure I'll be here next Easter," replied Siri, folding the letter into the envelope. "Aunt Joanna sends her regards."

Ellie nodded absently, then she lowered her voice. "Haven't you signed your contract?"

"I don't feel I can—not with Mother so ill."

"Scott was called away on a business trip—some property in Illinois to settle up." Ellie narrowed her eyes and said, "Darn you, you're supposed to ask when he is coming back."

"When *is* he coming back?"

"Your last week of school, Snow White!"

"What's the matter with you, Ellie?"

Ellie looked around the diningroom and saw that it was almost empty. "What's the matter with me!" she asked. "What's the matter with me!" She glared at the lone customer hidden behind a newspaper. "I'll tell you what's the matter with me!" Ellie rose to spindly heights, banging the counter. "I missed my train when I was your age—the best-looking, goldarned train that ever whistled down a pair of shining tracks—and what do I hear? Nothing but that eternal tootin' of regret. That's what's the matter with me!" The salesman's coffee cup clattered to the saucer, and he rose quickly, scattering newssheets to the floor and disappearing into the lobby. "See, child," said Ellie more gently, "what can happen to you when you grow old—even a loose-jawed, puffy-eyed blathering old fool can't stand you!" Ellie gave her a long malevolent stare and disappeared into the kitchen.

Soon the last week of school was upon them, and Siri's blackboards were chalked with tests. She watched her classes bent over their desks, ink pens scratching on white paper, hair ribbons bobbing up and down, middy blouses starched and fresh-smelling from wind-whipped washings. There they sat—the confident, the frightened, the shy and the bold—and scarcely a formal examination was needed to tell her the quality of their performances.

Scott was back by Wednesday morning, leaving a message for her to call at his office after school. When she walked into the building, she found Scott at his desk, preoccupied with papers. He rose and shook her hand, and the formality of the greeting appeared to put them both under some restraint. He held a chair for her and then went back to his desk. "Siri," he said, "we'll have to go out to Golag on Friday afternoon and help you settle what to do with Sophie and pay off a farmer or two who came up with a note. We can leave the checks with Egelmeier. He may be ruthless at times, but I have always found him honest. That should finish everything, so far as I can see at the moment."

"I don't know what I should have done without you," she said honestly.

"I'd like to hear that sort of thing the rest of my life," he said, looking at her soberly. "You're coming over for dinner, you know, on Saturday. Vinnie has contacted you, hasn't she?" Siri nodded.

Scott looked perplexed and said finally, "Is something bothering you, Siri?" She looked away, studying the grained pattern in his oak desk.

"End-of-school-itis, perhaps—a feeling of futility maybe."

"But why, Siri?"

"Well, to put it bluntly, I'm going home Saturday night, knowing that I'll have to face the sure knowledge of Mother's death."

"Yes, you are, my dear," he said rising. "It wasn't so long ago the same kind of thing happened to the Rittenhouses, you know." He set the ink pen into its socket with unnecessary force. "Siri, you are the most exasperating mixture of vitality and resignation

I have ever seen!" He came toward her. "You told me once about your grandmother and how she kept her vigorous identity through some rather disheartening experiences. I loved that old woman, just hearing about her. But, blast you, if you're going to be another Elisabet Vegg I'm well, I—"

Siri rose and stood facing him, her shoulders high and her brown eyes flashing. "Sometimes it takes courage to be an Elisabet Vegg!" she said. "How can you fight a land so big it dwarfs you and a man with a weakness so great that neither love nor anger can touch him! I think I hate you, Scott!"

He stood beside her now. He glanced briefly at the screen door leading to the street, then he leaned down and kissed the tip of her nose. "I'll pick you up Friday noon," he said. He watched her go out the door, her skirts swishing, her shoes tapping sharply.

Friday noon Scott's car was under the greening elms in front of the Lusk residence. Aunt Vinnie had packed a lunch for them, and Scott said he was going to take the old road past the Rittenhouse-Scott homesteads. "Who lives there now?" asked Siri.

"No one at either home-place, but there's a farm on a corner of Dad's old homestead." He went on to explain that the coming of the railroad had changed the aspect of things. "People sort of picked up their belongings and moved south a few miles to be near it." Siri watched the shadows of drifting clouds run swiftly over the green-gray hills, observed the antics of prairie gophers in their mounded village on a nearby slope, and saw the wind-sailing sweep of a hawk. "Beautiful, isn't it?" asked Scott, eyeing her upward glances.

"Beautiful," she said, "and so very empty." She gave him a swift, mischievous glance.

> "Some witch-wife's power,
> In evil hour,
> Made me leave home,
> And here to come!"

"What was that?" asked Scott.

"Something my father used to recite, something from *The Norse King Sagas*, I think."

"You know," he said, putting an easy arm about her shoulders, "I'd like to get into that medieval mind of yours. I never look at you but what I see foamy seas and wooded isles—"

"How nice, Scott," she said lightly. "It's cheaper than foreign travel." She watched him begin to brake the car and then its sudden acceleration. I've upset him, she thought, and that's all right, because he upset me last Wednesday.

They rode on in silence, until they heard the flap-flap-flap of a dispirited tire. Captives of the rutted trail, the wheels could not go anywhere, and Scott let the car jog along to the crest of the hill where rains and spring thaws had not washed deeply into the soil. "What do I do now?" asked Siri lightly. "Pull up the sleeves or give you the old university Rah-Rah?" She was already out of the car, lifting her skirts above the wind-blown grasses.

"Oh, just find a small hillock and say the proper incantations." She watched him open the tool box and find the necessary tools. He worked quickly, expertly, and seriously. She lay back upon the grass, hands under her head, recalling the time a year ago when Uncle Roald had taken them to the lake in his new car. They had camped out in a tent, and the night had been so beautiful that she could not sleep. She recalled tiptoeing out and lying in a hammock they had strung between two maples, where she could see the moonlight on the lake and on a woodless stretch of land that sloped below their camp. She had lain there for perhaps an hour or two, a raincoat thrown over her nightclothes, watching the night hours traveling slowly across the land. She had fallen in love with America that night—its immensity, its space, its serenity. But how frightened the family were to find her sleeping soundly outside in the hammock! Siri smiled to herself.

"And what's so funny about my changing a tire?" asked Scott, standing beside her with the lug wrench in his hand.

She sat up and said, "Oh, I was just recalling a motor trip last summer."

"And who was he?" asked Scott, setting down the wrench long enough to light his cigar.

"The family, that's all."

Finally they resumed their progress over the hills. "We're soon there," he said, observing her dream-lost mooning across the hills. "If you can take your eyes off me long enough to look, you can see the very smallest tip of Scotts Lake."

"But that isn't where Scotts Lake is supposed to be!"

"That's why you don't go off by yourself," he said. The car began to nose down now, and she could see a wooded cleft in the hills.

"Why a forest!" she exclaimed in fun.

"It used to look that way to Mother. You see that little valley down there and the windbreak of trees? The house stood there. If you look closely, you can see the traces of foundation."

"Was she alone much?"

"Most farm women are alone—much," he said.

When he had parked the car in the shade of the grass-grown windbreak, he took her around the place, showing her where the livingroom and the bedroom and the kitchen used to be. "And over there the barn." He stepped into the house-foundation and said, "Probably right here I was born."

She had grown very quiet. Finally she asked, "What became of the house?"

"We had it torn down. Dad and I could never stand skeletons that loom in lonely places and cry failure, failure!"

"Like Mother's place," she said.

He did not say anything, but took the lunch basket out of the car and helped her to a shady stretch between two rows of trees singing and rustling in the wind. He began to unpack methodically, handing her a sandwich wrapped in a linen napkin and pouring a cup of lemonade from a small quart-bucket with a snap-on lid. "There's some of Aunt Vinnie's cake here, too, and some apples, I believe." They ate in companionable silence, sometimes looking strangely at each other, sometimes gazing out to the level stretch of ground and its square of higher grasses bending to the will of the wind. When they were finished, he repacked the basket and stowed it in the car; and then he came to where she sat leaning backward on her extended arms. He sat down beside her, but turned a little so that he could look at her.

"Siri," he said, "I am going to tell you what I am going to do, and you listen carefully, without any bewitching little protests or

mischievous glances from those brown eyes. I am going to take
you in my arms and I am going to kiss you as I have never kissed
anyone before. Then because I think I am going to marry you, I
am going to kiss you again, and again. I am not going to make
any improper advances, as they quaintly phrase it, because I think
you will soon marry me, and believe me, I have plans for that moment too."

He looked at her long and steadily, and she met his glance without a sweep of her eyelashes, and then she said quietly, "What are
you waiting for, Scott?"

Later the car chugged up the straight road that led past Golag
to the Egelmeier farm. Siri sat in the circle of Scott's arm and
felt such an elation and contentment that she wondered why she
had distrusted him after their first kiss up on the hilltop. "When
these early settlers decided to go up a hill, they went up a hill,"
said Scott, putting the car into low and nosing it up toward a cloud.

"I noticed that," said Siri, "on my first ride with you." She found
herself suddenly remembering Leif and his road-building enthusiasm. He would go quite mad in this country, she thought. She could
think of Leif now without a tremor, and of their goodnight kisses
that had been childishly furtive in quality or merely playful—until
their last evening together.

The Egelmeier farm lay before them, scattered with a wide assortment of machinery, chickens squawking and flapping in the path
of the car. "I thought most German farmers were tidy," she said.

"Most, I'm sure. But don't underestimate his ability as a farmer,"
said Scott. "He's an amazing combination of sweat, beer, and clever-
ness." He honked his horn.

Mrs. Egelmeier's face and its several chins peered around a back
door. "I'll call him," she said, inviting them to get out of the car
and come to the front door. Almost immediately, however, they saw
the same back door slam and Mr. Egelmeier came out hitching up
his overalls and fastening his overall straps.

"Probably sat playing cards in his red underwear. He's so heated
up with beer most of the time, he could sit naked on a snowbank."

"What a place for Sophie!" she said, turning her face. In an open
place beside the barn she recognized the old carriage from the

farm, evidence probably, of some of Uncle Nels's depleted inheritance.

Mr. Egelmeier gave them each a hearty handshake and began to head them toward the house. Soon Siri found herself in a large frontroom with a nine by twelve carpet of violently pink and purple roses, an assortment of cane-bottomed chairs, a leather sofa rich with garish pillows, an organ, and many generations of Egelmeiers in a frame so high that a scaffold was necessary for a full appraisal.

Mr. Egelmeier requested that they sit down and asked immediately, "Peer?" At Siri's refusal, he called loudly, "Puttermilk, Ma!" He frowned at Scott. "You ain't going high and mighty on me?"

"I'll drink a stein with you."

"You ain't a Rittenhouse for sure if you don't."

When the refreshments had been properly received, acknowledged, and dispensed with, Scott said, "Guess you'll be glad to see us take Sophie, Herman. Aren't you a little tired of your visitor by now?"

Mrs. Egelmeier, who had joined them during refreshments, began to shake her head in a vigorous negative fashion. "Sophie, she stays here," said her husband.

"Where is Sophie?" asked her stepsister.

"She and dat damn boy is out in the fieldts chasin' rabbits."

"Should they always be out running together?" asked Siri.

"Don't vurry about dat!" exclaimed Mr. Egelmeier, holding his stein up to the pitcher his wife held. "Ain't eder of dem standt still long enough in vun spodt to get into drubble." Mr. and Mrs. Egelmeier shook with laughter.

"Excuse us," said Siri, holding a brief whispered consultation with Scott.

"She'd like to see Sophie. Can you get her in?" The Egelmeiers assured Scott that the dinner bell could be rung, so Mrs. Egelmeier left for the back part of the house and soon they heard the sweet pealing of a church bell.

Mr. Egelmeier caught Siri's startled look and explained that the bell had been salvaged when the Methodists in Golag "burndt." Finally the two children appeared, Sophie holding on to her friend's hand, and giving her stepsister a long, hard look. Scott glanced at Siri but saw that she was upset, so he said, "Sophie, we came to talk about something that can affect your entire life. You have a chance to go back with your sister when she leaves for Minnesota. The Gabrielsons have been kind enough to offer you a home and all the schooling you require. You must think about it carefully." He turned to Mr. Egelmeier and said that he had not gone into the situation legally but he felt sure that if a case were made of it, Sophie would find herself in Minnesota with her mother.

"Mother is quite ill, Sophie."

Sophie did not reply, but pulled on the lad's hand and drew him along toward Mrs. Egelmeier's side. "See?" said Mrs. Egelmeier, shrugging her fat eloquently. "She ain't your kind. Dat's all."

Siri looked doubtfully at Scott and said, "Well, let's leave it this way for the time being." She asked the Egelmeiers if Sophie needed clothes or anything else at this time, but both Egelmeiers declined with a frown. She thanked them for the refreshments and walked slowly out to the car, where a chicken sat picking at her feathers. She watched Scott as he and Mr. Egelmeier talked. She observed them shaking hands, finally, and Scott came over and began to crank the car.

As they drove through the yard, he said, "Well, it's all taken care of. I gave him the money for the other debts, so that's that, Siri."

"Some ghastly thing happened to that child at some time in her life," said Siri.

"Maybe something did. Maybe not. Dr. Rittenhouse diagnoses it as a simple case of an inheritance split right down through the middle." He smiled when he saw her raised eyebrow. "Fifty percent her father's stupidity, fifty percent her grandmother's guts."

On Saturday morning Siri had another letter from Joanna, mentioning their delight at the prospect of her coming home and adding that Elisabet had changed neither for the better nor for the worse. "I must prepare you for the fact that she and Leif have taken quite a fancy to each other. He brings her flowers and chatters to her in Norwegian—flatters her at every turn."

Late in the afternoon Siri walked up to the hotel to fetch Ellie. Having said goodbye to the Lusks and sent her baggage with Harald, nothing remained but the dinner with Vinnie and Scott. In the kitchen of the hotel Mrs. Swanson told Siri that Ellie would soon be down. Then Mrs. Swanson wiped her hands on a little towel she kept fastened to her waist and said, "Ah, tonight you go, Siri, and Harald and I vill be down to the train. He has a little gift he has made for you, and you mustn't mind an old fellow being a little in love vit you. It is a vay of remembering something vunce sveet in his own life."

At that moment Ellie came in, fit to kill, as she expressed it, in a tiered sheath and reeking of a scent she called New Mown Hay. "Someone ought to tumble in that!" she said gaily. Mrs. Swanson's laughter trailing after them, they set off down Main Street, with Ellie chatting, nodding, and waving, a new marten scarf thrown jauntily over one shoulder. "Mercer's will kill me if they see me in this," she said hopefully, casting bold eyes in the direction of the general store. "Sent to Fargo for this, I did." The sun at their backs cast golden shafts against windows and pink-pearled the sky in the east. The earth was rich with the smell of roots and new growth, and the lilacs shamed Ellie's perfume. "Quiet tonight, aren't you?" said Ellie. "Ha, Mrs. Poindexter's robins are back." She stopped short below a tree, her hands on her hips, the fur slipping down to an elbow, craning her neck at the limbs above. "You can't stand here all night," she said, giving Siri a little shove. They moved up the street and turned in at the familiar house where the twin globes shone feebly against the splash of color from the west.

Vinnie met them at the door with a kiss for each. "Scott's in the kitchen sweeping up broken glass. He's a bundle of something tonight," she finished, giving Siri a knowing glance. Apparently Scott had not heard them arrive, for they found him with a broom and dustpan. "Some witch-wife's power in an evil hour," he said, smiling oddly at Siri and dumping broom and dustpan into Ellie's surprised hands.

Ellie waited impatiently for the diningroom door to close on the two and whispered to Vinnie, "Something's happened between those two and I'll be darned if I don't hope they got careless."

"Ellie!" reproved Lavinia.

"Can't take any more of this lollygaggin' around. Good! Smells like prime rib. Right, Vinnie?"

Scott and Siri had wandered into the parlor. "See that gentleman up there?" Scott indicated a portrait of a stern-looking man with epaulets. That's my paternal grandfather. That fellow in kilts, my mother's grandfather. I think it's about time you met the family, Siri."

They walked a few steps farther, avoiding Vinnie's footstool with a sewing basket on it. Suddenly she was in his arms, returning his kiss with ardor, feeling her heart flutter like the sudden flight of a startled bird. She drew him down beside her on a sofa. "Scott, let's be honest about all this." She held on to his hand. "I'm leaving tonight, Scott, not knowing when I'll be back—and not as long as Mother is alive, anyway." She saw him begin to protest. "Mother will have to come first. We mustn't promise ourselves anything yet."

"How do you arrive at a conclusion like that?" She saw the sudden anger in his gray eyes and realized that Scott would never be put off with "just-becauses." She said seriously, "I have to be what I am, and how can you know what I remember?"

He took her roughly by the shoulders and asked, "Now what nonsense is that?"

She reached up and pulled his arms gently downward and then put her arms about his neck and kissed him softly at first and then with such longing and fire that she felt the surge of emotion in him and responded with such hunger and need she seemed to lose her self-identity. Finally Scott said, "This is not the kind of marriage I want, but this is the way it must be. Marry me now, and then you can go home in a few days and return in a few days."

"You would *let* me do that?"

"I would let you leave because my wife would not want to leave. You, Siri, want to leave." She looked at him with hurt and hopelessness, feeling that Scott was entangling her in specious arguments at a time when love, not logic, should grace their farewells.

"Would you be content with a *German* Lutheran marriage?" he asked. "Or shall we go to the county seat and petition the blessings of one of your sons of the North?" When he saw her eyes fill with tears, Scott knew that he had hurt her with his taunts. She rose with an averted face and walked over to the window overlooking the long stone-flanged porch and the darkening sweep of lawn below.

He saw her draw the curtains aside and look upward toward the still radiant evening sky. As he watched her, he knew that he had always seen her there, that she had stood so from the beginning— in his small-boy awareness of woman as he watched his own mother thrust the curtains aside and wait for his father's coming, in his youth and its romanticism; and Siri had stepped into the empty place as if the spot in front of the window had always waited for her. He came to stand beside her, not touching her, not saying anything.

They heard Ellie's quick steps. Siri put her arm in his, whispering softly, "Let's pretend we're happy, Scott, and show those two old darlings a good time."

It was Ellie, though, who flew the dinner hour on wings of laughter, reading into their glances a tale brightly told, not one needing telling. Vinnie seemed cheerful, although she was considerably disturbed over not having had a long talk with Siri. But what could she have said until Scott said, "I'm bringing her home on such and such a day"? She wanted the girl to know that the big old house would be hers to live in without an old woman's step on the stairs or her hands upon the kettles. She supposed the Rittenhouses had always been an odd lot in such matters. Though her brother Charles might bluster and storm about trade and politics, he always kept his Scotty, as he called her, and their doings close to his heart.

When they heard the quail and cuckoo clock strike eight, they scrambled up from their chairs with a look of surprise. Vinnie said she would stay and do up the dishes, but Ellie must go down to the train with them, so Vinnie kissed Siri goodbye and the three of them walked down the quiet streets to the depot. The little platform held the Saturday night banterers, the curious, and the lonely.

"Hi, Ellie! Leaving us?"

"Sure, Matt. Bought a hotel in Chicago."

Siri and Scott walked on into the depot. "Coming back next fall, aren't you?" the depot agent said. "Zelda took a real liking to English this year. Never understood diagramming before." He handed her an envelope. "Car 16. Lower berth."

Bugs was outside and greeted her shyly, returning to a group of boys and girls who pretended indifference, but followed Scott and her with watchful eyes. And then suddenly there was Mrs. Swanson, with Harald in tow, so scrubbed and washed and tailored that Siri scarcely knew him. "Yust someting I hacked out for you, See-re," he said, thrusting a package into her hands. She shook his hand and said "*Mange Tak.*" Then she laughed and said, "Don't forget to polish those jingle bells in case I go riding with you next year."

"You come back, See-re, I buy a new set for the sleigh—some Sviss Pole Shimes for a dollar and saxty-nine."

Then they heard the flyer and Ellie smacked her loudly and said, "Glacier Park next Easter!" and Mrs. Swanson kissed her and said, "Be good to Elisabet, God bless her!"

Scott and she walked down the platform to the sleeping cars. He nodded to the porter and said, "Take good care of this one." They moved through the vestibule and into the car. He set her suitcase down and said with a queer little twist to his mouth, "Sure hope you come back. Never understood diagramming before." Then he kissed her thoroughly and expertly and went down the aisle without looking back.

CHAPTER 19

The Dream

She stood in the dim light of the noisy train shed with Tommy on one side, Leif on the other. "Sure you'd know her after all these years, Siri?"

"Of course I'd know her!" she said, her mind wandering through the years to the same station and the same train on which Nels and Guro had brought her to America. *Anybody'd* know Kari Moen!"

Tommy winked at Leif. "Any moment now she'll have to prove it." The long train clang-clanged down the track, its dragon-eye sending a shaft of light to play upon the superstructure of its cavern. "Day coach or Pullman, Seer?"

"I don't know. I don't know."

"Now she doesn't know, Leif!" exulted Tommy.

"That's her. That's she. No. Yes. No. There she is!" Siri held on to her hat and ran flying down the length of a car. The boys saw her throw her arms around a little lump of a creature almost hidden under a merry widow hat. "Kari! Kari!"

Kari pulled a handkerchief out of her bosom and began to snuffle in it. "Oh, my, oh, my! Not surely our little Siri! Oh, this is more than I can bear!" Finally Siri escaped the damp embraces and made the necessary introductions. The boys soon took Kari by the arm, while Siri followed, attempting to hang on to what looked like an old egg basket from Fjeldstrand and a small faded black reticule old enough to have been on the voyage of Sigurd the Crusader. Kari, looking like a lumpy sack of potatoes equipped with short legs, tried to keep up with the long strides of the boys and at the same time keep an eye on Siri and her possessions. "You coming?" she called several times, attempting at the same time to listen to Leif's explanation of how her luggage would get from the train to their automobile.

"That's a pretty hat," flattered Tommy.

"I'll tell you how I got it." Then followed such a swift chatter of dialectical Norwegian that Siri could scarcely follow her explanations. She heard her finish with, "I bought it in Chicago so that people would not take me for a newcomer."

Tommy eventually deposited Kari in the front seat of the Gabrielson automobile, leaving Siri to fend off Leif's sporadic efforts at lovemaking and the bouncing luggage piled all about them. "How is Mikjell?" she yelled.

"I tell you for sure he is doing real good!"

"Where is Lars?" Siri pulled Leif's hand away from her neck.

"Lars, he's got six kids. And Gunhild, she says she is stopping at three, the last one named after you, See-re. But I tell you for sure that's not so easy to do as talk." Siri heard Leif's ribald ha-ha in her left ear.

"Mother can hardly wait to see you, Kari."

"Yes, poor Elisabet. She never had it good after you left." She became absorbed in her surroundings for a moment and then she heard Kari ask Tommy what he did for a living.

"I am with Dad in the construction and lumber yard business."

"How is it?" asked Kari pleasantly.

"Fine, Kari, fine."

"You want to keep good books in a family business. I knew a man who came from Stavanger once who went into the shoe business with the husband of his half-cousin, and there was nothing but trouble. You should figure it all down in pencil, Tommy, and sign a paper." She turned to Siri. "So my little girl is now a schoolteacher like her father Arne! Got any young men with serious ideas?" She eyed Leif through her crooked spectacles. "You two betrothed?"

"No!" shouted Siri.

"Then you should make him keep his hands off!" All four of them laughed uproariously, but Kari continued to look back from time to time until they reached the Gabrielson driveway. When Roald opened the door, she backed off for a full surveillance and then pronounced Roald more like Arne than not like Arne.

When Siri was helping Joanna prepare a late supper, her aunt asked, "Have you told her?"

"I will." She found Kari up in her room, where she had gone after a short reunion with Elisabet—supervised by Roald. "Kari," she said gently, "Mother is pretty sick at times, and once in a while her mind wanders. She has waited eagerly to see you, but we all have to be careful not to excite or tire her. You're a good nurse, Kari, and know how it is."

Kari put her merry widow on a closet shelf and said, "I have taken care of your mother and mother's mother and your aunt Guro. Have no fear, See-re, I can keep the proper silence." She asked suddenly, "Where is Sophie?" Siri tried to explain that she was temporarily living with a family out in Dakota. "No one ever understood that girl Sophie," said Kari, with a long sigh.

Kari's two days proved pleasant for both Elisabet and the rest of the family, and for the most part she kept her voice down and her handkerchief hidden. Siri or Joanna wandered in and out of the sick room, and when it became obvious that Kari was becoming too voluble, they called her down for a Kari-coffee-chat, listening to the old woman's prattle, and learning, of course, much about what had happened during the almost fifteen years of Siri's absence.

"The sexton—you remember him, Siri—is long gone, about the time your aunt Guro died of pneumonia. Now, Koppen is here somewhere in America. Well," she said dipping loaf sugar into her coffee cup and extracting the sweetened liquid with a soft whistle of breath, "he is married again. His first wife died." Siri observed how much Kari enjoyed her role of local historian. "I cannot say for sure, but it is rumored he found his old childhood sweetheart in America and they are living somewhere. Now let me see," she said, tilting her head upward and narrowing her eyes in thought, until the lashes almost disappeared in the puffs of flesh which were once lids, "I think the town is called Kalle-fjorna."

"But he preached so often against emigration!" exclaimed Siri, ignoring Kari's geographical ambiguity.

"Oh, about that I have no memory," said Kari, "but this I can say, that Mikjell and I, we shall look them up some time. And if he has married his old sweetheart, I can find out soon enough, for she was from Sogn and related to a second cousin of mine who corresponds with a first cousin in Bergen."

"Isn't that a lot of trouble?" asked Joanna innocently.

"Oh, no!" said Kari cheerfully. "It can all be done by letter in a few months." She put her plump hand on Siri's arm. "Yes, I suppose

you are your Uncle Nels's heir, for he told me on the day he took
the steamer to Bergen, and these are his own words, 'I am a useless
old sailor now, but perhaps I can leave a little for that girl of mine
in America, something she can remember her old Guro and Nels by.' "
Kari thrust out her chin and looked at Siri expectantly. Siri was also
aware of her aunt Joanna's look of surprise.

Later, when Kari had gone back into Elisabet's room, Siri said,
"I never wanted to tell you about Uncle Nels's inheritance, but maybe Uncle Roald and you should know what happened."

"And you never found out how much?" scolded Aunt Joanna when
Siri had sketched in the details, but her better sense soon prevailed
and she said, "You've done the right thing. It's better not to upset
your mother."

After Kari had left, the household settled down to its quiet
routine. Siri had a letter from Scott in which he threatened to start
meeting trains again if she did not come back soon. He went on to
say that he had been up to Golag once and that Sophie had taken
quite a shine to him, with Siri gone, sitting in the car one afternoon
for a short visit and confiding to him the news that she and the
Egelmeier boy were planning to get married some day. "I don't
concur with the Egelmeier consensus that those two can't get into
trouble."

The evenings seemed long and lonely, even with her family
around, and frequently she and Tommy took long rides together,
stopping at the confectioners or going down to a small lake where
the Gabrielsons kept a rowboat. Once when they were riding home,
Tommy said, "You ought to be nicer to Leif when he comes over.
He works in town now, and you can't help seeing a lot of each other.
"I can remember a time when you didn't go anywhere without Leif."

"And you didn't go anywhere without Georgia."

"Georgia's married now and living in Iowa." He drove on in
silence. Finally he said, "What's the matter with you Seer? We used
to have great times together, and I always took your side when
Brun got ornery. Remember the time he put your precious Troll
on the carriagehouse roof because you tattled on him? Who climbed
up there and got that dog down?" Tommy said abruptly, "I haven't

gotten over Georgia, Seer. I thought it might help if we doubledated. Leif knows a nice girl in St. Paul."

"Not Andrea?"

"So *that's* what's bothering you!" Tommy exclaimed. "That was over and done with several months ago." Tommy chuckled and said, "Guess they got in over their heads for a while—but he'd be the first to admit it."

"Boast about it probably."

"My guess is that *that* affair made you more precious to him. He's talked about nothing but you for the past few months." Siri knew that Tommy was trying to get her to talk about Scott, but she had the feeling that even to him she shouldn't admit her love for him, because he and Leif probably commiserated with each other like lovesick high school boys, so that even Tommy might not be discreet. Anyway, who had the words for what she felt for Scott and who would be foolish enough to share the yearning and the elation and the magic that swept over her whenever she thought of him?

In the morning when Siri was busy making her mother's bed, Joanna came in briskly saying, "Leif's mother is on the telephone. She wants you over for dinner tonight, Siri."

"I can't go, but tell her thanks."

She saw the timorous look in her mother's eyes and her downcast, slightly disapproving expression. "Oh, well, I'll talk to her." The upshot of it was, of course, that she was committed to go.

"I am so glad," said Elisabet, as Siri was dressing in the adjoining room. "You should get out and have a little fun, and Leif will make you laugh. Leif's a good boy. You must marry your own kind, and not be headstrong like Sophie who runs around with the Egelmeier boy." Siri was about to question her, but thought better of it. "Sometimes I cannot sleep at night, thinking about Sophie. You should have brought her back with you, Siri. Never would I have let them put me on the train had I known you would leave Sophie!" They had been through this so often that Siri did not even attempt a reply, but continued putting on her clean underwear.

"You are so much like your own grandmother," sighed Elisabet. There is a stubbornness in you, too, that makes me waken at night and fear you will go back to that terrible land. Promise me, Siri, that you will not go back."

"Oh Mother, how can I say what I will do?"

"You can say it. You can say, 'I will not go back, Mother.'" Siri saw her mother's eyes growing remote.

Siri slipped into a cool lawn dress Aunt Joanna had sewed for her during the past week. Then she came over to her mother's bed and sat down beside her. "I have time to read to you before I go."

Elisabet ignored the offer, saying, "I have not told you of the time I was alone for two days and nights, have I, Siri?"

"I think you have," she lied. "Look, Mother, here is an article about the harbor in Bergen."

"I will not sit there any longer," I said to myself. "It will serve them right if they come back from the Egelmeiers and find that I have gone to stay with Siri." Elisabet had resumed the monotonous, dreary tone of recollection. "I set out one night when there was a moon and started up the hill. Shep came after me." She tried to rise on her pillow. "You have not told me what became of Shep."

"Oh, Shep is with the family east of Golag. They also are Scandinavian." Siri put down the newspaper.

"Yes, you did tell me that."

"Mother, you mustn't tire yourself thinking about the past."

"Do you remember the lake where we picnicked?" she asked cunningly. "Well, above the lake, that is where Shep and I rested. I had walked myself quite out of breath, and so I sat down on a rock. The dog would not leave me and go back to the farm. I will go on, I said to myself, for I had a loneliness for lights and houses and people behind their doors. I was about to start out again, when I saw two long shapes moving along the lake. You remember where there are trees and bushes?

"Mother, would you like a drink of buttermilk?"

"I felt the fur on Shep's neck rise under my hand. The shapes stopped, and then I saw another shape come down from some rocks. Such shapes could be all around, I thought, and I held my hand on the dog's fur, for I did not want Shep to get loose and go down there. For if I lost Shep there would be no comfort in anything at all when I was alone, only the flame of a lamp on the table. You have no idea how lonely the place was at night." Her face brightened. "I was alone at Ørnheim once when I was a girl. I cannot think of the reason I was left alone, but I think it was to tend the creatures when Nels and Guro were gone. It was not a loneliness like the loneliness of Dakota, for there the stream talked all night and there was a singing in the trees." Elisabet sighed and pulled the covers up to her throat. "You can leave me now and let me have a short sleep. Sometimes when you talk so much, I am almost weary. You were always one to prattle when you were small—not at all like Sophie."

The Borland house was just as Siri remembered it: prim, clean, and woman-dominated, with its antimacassars, crocheted doilies, and embroidered mottoes. Mr. Borland appeared genuinely glad to see her and would have visited at some length about the Dakotas, but Leif's mother took her by the hand and settled her down in a kitchen chair. Leif wandered in and out of the rooms, obliged for the moment to accept a somewhat anomalous role in the proceedings. "Well, Siri, you're back again, like the good old days," said Mrs. Borland as she stirred egg into freshly ground coffee. "You mustn't run off again."

"I never did *run* off," said Siri with a good-natured smile.

"Leif missed you for sure," she said, having given the door into the diningroom a quick glance first.

"I hear he didn't miss me too much," said Siri, enjoying herself.

"He has told you about Andrea?" she asked, replacing the lid on a vegetable kettle.

"I don't know that anyone had to *tell* me," said Siri. "I thought everyone knew about Andrea."

Mrs. Borland scooped a heaping tablespoon of butter from a stone crock and said, "It was only because he missed you, Siri. Then that mother of hers wasn't any help, either—always hanging around here, drinking coffee, hatching schemes to throw them together! I don't give her the time of day now, I can tell you!"

"Who wouldn't you give the time of day?" asked Leif, opening the swinging door to the diningroom. "Ma, the chairs are around. When do we eat? I thought I was going to have plenty of time to take Siri for a long ride!"

Mr. Borland endeavored with more optimism than success to ask

Siri about the crops around Scotts Lake and the building business, but Mrs. Borland saved him from committing such dull folly by passing the plates of food around continually and offering Siri her recipe for this and that "when you have a home of your own." Finally Mr. Borland retreated obediently behind his new brown suit and his thick glasses and sat awaiting the moment of dismissal. Eventually the time came, and he recited a table prayer in such a pontifical voice that Siri concluded he was less in awe of the deity than his wife.

It had been a matter of some embarrassment to Leif that he had not been able to call for Siri in a car, for his college years had accustomed him to the sight and company of many of the privileged; but Siri took such interest in the old horse she recognized and in recognizing the old carriage, they finally drove off in good spirits, with Mrs. Borland running down the drive the last minute waving a blanket for Siri's knees.

Both Leif and Hester, the mare, possessed single-track minds, so it was no accident that the buggy was soon rolling through the trees toward the lake and the Olafson cabin. He took care, naturally, to angle off upon another road—for by now he knew them all—and chose a lonely one hidden by overgrown hazel bushes and native trees. He needed no stimulant to make love to Siri, but still he exercised a cautious restraint and made no overtures for the present beyond a vise-like grip on one of her shoulders. Finally he came to a secluded spot in the woods, where Hester would be obliged to start into the lake if she were going anywhere at all. He dropped the reins and tackled Siri in one sweeping embrace, saying over and over again, "Siri, Siri, be nice to me!" Caught completely by surprise, she had at the moment no hands to resist him and no feet for leverage because they had become entangled in Mrs. Borland's blanket. Finally she was able to make him understand that she needed to come up for air if not to salvage her dignity.

She moved as far away from him as the carriage allowed and began to rearrange her hair. Pity and laughter and an abiding fondness for him struggled within her; he was Leif and he was not Leif, as she was Siri and she was not Siri. Her natural forthrightness wanted to say, "I am in love with someone else," but her mother's nebulous hopes and her own caution prevented such a declaration. She could see that his pride was hurt, for his easy successes must have made him feel masterful. "Leif," she said, placing her hand on his—and holding it down firmly—"you are so changed, I hardly know you! Something has happened to you in the year we've been apart, something that makes me terribly afraid of you."

"I wouldn't hurt you, Seer. You know that." She sensed that he was beginning to recover his damaged pride.

"I've been through a lot, Leif, with Mother sick and all," she said, feeling like one of her least promising students in the senior play a few weeks back. "You'll just have to be gentle and understanding."

She watched him maneuver Hester back to the road, and when they were near one of the better-traveled roads, she tucked her hand into his arm and said flatteringly, "Something tells me a girl is going to have to be very careful out with you, Leif. I'm sure you don't know how overpowering you have become." The awful thought occurred to her that the next girl who went out with Leif might suffer unfairly for her flattery.

Leif had stayed quite late that evening he brought her home, drinking coffee and enjoying a long visit with the family, going upstairs to joke with Elisabet and putting her into such a good frame of mind that Siri felt her mother appreciated Leif more than the Gabrielsons, whose bounty she enjoyed. It was midnight before the family finally went to bed, and Siri was so tired that she fell asleep almost instantly

Elisabet, though, awakened some time before dawn with a pain so sharp that it was less like a pain and more like a shrill, suspended note hovering on the rim of consciousness. Before the pain or perhaps with the pain—how could she remember?—had come a dream less like a dream than an experience. "Look well," said a voice, "for this is the tree of your tree of life." And Elisabet looked out upon a vast meadow on which a great wind soughed, stirring fallen leaves so that they rose in a kind of panting rhythm at her feet. In the middle of this great grassy plain stood a tree, and on this tree hung one leaf.

"Look well," continued the voice, "for there hangs but one aged leaf upon this tree." Strange seemed the words to Elisabet and stranger still the voice which seemed to rise from the inner voice of the mind, carrying with it an echoed, diminishing quality. "You see the fallen leaves of your days," said the voice, "and should they be counted, they are all there, from the earliest to the last. Walk about them if you will."

"Not I," said Elisabet, searching about her shoulders for a warming cloak, for she was trembling and cold. "Yet if it is as you say that this is the last living leaf, fluttering strangely upon its small twig in the wind, then this is my last living day."

"It is your last living day." Thereupon the voice had seemed to recede, like a voice drifting down into a cavern or a well.

Then came the voice again or perhaps another voice with the cadence of the sea in it, muted and musical. "We have a journey together, you and I."

A petulant stubbornness stirred her. "I have just come here," she said. "From so far away across the sea that I do not wish to be hurried."

"Look down below you, Elisabet."

She saw the red roofs of the little farm glistening in the moonlight, and she gave a glad cry and began to follow the voice. Suddenly she found herself in an old familiar room; for even if she had been blind, she would have known it from the sea smell that lingered and the sharp pleasant odor of hearth fires burned out long ago. "Are you content, Elisabet, daughter of Olaf, now that you stand in this room again?"

"If you mean," she said, bending down to pry open a rusted lock on an old bridal chest, "do I have anything to regret, I tell you honestly I have no more to regret than any other. For twice I was a loving wife and twice a loving mother."

"Once you were a loving wife and once a loving mother."

She hid her face in her hands, and as she drew them away, she saw with surprise how wrinkled they were. "Why must you torture me? Who are you to know my inward thoughts?"

"They reside upon your face," the voice said sadly.

"If that is so, there is no help for it. Once I was a loving wife and once I was an obedient wife but twice I was a loving mother!" she said stubbornly

"Indeed?" said the voice with the wash of the sea upon it.

"You think because I sent a child away, I did not truly love her? I tell you, it took a greater love to send a child away than any man could know who stands and reads the tale upon my face!" He only smiled, but in his look she read a sad reproach. "Well, if the truth be known, I could not love the younger one as much as the one I sent away, for her presence was a reproach to me."

"We move on, daughter of Olaf."

"Then walk not too fast."

"Soon you will walk as fast as any," but still she struggled to keep up with the swirling cloak ahead.

"This is a strange journey," she said, "for it seems to grow easier as I move along." She could not be sure, but she thought she saw the slow nodding of his head. "My feet grow lighter and my breath grows longer. There was such a fear upon me at first," she said. The pathway led along a mist-swirled ledge, but out beyond, Elisabet could see a village lying with moon-silvered housetops and a church steeple shining like an inverted icicle. "I know them all down there," she said.

"They sleep whom you know," said the stranger who was not a stranger moving into the mist.

She could not remember whether she had cried out, although a cry seemed to hang in the air; and when she caught her breath she looked into the open room beyond her own and saw Siri lying with her arms flung upward, her long, brown hair in sweeping swirls about her face. She heard the clop-clop-clop of the milkman's wagon on the paving below. When she turned back to where Siri slept, she saw this child of Arne stretching so that an upper arm caressed the face upon which sleep and youth had left a rosy kiss. "Mother, why didn't you awaken me?" Siri sat up suddenly.

And so began a morning like other mornings on Lake Street; yet Elisabet alone knew that it might be like no other day of her life, but she kept her secret well, enduring the sharp pangs silently. One thing she had learned, she thought with a sense of bitter elation, was to keep things to herself—it gave a kind of meaning to her life, this endurance, seeming to unite all the bitternesses of the past into something which her own spirit could mold into a vessel about which she could say, "This is what I—Elisabet, child of Olaf and Bergit—have made."

"You must send for Sophie soon," said Elisabet, rousing from her reflections. "You must be near Sophie as much as possible."

"I will, Mother," said Siri, threading an embroidery needle.

"The poor child always lived in your shadow, and a big one it was for a little girl. Bergit always talked of her Siri and the old sexton, who never forgot you, always talked of your love of books."

"I suppose such things cannot be helped, but I understand, Mother."

"I supposed so once," said Elisabet gravely, "but now I know it could have been helped." She observed the fragility of her mother's blue-veined hands and the transparency of her small face in which the eyes had grown so large. "Tosten loved her except when there was a clashing of wills, and at such times there was a black grimness upon the household until one or the other had forgotten his anger."

Siri heard her mother's sharp intake of breath and listened to Elisabet's protest that she was comfortable. "How did you and Leif get along last night, Siri?"

"Fine, Mother," she said.

"It's well to marry a Norwegian," said Elisabet, looking hopefully into her daughter's face for signs of assent. Had it been anyone but her mother, Siri would have countered with a playful why—but she sat there passively agreeable, embroidering on a pillowcase for the bedroom of a Dakota house where elm trees sighed against the windowpanes. There was no sound from the bed for a few minutes, and Siri sat very still lest she disturb her mother. When she finished filling in a small design she glanced toward the bed. Elisabet's face hung like a withered flower upon a stem, and there was a silence upon the room that was more than silence.

Chapter 20

The Return

Unless one had known a great loneliness and unless one had
known space beyond space, thought Siri, it would be impossible to
understand how beautiful was the sound of a train upon the plains.
And on this—her wedding night—along with the noise of the train
was the sound of rain, beating and incessant. She had learned within
the space of nine months to like this country in all its moods and
recognized a kind of earnestness in the land: the storms of winter
had always been sweeping and thorough, and the rain which was
pouring down now looked as if it had a mind to wash the dust off
several prairie states.

Lulled by the rhythm of the train and the splash of wind-driven
rain against the windows, Siri recalled the difficult days following
Elisabet's death late in May: Joanna's hurt and puzzlement when
she discovered that Siri was adamant about a June wedding. "Wait
until we go to Livingston. We'll stop at the hotel and arrange a
right kind of wedding. This looks almost inde—, well, furtive, anyway," argued Joanna.

"I don't want a big wedding so soon after Mother's death. I just
want Scott." How simple it would be, Siri thought rebelliously, if
she could only step off the train into Scott's arms. She reflected that
Pastor Koppen and his black book and the wedding guests had not
been able to make a real marriage out of her mother's misalliance
with Tosten—but, then, she supposed, Aunt Joanna's sense of pro-
priety and Vinnie's labor over a wedding cake could not prevent
the ultimate consummation of her and Scott's love, only postpone
it. Like all lovers before her and all lovers after her, they would
endure the minister and his black leather book and the damp-eyed
wedding guests. Yet she found that her own thoughts would not
remain entirely within the small cubicle of her own private ecstasy,
but ranged to encompass many memories, accompanying her to their
hour of marriage like "a cloud of witnesses."

The heavy wash of wind-blown rain beating against the dark

windows set her to thinking of Joanna's worrying about her living in Dakota. "Poor child," she said, "you'll always think of your mother out in that lonely valley."

"I wish you would stop talking like that, Joanna," Uncle Roald had interposed, rising abruptly to knock the ashes from his pipe into the coal scuttle. She watched him come over to her and felt the strong comfort of his hand upon her shoulder. "Something tells me that this lass here will sail a steady course. The only thing I can't forgive," he said, winking at Joanna, "is our Siri not getting married in this house."

"Scott can't get away. He has a murder case. The first murder case he has ever had," she said with some pride. "In a small community like that such things don't happen very often."

"No," said Joanna, "I suspect they let the country kill them off."

"Well," finished Uncle Roald, giving her shoulder a final pat, "we'll stop off for a visit before we go out to Livingston for John's wedding. Some day, Siri, you must give us a chance to spoil our grandchildren."

Leaving Tommy had been as hard as anything she did. "I don't get a kick out of anything, Seer," he said, "after Georgia left." Once he had hurt her sharply when he suggested that she could not love as deeply as he had loved, that even Leif showed more feeling than she did.

"Words are not feelings," she said. "Somewhere, at some time, Tommy, I learned that. I suspect it was from my grandmother Bergit." She had tried to tell Tommy how it had been in those early years and how self-knowledge had come to sustain and guide her; how from her very smallness in a world where so many were big, she had learned to discover some strength within herself but which drew upon a source infinitely greater than herself, a source so great that the bigness of others grew sometimes small indeed.

The lights of a town too small for their stopping shone blearily through the wet windows. When she began to think of her mother Elisabet, she was moved by a loving pity for one who had been a mother and not a mother to her, for one who used words to conceal the thoughts that lay festering one upon the other. Was she wrong when she felt that her mother's cry, "There is a weakness in me— Oh, Siri, if I could only change what was—if I could only call back the years"—was essentially a cry against the world itself and what she had allowed it to do to her? Let Scott and her, she prayed, ever welcome the wind!

She saw the porter coming to brush her coat and gather her luggage. Why bother, she thought exultantly, for in less than an hour I shall be coming down a stairway in a wheat-colored dress of silk, and I shall have forgotten about a train whistling across the stormy plains. She smiled at him and tipped him generously, following him out into the chilly vestibule. "Coming home?" he asked.

"Coming home," she said. Soon he was helping her down to the rain-washed wooden platform, to the embrace of a tall, angular woman who cried, "I'm so danged excited, Siri! I've never been married before!" Harald took her luggage and helped them into a carriage made gloomy but dry by its sheltering side-curtains. Soon they were off with a sharp hissing of wheels in deep rain water. "You're mean, you're all mean," said Siri, "not letting Scott come down to meet me. How is he?"

"Fit to be tied," said Ellie, unable to conceal her maidenly delight. "Vinnie's leaving for Illinois on the morning train. She's sleeping with me tonight."

"I had a girl vunce—" began Harald, but neither of them was listening. He swung the carriage into the street leading up to the Rittenhouse residence, and Siri saw the familiar twin lights shining mistily through the rain. Driving around to the rear, he stopped beside the path leading to the back door, and Ellie whisked out her umbrella, the two women dashing through the dripping shrubbery and up to the long back porch, where Vinnie stood in the doorway waiting.

There was a swift rushing up the narrow back stairway to a bedroom and a bath with lavender soap. The two women, one so shrill and distraught by excitement, the other a Minerva of brisk efficiency, threatened for a moment to undo Siri, but she began to ride upon some inner quiet, almost to disengage herself from this body which the women were handling as though it were a mannequin in a shop window, until she heard Scott's voice downstairs as he greeted the German Lutheran minister—and even then she seemed to be two persons, the one standing aside with a cool and observing mind, the other all weakness and heartbeats.

*When she saw
Scott, she saw
no one else at all*

She heard them exclaim over the dress Dagmar had sewn for her; she saw their small frowns when she pinned an ancient *sølje* to the place where the collar points met. "Perhaps Scotty has something more fashionable," suggested Vinnie, but when Siri said that the dress had been made for the *sølje* the older women exchanged glances of fond amusement, Vinnie saying with quick tact, "Of course, dear." Then Vinnie led her to a long beveled mirror so that Siri could see the whole dress at once, but she gave her image scarcely a glance, beyond a swift look at the fit of the dress and the sweep of her hair. She was aware, instead, of the wind knocking against the window panes, the same wind, perhaps, which had only a few minutes ago swept its wet breath across a darkened little house in a lonely valley below Golag.

"Are you ready now?" asked Vinnie.

"Oh, yes," said Siri.

"Wait until you see Harald at the foot of the stairway," said Scott's aunt, "and then you take his arm and come into the parlor." She felt their kisses upon her cheek and heard the noisy rustle of their skirts as they went down the back stairway. She stepped out upon the carpeted landing: There was a sudden quietness upon the house. The voices below had grown still. For a moment she seemed to stand alone, with only the busy night wind shouldering the old house, and then upon the wind rode the voices of the past—her father's quiet tones and Bergit's deep chuckle and the small chiding whine of her mother Elisabet. She looked through sudden tears to the hall below and saw Harald waiting. As she moved toward him, it seemed strange to come in on the arm of Harald Haraldson, Mrs. Swanson's brother with the *yingle* bells; but then Joanna, who had directed the wedding by mail, and Uncle Roald, who had spent so generously, must have reasons why a girl who wore a Norwegian heirloom at her throat should be given away by a Swede. As she took his arm and they turned toward the parlor, she saw the Lusks and Mrs. Swanson, but when she saw Scott standing beside the minister, she saw no one else at all—not until a few minutes later when she trembled at his kiss, and the small gathering of friends came forward.

"Land sakes alive, I never thought I'd see *this* day!" exclaimed Ellie joyfully. "I wasted gallons of coffee on this romance!"

"I shouldn't think that would have been necessary," said the pastor, glancing at the young couple. "They look as if nothing could have kept them apart."

Mr. Lusk had cornered Harald among the potted ferns. "Did you ever read about the marriage customs of the Bavili?" he asked, peering sternly above the pinchers slipping down on his nose.

"My, my, what are you going to do with all this extra food?" asked Mrs. Lusk.

Vinnie remarked to anyone who might be listening, "I am so sorry the twins and Maude couldn't be here."

Siri put down her coffee cup and moved over to the footed glass plate on which the wedding cake rested. Taking a napkin from the table, she slid the silver spatula under a piece of cake. Ellie took it from her and said, "If sleeping on a piece of cake doesn't work, folks, I'm going to start meeting trains. Look what it did for Scott."

Vinnie heard the quail and cuckoo clock and said, "Ellie, we better get over to the hotel. Remember, I catch a train early in the morning." So they began to say goodbye as Harald went out to bring the carriage to the front. In the hallway closet Vinnie found her wraps and said to Siri, "Scott's going to be awfully good to you, Siri. You know that, don't you?"

A gust of cold air swept down the hall and the lights in a wall bracket flickered. Siri caught the older woman's hand and Vinnie placed a kiss upon her cheek. She looked up the stairway, past the landing, to a light shining from a room that was now Scott's and hers. "And I am going to be very good to him," she said.